THE LIE OF HAVING IT ALL

HOLLY RIDGE

MORGAN ELIZABETH

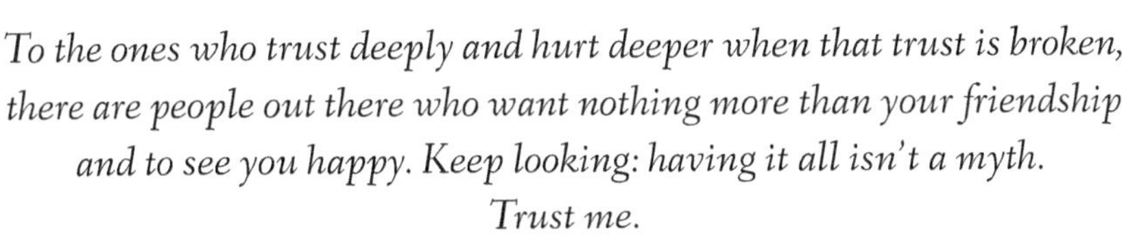
To the ones who trust deeply and hurt deeper when that trust is broken,
there are people out there who want nothing more than your friendship
and to see you happy. Keep looking: having it all isn't a myth.
Trust me.

PLAYLIST

Lucky - Britney Spears
You're Gonna Go Far - Noah Kahan
Born for This - Paramore
Wi$h Li$t (settle down version) -Taylor Swift
When Did You Get Hot? - Sabrina Carpenter
Sunrise Goodbyes - Houston Calls
Peace - Taylor Swift
Wannabe - Spice Girls
Butterflies - Kacey Musgraves
Attractive Today - Motion City Soundtrack
Honey - Taylor Swift
Maine - Noah Kahan
Where the Lines Overlap - Paramore
The Best of Both Worlds - Hannah Montana

A NOTE FROM MORGAN

Dear Reader,

Welcome to Holly Ridge! Whether this is your first visit to my cozy small town, or your third, I am so excited for you all to read Leo and Willa's story. I love this story so much, and it has been such a joy to bring these two characters who have been dancing around in the background of the Morganverse to the front and finally give them their own HEA!

If you know one thing about it, it might be that I am a people pleaser to a fault. Just like Willa, I have deep anxiety that often results in me being terrified to let those whom I care about down. Like Willa, this has led me to believe and trust in people who did not have my best interests at heart. In a way, writing this story was cathartic, and I hope you love it as much as I loved writing it. I feel like women as a whole are often told that having it all isn't possible, not if you want to have your dream career and a healthy relationship and stability and a family, and I am here to tell you that is absolutely a lie. You might have to find balance, and some days, it might feel so stressful and overwhelming, but you *can* have it all. Trust me.

This is a contemporary small town romcom, but it does touch on some serious topics like the death of a parent (off-page), narcissistic parents and parental figures, black mail. anxiety and on-page panic attacks, and adult language and situations.

As always, please put your mental health first when reading. It's supposed to be our happy place.

Love you to the moon and to Saturn,

Morgan

ONE

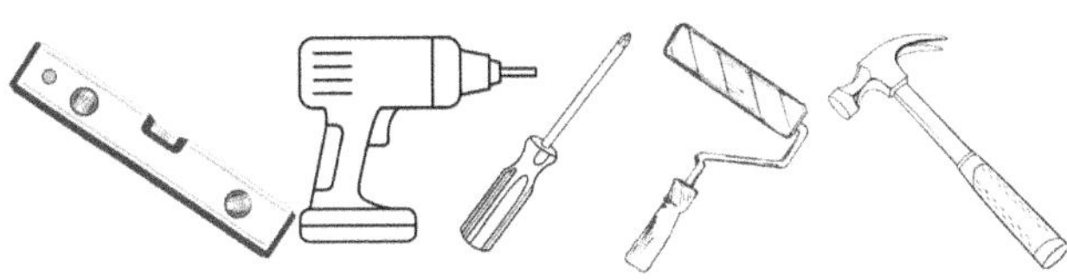

LEO

"Well, it's a shithole," I say, looking around. Cracked concrete slabs make up the front walkway, and a couple of weed-filled garden beds line the path. I'm sure the house was once quaint and well-kept, but right now it looks exactly as it has for some time—all but abandoned. The inspector told me the place was structurally near perfect, but unfortunately, no one has occupied the property bordering the Three Kings Tree farm for at least five years. The owners passed away and left the place to their kids, who never had the heart to sell it, despite living far away and barely maintaining it.

That is, until I came along with an offer they couldn't refuse.

I've always believed in my decisions, always going with my gut and following through on each and every one. When others think I'm about to fail spectacularly, I always have complete confidence in my choices and never second-guess my actions. But right now, as I stand on the front lawn of the run-down four-bedroom home on the outskirts of Holly Ridge, I'm wondering what the fuck I was thinking.

It was an impulsive decision, one encouraged by my client Adam Porter, who told me that when he moved here, everything suddenly made sense, and he felt a sense of peace. I thought it was bullshit, but when I looked at him, it was obvious. His eyes were clearer, the bags under them lighter, his shoulders less hunched. He smiled more, laughed, and joked. Looked at peace.

He was happy. While I've only recently become his agent to help him sell his songs, I've spent enough time in the same circles as the prolific songwriter and former rock band member to know that he'd been looking increasingly run-down over the past few years.

When my recent efforts to find my own sense of peace and calm hit dead ends over the past six months, each attempt railroaded by responsibility and my career, I realized I needed to take more drastic measures or else find myself following in my father's footsteps straight into an early grave.

"But it's *your* shithole," a now-familiar voice calls, and when I turn to give her a menacing look, the redhead just grins wider.

Hallie Young is possibly the most interesting woman I've ever met, all bravado and attitude and shit-talking in a way few people are willing to do with me. For that reason, strangely enough, I've come to enjoy her company. Her fiancé, Jesse, towers beside her, putting an arm around her waist and pulling her into him protectively, as if he's afraid her taunting will end badly.

"Hal," he says in a low warning, and she looks up at him over her shoulder, that smile taking over her entire face as if she is wholeheartedly entertained by this.

"What? It is. He bought the place; now it's his shithole."

In April, I asked Adam for his realtor's name before I came to Holly Ridge for a charity concert where Atlas Oaks was performing. I gave her a small but specific list of requirements, including land for relative peace and a long front drive to deter random visitors. I asked for a place surrounded by trees, just like my childhood home. I asked for at least three bedrooms, so I could have an office and a guest room, and I ended up with four. Despite her warning that the town's housing market was small, she managed to meet every one of those requirements with this place.

Unfortunately, I forgot to mention I would like the place to look well-kept and have up-to-date amenities. But when I scrolled through the photos and then checked out the property, I knew I couldn't pass it up: it was far too perfect.

It's the kind of place my dad would have seen the potential in.

"What are you even doing here?" I ask, finally turning to fully face her and taking in the small crowd that, for some reason, is here alongside her. "I invited Adam, not you."

She grins but doesn't speak.

"She found out I was coming and asked when and where," Adam explains for her.

"And you told her?"

He shrugs.

"She's scary. She threatened to torment me all summer if I didn't tell her when we were coming by, and she made sure to tell me it wasn't an empty threat."

"Smart man. It wasn't," Jesse says from beside his fiancée. "Once she threatened to turn my daughter against me to torment me."

"Because you were about to assault a deer!" Hallie says, throwing her hands in the air as if she's annoyed that she needs to clear her name. Jesse looks down at her with a bored look.

"Assault is a bit extreme. I was going to *scare off a deer*. With a pinecone."

"Po-tay-to, po-tah-to, same difference," she says.

"They are incredibly different, Hallie," Jesse clarifies. "You really need to stop telling people I tried to hurt a baby deer."

"The story is much more interesting that way. Plus, what are you going to do, not marry me?" The man lets out a deep sigh but doesn't argue. Instead, he pulls her tighter into his side. Hallie grins up at him before returning her attention to me. "Anyway, I wanted to make sure I was part of the welcoming committee."

"Welcome to Holly Ridge, where nobody does anything alone," Adam mumbles, and then winces when his girlfriend, Wren, elbows him.

"Are you telling me that if I invite one of you to something, I'm getting all of you?"

"Well, not all of us. Some of us do occasionally have to work. Colt wanted to come see the place, but he's getting a delivery today, so he has to stick close by. But yeah. Pretty much," Hallie responds with a shrug of her shoulder, as if this is totally normal. In fact, she gives *me* a look as if I'm strange for thinking that their clearly co-dependent behaviors are off.

"Hallie, come on. You're going to scare him off," Wren says in a chiding voice to her best friend, because she's not just Adam's girlfriend, but Hallie's best friend and Jesse's little sister.

The town is close-knit, if not a little too close-knit.

"What? It's true! You declared him one of us, so he might as well understand the consequences of that now," Hallie argues.

I sigh, but decide ignoring them might be the better option and make my way up the path without saying another word. As I do, I take note of projects that need to be done. Unfortunately, they're everywhere I look. The siding looks okay, but it needs a fresh coat of paint. The front door is a plain, generic slab that's seen better days, though it will suffice until I get around to replacing it with something more appealing. The front garden beds are completely trashed, with two half-dead bushes on the left and nothing but weeds and a few broken pavers on the right, which I assume were intended as a border. Internally, I sigh, knowing I'll have to hire out landscaping. While I grew up in a family of contractors who taught me how to fix up just about anything, I didn't seem to inherit a green thumb.

But the rest? The rest I can do. In fact, the rest I'm suddenly itching to do, despite the fact that I haven't picked up a hammer in years for much more than hanging the occasional frame. For the first time in a while, I feel the urge to get my hands dirty.

The key slips into the lock with no resistance, turning smoothly even though the door sticks just a bit as I open it and step into the empty entryway. The crew of intruders follows behind me, though I pay them no mind as I look around my new home. It's mostly empty, with a few pieces left behind, though considering I brought very little here, I'm grateful for that. There's a heavy dining room table and chairs I'm interested in stripping and refinishing, an old, beat-up coffee table that will work until I replace it, and a decent-looking dresser in the primary bedroom.

My dad would have seen nothing but potential within the walls, and right now, it's like I'm seeing it through his eyes. The bones are solid, though the floors need refinishing. The walls are in good shape, with just a few pieces of drywall that need patching, though every wall without gaudy wallpaper needs repainting. The ceilings have a few cosmetic cracks, which I know from my dad are from the old house settling over time, but nothing is outside my skill set.

"The inside's not much better," Hallie murmurs.

"Jesus, Hallie, stop it," Jesse says, but I ignore them as I continue moving through the house and into the sunken living room, until I reach a set of sliding glass doors. They stick and will probably need replacing, especially since the style is dated, but when I step out onto the pavers, I take a deep breath, relief moving through me.

More than anything, this is why I bought the place.

The outdoors hasn't been something I've enjoyed much in the past ten years, but as I take in a deep breath of fresh air, it feels like a new start, filling my lungs and sending relief buzzing through my veins.

"Okay, the inside is questionable, but this...this makes it worth it," Wren breathes, and I couldn't agree more. The entire property is lined by trees except for a large grassy plot behind the house. Privacy, nature, and a sense of peace remind me of my childhood, when things were simpler and easier.

To my left is a set of stairs to a deck, the door to which is through the dining room and is intended for an outdoor eating space, but it needs a ton of work.

"My God, that deck is gorgeous," Hallie says from behind me, as she steps out onto the patio. "And those trees! Imagine it in the fall! All the trees changing? It's going to be so pretty." The trees lining my property are a mix of evergreens and deciduous trees, making it the best of both worlds. A lush green in the spring and summer, and in the fall, I'll have a gorgeous burst of color. In the winter, with the evergreen trees, it won't be completely barren and will maintain my privacy.

Hallie takes a step towards the deck, but before she gets far, I reach over, grabbing her elbow to stop her. "Don't go up there," I say, shaking my head and letting go of her elbow. "It's old, and a bunch of the boards are rotting. It's not safe." Her eyes go wide, and she looks over at the deck. "It's one of my first projects. I don't think it can really bear weight at all right now."

Jesse moves over, taking the two semi-decent steps carefully before toeing the third and watching a chunk crumble off. "Yeah, this thing is fucked," he says, as if I don't know.

"It's about a third of the boards, so it's salvageable. Just need to rip them out, then replace them. Thankfully, the supporting ones seem to be solid. I can start tearing the bad ones out tomorrow, then I'll just replace the missing ones."

"How are you planning to get them here?" Jesse asks, still inspecting the deck.

"Not sure. My car isn't exactly built for it. I was thinking I'll probably have to rent something." I haven't needed anything other than small, sporty cars to navigate the city in years, but I know I'll have to replace it or get a second vehicle sometime before winter.

"I have a truck," Jesse says. "I could head down to the store with you, grab what you need, lug it back." Instantly, I shake my head, declining his offer.

"No, no, that's not necessary."

"I'm free on Monday," Jesse says, ignoring my rejection. "Madden'll help too. With the three of us, we'd get it done quick. Last summer, Mom had us build a deck on her place, so we're pretty well-versed in it."

Relief moves through me, knowing I have plans on Monday.

"I won't be around on Monday. I've got a meeting in the city. But thanks for the offer." My plan right now is to do as much cleaning as I can today before driving back home to my condo to wrap up any loose ends. Monday, I have one last meeting in the city, and after that, I'll be headed here to meet the furniture delivery. I ordered just enough to make the place livable while I clean and renovate it: a bed, a mattress, and a couch.

Up until just now, I was annoyed that I couldn't line up my meetings and the delivery so I could move in right away, but right now I'm actually relieved.

That is, until Jesse speaks again.

"I can move some things around. Thursday good?" I shake my head.

"Really, I appreciate it, but I can't—"

"I actually insist we do," Madden says with a grin. "Because mom is trying to wrangle us into weeding her flower beds, and if we're helping you, she can't hold it against us." I look to Adam, hoping he's going to help, but he just shrugs.

I came here to escape.

To be alone.

To work with my hands in silence.

Not to have my neighbors helping me with that.

"It's set," Hallie says with a wide grin, clapping her hands, ignoring my internal struggle. "The guys will come on Thursday to help with the deck. Then once it's all done, we can have a welcome party out here!" I open my mouth to argue about the plan or the party, I don't know, but I don't get the opportunity, regardless.

"Does ten work?" Jesse asks. I blink.

"Probably should do nine, since we might need to go to multiple stores, depending on what they have in stock," Madden says, tapping on his phone screen.

"Good call," Jesse says, then turns back to me. "So we'll be here at nine."

"I—"

"In the meantime, we have to head out. Emma will be getting back from a sleepover soon, and I promised we'd make cupcakes for family dinner tomorrow," Hallie says, stepping towards the side yard. Dazedly, I follow the crew, unsure of what's happening or how I got myself into this mess.

"What kind?" Madden asks, slinging his arm around Hallie's shoulders.

"Red velvet," she says, and they start to make their way towards the two vehicles parked in my drive that don't belong to me.

"My favorite. You really do love me, don't you?" Madden says. Hallie pulls her head back to glare at him, her look a brutal thing that could maim if it were tangible.

"Who said you're getting any?" Madden, clearly used to her killing glares and sharp attitude, rolls his eyes.

"You can't bring treats to my mother's house and not give me any, Hallie. I'm my mom's favorite," he says, and although I've never met Mrs. King, even I know that's not the truth. Jesse lets out a snort, confirming my assumption, and Wren looks at him, rolling her eyes, as we all follow Madden and Hallie.

"You're delusional. Right now, I'm the favorite King, since I'm making an honest man out of your brother. Then it's Emma, Wren, and Jesse. You're at the bottom of the pyramid."

"Oh, fuck off, I am totally above Jesse," he argues, opening the passenger side door of the truck and watching Hallie slide in.

"Oh, so you really *are* delusional," she replies as Madden follows her inside. Jesse, Adam, and Wren watch this without a bit of surprise on their face before Jesse shakes his head and makes his way towards the driver's side.

"Thursday," he says, then slides into his car, Hallie and Madden still loudly bickering inside, and drives off.

"What just happened?" I mumble to myself, staring at the taillights of the truck leaving my property. A small laugh comes from my side, and then a hand lands on my shoulder, Adam standing next to me with a knowing smile.

"Welcome to Holly Ridge, my friend."

Somehow, I don't think my retreat here is going to be nearly as peaceful as I had hoped.

TWO

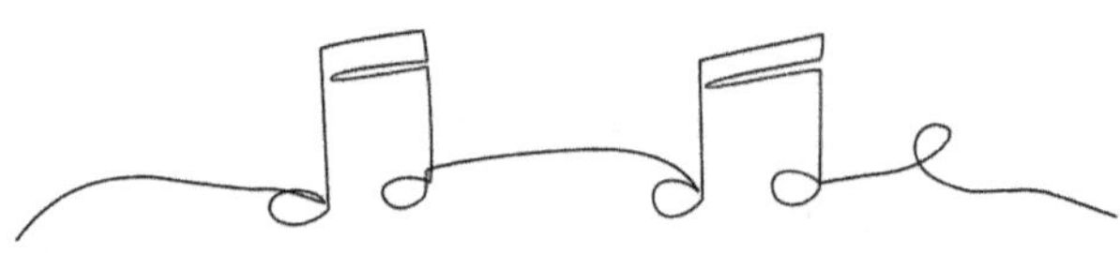

WILLA

"That's it. I'm done. Washed up. My career is over." I tear another sheet of paper from the notebook I have been doodling words and thoughts on, crumple it, and throw it at the wall. It circles the edge of the basket before falling to the ground. It feels like the perfect metaphor for how I feel right now: circling, spiraling, and ultimately creating a mess. I settle deep into the chair, tipping my head back, and groan at the ceiling before running a hand roughly over my face. If Jackie were here, she'd give me shit for it, telling me I'm going to get wrinkles, but what do wrinkles matter if my career is over and I'm never going to record another album?

Am I being dramatic? Maybe.

But I didn't get this far by being sensible.

"Okay, I wouldn't go that far," Adam says with a laugh and a shake of his head. "You're just...scattered."

That's the nice way to put the way I'm jumping from outlined track to outlined track, trying to cling on to some tiny bit of inspiration to get past this block and failing each and every time. I sigh, sitting up and frowning at him on the screen of my computer.

"I just...I don't know what to write. Nothing feels right. It all feels stupid and superficial." Creative block is a problem I've never run into before. Anytime I've ever been the slightest bit stuck, I've been able to pull inspiration from movies, art, or books to find the stories I wanted to tell in songs, even if they weren't my own. Though I tell fans all of my songs are written from personal experience, from my own struggles and wins in my quest to find true love, my love life is purely nonexistent. "Everything I write sucks. I'm totally fucked. This is it, isn't it? My career is over, and I've hit my peak, and I'm now destined for a life of C-list television theme songs."

"It doesn't suck," Adam says in his calm tone. I glare at him, and the edge of his lips tips up. "It's just very... sad?"

"Which is a problem." Running a hand over my face, I take a deep breath, trying to quell the panic building in my chest. I close my eyes, counting my breaths before I explain. "My last album was sad. My last album was my woman-scorned breakup album. This one is supposed to be a love album," I remind him, something he is well aware of since he wrote what will become the lead single.

In December, Adam, an incredibly talented songwriter, brought me a song he believed would be perfect for me. I immediately fell in love with it. *Are You Mine?* is all romance, all the butterflies of having a crush, of being unsure, of falling in love, and realizing they feel the same. When I heard *Are You Mine?*, I knew I needed it on my next album. I'm known well for writing most of my own songs, so while it's the perfect start, the perfect song to set the tone for the album, I need to write the rest of the songs myself.

At first, I was on tour, and when I sat down to write in my limited free time and found no inspiration, I figured it was because I was too busy. I was running from interview to meeting to practice to meet-and-greet to performance, each day in a new place, a new city. I didn't pay it much mind, even though in the past I'd always been able to write, no matter where I was. Instead, I made a vision board, a spread of words and photos and colors and even textures to inspire me, which is now hanging over my computer in my music room.

As I stare at it, once again, I know it's perfect, the exact vision I have for the album: a light, airy, love ballad-filled album about being afraid of love, finding it, and then being desperate to keep it. A color palette of pastel pinks and purples and blues and greens, a clipping of hands being held, a still of a couple passionately kissing. A couple of intimate snaps of a hand on a thigh, fingers indenting skin, of teeth on a lip.

Infatuation and love and attraction and need. That's the vibe for this album. Now it just needs to get written.

But I've been home now for two weeks and...nothing.

Not a song, not a lyric, not even a usable melody has come to me. Yesterday, I asked Adam if he could hop on a coworking call with me for a couple of hours to see if he could help shake some inspiration loose, but the call is now going on three hours, and I have nothing to show for it, other than a pile of crumpled-up papers and the anxiety stirring in my bones.

"I don't get it. I'm doing everything I normally do. I'm working out, I'm reading, I'm going through old notes. I'm meditating and journaling and spending at least three hours a day trying to write, but I've got nothing to show for it." He looks at me assessingly, head tipping to the side just a hair before he speaks with a gentleness I don't expect from him.

"Maybe that's your problem. You're trying too hard. You're too structured. Maybe you need to change up your routine."

Panic shoots through me at the mere suggestion.

"My routines are what help me write," I murmur, protective of the routines I've created. I like the predictability of a routine.

Routines are familiar.

Routines feel safe.

Routines help me stay in my groove.

Routines mean I am in control.

"Normally," Adam says, lifting a shoulder in a halfhearted gesture. "But maybe that's changed. Maybe *you* need a change." I scrunch up my nose, trying to push down how the mere idea of change unsettles me, and a chuckle fills the room. "I get it. I've been there, Will. Trust me. I was going on six months of no writing with my last block." My head snaps up, giving him wide eyes.

"*Six months?*" He nods, and I sit back, floored. Writing is as natural to Adam as it is to me. He, Riggins, and Stella Greene are the only people I've ever been able to write with, since they have the same consuming need to get words on paper as I do. "What did you do?"

"I panicked, for one. Tried to write even more, wasted time, paper, and energy I didn't have. I stressed enough to burn a hole in my stomach, I'm sure. Then I tried moving from LA to New York. Tried using a typewriter. I ran a fuck-ton. Watched movies, listened to music, and read books. Tried to...I don't know. Find myself? I cut myself off from everyone and everything."

I think about the hundreds of dollars I've spent on craft supplies, about the vision board I made, about the fancy notebooks that I've bought, thinking they might help, and the extra Pilates classes I added to my routine.

"But then I moved to Holly Ridge." He shrugs when I raise an eyebrow at him. "It was a random, spur-of-the-moment decision, but the best one I ever made. Maybe that's what you need."

"To move to a small town on a whim and fall in love? I'm sure Jackie and Leo would just *love* that," I say. He rolls his eyes through the screen and shakes his head.

"No, I don't think you need to up and leave everything you know. But maybe a change of scenery would help."

"I just came off a world tour," I grumble, drawing hearts in the margins of a piece of paper. "And I couldn't write while I was there. Not sure how a change of scenery would help." I know I'm being stubborn, and I know that he's just trying to help, and I'm grateful when he isn't irritated or offended by my arguments. Instead, he just shrugs knowingly.

"You may have been somewhere else physically, but at the end of the day, it was the same old, same old. Maybe change of scenery was the wrong word—You need a change of pace. Maybe you need to... I don't know. Disappear. Go somewhere new and just be...you. Not Willa Stone, the pop star. Willa Stone, the person." That knot in my stomach grows, swirling inward until I feel suffocated by it.

The truth is, I have no idea *who* I am without my external personality, without the version the world knows. I've been here for so long, grown into her, that I don't actually think there *is* a different version of myself hiding away.

But that's embarrassing to admit, to tell someone that there is no deeper version of yourself than the superficial one you've created to please those around you.

So, instead, I give him the logical answer.

"I don't think there's anywhere I can hide without having to be on all the time."

"You can in Holly Ridge," he says, with a small smile. "The Atlas Oaks guys were here not long ago; no one bothered them." I take in the sincerity in his voice, but don't speak. "If you ever want to come, get away for a bit, I've got a guest room you're more than welcome to. It's not luxury, but it's comfy, and Wren makes great cookies." His voice softens when he mentions his girlfriend, the muse for *Are You Mine?*, and I smile at that, so happy my friend has this... has found this.

Simultaneously, something ugly twists in my chest, something I recognize as jealousy, and I hate it. In an effort not to dwell on it, I nod. "I'll let you know. Maybe I'll come for a day, and we can write together in person. Maybe that will help knock this block out."

"Come for a while. A weekend or a week. You'd love it here. Wren's about to be off for the summer, and we have a couple of travel plans, but nothing crazy, so we'll be around. She would love to have you here. Though there would be a requisite visit to her niece." I never thought I'd see this, grumpy Adam Porter smiling and joking about this extended family of his, but it's clear before me.

Adam went to Holly Ridge, creatively blocked and emotionally cut off, and the journey transformed him. Even though I know it's impossible, I can't help but wonder if I could find the same.

"Hey, babe, I'm gonna go to the store, is there anything—" a pretty brunette says, walking on screen with her head down, a notebook in her hands. She stops mid-sentence, looks up, and gasps, her face going pink. "Oh, gosh, I'm so sorry! I didn't mean to interrupt. I'll just—" She starts to stammer and back up, but I shake my head.

"No, no, you're fine!" I say with a wave, secretly relieved for the interruption. I didn't want to sit with my thoughts or Adam's offer of a getaway much longer. "I was just whining to Adam. It's good to see you!" She comes closer, and Adam wraps an arm around her waist, tugging her down into his lap, and again, I feel that jealousy, guilt coming in on its heels.

"You too! How's it feel to have some time off?" Wren asks with a friendly smile.

"I was just telling her she should come here for a bit over the summer. She's creatively blocked, and I think she needs to change things up."

"Well, Holly Ridge is the best little town in the whole world. We'd love to host you! Being here fixed Adam's block right up."

I grin at them, but before I can say anything else, though, my phone beeps and a message from Jackie lights up my screen.

JACKIE

The meeting has been moved up by thirty minutes. Okay?

I sigh, tap out a response in the affirmative, and sit up. "That's Jackie—my meeting was moved up, and I gotta go get ready." I have at least an hour before I have to leave the house, but I'll need that much time to get the camera ready for the paparazzi who will inevitably be waiting outside to catch a shot of me. Adam nods, then gives me a stern look.

"We'll chat soon. Be easy on yourself, Willa. You can't force the muse." I give him a tight smile, biting back the instinctive response of reminding him that my label doesn't really care if my muse is taking its sweet time or not. "And think about coming to Holly Ridge."

"Will do," I say with a smile before wishing the couple goodbye and then signing off. Then, with one last look around my mess of an office, I sigh, do a quick cleanup, and move on with my getting-ready routine while mentally shelving my worries about my writer's block.

It's time to turn on Willa Stone, the pop star, and she never worries about anything. Why would she when she has everything she ever wanted?

THREE

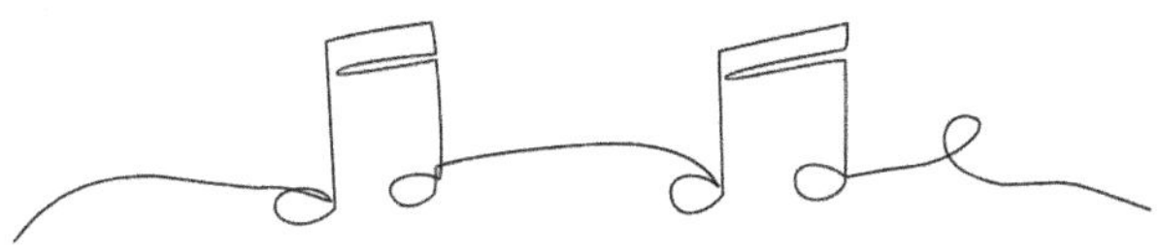

WILLA

As we pull up in front of the looming building in downtown Hudson City, the late spring sun glinting off the tinted windows, the lines of paparazzi with their cameras at the ready come into view, and I start my routine to center myself. Close my eyes, take five deep, calming breaths. Remind myself that my bodyguard, Gabe, is here with me. Remind myself that I have my armor on, my cool girl shield, that every hair is absolutely perfect. Remind myself that I've got this, that I've done this a million times, and I'm so curated, they won't be able to find a flaw.

By the time Gabe comes around to open my door, I'm in another zone, Willa Ston TM locked into place.

"Are you ready?" he asks, blocking the door for me. I take in one last deep breath, then let a wide, welcoming smile take over my face before nodding. He steps aside and offers me a hand, and finally, I step out onto the sidewalk and stand tall. I wave and greet the small crowd in front of the building, the mask hiding the nervous energy that hums in my chest.

I wasn't always like this, wasn't always so nervous and anxious and skittish when it was time to face the press. But something happens when the world begins to pick apart every photo that's ever taken of you, when every flaw is dissected and interpreted to mean something more. You become cautious, making sure every angle is perfect, choosing your words carefully, and learning to keep every single hair in place.

You build a shield, not to hide behind, but to protect yourself.

"Willa! Willa!" Voices call, camera's flashing, as they try to get the best shot, the one that will be posted to social media and splashed in multiple magazines next week, be it in a streetwear article claiming that some aspect of my outfit is trend forecasting or a post speculating what I'm currently working on right now, despite just ending my tour for my last album a week and a half ago.

I smile at the strangely familiar faces: I feel like I know every paparazzo in this town. "Morning, friends," I say in a cheery voice, lifting a hand and wiggling my fingers sporting a fresh manicure with nude polish.

"Willa! Over here!" one calls, and I turn my head toward him, smiling and giving him the shot he's looking for while Gabe slowly moves us toward the door.

"Willa! What's next?" another calls. I wink at her, then shrug.

"Going inside to figure that out now." More excited chatter, and I grin, knowing that it will get the fans and tabloids talking and build anticipation for my next project, even if it's not written. Gabe puts a hand on my back and guides me along as cameras flash and my name is called.

"Willa! Have you heard that Caleb is already dating someone else? What are your thoughts?" Caleb is the now-reformed bad boy I dated for almost six months, ending almost a year and a half ago.

"I wish him all the best. We had a great time together and ended things amicably. He'll always be a good friend of mine," I say graciously, always perfectly media-trained. Before they can ask anything else, Jackie waves at me through the glass walls of the building, indicating my press time is over. I give the crowd one last smile and wave before Gabe opens the door for me, and I step inside.

The doors close behind us, closing us in the building's silent, peaceful lobby, and I take my first full breath since leaving the car, the adrenaline abating just a bit. I brush a hand down my front, my shoulders relaxing just a bit as I revel in the quiet. Still, I remain fully aware that the crowd is still taking photos behind me.

"What are those?" Jackie, my talent agent and brand manager, asks as we walk down the marble entryway, staring at the brown heels on my feet. After my call with Adam, I got ready for today's meeting, putting on the outfit Jackie had set aside for me, labeled *Monday meeting*. A white, tight tank top, loose linen pants with a brown belt, chunky gold jewelry, and brown heels, though without even asking, I know why she's annoyed.

"Hello to you, too, Jackie. I'm great, thank you," I joke with a smile. Jackie is all business, all the time, and I can rarely resist the urge to poke at her a bit. "These are shoes. Brown ones. Peep toe?"

"Yeah, yeah, yeah," she says, an irritated look on her face as she guides me to the elevators. "But those are not the shoes I picked out for you." I lift a shoulder in a half shrug.

"The ones you left didn't fit. Too big."

"So you just picked out your own?" Jackie asks, clearly irritated. I roll my eyes at her dramatics.

"I have an entire closet of shoes. I'm an adult who can choose her own shoes, you know."

"It's..." she starts, then sighs and shakes her head as if I'm a child she has to calmly redirect. "It's fine, but I'd prefer we stick to the plan. We have to stick to the brand, Willa. It's crucial." I don't remind her that these shoes are the same boring brown as the others or that I really don't think a single streetwear shot of my shoes is really going to make or break my career.

The elevator doors slide open as we approach, and when we step in, Jackie presses the button for the top floor before they slide shut once more. Once the elevator starts moving, the shorter woman turns to me, a relieved sigh leaving her lips now that we're closed off from the cameras down below, and a smile on her lips.

"Morning, my girl, how are you?" This is my favorite version of my manager, the sweet one who feels almost motherly to me, the one I've known almost my entire life, the one who's been at my side since the beginning.

Jackie found me when I was barely seven, performing at a children's pageant my mom had signed me up for. At a young age, I was desperate to perform, and despite being a single parent, my mom was more than willing to feed into it, signing me up for everything and anything. Community plays, chorus groups, singing lessons, dance classes, and pageants. Any chance to show off her daughter.

I'd chosen to sing as my talent, and I don't want to toot my own horn, but even then, I was good and could capture a room. Jackie had been there by a stroke of luck, and after she sought me out. She told my mom she'd seen something magical in me, that she knew a few people in the industry, and wanted to see if they'd be interested in my trying out for a few parts. She gave Mom her personal cell number—she loves to tell this part of the story, adding that she didn't even have business cards yet, she was so new to the game—and told her to call her if they wanted to talk more.

A week later, my mom and I sat in an office and signed a contract for Jackie to become my talent agent. After that, I auditioned whenever I could fit it into my school schedule. I landed small parts, commercials, and extras, and even a few small roles, but I loved it. Within a year, we'd moved from our small town to LA so I could take on more auditions, and Mom quickly acclimated to the role of my manager.

When I was nine, I got my big break, a role on a family sitcom as the cute, quirky daughter, and became a fan favorite. But it was five years later, when I was fourteen and was cast in a large kids' television network's tween dramedy and got the chance to sing, that my career blew up. Four years after that, I released my first album and never looked back. Once I was of age and done with acting, Mom stepped down as my manager, retiring early and handing the reins to Jackie.

Through it all, Jackie has been my rock, the one always in my corner to cheer me on and make sure things move smoothly, and to make sure my career continues to grow.

"I'm good, Jackie. How are you?" She puts an arm around my shoulders and pulls me into her, giving me a side hug.

"Same old, same old. Nailing down the details for your next album release. Are you still on track for recording in November?" My stomach churns, but I hide my discomfort behind a shining smile.

"Absolutely." She looks me over for a moment, but then the elevator dings, the doors slide open, and both of us step out.

We walk right past the receptionist, Jackie leading us through as if she owns the place. I give a small wave to the receptionist, who smiles gently, despite glaring at Jackie. It's not unusual, since with her take-no-shit attitude, she often rubs people the wrong way. I try to offset that by being as kind as possible, and I hope we manage to balance each other out.

When I enter the meeting room, I try to mask the confusion on my face, as Jefferson Sterns is sitting beside Leo. Jefferson gives me a wide, friendly grin, while Leo barely even acknowledges our entrance. Some would find it rude, but I'm used to it from the brusque man.

Leo Sinclaire has been my publicist for years now, ever since he suggested my fake relationship with his client, Riggins Greene. After the scheme worked so well, it took my next album to triple platinum and skyrocketed me from arenas to stadium tours. Jackie reached out to him to ask if he'd be interested in working with me full-time. He's a stoic man, always looking rather irritated, but he's amazing at his job and, despite working in PR, has never made me feel like I'm selling my soul for my career.

His boss, Jefferson, though...

"Thank you both for meeting us today. As you know, the last album did absolutely spectacularly," Jackie says, avoiding any small talk as she opens her folder and begins going over numbers, ratings, and the reception of the previous album and the subsequent tour.

"Now it's time to talk about the strategy for the next album," Jackie says, and I nod, knowing that is the purpose of this meeting. "We're looking at a May release with the first single being 'Are You Mine?' Ideally, the album announcement would be in January." I nod, knowing all of these details already. "The next relationship should begin sometime in the fall; we're just waiting on final contracts."

"Who is this one with again?" I ask, unsure but not unsurprised.

"Chris Hill," she says, and I nod, remembering the headshot she showed me a few weeks ago. Dark hair, broody eyes...an actor, I believe. Another bad boy for me to reform.

"He's an actor who is about to be cast in a women's fiction movie as a loving, widowed single dad. Currently, he's been out breaking hearts, getting drunk, and partying, so we're hoping being seen out with you will boost his public perception to better fit the film's messaging," Leo says, folding his hands over his folder.

It will. We all know it will. That's how it works, after all. It's what I do, after all.

I date Hollywood's biggest scandals and reform their image in the media. While I'm at it, I collect inspiration for my next album, which the public will be waiting for with bated breath, desperate to get a bit of the inside scoop of my latest relationship and subsequent breakup. At the end, my faux-beau has a bit better standing, some of his misdeeds forgotten, be it a DUI, fighting in public, or being a menace on set, and I have something to keep my fans interested.

After all, no one wants to hear love songs from someone who has never actually been in love.

"In the meantime, I'd love for you to keep a low profile, really build up the intrigue before the big reveal," Leo says, and my eyes widen at the suggestion.

"You want me to hide?" I ask, shocked. Jackie's jaw tenses, and I wonder for a moment if she knew about this or if she's just as surprised as I am.

"No, I don't want you to hide. I just want you to lay low, giving the press minimal sightings, if at all possible. Let them wonder what you're doing, and more importantly, who you might be doing it with. I'm planning to strategically drop tips and hints to major publications about you being happy or flirting with someone new, implying that you might be feeling inspired, that kind of thing. The mystery will mean that when you do step out, everyone will be clamoring to see you and ready to listen to everything you're saying. Think of it as a press detox or a reset. You've been so heavily in the spotlight over the past year, we don't want to exhaust people's interest in you."

"They won't get exhausted by her," Jackie says, clearly irritated, and I think it's on my behalf. "She's Willa Stone."

"I agree that public interest in Willa has always and continues to be high, but we all know how these things go. The more we give them, the more they want. If we give less, then they'll be primed and even more excited to invest themselves into the relationship and thus, the next album," Leo agrees, his voice steady and firm, long used to dealing with my manager. Jackie is clearly unimpressed by the plan, but for a moment, light fills my chest at the idea of a break.

Hiding away.

No press.

No interviews, no scheduled appearances.

"And Leo's taking a leave of absence for the next few months," Jefferson says, speaking for the first time and cutting into my thoughts, his voice tight, clearly unimpressed. "That's why I'm here for today's meeting. I want to be fully in the loop for your next cycle, in case you need me. I'm planning to stay on top of Leo's clients while he's away." Now that is a genuine surprise to me, the idea of worka-holic Leo Sinclaire taking a leave of absence. But when I look at him, he's glaring daggers at his partner.

"It's not a leave of absence. I just won't be in the city," Leo clari-fies. With the venom in his voice, it's clear this is an ongoing conversa-tion between the men. Jefferson opens his mouth, but I speak instead, curious.

"Where are you going?"

"I bought a house," Leo says, jaw tight. He hates talking about himself, but I make it my mission to try to learn something about the closed-lipped man every time I see him. Most of the time, I fail, which is why, after nearly seven years of working together, I know that he doesn't like pickles (a crime), takes his coffee black (gross), grew up in Ocean View, New Jersey, and is an only child. I nod and open my mouth to ask another question, to see if I can get more, but he interrupts, redirecting the conversation.

"But I'm not requesting the low profile for my benefit. I will still be available if needed, and I am not far away at all. As your publicist, I would be your first line of defense for any kind of trouble." He doesn't say this to me, but to his boss, that glare locked in place one more. "This method has worked for you in the past: it worked with your third release, when you disappeared, then reappeared, dating Riggins. It would be a good time to switch up the process to avoid it getting stale or too predictable. Unpredictability with these kinds of things is incredibly important. We were able to divert attention after the Riggins incident, but we have to play this next one closely."

"Well, if Riggins hadn't gone off and—" Jackie starts, but I saw this coming and cut her off.

"Jackie," I say, firmly, because I'm not having this conversation again. When Riggins Greene, my very first fake relationship and now a friend of mine, went on a talk show to reveal that we had been in a fake relationship while he went to rehab, Jackie wanted to throw the book at him, sue him for breach of contract. With Leo's help, I managed to convince her otherwise, reminding her it would reveal more than we wanted. Instead, we twisted the narrative to tell the media that I was unaware of his marital status before beginning my relationship with Riggins, and that it was a turbulent time for all of us involved, then wished him and Stella all the best.

"I think it's smart," I say, turning to Jackie. "I can't go from relationship to relationship nonstop, and we all know that if I'm out of sight, the fans speculate and build up the suspense." I turn back to Leo. "I do have my mom's charity event in early October, though, and

I can't miss that." When my mom retired from being my brand manager, she joined a few charity boards to keep herself busy and, more importantly, relevant and connected, so a few times a year, I'm expected to donate to auctions or, if I have no other scheduled events, I'm expected to attend the galas she is helping to run. Leo nods.

"That will be fine, I've already included that in your schedule, and we should have the relationship moving by then. And if not, being spotted here and there is good. We simply want to minimize exposure."

"I do want to make it clear that if you're not comfortable with this plan, you can let me know at any time. Chris is my personal client, and I know we could easily bump up the schedule. We don't have to work on Leo's timeline," Jefferson says with that same sickly-sweet smile on his lips.

My ick fully triggers. I don't like something about his tone...or maybe it's the way it feels like he's using me to get at Leo. I put Willa Stone™ back on. My shoulders straighten, and I look down my nose at the man before me.

"We're not working on Leo's timeline: we're working on my time-line. My music isn't ready anyway, so there's no point." There's a sharp pain in my ankle as Jackie kicks me beneath the table, since she's always warning me to lock my attitude in a box. You can't be America's Sweetheart if the public thinks you're a bitch, after all, but I don't drop my stare-down with Jefferson.

"Of course, of course. I was just throwing it out there," Jefferson says, brandishing his hands in surrender, and an awkward silence fills the room as I continue to stare at him.

From across the way, there's a small sound, a snort coming from Leo's direction, and I finally break my gaze from his boss to look to him. Entertainment is written across his face, but there's something else there too, a flash of something in his blue eyes, not quite relief or gratification, since I don't think the man is actually capable of either of those things, but something close to it. I give him a smile, hoping it looks genuine, before Jackie speaks.

"Well, I don't want to waste more of your day, Willa. I think we can probably end things here," Jackie says, a fake pleasantness in her words. "But Jefferson, I would love to chat with you some more about Chris and his goals and expectations for this collaboration. Are you open for lunch today?"

"For you? Always," Jefferson says, then stands. "And remember, Willa, anything at all, feel free to reach out." I smile and nod, staying seated as they leave. Once they're gone, I stand, grab my bag, and follow Leo out, my mind still reeling from that meeting but eager for an opportunity to get under his skin.

FOUR

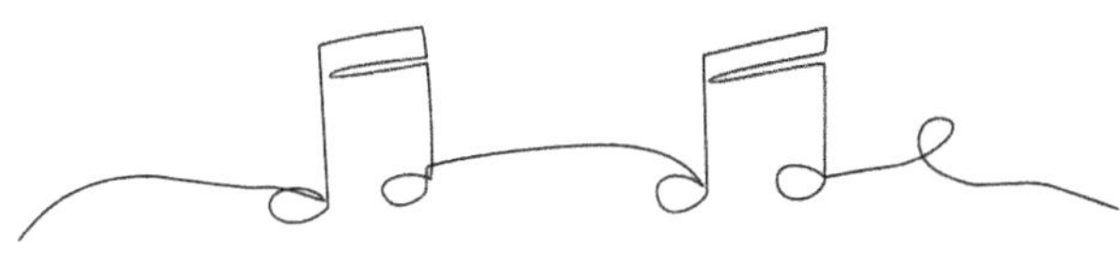

WILLA

Leo's steps are long strides, and it takes at least two of my own to match one of his, but I reach him and then smile up at him, desperate to talk to *somebody* about that meeting.

"That was weird, right?" I ask as we wait, side by side, for the elevator. Leo looks at me for a single, irritated moment before looking back down at his phone. I can't help it; a small smile tips onto my lips at the look.

I have always deeply annoyed Leo Sinclaire from the moment we started working together, and despite my brand being *everyone-likes-me*, it's been a breath of fresh air to find someone who isn't constantly striving to kiss my ass.

"Jackie and Jefferson?" I ask, continuing despite his silence. "I think they might have been flirting." He stays quiet, tapping on his screen as we wait for the elevator. "Do you think they slipped off to have a nooner?" That gets his attention, and his head snaps up to look at me.

"Did you just say *nooner?*"

I bite back a laugh and respond with a straight face. "What else would you call a mid-day hookup?"

"Not a *nooner*," he says, and for a moment, a glimmer of the man I met long ago, the one the hopeless, idiot part of me thought meant something, shines through. It's gone in a flash, and he turns back to his phone. He's always on his phone, always putting out some kind of fire or threatening some tabloid, I'm sure.

"Are you and Jefferson on the outs? I thought he was going to explode when I said I was fine with the updated timeline." I ask, always trying to find out some tiny bit of information about the man.

"Why'd you do that?" he asks, looking to me. My face goes as neutral as I can manage before shrugging.

"I think your plan is sound. Jackie doesn't like anyone saying anything that might hurt my feelings, but you're right; too much exposure breeds expectations and boredom. If we want the marketing for the next album to hit hard, we need to preserve a bit of that mystery."

He looks at me, something new crossing his face that I've never seen before, like he's seeing me for the first time, and it makes me feel far too exposed.

I pull up my shield, turning flirty, fun, friendly, and just a bit ditzy.

"Plus, a couple of months on some island would be nice. Maybe I can hook up with some cabana boy, have a torrid affair, and use that to write my next album." His shoulders go tight with my words, and I try not to smile too wide at the fact that my words had the desired effect.

For as long as I can remember, I've loved teasing Leo Sinclaire. It's hard to do, nearly impossible to get a rise out of the even-keeled, closed-off man, but when I can, it feels like I won the lottery.

"No," he says, words firm, sliding his phone into his pocket for the first time and turning to face me with his jaw set tight. He crosses his arms on his chest, and his suit jacket pulls tight across his chest. I wonder, not for the first time, if it's just a well-fitting suit or if he really does have the broad shoulders and toned arms the suit promises. "No cabana boys. No affairs. You are to stay out of the public eye, avoid the tabloids, and not create a fucking scandal." I lose the battle to bite back my smile as the elevator doors slide open, and we both step in.

"Okay, okay, no cabana boys." His glare as the doors shut us into the elevator is still searing, so finally, I give in. "I was just joking. When have you ever known me to do that?"

His eyes narrow, but he doesn't respond, probably because we both know the answer is never. He sighs, a deep sound that seems to be coming from him more and more lately, before he turns to me fully.

"Just stay out of trouble, okay?" he asks, sounding exasperated. My brows furrow.

"Out of trouble?" I ask, unsure.

Mostly because I've never actually *been in trouble.*

"Yes. Stay out of trouble. The goal is to stir up interest with you being off the grid. I don't want to have to deal with cleaning up your messes during that time." I stare at him, fighting back the irritation in my veins.

"I've never actually needed you to clean up my messes," I say low. "I always follow what you guys ask me. And the problems you've had to deal with are from someone else." Finally, he looks at me, a blank look on his face, and any of the remaining joy from messing with him is fully gone.

"Good. Let's keep it that way, okay?" I stare at him, unsure of what to say, but before I can think of anything, the elevator dings our arrival.

I'm still stunned silent when the elevator doors slide open, and without another word, Leo steps out, head down as he stares at his phone screen once again, and walks off with purpose. When I follow much more slowly, Gabe is already waiting for me, giving me a nod and a soft smile, which I return. I follow him to the front doors, and when I spot the paparazzi still outside, that familiar panic stiffens in my chest. Gabe steps out before me, and I use that time to bury my nerves, closing my eyes and taking a deep breath. It took a while to get used to this, to the crowds and the cameras and the attention, but after years of it, I've gotten used to it, creating a routine for handling it: Pause, deep breath, know how long I'm going to be out there, and put on my shield.

By the time I open my eyes, a grin is spreading over my lips, and I'm taking a step out to the door, Willa Stone™ firmly in place, and Gabe is nodding for me to follow. I wave as I step out, cameras flashing and my name called from all directions. I hold that smile until I slip into the car, and the door slams shut behind me.

With the sound shut off, a wave and calm floats over me, washing away the panic and unease that always comes. My shoulders drop, my face relaxes, my eyes close, and I sit back, taking in a deep breath. Gabe drives slowly off the property, a few flashes still ticking, but I don't fully relax until we merge onto the highway and make our way home. But as the adrenaline washes away, relief fills in the cracks, and I can't help but smile a real smile, thinking that may have been the last time I have to do that for a while.

The next morning, my alarm goes off at what once felt like the ungodly hour of five thirty a.m., but I've had the same morning routine for almost seven years now, so I roll out of bed without issue. After my normal bathroom routine, I brush my blonde locks into a sleek high ponytail, pop in my blue contacts, and swipe on a light layer of makeup, just in case the press catches me. In my bedroom, I throw on an all-black workout outfit and then head down the stairs.

I grab a glass of water and a pre-bottled green juice from the fridge, grimacing at the bright green color before sighing and chugging it. It tastes absolutely disgusting, but according to my nutritionist, it's perfectly formulated for my own metabolism and great for my hair, skin, and nails, or something like that, so I drink it like clockwork every morning. When I'm done with the goo, I shiver, then slide on my shoes and head to the door.

"Morning, Gabe," I say with a soft, genuine smile when I see him already waiting for me. He's been with me for about two years, going on tour with me when his boss, Jaime Wilde, and head of Wilde Security, stepped down from personal bodyguard jobs. He tips his head stoically, then opens the car door for me, waiting for me to slide in before closing it behind me, and then takes me to Pilates.

Ninety grueling minutes with my personal trainer later, I'm back in the car and headed home for a shower, a change, and breakfast.

And there, for the first time in forever, my routine ends.

Normally, I have something going on. Normally, I'd put on a carefully crafted outfit and greet my hair and makeup artist at the door for full glam before interviews, meetings, or some staged outing. Other times, I'd head to the studio to brew up some buzz for the next album. If I'm in a relationship, I'll have a date scheduled. If I'm on tour or prepping for tour, I'd have practice, meet-and-greets, or... anything.

But right now, with this new plan, my schedule is wiped clean.

So I clean up after breakfast and realize my spices are a mess, in need of organization. While doing that, I notice the pantry could use a spruce-up, and while I'm at it, why not tackle my bathroom closet and the linen closet?

Three times, I walk past my music room, but three times, I find an excuse not to enter.

But eventually, when all the closets I can think of are organized and cleared out, even though they're already pretty tidy, I grab my water and notebook and brave my music room to write.

And I sit there.

And sit there.

And sit there, praying for inspiration to strike. My fingers move on strings. I try to write things down, feelings of falling in love, of having a crush, anything that aligns with the direction I have for this album, but nothing fucking comes.

All I can think about is my conversation with Adam the day before.

After an hour of sitting at a blank sheet of paper, all I've got to show for it is a couple of doodles in the corners, the word love and crush written a dozen times, along with a couple of other words I'd hoped would spark an idea before I sit back with a resigned sigh. A small yawn leaves my lips, and when I look at the clock, I realize it's time for my afternoon coffee. I stand, about to make my way downstairs to make it for myself, when I pause.

Get out of your routine.

Maybe Adam was right.

Maybe I just need to switch up my routine a bit.

Picking up my phone, I tap the screen until I get to Gabe's name, then hit send. It rings just once before he picks up.

"Hey, Gabe, can we go to the coffee shop downtown? I want to get a drink."

"Of course. When?"

"Uh, now?" I ask, walking towards the door and my shoes.

"No problem. I can be there in five."

Excitement fills me at the prospect.

"Or I could go get one and bring it back to you," he offers.

"No, no. I want to get out of the house."

"I'll be right there." He clicks off.

Change your routine.

For as long as I can remember, my life has been structured. A strict morning routine, gym routine, followed by practices and interviews, and strategy meetings... Each day is perfectly lined up, crafted to turn me into the powerhouse I've become.

It's still moving through my mind as I slide into the back seat of the G-wagon, a requirement made by Leo Sinclaire, even though I have always hated the feeling of being driven around. But in the front seat, the windows can't be tinted, so the cameras can get a snap of me in a moment when my guard is down, something that will inevitably be torn apart by the media that seems to control my life.

When we pull up to the coffee shop, Gabe gets out first before opening my door and guiding me in. There are a few whispers, and the cashier clearly recognizes me as I place my order, but when I give her my name, she squawks at the confirmation. I let out a little laugh and take a photo with her, and then the rest of the staff while they make my drink.

Once it's in hand, I wave goodbye to my new friends, and suddenly, I'm excited to get back home and try to write again. The hint of melodies plays on the edges of my mind, and I wonder if maybe this is exactly what I need: a bit of a change-up. As I move to the door, I contemplate if maybe this could be a new part of my routine, a mid-afternoon pick-me-up to break up my day.

"Ready?" Gabe asks, and I nod, though when I look out the door, I bite my lip, seeing a handful of paparazzi outside. I thought I'd have time, that I could get in and out before anyone reported I was here, but clearly not.

I suppose the thought of coming every day is out the window. I'll have to opt for the drive-through next time, or else I'll get bombarded every time. With a hint of disappointment, I take in a deep breath, closing my eyes and centering myself, putting the shield up before nodding to Gabe, who pushes the door open. I smile and wave at the paparazzi, making sure each gets the photo they need as I move toward the car, Gabe at my side, a hand hovering over my lower back.

"Willa, one moment, please!" a man holding a large camera calls, stepping closer. "Just a few questions!"

"I'm sorry, I have to head out," I say, giving the man a tight smile. I don't recognize him, but the tag on his chest is for one of the more well-known tabloids. While I can probably talk my way out of getting spotted this morning, stopping to answer questions would absolutely not please Leo.

"Come on. You spent a while in there with the staff." I grit my teeth at his entitlement but force the soft smile to stay on my face, no matter how much I want to curse this man out.

"I was just chatting with some fans while I waited for my coffee," I say, lifting the drink up and taking a step towards the car.

"I'm a fan, too. Give me something. When's the next album

coming out? Are you dating anyone?" He steps closer, crossing the line that isn't so much required as implied. All of the paparazzi in town know not to get too close, to respect personal space, but this man is new and clearly doesn't.

"I really—" I start, unsure of what to say or how to get out of this, but then he reaches for me, his fingers just barely touching my upper arm before Gabe pulls me back and behind him.

"Get back," Gabe says, voice firm as he steps closer to the man and me.

"Oh, come on, she's not in a rush, she just spent—"

"I said, get back," Gabe says, voice rising.

"She's being an uptight bitch," he says, and despite everything, despite knowing the man is an asshole, it stings. I try to tell myself that nothing they say can hurt me. I have my shield on, because they aren't saying it about me: they're saying it about my shield. About the person, I show them.

But it still stings every time.

"If you don't back off, I'm going to be forced to call the cops for harassment."

"She's a celebrity, this is what she signed up for," the man says, and that familiar panic fills me, brewing and swirling in my chest. No amount of deep breaths will counter this; the only thing that will work is silence and a door between the crowd and me. Instead of responding to the man, Gabe looks at me, reads my face, and sees it.

"Car, now," he says, moving and opening the door, letting me slide in. I don't argue, not as he slams the door shut, then returns to arguing with the man. I'm sure the press is going to have a field day with this, framing me as a self-important diva who is rude to fans, but I can't focus on that right now. Instead, I close my eyes, take deep, measured breaths, and remind myself that I'm okay in this moment, that I'm safe.

After a minute or so, Gabe slides into the car wordlessly and then drives off. Once we're far enough that he feels comfortable, he pulls over to the shoulder and calls Jaime on the car's Bluetooth. He fills his boss in on what just happened, but my mind is still swimming, so I barely listen to their conversation. The call ends, and silence fills the car once again.

"Are you okay?" he asks, and I nod, even though he can't see it before I speak.

"I should have just talked to him," I whisper, my voice fragile even to my own ears.

"Willa—"

"He has a job to do," I continue. "He has bills to pay, and if I had just—"

"His job is to respect boundaries. Everyone else can do it just fine. He should have respected both your time, personal space, and the fact that you were on private property."

"But—" I start, but Gabe isn't having it, his face firm.

"No. You've gotten way too comfortable with letting people push you around and thinking you need to accept it."

"It's all part of the job—" He turns in his seat, locking eyes with me and shaking his head.

"No, it's not. I know Jackie tries to make it seem like your life isn't your own, but there are hundreds of celebrities out there who don't make themselves as available as you do. You should be able to do something for yourself, to get a goddamned coffee, without them harassing you." I lift a shoulder half-heartedly.

"Well, after that, Leo's probably going to send me off to some far-off land where no paparazzi can get to me until he's ready for them to see me." Gabe looks me over, his face going just a bit soft before he speaks.

"Maybe that would be good, Willa. Maybe you need that." His words shock me to my core, and I don't respond, too lost in my thoughts, but Gabe doesn't push it, doesn't try to get me to talk more, and I'm grateful for his ever-present silence. After a moment, he turns back around and drives me home. My hands shake the entire drive home, and I barely drink my coffee, and by the time I make it home, the only thing I can think about is getting out of the city.

FIVE

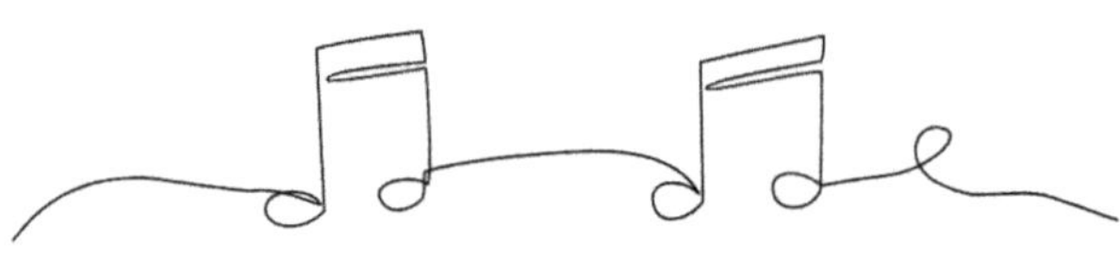

LEO

On Tuesday evening, I sit with a beer on the Adirondack chair I'd assembled that morning, enjoying the quiet of my backyard. Despite needing to reset the pavers and weed like wild out here, I know I'll be spending a lot of time out here. Eventually, I'll get an outdoor dining set and a grill, making it a space for entertaining, even though I don't really have anyone to entertain.

Except, I might actually, because although I've done my best to stay away from Adam's new friends and pseudo-family, it's becoming increasingly obvious that it will be impossible here in Holly Ridge. On Monday, I got home from the city with barely any time to spare to meet the truck delivering the bed, mattress, and couch I'd bought to make the place livable while I work on it. Not five minutes after they drove off, I got a text from an unknown number.

UNKNOWN

Do you need help with your furniture?

Because I can send Jesse over if you need.

A creeping knowing stirred in my gut, but I asked anyway.

. . .

Who is this?

Hallie. Do you need help? I just saw a
furniture truck drive down the road.

My first instinct was to argue with her, to tell her it was a breach of privacy, but I've heard enough stories from Adam to know it wouldn't be worth the energy. Instead, I gave her a polite dismissal.

No, thank you.

Where did you get my number?

Wren

I should have known. And since the woman has never contacted me personally, I'm pretty sure she got my number from Adam, the traitor. I sighed, realizing my new reality.

Let me know if you need anything. Once
you're settled in, I want you over for dinner.

It was less of a request and far more of a demand. I gave a thumbs-up, deciding that responding as little as possible without being rude was the key here. When she didn't text again, I think I may have made the right choice.

Then, this morning, there was a knock on my door, which, at first, concerned me since this place isn't necessarily easy to find. But when I opened the door, there was a smiling Wren King on my front step, her signature ribbon—this one a pale blue—in her dark hair, a wide, friendly smile on her lips, and a plate of cookies in her hands.

"For you!" she said, handing the dish to me after I greeted her. "Welcome to the neighborhood!" I didn't bother to remind her that her neighborhood and mine were on opposite sides of town. "Don't worry, I'm not here to bother you. I just came to drop these off. Gotta head into work now."

"Oh, uh, thank you?" I asked, unsure. I've never been hand-delivered a plate of homemade cookies. If it were anyone else but Wren, I would probably throw them out. But the Atlas Oaks guys bragged about trying her cookies when they went there for dinner when they were in town for the festival. I opted out in favor of working in the hotel while we were in town, and I'd been curious ever since.

She took a step back, that grin still wide on her lips as she waved a hand. "No need! You can keep the plate, too. But I did want to invite you over for dinner sometime soon." I don't respond, my mind blanking on reasons to bow out, but she opened her car door before I could. "I'll have Adam reach out, set something up." I nodded, then watched the little whirlwind of a woman slide into her car, give me a wave as she executed a K-turn, and drive away.

Still, despite the well-meaning interruptions from my new, far-too-friendly neighbors, I've felt a long-forgotten sense of peace since officially moving to Holly Ridge.

As I sit eating one of the admittedly delicious cookies, I let that feeling sink further into my bones as I stare at the trees, picturing them in various seasons once I settle in, and thinking once again that my dad would have loved this place.

He loved being outside and working with his hands, and long before I was born, he built a construction company with my uncle. When my mom was pregnant with me, he bought a rundown place in the middle of nowhere and fixed it up, and that's the house I grew up in, and my mom still lives in. It was similar to this place, surrounded by trees, just far enough out of town to be quiet, but not so far out that mom couldn't have little luxuries, like shopping or a nice dinner out.

I grew up around power tools, home renovations, and, most importantly to my dad, nature. The smell of wood always sends me back to those days, to summers working for my dad, painting rooms or installing trim or adding finishing hardware, or, when I got older, making cabinetry since carpentry was my dad's specialty, a skill he was determined to pass down to me. Those skills have gone unused, but now, here, as I work on this place, it's all coming back to me like second nature.

When my phone rings, a group of birds I'd been watching flies off, and I sigh, coming back to reality as I reach over for my phone. When I see *Jackie Klein* on the screen, I groan, rubbing a hand over my face.

I do not want to talk to Jackie right now.

I don't really *ever* want to talk to Jackie, whom I find myself butting heads with more and more lately, but I really don't want to right now, the day after I told her that Willa is to lay low. That being said, I know that if I don't answer, she'll call Jefferson, and I don't need to give him any further opportunities to shmooze her. Monday was another blatant sign that Jefferson is trying to secure my clients for himself before my contract is up, and despite her manager being a pain in my ass, I don't trust Jefferson to take on a star like Willa without being incredibly detrimental to her career and brand.

Though that's more about not wanting to ruin my hard work than worry about the woman myself, of course.

"Hello, Jackie," I say, trying to maintain neutrality as I answer. "To what do I owe the pleasure?" Jackie doesn't bother with niceties, instead jumping right into what she needs. It's probably the one thing I *do* appreciate about the woman.

"A paparazzi harassed Willa today and got his hands on her. I need you to kill a story on it." I sit up straight, my heart sinking to my stomach at the thought of Willa in a situation like that.

"Fuck, Jackie, is she okay? Where was it? Was Gabe there?"

"What? Oh, yeah, she's fine, probably learned her lesson." Her voice is casual, as if her primary client wasn't just in a precarious situation. If I were talking to anyone else, I'd think I might be overreacting, and the situation wasn't that bad, but this is Jackie I'm speaking with.

A few years back, Willa had a stalker, and Jackie let it trail on for a full week despite knowing who it was because *any press is good press*, especially if it can win America's Sweetheart some pity points. I remember the look of panic on Willa's face every time the cameras weren't on her during that time, the way she was so pale and nervous at all times. Eventually, I was fed up with it and filed an anonymous tip, ending that nightmare.

"Learned her lesson?" I ask, a sour feeling of disgust curling in the pit of my stomach. Jackie sighs, papers moving in the background as if this call is already going on longer than she would like.

"You told her to stay under wraps, and this wasn't an activity on her normal schedule. She went to a coffee shop on a whim, spent time there lollygagging with the staff, so by the time she left, there was a crowd. She didn't even have on a branded outfit; she was just wearing *workout clothes*. Really, what did she expect?"

I do my best to read between the lines there and get the idea of what happened: Willa, being sweet Willa, went to get a coffee and then chatted with the staff, probably signed some autographs and took some pictures, and it took longer than expected to get in and get out, giving time for a crowd to form, including an overzealous pap.

"So, what's going on?" I ask, standing and moving inside to my computer.

"I got a heads up from my contact at *Fan Magazine* that they've got footage and are going to spin it as *America's Sweetheart snubs a fan.*"

"A fan? I thought he was a paparazzi?" I ask, a hand lifting to my temple as I feel a migraine coming on.

"He is, but they've chopped the clip to him telling her he's a big fan and asking for just a minute of her time. They're going to say she's a man-hater and only likes her female fans." I close my eyes and sigh at the true ridiculousness I have to deal with on a daily basis. "I need you to contact them and kill the story in the next twenty minutes. Once you've completed that, send confirmation that the task is done." Despite the demand, she sounds bored, and irritation bubbles to the surface of my currently roiling emotions.

"I don't work for you, Jackie," I remind her. "I do not have to complete a task the second you request it, nor do I have to report to you when I've completed an assignment you give me." I, of course, will be doing it regardless because I'm good at my job and protect my clients at all costs, no matter the headache their team gives me, but I find it vital to continuously remind Jackie of that line. A sigh fills the line and her voice goes sweet in a way that sounds completely unnatural on her.

"If you don't have the time, you could share your contact info for *Fan Magazine,* and I'll do it myself. I know you're on your little break or whatever, but these things need to get done."

There is no universe in which I would give her my press contacts, and despite her giant ego, she knows it. I don't trust the woman as far as I could throw her.

"Send me the details, and I'll make some calls," I say.

"Are you sure? I don't—"

"I've got it," I say, cutting her off. She doesn't speak for a moment, and I can picture her pinched, irritated face. Her annoyance brings me a spark of joy, though it also sets off an alarm in my mind, a whisper of a question that this was all a ploy to get my info. A setup, maybe?

I brush that aside as the nonsense, conspiracy-theory-type shit it is.

"Fine. Please let me know once you've finished," she says, irritation clearly in the words, as if I'm her assistant. I open my mouth to argue and remind her *once again* that I do not work for her, but the line is dead before I can get a word out.

With a sigh, I sit back and stare at the sky. A minute later, my phone beeps with a new email from Jackie with details and two video clips. One is edited, with clips spliced together to make Willa seem like a stuck-up snob, but the other, an original from an angle other than the tabloid one, makes my stomach churn.

Her smile when she steps out of the coffeehouse is glowing, a coffee in her hand, her blonde ponytail swinging from side to side as she moves. Like she always does when paparazzi gather, trained to do so, she steps carefully, moves slowly, making sure everyone gets the shot they need. She waves and smiles, a black tank top and legging set hugging her curves as she moves toward the camera. A paparazzi I don't recognize, wearing a Fan Magazine lanyard, calls her name and says something I can't quite catch. Willa gives him a soft smile and shakes her head graciously, but unease is clear in her eyes. The man continues to harass her, and Gabe steps in, but the man doesn't stop, going so far as to try to grab her arm before Gabe successfully gets her into the car.

When she slides in, the camera gets a glimpse of her face, and the smile is gone, fear and panic written plain as day across it, and anger blooms in my chest.

Before the videos hit my inbox, I thought I would feel frustrated she didn't take my advice, didn't stay out of the cameras, but instead, it's anger that some asshole put that look on her face.

I let that fuel me as I tap on the screen of my phone, calling up my contact, the editor-in-chief at *Fan Magazine.*

"Leo Sinclaire, how are you, man?" Jackson Smith says, but I'm not in the mood for small talk and niceties. Unfortunately for him, I made this call already pissed the fuck off, and I have no other outlet for it.

"Kill the fucking story, Jackson," I say, letting my voice crack like a whip along the line. I'm known for my temper, my sharpness, and my lack of mercy when it comes to protecting my clients.

He sighs, then answers, clearly already knowing what story I'm speaking of. "I can't do that, Leo."

"You can, and you will," I tell him. "You and I both know that story is bullshit, and your man is in the wrong. I want confirmation that the story has been killed within the hour. Then I want that man fired, and I want a formal apology printed on your website in the next twenty-four hours."

"Leo—"

"An hour, Jackson."

"Come on, Leo. Don't be rash," Jackson says, the good old boy out of his voice and tinged with a hint of panic, but clearly not willing to throw in the towel just yet. We both know a story like that could sell hundreds of thousands of copies and rack up millions of views on socials. "You know I can't do that. It's a good story."

"There are a million stories out there. A million celebrities, more than happy to be followed around. It's clear that Willa did not want to be. She politely declined talking to him, and he decided to verbally harass her and tried to put his hands on her. Now, if I don't hear that you're letting him go in the next twenty-four hours, you will no longer be on my short list of magazines to send intel to. You had the exclusive of Wes and Harper's wedding. I gave you the info on Willa's breakup before anyone else. You knew Courtney was pregnant first and got the baby announcement before she even told her fucking parents. That will all end."

"Come on—"

"Is this one story worth a dozen more?"

There's silence before he speaks. "I could go to Jefferson." Irritation flares within me, but it's the jaded kind, the kind that makes me want to ruin his career just to prove I can. "We both know he doesn't have the same qualms about morals that you do." I push down that feeling and force myself to think rationally.

"And we both know that Jefferson's clients are not Willa Stone or Atlas Oaks. We both know that Jaime at Wilde Security fucking hates his guts. We both know that he hasn't given you a tip in at least a year, because he has nothing to give you. Now give me what I need, Jackson, or you're done. I want confirmation in an hour."

And then I hang up.

When I do, my chest tightens, and I work to lower my heart rate by taking deep breaths. I stare out at the trees, trying desperately to find that peace I'd had not long before, but realize it's a lost cause. Instead, I stand and head inside to keep working and distract my mind.

Thirty minutes later, I get a text confirming the story is killed, and he's running the firing through HR right now. With a sigh and a healthy amount of satisfaction at putting the fear of god into yet another scumbag tabloid owner, I pick up my roller and continue my effort of priming my guest room. I only get one wall finished when my phone rings again. Since my phone is on do not disturb, it means one of the few people who's allowed to get through is calling.

"Oh, come the fuck on," I grumble, setting the roller in the paint tray and sliding my phone out of my pocket. My earlier irritation flares brighter when I see the name on the screen.

Just like when Jackie called, I contemplate ignoring it, but there's always a small chance that there's a real issue I'll need to sort out, so I pick up the phone.

"Jeff," I say, balancing the cell between my shoulder and ear as I make my way to the kitchen for water. He hates when I call him Jeff, usually correcting me quickly, so I can tell he's extra pissy when he doesn't.

"Why am I hearing that you just threatened to blacklist *Fan Magazine*?" he asks as I reach up for a glass in one of the cabinets in order to keep myself calm and steady.

"Because I just threatened to blacklist *Fan Magazine*," I explain before putting my glass beneath the faucet and filling it. Once that's done, I lean back onto the counter and focus on the call.

"You can't do that, Leo." I shrug, even though he can't see it, and take a long sip before responding.

"Strange, I believe I just did. His employee touched one of my clients. I told Jackson he needs to let him go, or I'm blacklisting the entire paper." A heavy sigh, one I've heard more and more over the years, leaves Jefferson's lips.

There was a time when I was Jefferson's star employee, the one he would point to in meetings to show what people should strive for, the one he promised partnership and cooperation with. There was a time when I didn't absolutely despise Jefferson Sterns, but those days are long gone

Now we tolerate each other, stuck in a stalemate neither of us can leave without imploding.

"What happens if they keep him around?"

"Then I blacklist him, Jefferson," I say as if he's a child who doesn't understand the basics.

"You can't blacklist one of the most popular tabloids in the country, Leo."

"I can, and if they continue to work with paparazzi who feel it's acceptable to lay hands on my clients, I will, in fact, be doing that."

"We need them, Leo."

That right there is why his firm, Perfect Image, will fail the moment I leave this company. He gives the media, the tabloids, the press far too much power, too much sway. His need to keep them on his good side, instead of the other way around, is part of what's turned his morals inside out, what's made him someone I despise being attached to.

"There are a dozen other tabloids desperate for exclusive information on our top clients. I'm not worried about this one."

"You've fucking lost it. I knew it when you said you were going to disappear, but now it's affecting my bottom line. I was speaking with Jackie, and she thinks you're getting a bit soft. Your contract with Willa is up soon, and—"

"Now, Jefferson, I would be really careful of any threats you might want to throw my way," I say, standing up straighter now. This has been coming for some time; we both know it, but I've been holding it close to my chest.

The truth is, Jefferson knows I want out.

I joined Perfect Image as a publicist ten years ago, fresh out of school and eager to prove myself. I started with clients no one else wanted, proved myself, built my client list, and brought in the firm's highest earners, including Willa Stone and Altas Oaks. While Jefferson does have some big names, we both know that the ones I have and the contacts I have are much more lucrative for the firm than anyone he has ever brought in. When I leave, the business will probably crumble in the years that follow.

We are fully aware know the only reason I stay is I have an iron-clad non-compete clause in my contract barring me from quitting and starting a business with any clients who are on current contracts with Perfect Image, and the only reason he doesn't fire me is because if he does, that same contract states that if I'm fired outside of the well-laid out terms of stealing, breaking my contract, or sabotaging the company, that non-compete is null and void. And more importantly, Jefferson knows that I won't do anything that could risk my clients' reputations by leaving their publicity solely to Jefferson.

"Now, I've got things to do," I lie. "And I would like to do them. If you have any other questions about my business or my clients, I might suggest simply not worrying about them and instead focusing on getting some high-earning clients of your own. I know that's a foreign concept for you, but maybe if you had some, you wouldn't have to use my clients to fix yours."

"Oh, fuck off—" he starts, but before he can say anything else, I hang up, then turn my phone to do not disturb, fighting the urge to throw it at the wall.

Then I step back outside, the sky dark now, and try to take a few deep, calming breaths to slow my heart rate and center myself. Days like this only cement the fact that I need to follow the exit plan I've laid out, take the time out here in Holly Ridge to find myself, and figure out what's next. Figure out who I am—what I want to be—without work. I've spent so much of my life hustling, building the publicity firm I love with everything I have, but every day I realize it brings me more stress than joy.

It started last November while trying to find a solution for a client of Jefferson's who was accused of domestic abuse. I was on the phone with him, arguing that we should drop the client because the evidence was substantial, and he refused. After some choice words, I hung up on him. As I stewed over the bleak outlook of my career and the fact that I was essentially tied to this sinking ship with no other option in sight, my chest tightened, and I couldn't breathe. Panic shot through me, and I was sure that was it. My assistant later told me that all the color left my face, and she called an ambulance before saying a single word to me.

In that moment, I was sure I was having a heart attack just like my father. My father, who worked his entire life to give my mother and me everything we needed and wanted, only to die of a heart attack when I was sixteen. Worked himself to death, my mother loves to say.

As the ambulance sped through traffic, as the EMTs murmured to one another about blood pressure and radioed in words and numbers that meant nothing to me, all I could think was *what was I leaving behind?*

My father left behind a legacy. A construction company co-owned by his brother that, to this day, still keeps my mother's bills paid. A wife who loved him so much, she never moved on, never dated again. A son. A family.

In contrast, while I have a handful of friends and acquaintances, who in this world would truly miss me? Sure, a headshot of me smiling would be on some montage of people lost over the last year during an awards show, and people would clap, and there would be some social media posts, but other than that. Nothing.

I'd be leaving nothing. I've worked myself to the bone, but that was all I had.

Thankfully, a few hours later, I learned that I wasn't having a heart attack: I was having a panic attack, spurred by the stress of my job. Although I was somewhat embarrassed, a doctor sat me down to tell me it was a sign, and that if I continued down the path I was going on, I would wind up here with a real heart attack, considering my family history.

Soon after, I did what I could to try to relax. I tried taking a vacation, yoga, meditation, and therapy, but I knew it wouldn't fix everything and surely wouldn't give me what I realized I needed: a life.

I started cutting back, offloading some of my clients to other publicists I trusted within the firm and keeping my main accounts, whom I'd worked with so closely for so long, so that most of them weren't even a headache anymore. I started taking on agenting work, carefully selecting clients I saw had potential. I already had the connections, so it made sense to use them, since I couldn't take any of them on as new PR clients, given my current intention of leaving Perfect Image once my contract was up and starting my own, smaller boutique firm.

I made an exit plan that led me here, and despite the fact that my work does, in fact, follow me wherever I go, as I stare at my new backyard, I know in my gut I'm on the right path.

SIX

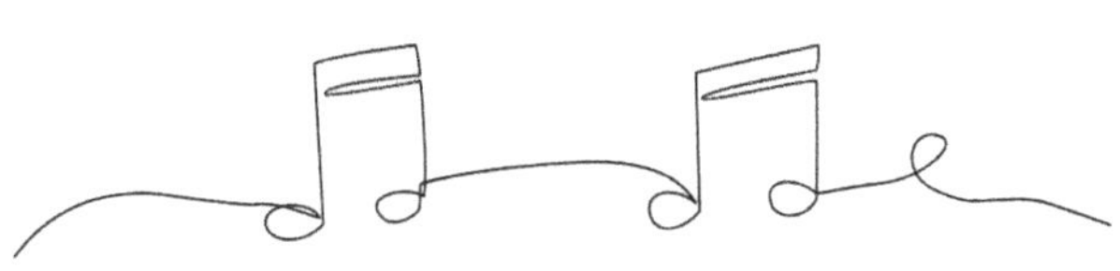

WILLA

I have to fight back an uneasy rise of panic as I park in front of a cute gray house the following afternoon. I tell myself it's residual adrenaline because I somehow drove from the city to Holly Ridge by myself, no bodyguard in sight. The decision was impulsive, but after stewing on it all night after my run-in with the paparazzi, the subsequent lecture from Jackie, and the awareness that my writer's block isn't improving, I decided I needed a change.

The conversation I'd had with Adam ricocheted through my mind as I tossed and turned all night, pinging back and forth and hitting each and every sore spot I'd been hiding for the past few years — all the loneliness, anxiety, and nerves. The fake nature of my life. The burnout I'd been ignoring. The lingering unhappiness closely followed by guilt whenever I acknowledged it.

This morning, I called Jaime Wilde and asked what he would need to feel comfortable with my being bodyguard-free for the next few months. I thought he'd be aghast, tell me it was impossible to travel without someone around all the time for my own safety, but when he heard where I was going, he was surprisingly okay with it, saying Holly Ridge was a bit of an anomaly, and so long as I stayed in the town, I could go alone.

Without a second thought, I packed a couple of suitcases, loaded them into the trunk of the car I rarely drive, entered my destination into my GPS, and headed out without a word to anyone else or a moment to second-guess.

Now, I'm here in the small town of Holly Ridge. It's just as cute as I've heard, and when I look next door, it's clear that while I'm sitting in front of Adam's house, the cute house beside it is Wren's. It's currently decorated with gorgeous, colorful blooms of flowers in the gardens and well-maintained, with a *Welcome Spring!* flag blowing gently in the wind. The porch is twined with what I think are fairy lights, and I'm suddenly desperate to know what it looks like when it's dark. It lacks the elegance or the extravagance of the homes I'm used to, but somehow, it's even more beautiful because of it.

Come on, Willa, I tell myself, taking a deep breath and looking back to Adam's boring-by-comparison front door. *You've got this. What's the worst that could happen, anyway?*

Well, I tell myself. *Adam could look at me like I'm out of my mind for taking him up on his offer to visit him in Holly Ridge.*

He could act like he's never seen me or tell me he was joking.

Even I have to admit the irony that, at any given moment, a magazine or newspaper is probably posting every intimate detail of my life, but walking up the front steps of a friendly acquaintance I've worked closely with is what makes me nervous.

With one final deep breath, I grab my keys and then step out of the SUV. My hair is pulled into my normal ponytail, but I'm wearing a hat that I dug out of the depths of my closet. I'm not wearing the blue-tinted contacts I always wear when we're out and about, which were given to me as a kid when I was on a popular family sitcom, and they needed a blonde hair, blue-eyed girl. I'm in a pair of my black leggings and a white sports tank, with pristine white sneakers on my feet. If Jackie saw me out and about in this, she might have a heart attack, but there are no cameras here, so I should be able to avoid her wrath.

Slowly, hands shaking, I make my way up the sidewalk, stepping up the three steps of the front porch carefully before taking in one last breath and ringing the doorbell. Then I step back, waiting patiently and trying to regulate my breathing.

Then I wait.

And wait.

Biting my lip, I wonder if maybe the doorbell doesn't work. That happens, right? People knock on doors in the movies, so maybe I should try that. Breathing in deep, I knock three times, trying to add as much confidence as I can to the move.

Again, nothing. I glance over to the empty driveway. I thought the car might have been pulled into the garage, but maybe he's not home? Wren mentioned that they are going on vacation sometime soon, so maybe they left?

What do I do if he's not here?

I'm trying to sift through my thoughts, or rationalize and organize them, when I hear it.

"Willa?" a voice calls from next door, and panic scorches through me. Why did I ever think I could blend in and disappear into this small town? Maybe I should have brought Gabe with me after all. I take in a deep breath and put my mask on, happy, slightly stupid Willa Stone TM, and turn towards the speaker before starting to make my way down the steps.

"Hi—"

"Oh my god, it is you!" a pretty brunette says, moving down the wide walk in clapping flip flops. She's in a pair of worn-in jeans and an oversized T-shirt that reads, *Holly Ridge Elementary,* as she makes her way over. I can't remember if I have a Sharpie in my bag or if I—

"Adam didn't tell me you were coming!"

She moves across the sidewalk, and I walk more slowly towards her, but when she finally comes into focus, I realize it's not a fan, excited to see a star out in the wild. It's Wren, Adam's girlfriend.

I feel it when it happens, when my easy, public smile turns genuine and spreads across my face. It's the wonky smile that my team has told me isn't cute, showing the one slightly crooked tooth on my bottom row of teeth that, despite Jackie's insistence, I refuse to fix. But right now, I hope it shows Wren just how happy I am to see a familiar face, that the relief coursing through me is genuine.

"He didn't know I was coming!" I say with a laugh and a shake of my head. I move down the sidewalk, meeting her halfway, and try not to be surprised when she pulls me in for a big hug. She's a few inches shorter than my five feet eight inch frame, but then again, most everyone is shorter than me, so it's nothing new.

"Oh my god, it's so weird to see you here!" I bite my lip nervously, and she reads it instantly. "Oh, no, not like that, I just mean...this is Holly Ridge."

"Well, I've heard great things about it. I figured I'd come and see what all the hype was about." She nods eagerly, grabbing my hand and tugging me away from Adam's place toward the house she came out of.

"Adam's over here," she says, turning up her sleeve. "He doesn't live there anymore."

Jesus, Willa, you almost completely blew everything.

"He just signed the lease yesterday to rent it out; the new tenants are moving in next Monday. He's living at my place now."

"Oh," I say, confused and flustered as she moves me to the door and ushers me in.

"Babe!" she calls as soon as the door closes behind us. I stand there, confused. "You'll never guess who is here!" she calls.

"Hallie?" he asks, exhaustion in the word, and Wren laughs, but before she can correct him, he comes down the stairs and catches sight of me. "Willa?"

"Hey, Adam."

A hesitant smile crosses his face.

"Hey! Wow, you're here. What are you doing here?" he asks, wrapping a gentle arm around Wren.

I shrug, suddenly embarrassed. "You said any time."

"I guess I did," he says with a laugh. "Can't say I actually thought you'd take me up on it." Slowly, dread curls in my gut. *This was so stupid. I should have called. I should have warned him. I should have sucked it up and stayed home.*

"I'm sorry, this was–"

He shakes his head quickly.

"No, no, it's totally fine. I didn't mean it in a bad way, and I just can't believe you're here in Holly Ridge."

"Have you eaten?" Wren asks, and I'm grateful for the diversion. "Lunch. Have you eaten?" I look around her small kitchen and shake my head.

"No, I–"

"Perfect! I'll get lunch started, and you can tell us all about your plans!" Wren says, excitement written clearly across her face.

"That's really not—"

"I promise it's easier if you just let her take care of you," Adam says, voice low as he leads me into the kitchen. It's strange, this interaction, the normalcy of it, but I chose not to look at it too closely.

"Is there anything you don't eat?" she asks, opening the cabinets and looking over her shoulder at me. My mind instantly goes to the most recent diet my nutritionist had me on, a dozen things I shouldn't eat on it. She called it an anti-inflammatory diet, something people who have allergies usually are, though I have none.

But the point of this is to find myself, right? I smile. "Nope, I'm not picky," I say.

"Perfect."

Thirty minutes later, I'm incredibly pleased I didn't give her any restrictions because the half-eaten sandwich before me is the most delicious thing I've had in some time. She told me she grabbed the bread from the town's farmers' market as she cut thick slices of the sourdough for me, herself, and Adam. Then she layered thick, fresh tomatoes, lettuce, and more bacon than I've ever seen in one place on the sandwich, adding fancy toothpicks to keep them together before sliding it across with some bagged chips that I don't think I've eaten since I was a kid. They crunch deliciously, and the salt and oil are addictive, just like I remember.

"So you convinced Jackie to let you have a break?" Adam asks after I tell them that I'm essentially off for three months, a teasing smile on his lips.

"Not quite," I say with a smile. "Leo kind of insisted on building intrigue for the next album. My next relationship doesn't start until September, so he wants me to lay low." Adam nods with understanding, and Wren looks over her shoulder at us, a look I can't quite decode. "But I'm glad. At first, I wasn't sure what I'd do with the free time, but now I'm kind of looking forward to it. I've been under the spotlight nonstop for..." My words trail off, unsure of exactly how long it's been. "A long time."

"I know," Adam says, understanding more than most people. "So what are you going to do with all of your free time?"

"Oh, I..." I start, and then I laugh. "Honestly? I'm not sure. I haven't had time off in a long, long time." I lick my lips, popping another chip in my mouth and chewing thoughtfully before expanding, "I knew I was going to drive myself insane at home alone the whole time. You said this place was great for your writing block, and I figured three months could give me the full Holly Ridge experience."

Adam nods, a small tilt to his lips seeming to approve.

"Where are you staying?" Wren asks. I bite my lip and lift a shoulder.

"Not sure."

"You're welcome to stay here," she says, looking towards the stairs. "One guest room is Adam's office now, but we have three. I can move my crafting supplies to the one closest to our room so you're not right next door..." The cutest blush burns on her cheeks, and I fight the laugh bubbling in my chest.

"Don't worry, I won't be staying here. I'm going to go look for a hotel." Wren's nose scrunches up, and Adam's lips roll inwards. "Or maybe not...?"

"The hotel here is small, not something you'd really want to stay in full time. There's no kitchen or anything, so if you're planning to stay longer than a week, it wouldn't really make much sense." There goes that plan. I bite my lip, trying not to look as thrown off as I feel.

"Well, then maybe I'll look for some kind of long-term rental?" Now it's Adam's turn to look unsure.

"Rentals are far and few between here in Holly Ridge. It's why my place got booked so quickly. It doesn't really exist."

"And Colton already filled his place," Wren says low, a finger moving to her lips, though I have no idea who Colton is. Her lips purse, as if she's thinking, and from what Adam has shared with me, it makes sense. Apparently, Wren can't stand the thought of not helping and needs to find a solution. Desperate not to further inconvenience her, I start to speak.

"I promise I can figure it out, there's no need—" But suddenly, her face lights up an idea clearly hitting her. A red-tipped, blunt finger taps at her chin, and she grins.

"You know, I might have a place for you," she says.

"Really?" Relief washes through me, and it leaks into my words.

"Yeah. It's small, but no one's living there right now. And it's furnished! No one will be staying there, so if you want to spend the whole three months here, you totally could." Her own excitement is brushing off, and I sit up straighter, my smile widening as understanding appears to strike Adam.

He seems to contemplate her words before speaking. "Hallie's old place at Three Kings?"

Wren nods, and he turns to me with a wide grin on his lips.

"You said you wanted the true Holly Ridge experience, right?"

SEVEN

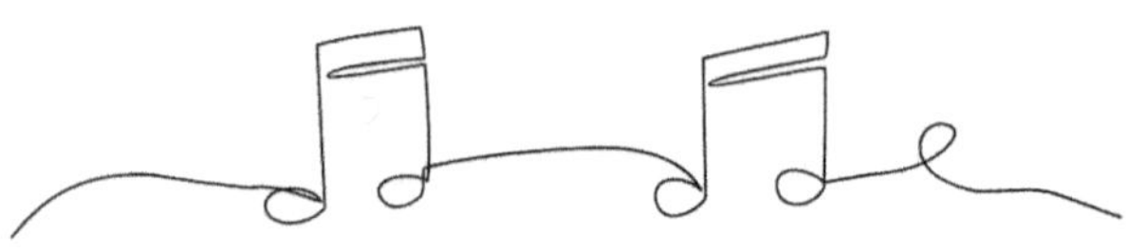

LEO

If you had told me two months ago that I'd be standing on my property in the woods in the small town of Holly Ridge, watching two grown men—brothers, no less—argue about the best way to carry a plank of wood, I'd tell you that you needed to be checked out.

But here I am.

"I can't help that you're a fucking idiot, Madden," Jesse says, a stack of five long planks of wood in his hands, his brother holding the other side as they unload the extra wood that we didn't end up needing to my garage, which is currently holding all of my projects and tools.

"Me? You're the one who thought Hallie and I were into each other for a year," Madden says, a smile on his lips. Jesse's phone lets out a *bing*, and he lets go of the large piece of wood, letting it drop to the ground and making Madden's body lurch as he takes on the bulk of the weight. "What the fuck, man?"

"Sorry," he says, the smile on his lips conveying the exact opposite. "Could be an emergency."

"Oh, fuck off," Madden groans, rubbing at his shoulder dramatically. I continue running the pieces of half-rotted wood through the table saw to cut it into smaller chunks for easier disposal.

It's been like this all day. Even though the family dynamic is incredibly strange, and the constant bickering is almost alarming, I feel oddly at home here. Being around Atlas Oaks for so many years and watching four grown men act like bickering siblings all day long, it's almost like I'm used to this back-and-forth.

I had almost forgotten about Hallie's little intervention until a truck rolled up to my house at eight a.m. on Thursday morning, and Jesse and Madden King hopped out with wide, nearly identical smiles on their faces. Even though I told them they didn't really need to be doing this, they shook their heads and asked what other projects I might need supplies for. With a reluctant sigh, I moved around my property, showing them the back deck and the boards that needed replacing. I'd managed to take out the weak and rotting ones while salvaging most of the structure on my own, but without a truck, I couldn't get the boards needed to replace them.

Soon after, we made our way into town, bought boards, bags of leveling sand, and pavers to start replacing the broken slabs out front. Then we spent the morning and afternoon replacing the boards and staining it. In less than a day, I have a fully functional back porch, and even though it's a small project compared to all the work needed here, it's nice to have something completed. Quietly, I'm looking forward to coming out here tomorrow morning with my coffee and relaxing in my own yard.

Though that relaxation won't last long, not with Madden and Jesse planning to come back here on Friday to help me out with the front walkway. As much as I insisted that I don't need their help, they won't take no for an answer, and I know that on Friday morning, I'll see Jesse's truck in my front drive early. I plan to take my car into town tomorrow to buy a propane grill and barbecue stuff. If they're going to be helping here, I might as well feed them.

This is what I'm thinking about, lost in my own thoughts, when Jesse groans loudly, drawing my attention. As I look over at him, his eyes leave his phone screen, and his head tips toward the sky, irritation written all over his face, lips moving as if praying for a solution. After a moment, his head tips back down, and he shoots me an apologetic look.

"I gotta go. Hallie just asked me if I have a dolly somewhere and if she can use it to move a bed."

"A bed? She's trying to move a bed?" Madden asks with disbelief in his voice, but his face has a knowing smirk on it. I don't understand these two in the least, but Jesse seems to. "And how does she expect to load an entire bed onto a dolly?"

Jesse shrugs, then slides his phone into his pocket.

"It's more of a threat than an actual question," he says, moving to his things and sliding items back into his toolbox.

"She's threatening to move a bed?" I ask, not understanding their relationship at all.

"No, she's threatening to do it herself and probably hurt herself in the process if I don't come over to her old place to move it myself." An irritated look flits across Jesse's face, but there's also an amused smile on his lips at the thought, as if he finds her threats endearing rather than annoying, like a normal person would. Before I can say anything, though, Madden speaks.

"Are they moving Willa in already?" Madden asks, and with his words, every part of my body stills. The King brothers don't register my shock at all, though. Jesse reaches up to pull his hat off, flipping it so the brim faces forward once more.

"Yeah. She stayed at Wren's yesterday, but since Nat is off today, they're all hands on deck moving her in."

I force myself out of my shock and ask a clarifying question, trying to fight back the irritation.

"Willa?" I set my hammer down and straighten. *Don't panic.*

Both brothers look at me, a hint of confusion on their faces.

"Yeah, she came in yesterday to see Adam. Apparently, she's planning to stay here for a while, write her next album with Adam." My chest tightens further as I see my peaceful retreat melting away.

"Willa's here? Like, Willa Stone, Willa?" It's an incredibly common name, after all. It could refer to anyone. I'm sure there are at least four different Willas in Holly Ridge alone.

It's a lie, of course. I've only ever met a single person named Willa. Still, I believe it for a blissful three seconds before Madden turns to face me and take in my face, which I'm sure is stricken with pure and utter alarm.

"Yeah. I thought you knew. Aren't you her publicist? I would have thought they would have updated you on that."

"Yeah, but..." I start, but don't finish, because how would I finish that sentence?

But she is supposed to be home for the next three months?

But she's supposed to be far, far away from me for three months?

I don't finish my sentence. Instead, I shake my head and take a deep breath, trying to calm the pounding in my chest, but it does nothing to soothe my panic.

Then I speak. "Mind if I come with?"

Even though my place is right next to the Three Kings property, it takes about ten minutes to get there since you have to drive down my winding drive, then back up the farm's entryway. We pass the tree lots and a few closed-down Christmas-themed buildings, drive just beyond what Madden points out to be Jesse and Hallie's place, then park out front of a small cabin-looking home with four cars parked out front. One is a brand new all-black G-wagon that makes my stomach twist once more, and three other much older-model cars. The front door of the house is wide open, and when the tires crunch on the gravel drive, a familiar redhead looks out the door, a wide grin spreading on her face before she steps out.

"She's such a brat," Jesse grumbles, but there's no real irritation on his face. I've noticed that even when he's full-out complaining about his fiancée, Jesse never actually looks mad or irritated or even inconvenienced.

He looks *entertained*.

The man is clearly out of his mind.

He puts the truck into park, kills the engine, then opens his door and slides out. Hallie is already halfway to us, and when they meet in the middle, Jesse pulls her in close, a hand sliding up into her hair to angle her head and press a kiss to her lips. I look away, an uncomfortable pit in my stomach that I don't enjoy.

It's there every time I see them or Adam and Wren together. When I felt it around Stella and Riggins, or Wes and Harper, I had chalked it up to irritation, knowing they were bound to make my job more difficult, since both of their relationships have been in the spotlight in one way or another.

But now, with people who barely, if at all, impact my job and surely don't add more to my already full plate, I wonder if it's something different. Something worse.

Something closer to jealousy, an emptiness I've been ignoring for years now.

Being around so many happy couples has made me wonder whether that's what's missing from my life.

But that feeling is long forgotten when an all too familiar, tall blonde steps out of the house behind Nat and Wren, a hesitant smile on her lips. White teeth come out to press into a full, pink bottom lip, something I don't think I've ever seen the meticulously put-together woman do. She scans the area for a moment, taking in the new arrivals, then waves at Madden, who approaches his sister and slings an arm around her shoulders. He says something that makes Nat roll her eyes and shake her head, and Wren laughs. Her eyes continue to scan, softening when she sees Jesse and Hallie, before her gaze stops on me.

For a moment, there's confusion, the same confusion that's moving through me, but then her face lights up.

A mix of relief and happiness moves over her face before she steps in my direction.

For a moment, she looks at me, and the breath leaves my lungs.

For a moment, I almost don't recognize her, instead seeing someone different altogether, someone I knew for the shortest time before reality crashed down around us.

For a moment, I almost smile.

That is, until the irritation comes barreling in.

She is here.

Willa is here, in Holly Ridge.

Apparently moving in.

Right next door.

I'm breathless.

I'm in awe.

I'm absolutely furious.

"Leo!" she says, moving my way. Her blonde ponytail sways from left to right as she walks in my direction. "I didn't know you'd be here!" Her blonde hair is pulled into her signature neat ponytail, which she wears whenever she's not on stage or at an event, but her eyes are brown rather than the captivating blue magazines and tabloids talk about nonstop. She's in a pair of shorts that are almost impossible to see beneath a worn, oversized Atlas Oaks T-shirt in a dark navy blue. I don't know if I've ever seen her wear that color, but it suits her.

Or maybe it's the genuine smile on her lips.

"Is this where you bought your house?" I continue to stare, unable to process her question before she continues.

"I can't believe you're also here! It's like our own little crew is fleeing to Holly Ridge."

"What are you doing here?" I ask, looking around.

"I came here to hide away for the summer." Her words are filled with excitement, but all I can feel is dread.

I came here to escape, and now the exact life I've escaped has followed me here.

Even worse, it has to be fucking *Willa*, a temptation who has always plagued me and a temptation I can never have.

"Why?" I ask, and she gives me another one of those stunning smiles, this one tinged in humor, before she explains.

"Well, I've been told I need to keep myself on the down low, and I was going stir crazy in my apartment. Adam suggested a change of scenery to deal with my—" She hesitates, the faintest blush blooming on her cheeks. "Boredom. I showed up yesterday, and Wren said she knew a place I could stay."

"You came to Holly Ridge to avoid being *bored?*"

Something crosses her face before it shifts behind her expert-level mask, gone as quickly as it came.

"Well, you told me I couldn't be in the spotlight."

Without meaning to, the stress-induced frustration breaks free from my normally cool demeanor, and I snap. "I meant go out to dinner without Jackie calling up the paparazzi, not *move*." There's a momentary freeze, a shift that if I weren't so frustrated, I might take better note of and ponder why she looks almost confused, but I'm not, so I don't. "I meant stay away from premieres. I meant don't start dropping hints about your next fake relationship for a bit. I did *not* mean to go to the small town; I came to avoid work, primarily *you*."

It happens right before my eyes, in a devastating show of emotion on her face: the tentative excitement melting away and turning sour, a wall rising that I realize now is always there.

I don't pay any mind to it, continuing my accusations.

"Did Jefferson send you here?" I ask, trying to find an explanation for this, to understand what's happening because fate can't possibly have this fucked up a sense of humor, can it? To guide me to a small town to escape the stress of work, only to lead my biggest stressor right to my doorstep?

I've spent the last eight years maintaining a strictly professional relationship with Willa Stone and succeeding. I've done that for countless reasons, all of them sound and well-thought-out and incredibly important both for my career and my sanity, and yet here she is, standing toe to toe with me, confusion written clear across her face.

"What?"

"Jefferson. The owner of Perfect Image Publicity. My boss. Did he send you here? He knows I'm here, and he's pissed I told you to take a break, pissed you're my client and not his. Did he send you here to piss me off?"

"What? No. I don't even know if *Jackie* knows I'm here." A blush burns over her cheeks, and she bites her lip. "It was kind of a last-minute decision."

Well, that's an interesting turn of events. Jackie knows when the woman breathes wrong, keeping her on a tight leash and an even tighter schedule of appearances, new releases, and what she calls *brand-building moments.*

So she's not here as a punishment. If I take a moment to think about what she said when she saw me, I don't think she even knew I was here. According to her, she's here to relax and write her next album, to lay low somewhere new. The too-familiar grip of my anxiety around my chest starts to loosen, and I take in a deep breath, trying to think rationally.

Willa is here, but I'm overreacting. It's not a big deal. How much of a problem could she be? Hell, I bet she's less likely to get hounded by the paparazzi in a middle-of-nowhere town than in the city. Maybe this will actually work in my favor.

"Fine. But can you please stay out of trouble while you're here?"

She blinks at me once, twice, three times before she speaks, confusion in the words. "Stay out of trouble?"

"I came here to avoid work, and you've followed me here. The least you can do is make it so I don't have to swoop in and clean up any messes you make."

Again, silence and staring before she speaks, her words slow and chosen meticulously.

"What messes of mine have you had to clean?"

I stare at her, confused for a moment, and that confusion only deepens when I take in the foreign expression on her face. It looks like it's not just foreign for me to see, but for her to feel, as well. It looks so out of place that it takes me a moment to realize what it is I'm actually seeing: utter irritation. Frustration. *Anger.*

Willa Stone is standing in front of me, hands on her hips, *angry* at me.

"You can't think of one. Because I might have a lot going on and put work on your plate, but I *never* get into trouble. I follow the plan, I do what you say—what *everyone* says—and you never have to come in and *clean up my messes.*" Her face is going a bit red now, her words coming out faster. "I'm not some headache, going out to bars and dancing on tables and getting hammered. I've never even been drunk, because it wouldn't fit the *brand.*" She steps closer, poking me in the chest, and I stand there, completely silent.

The woman in front of me is not America's sweetheart; she isn't the delicate flower that the world sees, the loveable girl the world can't help but fall for. The woman in front of me is not the yes-woman who agrees to everything everyone says. She's not fragile or quiet or meek.

She's fierce. She's strong.

She's fucking beautiful.

It's the woman I met in a coffee shop years ago.

"But don't you worry, Leo. I won't get into any trouble, and if I do, I won't make it your problem."

I'm still in awe when she turns on her heel, her jaw tight, and I try not to watch her as she goes. I try to ignore the way her long pony-tail swags along her shoulder blades, exposed by the backless sports top she's wearing with some kind of halter neck. I try not to wonder if I've ever seen her this casual—even in her press photos on her way in and out of the expensive Pilates classes she takes, she's done up, makeup on, hair perfect, those annoying blue contacts in place.

"Looks like you've got your hands full with that one," a voice says, knocking me from my dazed state, and when I turn, Madden is walking toward me, hands in his pockets, a grin on his lips.

"What?"

"Willa. She's a handful." I shake my head.

"Not my handful."

The smirk on his lips turns into a full-blown grin, clearly not buying what I'm selling.

"Sure, she's not," he says, slapping a hand to my shoulder. "I forget this is how this always starts." With one last laugh and a shake of his head, he walks away to where Wren is calling his name.

I don't bother to ask what he means—something tells me I wouldn't love his answer.

EIGHT

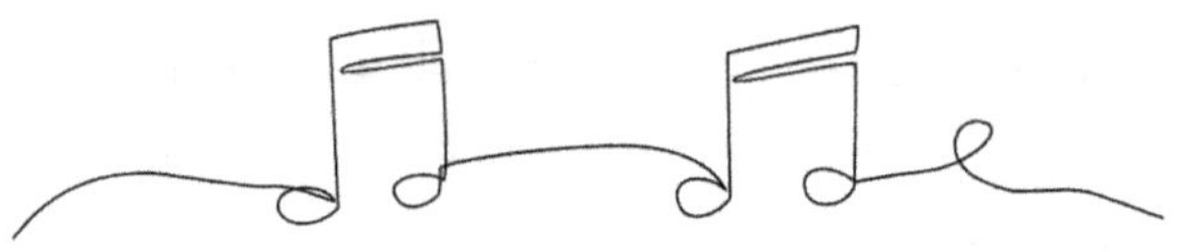

WILLA

Even though I've received at least three different offers for dinner, I politely decline Hallie, Wren, *and* Nat's offers, telling them I'm planning to just hang out and settle in for the night.

And while that's the truth, it's not completely the truth.

The real truth is that I need time to decompress and be alone after nearly two full days of excitement, and maybe, hopefully, possibly, write something.

Unfortunately, when I sit down to write, nothing comes.

Well, actually, that's a lie.

Things are coming. Lines and lyrics and even a couple of melodies, but none of them are what I need. Instead of hopeless love and sweet crushes or even saucy, heated innuendos, everything sounds... annoyed.

Angry.

Frustrated.

And even more unfortunately, I know the exact reason.

Every time I close my eyes, I see Leo and that irritated look he gave me when he saw me walk out of my house.

I feel the heat emanating off his body, the fury rolling off him in waves when he stands, towering over me.

My emotions went from excited to see a familiar face to annoyed that, while I came here to escape the pressure and expectations, here was yet another person telling me how to act. And it was honestly disappointing that Leo seemed so miserable that I was here.

I haven't thought about Leo Sinclaire this much in years, a very careful decision I made forever ago, not long after I met him.

But today, I let my mind drift back there for the first time in a long time, to eight years ago

Because there was a moment, a brief glimpse in time, when I thought Leo Sinclair and I could be something.

I met Leo as *just Willa*, nearly eight years ago, when I was barely twenty. It was a bit after my second album came out, and that morning, Jackie was trying to convince me into participating in what would end up being my very first fake relationship.

The first of many.

"At the very least, go to this meeting," Jackie said that morning, her voice low and a bit irritated. "Go in with an open mind. I think they have a really great plan and that you could really benefit from it."

The *plan* she was talking about was a fake relationship with Riggins Greene to build public interest in a whirlwind romance and, by extension, in my third album. It seemed that Riggins had a drinking problem and was headed to rehab, but the label was desperate to keep that out of the media. His publicist was suggesting a fake relationship with a sweet, wholesome child star-turned-pop star to balance it out. My second album had done substantially worse than my first, and Jackie was sure that creating interest in a relationship, and then writing an album around it, would be the key to the stardom we were after.

I wasn't fully on board, still a hopeless romantic at heart who wanted to write songs about my *real* life, including love. I'd told her this before, but she was pushing harder than ever. "Jackie—" I started, but she cut me off before I could give her my normal argument.

"One meeting. If you say no, then that's it—I won't bug you about it again." With a sigh, I nodded, then agreed verbally.

"Fine... One meeting, but no promises. I'm serious, Jackie, don't get your hopes up."

"Of course. Of course!" she said, and I smiled to myself, shaking my head at her clear excitement. "Okay, the meeting's at one, and I'll be at your place in an hour and a half?" I agreed, she said goodbye, and hung up.

Knowing I had a long day ahead, I decided, more than ever, that I needed my Monday morning sweet treat. Back then, every Monday before my day really got started, I would sneak to the little coffee shop down the street for a coffee and a cookie. I slipped down there that morning in a baseball hat, my hair in a low ponytail at the back of my head, no makeup, and an oversized sweatshirt and sweats. Back then, before I was *Willa Stone*^{TM}, in the hustle and bustle of the city, I could slip in and out of places unnoticed. I didn't have near the level of media intrigue, and I surely didn't have a bodyguard following me around.

It was late fall and unexpectedly freezing—I remember that most of all, because when I stepped outside, I thought I should have worn a jacket, but since it was just a few blocks, I figured I'd be fine. I got my drink, an iced concoction that the place was best known for, despite the cool temperature, as well as a chocolate chip cookie, and turned to head towards the door. That's when a man ran into me, not paying attention to what he was doing. He had dark glasses on and a sweatshirt of his own, and despite his irritated look, the second he realized he'd effectively drenched me in cold coffee, he stopped, his face going aghast.

"Fuck, I am so sorry," he said, sliding his glasses to his head. His eyes were sky blue. I remember thinking that's what my contacts were supposed to give me. "I didn't see you there." I lifted my eyebrows in challenge, and he gave me a sheepish smile before confessing. "I was out last night celebrating, and I might be a bit hungover. I wasn't paying attention in my quest for caffeine." I give him a small smile and a nod.

"Totally understandable," I lied, because I had never been hungover, so it *wasn't* understandable to me. "No worries at all."

Finally snapping out of my daze, I tossed my now-empty cup in the trash and moved to grab napkins. He did the same, moving to sop up the coffee on the ground as I got what I could off my sweatshirt, pulling it away from me so it wouldn't sit against my tank top and soak it, too.

"Shit, you're drenched," he said, eyes moving over the light colored sweatshirt now covered in a brown stain. I shivered, then decided the sweatshirt needed to go—it was doing more harm than good. I tugged it off over my head, then draped it over my arm. "I'm so fucking sorry."

"It's fine, really. I don't live far from here," I said with a smile. "I won't be in the cold for long."

"You walked here?" he asks, looking confused, brows furrowing.

"Uh," I start, biting my lip, because every safety conversation I'd ever had told me disclosing that would be a terrible idea, even though everyone walked there. But right now, I was *just Willa*. But he shook his head quickly.

"Not in a weird way, I just...you can't walk home in your wet sweatshirt, and it's freezing outside." I looked down at my balled-up sweatshirt and smiled, giving him a small wave of my hand.

"I'll be fine, seriously." He shook his head and sighed, rubbing a hand at his temple, and I wondered if the headache was his hangover or mine.

"Are you always this stubborn?"

"Do you always spill coffee on unwitting suspects?" I countered with a smile and a raised eyebrow.

"Touché," he said with a grin. Just then, someone walked in, a cold rush sweeping in and carrying a fierce, cold breeze. I was in just a tank top and leggings, and I shivered. His face went contemplative, his lips tightening with dislike. "You can't walk home in that." I opened my mouth to argue, but before I could, the man was reaching behind him, tugging off his own sweatshirt, and handing it over to me.

He was giving me the literal shirt off his back.

"Take this."

I stared at him, baffled and awestruck.

"What?"

'It's the least I can do. I can't have a pretty woman freezing to death on my conscience."

I shook my head.

"Oh, I couldn't—"

"If you don't, then we'll both just freeze." Without meaning to, I looked over the plain white T-shirt he was wearing underneath, which fit and showed off every defined muscle hidden beneath the sweatshirt. Another shiver went through me, but this time, it had absolutely nothing to do with the cold. "Come on. Put it on," he said, misunderstanding my chill. His voice was low and smooth, and that rolled through me as well, and without giving it another thought, I threw the sweatshirt on. He smiled at me, another panty-dropping one, and then nodded like he was happy I was now safe and sound and warm. "What were you drinking?"

"I'm sorry?" I asked, still in a daze.

"I just made you lose your drink. What was it?"

"A, uh, cookie butter latte." He nodded.

"Iced?" I bit my lip, then smiled.

"I think a hot would be better this time." A small laugh left his lips this time.

"Fair enough." I stopped and stood there like an idiot, watching as he walked back into line and ordered. I stepped aside and apologized profusely as an employee came out with a mop, but they waved it aside, and I made the mental note to leave a huge tip next time I came here.

"Are you in a rush?"

"What?"

"Are you in a rush to get back to wherever you were headed?" I checked my phone, biting my lip. Jackie would be at my place in an hour and a half, but it was less than a 15-minute walk back, so I should be more than fine to stay for a coffee.

And with the way my heart was racing, I really didn't want to leave just yet.

"No," I say. With the single word, I broke into a wide, happy grin.

"So, you'll have coffee with me?"

"If you tell me your name."

Without a moment's hesitation, not even bothering to play it cool, he put a hand out to me. "I'm Leo."

Leo.

I loved the name instantly. Simple and strong, different enough but not too far out there.

Kind of like Willa.

But Willa was too obvious, and since it was clear this man had no idea who I was, and I was giving into the fairy tale of meeting him here, I decided to do what I hated to do: lie.

"Marie," I said, giving him my middle name. Giving it dimmed my joy just the tiniest bit, even though I knew it was a much-needed deception.

"It's nice to meet you, Marie." The barista called his name, sliding a hot paper cup across the counter, and he stepped away to get it. Then he was back before me, holding both cups, and tipping his head toward an empty table in the corner. "Come, sit," he said.

I lifted an eyebrow, challenging. I'd always been a shy person, one who hated to rock the boat or be an inconvenience, but something about this man made me want to be different. To poke and prod and see how he would react. Maybe it was that he didn't seem to recognize me or know who I was, which felt freeing. I couldn't remember the last time I met someone without an introduction that created awkward expectations.

"Do I look like a dog?" Jackie always told me men didn't like women to talk back, that it would scare them away, and I should play into the soft, sweet aspect of myself. But instead of being turned off, he seemed fueled by my sass, and there was a spark in his blue eyes when he responded.

"Would you please sit, Marie, and enjoy a coffee with a stranger?"

I grinned then, enamored by him and his wide smile and his messy hair. His sweatshirt smelled good, like expensive cologne and men's deodorant, and I had the urge to sniff it.

We sat there until long after I had drunk my entire coffee and split my cookie, talking about everything and nothing at all the entire time.

I hadn't had as much fun in years.

"It's like those packets of frosting they give you for Toaster Strudels. What the fuck is that? That's not nearly enough frosting for one pastry," he said an hour later, clearly very passionate about the topic.

"A toaster strudel?" I asked, staring at him, confused. "What's a toaster strudel?" His eyes bugged out, shock written across his face in the most dramatic way, and I snorted out a very unladylike sound.

"You've never had a Toaster Strudel? The frozen pastries with jam in the middle? You toast them up, then put the little packet of frosting on?" I shrugged, suddenly feeling embarrassed. "Oh, honey, I have to widen your pastry horizons," he said, and I don't know if it was the low tone of his voice or the way he called me honey, but I liked it a lot. Heat moved through me, melting the embarrassment out of my body.

"Well, maybe—" I started, but then saw my screen flash from the corner of my eye, Jackie's name on the screen. "Shit." I grabbed the device and cursed again under my breath. "I have to go." Somehow, I'd missed two texts from Jackie and a call. She was going to absolutely *lose* it. "It was great talking to you!" Then I stood and left. It wasn't until I was halfway to my place I realized I should have gotten his number, but for some reason, it didn't even faze me; there was no disappointment rushing through me.

There was a spark, the universe pushing me towards him, and I knew in my gut we'd meet again.

It was meant to be.

Back then, I was still a hopeless romantic, still believed in true love, still believed I could have it all: the career of my dreams and a love that took my breath away. I'd thought I'd found it once before with a co-star, but I was young and stupid and a bit delusional, and it ended in a blazing tabloid mess. Still, that didn't mean it didn't exist.

Even though Jackie looked absolutely irritated when I showed up, profusely apologizing, there was an air about her, an excitement that rubbed off on me. Or maybe it was the fact that I'd just had the most memorable morning of my life. I planned to head down there again tomorrow morning, ask Sally, the barista, if she knew the man I'd been chatting with. See if maybe, just maybe, I could bump into him again, because an encounter like that was for books. Sweet and romantic, and the perfect "how we met" story.

I jumped into the shower, carefully folding the sweatshirt and hiding it in the back of my closet, then got ready. I was still floating on cloud nine. The usual anxiety that crept in when I heard the paparazzi's call and saw their flashes didn't even touch the joy I was feeling. In fact, despite knowing I was headed into an important meeting, I could only think of one thing—going back to the coffee shop the next day to find out who the man was.

And then I walked into the room, and my heart skipped. Sitting at the table was the man from that morning: Leo. He looked a bit different, his hair brushed and dressed in a suit, more put together, his face sterner, less joking, and guarded, but I recognized him all the same. My heart beat faster, my ears ringing as I realized I was right: the universe would bring me to him, though I didn't expect it would be that soon.

I followed Jackie into the room, smiling so wide it hurt my cheeks, but some of that glow faded when he gave me a small, friendly but curt nod, and began moving to his papers and shifting things around.

As if he didn't know me,

As if he didn't recognize me.

I sat, trying to catch his eye to remind him naturally who I was, but moments later, Jackie was introducing us. Finally, Leo looked at me, and I still didn't see any recognition on his face, just a blank, business-like slate.

"Hello, Ms. Stone. My name's Leo, I work with Perfect Image Publicity and represent Atlas Oaks. I'm excited to speak with you about a media relationship that we believe would be greatly beneficial to both parties."

His eyes were on mine, but they were blank, businesslike. There was nothing there, none of the kindness or intrigue I saw that morning, and I realized I had once again completely romanticized the moment.

I had thought there was something

Clearly, I didn't have the same impact on him.

So I threw up my shield, the business one Jackie taught me to curate for the cameras, and I put that morning into a box in my mind, locking it in a safe and hiding it away. He wasn't my dream man after all.

At the very least, if I was going to fall head over heels for a man at first sight, I wanted him to be able to recognize me outside of my glam.

It was the sign I needed, the realization that I could have the fairytale romance or I could have the career, but I couldn't have it all.

"Okay," I murmured with a nod, keeping my eyes down on the lengthy contract that was slid before me after the entire scheme was explained to me in lengthy detail, the benefits for my brand, the in-depth press plan, and even some projected results. It was black and white before me, the ending of any romantic ideals I had, and the decision to choose my career instead. "I'm in."

That was the day I came to terms with the fact that the concept of *having it all* is a lie.

What they don't tell you about *having it all* is that you *can* have it all, but you have to choose what version of *all* you want: you can't have it all in all aspects of your life. You can have a career or a love life. You can have fame, or you can have comfort. You can have peace and quiet or adventure and success.

The world tells us the lie of having it all so that we keep going, of how to keep striving when life gets hard. But the people at the top, the ones who are the most successful, will all tell you the same thing —at some point, you have to choose. You have to choose what you want most of all and how to be okay with everything else falling behind.

That was the day I chose my career. I chose performing and my fans and success over finding that foreign, mythical, all-consuming love that songs were written about.

And up until recently, I never, ever regretted that decision.

But here, in this small town, surrounded by people who seem to actually have it all—the career, the love life, the family, the friends, I wonder if all this time, maybe I had it wrong.

NINE

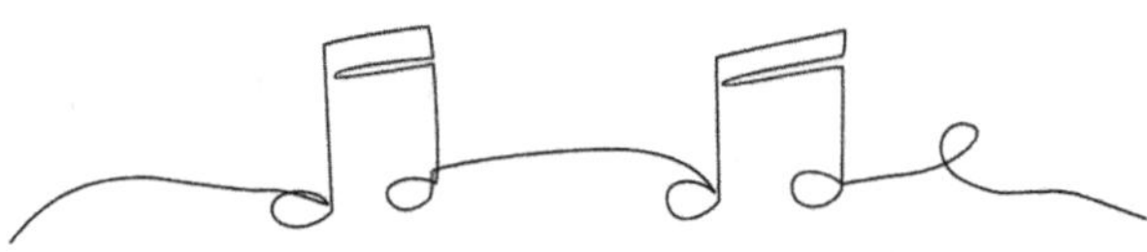

WILLA

On my first full day in my new place in Holly Ridge, I wake up early on instinct and go about my usual routine, determined to get myself back on track. Now that I have peace and a new setting, I just need to fall into my routine, and I'll be able to write.

At least, that's what I convinced myself of the night before.

Like clockwork, I wake up, get dressed, drink a glass of water, then my green juice, do a virtual Pilates class, shower, and have breakfast. Finally, I sit, ready to write, with my guitar in my lap. I'm hopeful, determined to believe that if I just fall into old patterns, it will happen. On instinct, my fingers start to move, humming to an old Atlas Oaks song, and my chest feels lighter, my day brighter. As my fingers move gently over the strings aimlessly, I wonder when the last time I did this was...just playing for no real reason. I used to do it all the time, just sit and play random songs, my own and other artists, just for the fun of it.

That is, until the guilt barrels in, reminding me that I *should* be writing, not goofing around. I *need* to be crafting my next big album. I *need* to make it bigger and better and flashier, to pull out all the stops, and it always starts with the tune and the lyrics.

Reaching for the pad of paper, I pull it closer and start writing down emotions and thoughts about falling in love, hoping it will spark something. I shift in my seat, my top cutting into my side, and realize maybe that's my problem. Maybe I need to change into comfier clothes, something loose and comfortable and familiar in order to tap into my muse. Eager for any excuse, I set my guitar aside and walk away, my chest lightening with each step I take away from my work, something I ignore fervently. When I step into my new room and open the small closet, I look around, seeing taupes, browns, creams, and blacks. My tour and red carpet outfits are often filled with color, denoting whatever each album vibe is going to be, but my "streetwear," as my stylist calls it, is mostly neutrals, meant to complement my hair and skin, apparently, so my entire closet is perfectly curated cool girl outfits chosen to become inspiration for everyone.

My fingers freeze over the fabrics, guilt rearing up as I take in the extravagant wardrobe. All of which, in this moment, I realize I don't even really like.

They aren't *me*, Just Willa. They're *Willa Stone TM*, the brand.

And even though the brand is what sells it, the brand isn't who *writes* the music. My mind drifts, stumbling on another idea: I wonder if my clothes are contributing to my writer's block. Nothing I wear lines up with the muse I'm working with—there's no color, no softness, no comfort.

That's an easy change to make.

Decision made, I dig through to the back of my closet, finding a far too familiar oversized navy blue sweatshirt. Leo's sweatshirt. I should have thrown it out a dozen times over, and I don't quite know why I chose to pack it up when I came to Holly Ridge, but I did. Forcing myself not to overthink that decision too much, I grab the sweatshirt off a hanger, followed by a pair of comfy bike shorts, and change.

After, I catch sight of myself as I head back into the living room, and decide I need another change—my eyes. Quickly, I take out the blue contacts I put in as part of my normal routine. I don't need them to see, so there's no point in having them in right now. Finally, I undo the tight ponytail I'd put in out of habit, brushing out the gel I'd used to slick it back before sitting down at my computer.

Then I go shopping at a popular athleticwear company.

When my cart is filled with pinks and purples and blues of all shades, all the colors I envision for this next album, I hit next-day delivery and sit back with a smile.

I'm still avoiding my music hours later, instead searching online for some kind of craft or hobby to pick up and placing random orders, when there's a knock on the front door. My back straightens, my chest tightening as I look around, panicked.

Who is at my door? No one even really knows I'm here, after all.

What if it's a paparazzi or some rabid fan who found me here?

Maybe I really should have brought a bodyguard, or at least had Jaime install some kind of security system, or—

The pounding knock comes again, but this time, a voice accompanies it. "Willa! Open up, it's Hallie! We brought dinner!" The nerves melt away as I stand and tentatively walk to the door. When I open it, Hallie and Nat are smiling at me.

"What are you guys doing here?" I ask with a laugh, stepping aside as the women walk in, Hallie holding a stack of pizza boxes, two white paper bags on top. Nat is carrying a bunch of bags, and I stare at them in awe as they move through, straight to the kitchen

"Girls' night," Nat says.

"Poker night is happening at my house, and the testosterone was suffocating me, so I called up Nat, and we decided we'd come here and hang out. Plus, we had a bunch of stuff to bring here, decorations and whatnot," Hallie says, lifting one of the bags. When I step closer, I realize it's filled with home goods—a throw blanket, some art prints, and a bunch of knick-knacks.

"Decorations?"

"This place is empty and boring. You came here to write—I can't imagine you find it very inspiring," Hallie says with a shrug.

"I can't possibly—" I start, shaking my head, but Nat just smiles at me, putting a hand to my forearm.

"You're going to hurt Wren's feelings if you turn them down," she says low.

"She's not even here," I say, looking around.

"Yeah, she has a meeting to help plan the summer festival. But that's neither here nor there. She'll find out you didn't take them and then be offended."

"So I just...accept it?"

She shrugs with a smile.

"Welcome to Holly Ridge, babe," Hallie says. "Now let's eat."

Two hours later, I'm full of pizza, salad, and some of the best garlic knots I've ever had in my life, and the little cabin is completely decorated. The walls are covered with various art pieces and prints, and they even helped me hang the big mood board I made for the album, which I felt was imperative for getting inspired.

I love it. Every single inch of it.

It's not necessarily what I ever thought would be my style, but the truth is, I'm not even sure what my style *is*. Maybe this mish-mash could be me.

"Thank you, guys, for this," I say, looking around in awe, my heart full from their generosity.

"Are you kidding me? This was a blast!" Nat says with a grin.

"Nat loves any excuse to take over and give people some kind of style," Hallie says, and Nat rolls her eyes.

"You say it like it's a crime."

Hallie just shrugs, neither confirming nor denying the accusation, and I smile at them. But even as I do, an ache burns in my chest.

I've never had a group of girlfriends who tease and joke and drop everything to help one another. I've read about it, and I've acted it out, and I've even pretended to be part of a celebrity girl gang a time or two, but I've never actually *had* it.

I'm lost in those thoughts when Nat reaches out, fingers grazing the strands of my hair, a thoughtful look on her face. "You know, you'd look good with some low lights. I've always thought that, but now that I see you in person, I can't stop thinking it." I reach up for a lock of my hair, pull it forward, and look at it before giving her a thoughtful look, and her face goes nervous. "Not that I'm saying your hair isn't gorgeous, of course. I just... Fuck, I'm an ass. You have a lot of people to deal with, and I'm just a small-town hair stylist, I—"

"No," I say with a shake of my head, the smile spreading across my lips. With that, Nat's nervousness fades a bit. "No, you're not out of line or anything. I agree. My natural hair color is closer to a dirty blonde than this." I grab a few locks and pull them in front of me, inspecting the too-blonde strands. A wide grin spreads across Nat's lips. "My mom's hair has been a darker blonde most of my life, but they've been keeping it light since I was a kid, and I've kind of just leaned into it."

"We should do a spa day, give you some low lights, freshen it up. I mean, if you're here for a while, you're definitely going to need some-thing, you know?" I sigh, knowing that's not an option.

"I'm pretty sure dyeing my hair doesn't fall into the strict instruc-tions Leo gave me."

Hallie raises an eyebrow, the words clearly piquing her interest. "Instructions?"

"He told me to stay out of trouble while I was here so he wouldn't have to deal with me." Her eyes widen, and without meaning to, I continue ranting. "Which is bullshit because it's not like I ever *get* into trouble. Like, ever. I don't do anything that isn't for my tour or for promo. When *would* I get in trouble? With all of my free time?"

"Why would he say that?" Hallie asks, annoyed on my behalf.

I groan and sink back, the familiar irritation rising once more

"Who knows, but it's so annoying. I came here because I need to *stay out* of the spotlight. Not to mention, throughout my entire life, I've worked to maintain my image. America's sweetheart can't *get into trouble*. I have sacrificed everything to build that. Why would I do anything to jeopardize that?"

"Is that why he looked like he was constipated the entire time he and the guys were here?" Hallie asks. I shrug.

"I guess. He's mad I'm here. Did you *see* him pull me aside when he got here?" I ask, still annoyed, and Hallie nods. "He's acting like he's my dad or something, like he needs to keep me in line. All I've ever done is stay in line!"

"It's a bummer he's kind of a grumpy asshole. He's pretty hot," Nat says. "Kind of like if you mixed Madden and Jesse's style and got the perfect mix of both."

"Yeah, I can see that," Hallie says. "When he was here for the festival, he was all button-down shirt tucked into slacks, which sounds out of place here, but on him it worked. But since he's been here, he's all dressed down, working man. Hot."

"He's usually wearing these suits and looking all angry and yelling at people." My mind moves to the white tee he was wearing, the way it hugged his chest, the way those jeans fit just a little *too* well. His hair is always combed back nearly, but it was clear he hadn't put the same effort into combing it back like he does when he's on the job, and the whole look was very, very appealing. "Which, like, hot, I guess, but I've never seen him like *that*, you know? He's never dressed down."

I never thought I had a type, but the way my heart and other places responded, I might after all.

"Do you mind if I ask...have you two ever..." Nat asks, her voice trailing off before a blush burns deep on her cheeks. "Oh my god, I can't believe I just said that, I'm so sorry. I've been around Hallie far too much and—"

I let out a laugh and shake my head.

"That was one of the most politely asked personal questions I've been asked over the years. Tabloids and interviewers *love* to try to corner me and ask the strangest questions."

Nat scrunches her nose in disgust, and I shrug.

"Okay, but that wasn't a no...?" Hallie says, voice trailing off with a bit of irritation. I let out a laugh and shake my head.

"No, no. Leo and I have never and will never. The man can barely tolerate me." They look at each other, a knowing smile I can't decode shared between them.

"Wren thought the same thing about Adam, you know," Hallie says eventually.

"What?" I ask with a laugh. "Adam, who basically kisses the ground she walks on?" Hallie smiles wide and nods.

"Yup, couldn't stand her when he got here. And Jesse was a total grump when he and Hallie were forced together," Nat says

"Seems to be a trend," Hallie says, a playful smile on her lips, giving me a knowing look, and I finally understand what they're implying.

"Well, I love that for you guys, but I wouldn't hold your breath. Leo can't stand me. It's purely business between us."

There's another beat of silence before Nat speaks. "Should we tell her?"

"Tell me what?" I ask, confused, staring between them. Nat opens her mouth, but Hallie slaps her hand over her mouth and shakes her head.

"No, no, it's more fun this way, if she thinks he really hates her."

"Should I get the popcorn now or...?" Nat asks, and Hallie laughs.

"Why does everyone in this town talk in riddles?" I ask, fully confused.

Hallie shrugs. "Part of our small-town charm. But you know what I think? I think you should tell Leo to go fuck himself."

"What?"

"I think this would be a great time to get into trouble."

"Get into trouble? That's exactly what I was told *not* to do."

"Exactly. I mean, do you always do what Leo tells you to do?"

I bite my lip nervously. "Not *Leo*," I say.

Nat's brow furrows.

"But you let other people tell you to do?"

I sigh, unsure of why I'm even entertaining this.

"It's complicated. I don't exactly live a normal life." There's hesitation, and I hope she doesn't dig any deeper, since I'm coming to terms with a lot these days, and one more thing might send me over the edge. I'm relieved when she nods, clearly deciding not to press it.

"Okay, well, we're gonna be living a normal life for the next three months. And that's going to start with getting into some trouble."

Hallie sits up and moves to the edge of her seat, a light sparking in her eyes, and I can see an idea forming in her mind. Part of me knows to be nervous of it—that look in her eyes—but I can't seem to. Instead, excitement brews in my veins. "How? As fun as it sounds, I can't be getting arrested or anything." Hallie rolls her eyes.

"In order to get arrested, you'd first have to do something that would make Leo actually want to call the cops, and then he'd have to deal with your drama. Kind of counterintuitive, you know?" I stare at her, seeing her logic, and it's clear my moment of hesitation fuels her. "Actually, it's genius. You can have fun and be silly and get into trouble for the first time, but in a controlled way. It's kind of foolproof."

"I don't know—"

"I do," Hallie says, standing.

"Come on. It's not actual trouble. It's...good trouble. Like a white lie."

"What are you thinking?" Nat asks, clearly on board.

She turns to me with a widening smile, mischief written all over her face. "Ever toilet paper a house?"

TEN

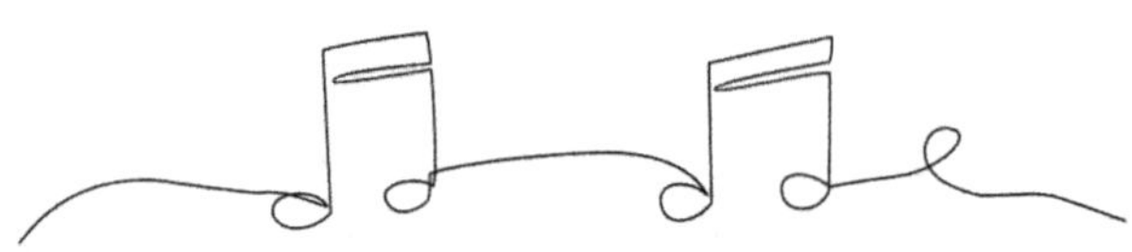

WILLA

"Are we sure this is a good idea?" I ask, biting my lip as I stare at the UTV now parked outside my new place. Nat's in the back, a twelve-pack of toilet paper beside her, and Hallie's in the driver's seat. Once again, she pats the seat next to her, where I guess I'm supposed to be.

"No."

My eyes go wide, and panic is written all over my face. When Hallie sees it, she lets out a bark of a laugh. "It's a *great* idea. Come on, Willa. It's basically an American tradition."

"Wasting toilet paper by throwing it all over people's houses?"

"Yes. And right now, Leo is at my place with Jesse, so we have time to get the job done."

The premise is simple, something I've seen in movies a million times but never realized people actually did. Once I was grudgingly on board, Hallie went over to the main house on the Three Kings property to get a dozen toilet paper rolls, since, according to Hallie, Mrs. King hoards them. Nat stayed with me so I wouldn't chicken out. She returned quickly and handed them over before juggling keys to a UTV she stole from her fiancé. According to her, Leo got wrangled into poker night, so we had some time.

"He doesn't get to tell you what to do, Willa. You're here to have fun, and he's just going to have to deal with it," Hallie says, and I stared at her for a moment, running through my options. But after a moment, I realized she was right: who the hell was Leo Sinclaire to tell me what to do?

I nodded, then slid onto the seat beside her. She squealed with excitement, and Nat clapped, hooting once when we took off. Hallie drove us through the woods, a half mile to the east, until we got to Leo's place. Now we just need to deck out Leo's place with the toilet paper and leave before he gets back. According to Hallie, we'll be in and out before Leo gets home, much less before he's able to realize who actually did it.

I sigh, knowing there's no talking her out of this. "So, how do I do this?" I ask, holding the toilet paper roll she handed me. From the corner of my eye, Nat is already at work, wrapping the fence in white streaks that glow in the dim moonlight.

"So you grab this end," Hallie instructs, taking her own toilet paper roll and grabbing the loose end. "Hold it tight, and then chuck the roll up." She does as she instructs, and I watch the roll rise, loop over a tree branch, and come back down, leaving a long strand of toilet paper in its wake. She grins mischievously, then repeats it on another branch. "Keep going until we're all out." We both stare as it sways in the gentle breeze, and I try to fight back the childish excitement bubbling up, tempered by a healthy dose of skepticism and common sense.

"What happens when he comes home?" She shrugs as if it's no big deal.

"He'll probably call Madden or Jesse."

"And they'll...?" I ask.

"Play dumb. Tonight, Jesse will probably interrogate me to figure out if it was us. I've got a good poker face, but not with him," Hallie says with a grim face that doesn't look nearly as fearful as I think it should.

"What she means is Jesse will tease her and practice orgasm withholding until she confesses," Nat says from a few feet away, tossing her own roll up and over the porch of Leo's house.

"What?" I ask, eyes wide. Hallie just beams in my direction, bright and happy and full of mischief.

"Can't lie, Will, this is kind of a double-duty task for me. You get to be bad, and I get to be *bad*."

I continue to stare at her, baffled, but clearly, Nat is not as shocked as I am.

"Please take notes; I'm dying to know all the dirty details," Nat says. "You never tell me anything anymore." She's nearly pouting, and Hallie rolls her eyes dramatically before throwing the roll of toilet paper again.

"I can't share when Wren's around. We made a pact."

"You guys...share?" I ask, somehow even more confused and shocked. But Nat shakes her head.

"We trade sex stories. Got any good ones?"

I think back on my lackluster experiences with random celebrities and one-night stands.

About four years ago, I decided it wasn't worth it: I had much more fun with a vibrator than I ever had with a man. I have to admit, I thought that, just like soulmates and toilet papering houses, amazing sex lives and girlfriends trading stories were some kind of myth, a fake pastime movies and shows made up.

But that suddenly feels unbearably embarrassing, so instead, I move on with the task at hand, choosing the lesser of two evils.

"Aren't we on a time crunch?" Grabbing the edge of the roll, I toss it up. The roll moves to the roof and then pauses for a moment.

"Jesus, Willa, you've got a freaking arm on you," Hallie says with a laugh.

"I take Pilates classes five times a week and strength train twice a week," I say offhandedly.

"Well, if the music thing ever stops working for you, consider a career in softball." We watch as the roll slowly moves again, rolling back down and leaving a long line of toilet paper. When it falls back to the ground, I can't say I don't feel a bit of a thrill at the way it looks.

It's going to be a huge mess for Leo to clean up, but it's the least he deserves. I mean, if he's going to accuse me of being trouble, I might as well live up to the accusation.

I'm giggling as I pick up the roll and throw it again, and then again, and again, until the house and surrounding property are absolutely *covered* in the stuff.

"Shit," Hallie says as I finish my last roll. Everything is covered in thin strands of white paper, and I keep giggling to myself as I look around.

I can't even begin to remember the last time I had so much fun.

"Shit?" I ask, turning toward where she is, but I don't need her to explain, not when I can see pinpricks of light in the distance, quickly getting larger. I'm frozen for a moment before I realize a pair of head-lights is approaching, moving up the driveway toward us.

"Go, go, go!" Hallie says loudly, waving her hand toward the UTV at the edge of the woods, and it feels like some kind of military drama. My heart drops and my pulse races as I realize what's happening: Leo is back, and he's about to catch us in the act.

I bend, scooping up the trash of empty toilet paper rolls, but Hallie shakes her head and starts running. "No! Leave them! Go!"

I don't question her, not as the light begins to move up and over the driveway, illuminating my legs. "Ahh!" I shout as if it's a sci-fi movie, with the light a laser. That's when I start running in earnest. Nat is a few feet ahead of me, and I'm moving quickly and closing in on her when I drop my phone.

"No!" I shout, moving back to grab it.

"Willa!" Nat yells, pausing to look back at me.

"Go on without me!" I yell dramatically. If my pulse weren't pounding a million miles a minute, I might laugh at how bananas this is. But instead, I wave towards her. "I'll catch up!" She nods, then turns back towards the woods, sprinting towards the UTV.

"Hallie! Start her up!" Nat yells.

"What the fuck is going on here?" Leo calls from a distance, keys jangling as he jogs toward us.

I reach for my phone and start back toward where Hallie is sliding into the UTV seat and starting the engine, Nat just a few feet away from freedom. I start moving again, forcing my legs to pump harder, to go as fast as I can, but suddenly, I'm not moving.

Suddenly, the distance between the UTV and me is no longer lessening because a hand has grabbed my wrist, and I'm being pulled backward, into a brick wall.

No, not a brick wall.

A chest. A hard chest. A heaving chest. My hand slams into it as I stumble a bit, and on instinct, my head tips back. I meet Leo's eyes, and my breath catches in my lungs.

I'm tall.

Not crazy tall, not six feet or even five-ten. Just five eight, but considering women in Hollywood tend to be cute and petite, considering the average height is much shorter, it's rare that I have to tip my head back to look at someone. I remember that on my second fake date, the guy had to wear lifts to be taller than me in my heels for red carpet appearances.

But in this moment, I find myself thinking I wouldn't have that issue with Leo.

No, it wouldn't be a problem, because Leo towers over me, and I fight the urge to ask him how tall he is. I bet I could wear six-inch heels and still not be taller than him.

It's not something I should be focusing on, especially not with the adrenaline coursing through me or the angry look on his face, but it's all I can think of. That, and the way his chest is hard and warm beneath my hand.

"What the fuck are you doing here?" he rumbles. I stare at him, shocked into silence as I take in his face. It's confused and angry and so fucking handsome that I can't focus. His arm burns a line along my lower back, and my lungs are panting, though I don't know if it's from the way he's looking at me or the run or the adrenaline coursing through me,

When I don't respond, he repeats his question. "What are you doing here, Willa?"

"Having fun," I say, the words coming out as an almost-whisper, and even in the dim moonlight, I see his eyes widen in shock and disbelief.

"I told you to stay out of trouble," he says.

That familiar irritation rolls through me, and I speak without thinking.

"You can't tell me what to do."

His face changes again, and part of me says to run. He's not holding me tight, and it wouldn't be too hard to slip out of his hold and book it towards Hallie and Nat. I tell myself that I'm not so Hallie and Nat can get away, but I don't even know if I'm buying that right now.

"Well, someone has to."

My heart rate speeds up, my gaze dropping to his full lips without my mind's permission.

"And you think *you're* the man for the job?"

He seems to be just as shocked as I am, but it doesn't last long before he volleys back at me. I fight a smile. This...*this* is what it felt like in that coffee shop all those years ago, the ease of it, the humor, the banter. This is why I was so torn up when he didn't even notice me.

"I can't think of anyone else better for the job," he says, his voice low, and my pulse starts to pound in a way that has nothing to do with the adrenaline coursing through me from our sprint. His eyes are burning in a way I've never seen directed at me, and my breathing goes shallow. His veiled threat settles low in my belly, churning up ideas that I thought I'd long, long buried.

"I'll believe it when I see it," I murmur.

"You're such a brat." He smiles when he says it, like he thinks he's winning this battle, like he thinks he's caught me off my guard.

"What are you going to do about it, Leo?" My words are loaded with innuendo, and when his eyes widen and his lips part, I'm pretty sure each one landed.

We stand like that for a moment, both of us stunned into silence, and he shakes his head.

His eyes drop, moving from my eyes to my lips, then down my body, scanning and assessing, before coming right back up. Each inch he covers, my pulse pounds harder. It feels like some Wild West showdown, and I don't know whether I want to win or lose.

"GET ON!" a voice calls, snapping me back to the here and now, and I whip my head to the side to see Hallie and Nat coming our way on the UTV. She stops, reaches over, grabs my wrist, and tugs until I'm sliding my ass onto the seat as she hits the gas and we're moving. "Later, Leo!" she says with a laugh. Looking over my shoulder, I catch Leo watching us drive off, the same shocked and confused look on his face as before, but there's no irritation there anymore. Instead, just a hint of amusement.

"What the hell was that?!" Hallie yells, a wide, excited smile on her lips as she drives through the woods, Nat laughing as we go. "With Leo?"

"I...." I say, still dazed now that the high of battling with him has worn off, confusion taking its place. "I have no idea."

"Told you," Nat says with a laugh. "I'll make sure to get the popcorn ready." This time, I don't ask what she means. Instead, I play the look he gave me over and over in my mind, dissecting it, trying to find excuses and meanings that fit my previous understandings and experiences, and somehow missing a piece.

That night, I don't go to bed at my normal early hour.

That night, I throw my entire routine out of whack, and I stay up late, basking in the glory of getting one over on Leo, of a night of chaos with my friends.

But most importantly, I stay up late, eagerly writing down lyrics and lines, snippets of a new song. It comes easily, as if my muse has returned with a vengeance, and when I finally pull my exhausted body into bed, I think that moving to Holly Ridge just might have been the best first choice I've ever made.

ELEVEN

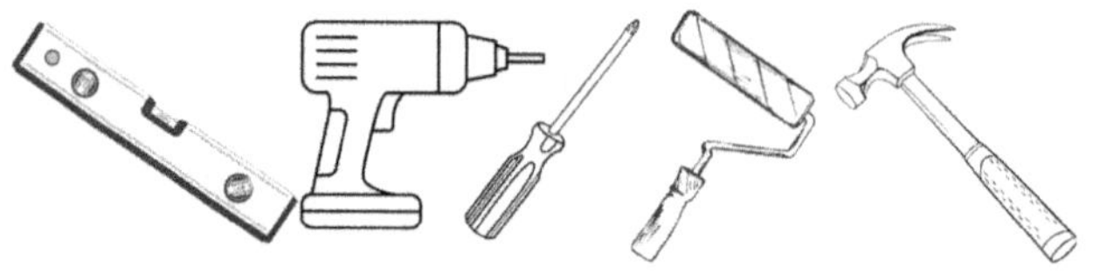

LEO

There are a million reasons I've kept my distance from Willa Stone.

She's a client.

She's *Willa Stone* and absolutely untouchable.

But tonight, I held her in my arms while she wore a sweatshirt I gave her years ago, and I nearly forgot each and every one of those million reasons.

I am so completely fucked.

TWELVE

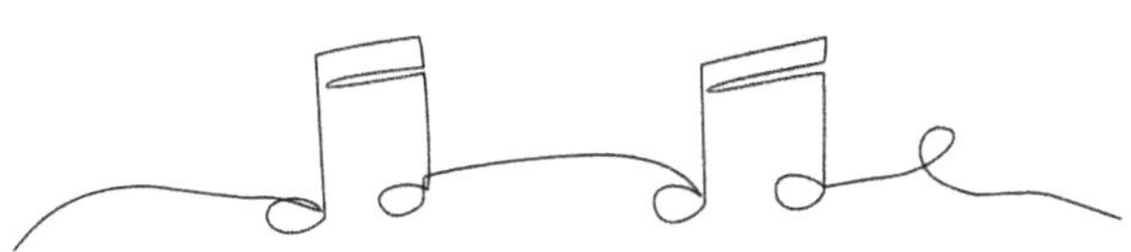

WILLA

The next morning, I woke with an unfamiliar exhaustion that ached in my bones. I lay there for a moment, confused, before it all came back to me: not a wild night of drinking or partying, as one might expect from a pop star, but a night in a small town with women I had just barely met, adrenaline pumping through our veins as we vandalized a man's house. The man who grabbed my wrist when I tried to flee the scene of the crime and tugged me into his chest before looking down at me with a heated glare.

For the first time in years, Leo Sinclaire had looked at me with something other than the cool indifference he always showed me.

A shiver rolls through me as I remember how he looked at my lips, how he held me tight, how his body felt against mine.

Once I push past those memories, I stumble across the next, more important one: I started writing a song last night. At that reminder, excitement courses through me, and I roll out of bed, eager to get on with my morning. I speed through washing my face and brushing my teeth, and head to the kitchen for water and my green juice. When I pour it into a glass, I stare at the goo for longer than usual, a grimace on my face.

Do what you want.

One thing I know I *do not* want is to drink this green sludge, and in a moment of impulsivity, I upend the glass over the sink and drain it.

A wave of excitement rushes through me, and I'm nearly giddy as I move through the pre-recorded online class on my computer before taking my shower and having a quick breakfast.

Then I sit down in front of my guitar and paper and take a deep, nervous breath before reading over what I jotted down the night before.

For a moment, I fear I'll be back where I started, that what I wrote will have been shit, but instead I realize I've finally got something. I spend the entire day adding and tweaking the lyrics and adding a bridge. Joy fills me as the vision I'd already had for the album grows and takes shape, becoming almost tangible.

Each of my albums tells a cohesive story, so if this is the first track for the album—a night out with your friends and getting into trouble—then track two would be about meeting the person you're about to date, about knowing from that very first glance you wanted to learn more about that person.

Halfway through the day, my clothing delivery arrives, and I excitedly put on one of the colorful sweatshirts and a pair of comfy lounge shorts before finishing the first song over leftovers from the night before.

I head to bed that night feeling more hopeful and inspired than I have in months.

The next morning, I wake up and start my routine, though today I don't even bother cracking the seal on my green juice. By eight, I've worked out, showered, and eaten, and I'm sitting on my couch with my guitar in my lap, ready to start writing.

That's when the panic drifts in once more.

I thought that since the previous song came so quickly, I was on a roll and the rest would finally start flowing in.

I was so horrendously wrong.

I sit down to work on the next song, one I decided would be about meeting someone and having a crush on them, that butterfly feeling in your chest that accompanies it. I know the vibes, the general idea of the song. I've written down words to spur anything on, but just like before I wrote "Good Trouble," I get *nothing*.

Nothing comes to me.

At first, I think it's a fluke. At first, I thought I might just need to rest and get some space between the first song and the next, but then the same thing happened on Friday.

And Saturday.

And Sunday.

On Monday, I head to Adam and Wren's house, and he helps me refine "Good Trouble," then records the track in a messy first draft. That goes smoothly, and I think maybe it was just being alone that had me stuck, but on Tuesday, when I try to write the next song with Adam, I hit that same stupid wall.

I hate everything I write.

It's all terrible.

By Thursday, I'm back to writing alone and crawling out of my skin, trying to find that thread of inspiration, when Nat calls. Eagerly, I answer, desperate for any kind of distraction.

"Hey, how's it going?"

"We're going out tomorrow," she says with no fanfare, no pleasant small talk. My brows furrow in confusion as I stare at the blank wall before me.

"Out?"

"To The Mill."

"The Mill?" I ask, feeling like a parrot as I echo her words.

She doesn't seem to mind, patiently explaining. "It's a bar in town, owned by Hallie's brother."

"Wow," I say with a laugh. "Do you know everyone here? Is everyone related in some way?"

Nat lets out a melodic laugh. "I mean, kind of? It's a small town; everyone knows everyone."

I sit back on the couch, folding my legs beneath me. "It sounds fake. Like some kind of shitty made-for-TV movie."

"Close enough," she says, and even though I can't see her, I can picture the shrug. "Anyway, are you in? We're thinking seven, but we'll go to the diner before, at, like, six to make sure we're not drinking on an empty stomach."

"I don't know," I say, biting my lip.

"Come on. What else are you going to do? You came here to have fun, right?"

She's not completely right, since I came here to lay low, but considering how stuck I am, I don't correct her. Instead, I think of how the last time I went out with her, I wrote a song and got inspired, and I would do just about anything for some inspiration right now.

"The girls will all be there. It'll be a blast," she says as if she can sense my hesitation.

For a split second, Leo's warning not to get into trouble moves through my mind, but instead of driving me to the smart answer, it does the opposite.

"Okay, I'm in," I say, a small smile on my lips.

"Really?" she asks, then squeals in excitement. "Oh my god, yes! I can't wait! We'll get ready at your place. We'll be there at five. Gotta go call Hal, later!"

And before I can argue, the phone goes dead, as if she doesn't want to give me any chance to reconsider.

Another thing I've always thought was a cinematic exaggeration was the non-stop laughter of a group of girlfriends getting ready for a girls' night out. You know the kind...the giggles that start at the slightest little thing and never seem to stop? Turns out that's real, too.

But the next night, when Nat, Hallie, and Wren all come over to get ready for a night out at a small-town dive bar, I experience it for the first time. Sharing lipsticks and borrowing tops and laughing so much, I had to wave my hands at my face so as not to ruin the perfect face of makeup that Nat did for me.

It's real, and it just played out at my place tonight.

"Will, are you ready?" Nat calls from my living room. "Jesse's here."

"Coming!" I shout, then stare in the mirror for another moment. For the first time since I arrived here, I do my centering routine: close my eyes, take in five deep, calming breaths until the butterflies in my chest slow. This time, though, I don't remind myself that Gabe is here, because he's not, and I don't have to assure myself that I have my cool girl armor on, because I don't.

But that knowledge doesn't leave me more nervous: in fact, it makes me feel even better.

Instead of a fashion-forward, paparazzi-friendly outfit, I'm wearing a casual top I borrowed from Hallie, a pretty powder-blue one that looks amazing on me and complements my hair perfectly. I'm not wearing my headache-inducing slick ponytail because Nat insisted on doing my hair and makeup. Instead, my hair flows down my back in loose waves, and my makeup is light with a brighter blush than I would normally wear, something from Nat's own collection. I don't have my contacts in, and instead of my signature neutral smoky eye, I'm wearing simple eyeliner and mascara.

When I open my eyes, I don't see Willa Stone TM, ready to trick the world into thinking I have it all together, in the mirror.

Instead, I just see myself.

Instead, someone familiar and friendly stares back at me.

I smile at the woman in the mirror, then step away to head out with my friends.

Hallie insisted that Jesse drive me home tonight, so I could get crazy, and I didn't have the heart to tell her that it probably wouldn't happen. Nat is planning to take a cab to her house, located not too far away from the bar, and Adam is meeting us at the Mill, so he'll be taking Wren home, but we all pile into Hallie's car with Jesse driving us to the diner. We eat in utter chaos, Hallie and Jesse bantering nonstop, which Nat tells me in a hushed tone is their own personal version of foreplay. Nat argues with Madden, who shows up a bit after us, and Wren eagerly fills me in on all about her and Adam's summer plans over the loud chattering.

After dinner, we head to the Mill, which is in the center of town. It's dim, with dark, dark hardwood floors and beams throughout, and tables of various sizes and heights lining the sides of the room. To the left is a bar with bottles lining the walls and half a dozen stools. Music plays from a jukebox—an actual, real-life *jukebox!*—in the corner, and it looks exactly what you would picture if you thought of a friendly local bar in a small town.

I *love* it the instant I step inside.

The bell over the door rings when we step inside, and the bartender gives us a wave. My companions all wave back, giving various greetings. He's tall and grinning wide, hands holding a glass that he's drying, and he looks sort of familiar. After a moment, I realize he must be Hallie's older brother, Colton. That's confirmed when Hallie veers away from the group, moving to the bar and reaching over to hug him while we all move towards a large table that Nat tells me is *theirs*. Once we settle, Jesse asks everyone for their drink orders.

"I'll just have a diet soda," I say when his eyes hit me after getting Nat and Wren's drinks. I expect an argument, for Nat to tell me I need to have fun or that I need to let loose, but there is none, just a nod from Jesse, who moves to get his brother's order before walking over to Hallie. He places a hand on her lower back, and she turns to him with a soft look before leaning into him. I try to ignore the ache in my chest as I avert my gaze and look around the bar.

The bar isn't packed, but it's definitely busy, with most tables having a few people seated or standing around the high tops. Something feels strange, different, and a bit unsettling as I look around. I can't put a finger on it at first, but then it clicks.

No one is staring at me.

I can't remember the last time I went somewhere without having to be on, knowing phones were lifted and turned toward me, ready to capture any misstep or embarrassing moment. When I think back, I realize that the same thing happened at the diner, to a degree, but not nearly like this. Here, it's like I'm...no one.

"You look like you just saw a ghost," Adam says with a laugh. I blink, trying to come back to myself, but the truth is, I feel like I did: the ghost of some life I never knew existed, one where I'm normal, where I'm a no one.

When I look back at them, I realize he's grinning at me, thoroughly entertained. A blush blooms over my cheeks as I bite my lip. "I promise I'm not trying to be full of myself, but...no one's staring at me."

"And they won't," Adam says with a shrug, settling into the chair beside Wren and across from me. She smiles sweetly and leans into his side, but I'm stuck on his words.

"What?"

"They won't stare at you. I mean, you'll have a few here and there who want to talk or ask for a photo or a signature. But it will stay within the town. No one will bother you here, not unless you want to." I stare at him, disbelieving.

"We take care of our own," Wren says with a shrug.

"But I'm not..." I start, then bite my lip. I've been doing that a lot lately, and I suppose without Jackie here, I have no one to stop me. "I'm not..." I don't have to finish because Wren understands.

"You're part of the town. You're here at the Mill with us, so it's clear we've claimed you," she replies as if it's pure logic, and warmth floods my system at her simple, sweet words.

We've claimed you.

People have 'claimed me' or befriended me a hundred times over in my life. But they've always had an ulterior motive, always were looking for some kind of connection or favor. But as I look around this table, I realize that no one has asked me for anything, except once Adam asked me to FaceTime a twelve-year-old, which I was more than happy to do.

"So I can..." I ask, my words trailing off. Jesse and Hallie come over, setting drinks down, and I absentmindedly take a sip from my drink.

"You can let loose," Adam says simply. Instantly, my mind moves to Leo's insistence that I stay out of trouble and the subsequent chaos. I haven't seen or heard from him since, though with the way his arm felt on my waist, the unhinged and entirely inappropriate thoughts that went through my mind, I am more than happy with that. "And if you do, no one will be the wiser."

"No one would risk the wrath of Colton," Hallie adds, picking up on the conversation effortlessly.

"The *wrath of Colton?*" I ask, trying not to look at the bar where the large teddy bear of a man stands.

"Oh yeah. He's tough," Hallie says. "Will kick anyone's ass who gets on his bad side." As seems to be the way, I can't quite decode Hallie, though there's a tiny quiver to her lip as if she can't hold back much longer. Before she cracks, Wren rolls her eyes and sighs.

"He'll just blacklist them. Hallie just loves dramatics." She lifts her bright red drink and takes a small sip. "There aren't many bars in town, and this is really the only good one if you're under the age of sixty. So if you get kicked out for good, you're kind of out of luck in terms of socializing."

"Huh," I say low, mind reeling.

Just then, the song changes, turning to some upbeat summer song from a few years back, and Nat turns to Hallie with wide, excited eyes.

"Dance?"

"Hell yeah," she says, chugging her drink until it's nearly empty, then standing. "Willa?"

I shake my head. "Maybe later."

Nat glares. "*Definitely* later. You're having fun tonight."

"Let her be," Adam says, surprising everyone. "Let her settle."

Nat takes us in, then rolls her eyes and nods before skipping off to the center of the room to dance with Hallie, and I sit back and bask in the magic of Holly Ridge.

Thirty minutes or so later, I'm still nursing my drink, now mostly ice and watered-down soda, when it happens. Some kind of energy shift, the door opening, and a bell jingling over the door, still heard despite the low music that's playing. Hallie promised me it gets louder, that she could probably convince Colt to allow karaoke again (something that, apparently, she and Wren managed to get outlawed two years ago after a very boisterous round), and every head in the bar turns to the door.

Leo walks in, gaze scanning the bar hesitantly.

My heart skips a beat, the same way it did when I saw him outside the cabin when I moved in, the same way it did when he caught me after toilet-papering his house.

The same way it did when we spent an hour chatting in a coffee shop years ago.

And just like that day, my eyes take him in, completely in awe of him. It's absolutely rude for a man to be such an ass *and* be that hot. He's in well-fitting jeans and a tight white T-shirt that shows off muscles I didn't know he had across his chest, stretching the arms of his shirt. He's wearing fucking *work boots,* which feels almost illegal to see in the wild considering I've only ever seen him in custom-made shoes.

It's like seeing Superman out of his costume or a lion without its mane. Like this, totally out of his fancy, expensive suits, his normally neatly-coiffed hair a bit messy, like his hands have been running through it nonstop, pushing it back to keep it out of his eyes—he looks nothing like the man I sat across from in a business meeting.

"Leo!" Madden calls from the other side of the table. Leo's pleasant look as he waves to Madden melts off when his gaze slides to me. His face transforms, expressions moving from confusion to shock to frustration in the blink of an eye. When he recovers, his steps quicken, eyes narrowing on me. I watch in utter fascination as the gap between us closes before he stops just a foot from where I'm sitting on a tall stool.

"Hey, Leo," I say, trying to sound casual.

"What are you doing here?" he asks, irritation rolling off him in waves. I roll my eyes, whatever awed stupor he put me into upon walking in fading quickly with his attitude.

"This is getting kind of old, Sinclaire," I say with a sigh. For a moment, when his face screws up in irritation, I second-guess myself. But then Nat snorts out a laugh beside me, and it fuels my sass.

I'm starting to like this new version of me who gives zero fucks, who doesn't baby everyone or worry about how her actions will impact them.

I'm not hurting anyone, so what should matter?

"I'm staying in Holly Ridge to write with Adam, remember?" I say slowly, as if he can't understand my words. He sighs, eyes drifting shut as he takes a deep breath before he speaks again.

"Yeah, I know. What are you doing here? This is a bar." I look around, pretending to look shocked.

"Wow, is this what this place is? I didn't know. I've never actually seen one in real life."

"Drop the fucking act, Willa. You know what I mean. You can't be out at a bar," he says, and that now-familiar irritation brews in my veins, further pushing me to do whatever it is Leo tells me I can't do.

He's not my dad. He's not my mom. He's not even my *manager*.

"Well, I'm here. What are you going to do, throw me over your shoulder and take me home?" A laugh bursts from someone behind me, but I don't break eye contact with Leo, unwilling to lose this stare-down. I've never had anyone pull this kind of reaction from me, never felt the consuming desire to argue and go toe to toe and prove someone wrong, but for some reason, I feel it surging anytime Leo opens his stupid mouth.

And it becomes even more pressing when his jaw goes hard, and his eyes flare with irritation.

"If I have to."

My breath hitches at his words, and then the strangest thing happens.

His eyes drop, moving from my eyes to my lips like he's watching where my gasp came from. For the smallest moment, I think his eyes heat, but it's gone so quickly, I think I must have imagined it.

"You know what would loosen up this tension right now? Shots!" Nat shouts, and Leo looks away, then, shifting his glare to her. I laugh and start to shake my head because, despite feeling comfortable at this bar, I don't know if I'll ever feel comfortable enough to completely let go like that.

The one and only time I got drunk was my twenty-first birthday, and every paparazzi in a one-hundred-mile radius seemed to catch me stumbling about, taking shots, dancing with everyone and anyone, and generally having a good time. The next morning, I was so terribly hungover, but it was the lecture Jackie gave me about messing with the brand that made me realize it just wasn't worth it.

America's sweetheart doesn't get shitfaced drunk and grind on strangers, after all.

"Absolutely not," Leo says before I can respond. I narrow my eyes at his tone, so firm and unwavering.

And I say fuck it.

"Hell yeah!" I shout, lifting a hand in the air. Leo's mouth opens to argue, but Hallie and Nat grab my hands, and we nearly skip to the bar, where Hallie orders something and Colt lines up three shot glasses. Leo's gaze burns a hole in my back the entire time, but I don't turn to check until the girls, and I tap our glasses in a cheers. Only then do I turn to look at Leo, then hold his gaze as I lift the small glass, gesturing toward him in a toast with a small smile on my lips before I down the drink.

And even if I refuse to admit to myself, I don't think the burning warmth in my belly is from the liquor.

THIRTEEN

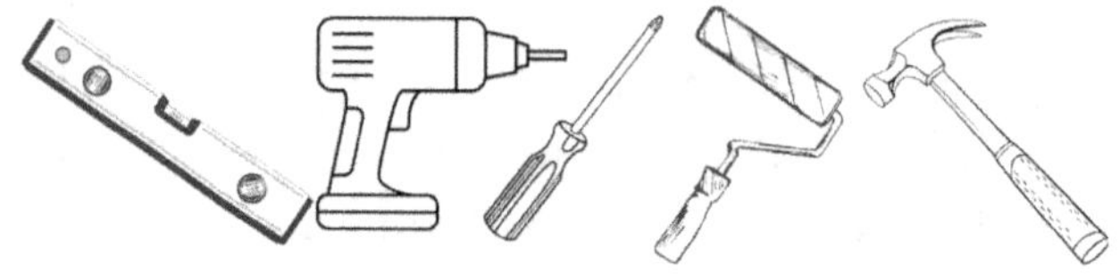

LEO

I should have said no.

When Madden texted to ask—no, demanded, since I don't think the Kings know how to politely request anything from anyone—me to come down to The Mill for a drink, I should have said no. In fact, I had typed out a polite but firm "no thank you," but before I could send it, an email hit my inbox, with "URGENT" in the subject line and Jefferson's name in the sender box.

Ignore it, I told myself. *Ignore it. It's a Friday. If it were actually urgent, he would call. Willa is here, and if there were an issue with Atlas Oaks, Harper, or any of your other clients, they'd reach out to you personally.* None of his clients likes dealing with Jefferson, either.

But I couldn't resist, being a glutton for punishment and a workaholic, desperately trying to recover and failing miserably.

Hey Leo—

Jackie just informed me Willa has found a place to stay in Holly Ridge, where she'll be working on her next album. She has requested that Jackie allow her stay there without anyone managing her. Since you are currently residing in Holly Ridge for the foreseeable future, I expect you to do your job and ensure that Ms. Stone stays out of trouble. Any shortcomings on that will be discussed at your next performance report. She has created an image of herself, and to ensure a successful campaign with Chris Scout, we need to maintain that image.

—Jefferson

I read between the lines the way I always have to with him. Despite being a jackass, he's a smart businessman with far too many high-powered lawyers in his pocket, and he knows not to put his threats on paper.

Keep Willa in line, or somehow, someway, I'm going to make your life an even bigger hellscape than it already is.

In that moment, I remind myself of my exit strategy and that I won't have to deal with him forever. I have less than two years with Perfect Image before my contract ends, when the ironclad non-compete I signed expires in full. After that, I'll be able to leave with my client list and start my own firm.

It's why, despite his not approving of many of the decisions I make for *my* clients, Jefferson won't fire me. If he were to do so without merit, which I'm careful never to give him, that clause would be null and void, and I'd be able to take whichever clients with me I wish, including Atlas Oaks, Stella Greene, Harper Holden, and a line of the other high-profile clients the firm boasts. While Jefferson and the other publicists represent many other stars, none hold the power that my clients do.

Unfortunately, Jefferson is more than aware of my plan, which is why, when he showed up at my meeting with Willa, irritation flooded me. I don't know where Willa will stand when I leave the firm, but it's clear Jefferson is trying to ingratiate himself with her manager. For the next two years, he'll be doing everything in his power to pull Jackie to his side by the end of my contract, so as not to lose Willa.

Apparently, that includes getting me to keep an eye on her client.

It's not even that I'm annoyed he's asking me to be a glorified babysitter. It's nothing I haven't done in the past for other clients—hell, there was a time when I was the only thing stopping Atlas Oaks from having a complete media crash out.

The truth is, if he'd asked me a year ago, I'd have been fine. If he'd asked me six months ago, I would have been fine.

Then. Willa was in a professional box that I could not even approach, with nothing but business between us, the way I had carefully crafted it over the last few years.

But now she's in the same town as me.

Now, we're somehow sharing friends.

Now, she seems to have found the backbone she's been missing and is showing it off with me in a way I find myself liking far too much.

Now, I know what she looks like when she's in shock, know what she feels like when I have her in my arms.

Fuck.

As I stared at the email, I attempted to regulate my breathing, taking the deep, measured breaths my therapist recommended, counting to ten with each one, when my phone *bings* with another text. That dread curled in on itself, anticipating a follow-up text from my boss.

But it wasn't from Jefferson or Jackie or anyone work-related.

MADDEN

Hallie insists.

Two words that held a subtle yet effective threat: Hallie insisted I come, and if I said no, I could expect some form of backlash. With a sigh and deciding I could use some time out of my house, without overthinking it, I replied with a one-word text.

When?

I would go to The Mill for exactly one drink. One beer, less than an hour, then head home. It would be a double-duty task, getting Madden and Hallie off my ass for not hanging out with them, and it would give me time to avoid replying to Jefferson's email the way I really fucking wanted to: with a bolded ***fuck off.***

Now!

With a sigh, I closed my laptop and quickly changed out of my paint and sawdust-speckled clothes, slipping into a clean pair of jeans and a T-shirt, sliding on some shoes, and grabbing my keys before making my way down my long drive.

My plan goes up in beautiful, searing flames the moment I step inside the bar and scan the room to see Willa Stone sitting at a table between Nat and Madden, a drink in her hand and a wide grin on her lips.

"Leo!" Madden calls, and without conscious thought, my feet move, eyes locked on Willa.

Then I do what I found myself doing the last time I was surprised by her: I argue with her. I challenge her.

And just like last time, she shocks me by not backing down. For once, she stands up for herself and gets *annoyed* with me.

When she runs off to take shots with Nat and Hallie, I groan but can't help but watch her ass in the little shorts she's wearing. I watch her back the entire time as they chat with the bartender, who is already lining up shot glasses, but I can't see her face until the girls clink glasses.

That's when she turns, scanning the bar and finding me, then holding my gaze as she lifts the small glass, gesturing toward me in a toast with a small smile on her lips before she downs the shot.

"Not your handful, huh?" Madden asks, echoing my words from the other day with a laugh. I turn to him, giving him a glare that makes tabloids and paparazzi cower in fear, but just makes him laugh before he pats me on my shoulder. "What are you drinking tonight, brother? I think you're going to need it."

Willa takes three more shots over the next hour, and I do everything in my power to remain calm, cool, and collected. Maybe that's the key, not giving into the bait she's clearly dangling, not rising to the challenge. Maybe if I pretend to be unfazed, she'll lose all interest.

But after the fourth shot, I decide I don't care. In fact, it's just minutes after that fourth shot, when she stumbles and falls to the ground in a giggling heap on the makeshift dance floor after Hallie attempts to twirl her, that I lose it. My stool scrapes as I stand, then take long strides to her.

"Leo! Are you here to dance with us?" she asks eagerly, with a giggle that would be cute if she weren't her and I weren't me and we weren't what we are. I grab her hand, and she takes it willingly as I help her stand, then guide her into the quieter hallway at the back of the bar, where people can hang coats. She's still giggling as I turn her, put her back to the wall, and stand a foot in front of her.

"You know, the caveman act is kind of hot, but if you wanted me alone, you could have just asked. I would have come with you," she says, and I push that back, trying not to focus on the words or the hidden meaning.

"What the fuck are you doing?" I ask in a hushed, angry whisper. Her dazed eyes go confused, brow furrowing as she looks at me.

"What?" Her joy has melted away, and despite my anger, guilt seeps in, though like so many things tonight, I push it back, letting logic and duty remain front and center.

"This isn't you, drinking and being loud. What are you doing?"

"Not me? You don't even *know* me," she mumbles, but then answers my question. "I'm having fun, Leo. I'm having fun for *once in my life*," she says, and confusion wracks through me.

"Willa—"

There's another shift on her face, each of them happening so fast, I almost can't keep track of the changes. She shakes her head, her hair swaying from side to side as she does. It's down, and this close, I allow myself to take in the other changes, like the simple makeup that enhances her natural beauty instead of trying to make her look like a perfect doll. Those god-awful contacts are gone, and she's in a soft-looking blue shirt that I've never seen her in, a casual top that I doubt her stylist chose for her.

"I never get to have fun like this. I just want one freaking night. One night where I can be normal, and I can be happy and have fun, and where I don't feel *lonely*."

That last word carries so much emotion, weighed down with yearning and grief, and when paired with the lost look on her face, it shocks whatever anger was still lingering in my system out.

"Willa," I say, my voice suddenly soft even to my own ears as she unloads this onto me, as she throws me back with her words. She shakes her head, then continues.

"Do you know what it's like to feel so lonely all the time? To be in a room filled with people who know your name and still feel like you're all by yourself? Like, no one in the entire world actually knows you? Everyone puts me on this pedestal, everyone keeps their distance, and I'm *so fucking lonely*." Her voice cracks, and when it does, my chest cracks, too. Her eyes are wide and glassy, reflecting the sadness in her words. "I'm so lonely, Leo. It's crazy, because everyone wants a piece of me, everyone wants to talk to me and use me and find out how I can help them, but I...I'm so lonely. And here, for the first time, I don't feel that. I just want to feel like I belong somewhere for once in my life." I don't know what to say, not when her face is so open, so I don't say anything.

In the next instant, her face changes, those emotions pushed back to hide under some shield she's erected before she pushes at my chest.

"And *you* are trying to get in the way of that. I'm a big girl, Leo. And I'm tired of people telling me what I can and can't do." The song out in the bar changes then, a familiar tune drifting into the hall. It's one Willa wrote for another pop artist, though she didn't record it herself. She grins when she hears it, any anger or sadness replaced by the happy-go-lucky party girl I pulled into here. It happens so quickly, I wonder for just a moment if I imagined the other versions. "Now get out of my way. My song is on."

When she pushes at me this time, I don't resist, instead stepping back as she moves away, nearly skipping back into the bar. I can hear when the girls must spot her because a loud cheer fills the room before they all start singing together, but I stay in that back hallway for a long moment, her words running through me and leaving me uneasy.

Do you know what it's like to feel so lonely all the time?

In a strange way, the drunken pop star put into words all of the things I've been feeling lately, the loneliness despite everyone always needing something from me, and the strange desire to just *be*.

How the hell am I supposed to balance doing my job and giving her whatever it is she wants? Because if she ever looks at me with that sad look again, I know I would give her the entire world on a silver platter.

FOURTEEN

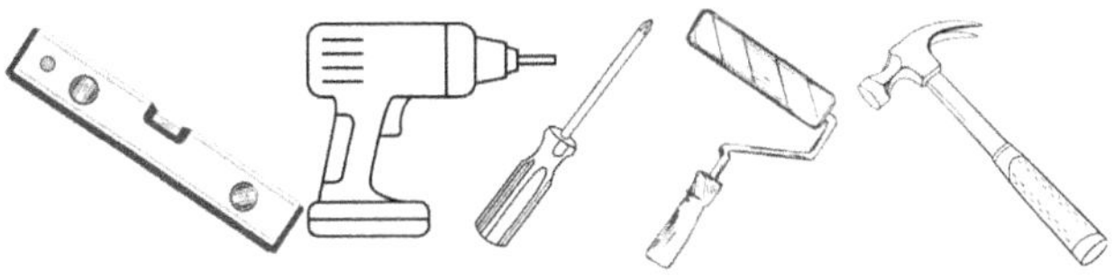

LEO

An hour and two more shots for the girls later, I'm still nursing the one beer I won't finish because I need to keep my mind alert. Willa and Wren twirl one another as music plays and each time she stumbles, I fight the urge to stand up, throw her over my shoulder, and take her home to sleep it off in the safety of her home.

"You look like you wish your eyes had laser beams," Hallie says, and I stop watching Willa to glance over at the redhead. I try to harness the lasers she spoke of to get her to leave me alone, but I fail. She must have some kind of killer armor, because instead of crumbling, she grins wider and sits on the stool beside me. Her fiancé stands behind her, a hand on her waist, and Nat sits on my other side.

It feels like an intervention, and I don't like it. Still, once I note them all blocking me in, my eyes move back to Willa.

The worst part is that as I watch her tip her head back and laugh, hands holding Wren's, I don't think I've ever seen her look more beautiful. Her hair is half down, the top half braided and knotted at the back of her head, the rest flowing down her back in loose waves instead of her normal severe ponytail. She's in a light blue outfit, the end of it just barely touching the top of her tight white shorts with a brown belt. When she twirls, the bottom lifts, showing a sliver of her tanned, toned stomach.

I could lie and say I haven't been watching, haven't been keeping track every time Wren spins her out for a glimpse at it, but I'd be lying.

Fuck, I'm pretty sure every single man in this place is doing the same, a fact that makes that familiar irritation brew in my chest.

"You have to stop looking like you're constipated every time you see her," Hallie says.

"I don't—"

"You totally do," Madden says, coming over to our growing group.

"I give him a month before she's over his shoulder," Nat says, sipping a drink from a thin straw, a smile on her full lips.

"A month?" Hallie says, disbelief in her words. "I give it two weeks."

"Nah, six, at least. He's still too far in denial," Jesse says. Hallie looks over her shoulder, raising one perfectly arched eyebrow at her fiancé.

"Unlike you?" He grins, pulling her further into him and pressing a kiss to the top of her head.

"Unlike me. I was long gone for you well before I carried you out of here."

"Adam only took, like, two weeks," Nat says, and somehow, my confusion only grows deeper.

"Yeah, but the first time he did it, they didn't fuck after. So does it count?" Hallie says, seemingly to genuinely wonder.

"Can we not talk about my sister getting fucked?" Madden asks, face a bit green.

"Are you all out of your fucking minds?" I ask, interrupting the strange conversation.

"You get used to it," Adam says with a sigh from the other side of the table. "But they're right: you gotta stop glaring at her. It's getting weird." I try to school my face, then finally turn away from the women dancing.

"I'm just worried. She's lived a sheltered life. She's never been drunk to my knowledge."

Hallie tips her head before challenging me.

"You know, she wasn't even drinking earlier," Hallie says, a smile in her words. "When you came in? She was nursing a soda." I turn to her, confused, and a wide grin spreads across her lips, like she's greatly enjoying dropping this bombshell. "But you came in, went all crazy caveman, argued with her, and essentially pushed her hand."

My eyes widen, and I move to stand, deciding then and there that this stupid game needs to end, but Hallie's hand moves to my arm, gripping with surprising strength and forcing me to sit back down.

"If you go over there and tell her to leave, she's just going to fight you harder, do exactly what you tell her she can't do. She's like a teenager with her first taste of freedom," Nat says, and even though I want to, I can't argue with her logic: I've seen it play out a few times already.

"She's having fun, Leo. There are four completely sober men watching her every move and committed to keeping her safe, and Colt won't let anything bad happen here. You said it yourself: she's lived for the brand most of her life. She's never been free to have fun, to explore. This is a safe place for that to happen."

"She's safe here, Leo. This is the best place for her to let loose. She can't live her entire life cooped up. She needs to have the opportunity to live."

I sigh, then lean back and cross my arms on my chest. "You're kind of good at this," I say begrudgingly.

"My brother's a bartender," she says as if that explains everything, then lifts a shoulder. "And my mom didn't love me."

"Jesus, Hal, you can't just dump that on people," Jesse says with an exasperated sigh, but he's still smiling, as if this entertains him. She turns to her fiancé, a fierce look on her face.

"Why not? It's the truth!" She seems strangely okay with this information, and I have to wonder if it's some kind of inside joke. Hallie turns her assessing gaze back to me. "And because of it, it just means I can see damaged people a mile away. You and Willa? My people."

"My parents love me," I argue.

"But...?" Her ability to read people is actually alarming. "I can smell a but." I roll my eyes and sigh.

"But my dad's dead," I admit.

"Ooh! Dead dad club!" Nat says, clapping before she slings an arm around my shoulders. I turn to her, a bit confused because I've never actually gotten *that* reaction to telling anyone my father is dead. "Finally! Someone for me!"

"For...you?" I ask, lifting a suspicious eyebrow. The longer I'm here, the more I wonder if *anyone* normal lives in Holly Ridge.

"Everyone here has dads. Even Hallie and Colt, though their's kind of abandoned them once Hallie graduated. The Kings have the *best* dad, which, honestly, is a stab to the heart, ya know?"

"You all are out of your damn minds," I grumble.

"Ah, yes, because you're just the *picture* of mental stability," Hallie says with a laugh. I don't have time to say anything else because just then the song ends, and Wren and Willa stop dancing and start making their way to our small table. I watch Willa like a hawk, and when she stumbles, my entire body jolts toward her as if controlled by some ghost before she catches herself, steadying her feet. A moment later, she and Wren start laughing hysterically before hugging one another.

Beside me, Hallie lets out her own loud, entertained laughter, and when I notice she's looking at me, laughing at *me* and my unintentionally protective manner, I realize just how fucked I am. I don't even realize my shoulders are tight with anticipation until Willa sits down safely beside Wren, and the tension leaves them.

"You know, the house is empty tonight. Emma's at your parents' place," Hallie says, thirty or so minutes later, turning to Jesse and putting a hand to his chest. "Maybe I should try to pace the girls, and you can take me out of here on *your* shoulder tonight."

"Do it," Jesse says, a mischievous look in his eyes, and Hallie's face lights up.

"Couch sex?"

He doesn't answer, but he doesn't have to. The look on his face says it all.

"I need another drink for this," Wren groans.

"Me too!" Willa says, standing and wobbling a bit.

"You should drink some water," I say in a low voice, trying to keep it a gentle suggestion. "You don't normally drink like this and—"

Her nose scrunches up, and I realize I said the wrong thing once again.

"You don't get to tell me what to do." She takes a half step towards the bar, then looks to me, a mischievous look on her face and a glint in her eye, before she calls over her shoulder. "Hallie! We're taking another shot!"

"Coming!" she calls, then skips towards the bar. As she moves around the table, Willa stumbles, though Madden thankfully catches her by the shoulder. She and Wren lock eyes and instantly burst into hysterical giggles before they finally reach the bar.

I watch in utter misery, completely out of my depth.

"Let her live her life," Madden says. "Anything goes wrong, enough of us are here that we can get her out quick and easy before it gives you a headache." I shake my head and speak without thinking.

"Willa doesn't give me a headache," I admit, because she doesn't. "She never has." Her manager might, and my boss might, but if I'm being honest, Willa doesn't. She was right: she doesn't ever get in trouble. She stays well within the bounds of what everyone expects of her, maintaining that America's Sweetheart persona that she's built over the years.

But without the spotlight, without the eyes, I'm learning that she's brighter. Happier. Lighter.

In fact, right now, I'm the only person dragging her down.

"She just drives me crazy."

It feels like I spend an eternity at the bar, watching Willa get more and more drunk, though my nerves are appeased when time and time again, it's proven that everyone was right about this place: it's safe, not just physically for Willa, but from the media. No one has approached her outside of our small group, and I haven't seen a single phone lifted to take a sneaky photo or video. Whatever fear Colton puts in his customers, they have respected Willa's privacy, and for that, I'm grateful.

"I gotta get her out of here before she gets too wild," Jesse says, watching his fiancée, who has made good on her promise and caught up with Nat, Wren, and Willa. When I turn to him, I don't see the irritation I might expect. Instead, there's a pleased smile like he loves this about her, as if he knows who she is and accepts it because it's something he loves.

I turn back to the girls and take them in, all four of them screaming a Spice Girls song at the top of their lungs.

I've never seen Willa this free.

"You're supposed to take Willa home?" I ask. He nods, though for the slightest moment, disappointment flashes on his face. Considering every time Hallie's been within touching distance, he's had his hand on her and murmured until she blushes, I can assume why. "I'll take her."

"What?" he asks, turning to me.

"I'll take her home." Jesse's face goes unsure, and despite the mild irritation of that, I can't help but feel that now familiar gratitude move through me. It's clear this crew has taken Willa in as one of their own, and that means they take care of her.

"She's really drunk, I don't mind—"

"It's cool," Madden says to his brother. "Leo's got her. He's been taking care of her longer than any of us has even known her." The oldest King takes in his younger brother, then the women, and finally looks back at me. I could lie, tell myself that I only offered to help because I want to do the man a solid, but I don't know if it's even worth lying to myself anymore.

"If she's okay with it, then okay. But if not, I'll just take her home. It's not far for me." I nod, then look to where Willa is, take in a steadying breath, before making my way to her. She catches sight of me, and her face goes beaming, the biggest wonky smile gracing her drunken face as she throws her arms into the air.

"Leo! King of boredom has come to dance!"

"No, no, I—" I start, but she trips into me, her chest hitting mine, her arms looping around my neck, and on instinct, my arm wraps around her waist, holding her to me.

In an instant, her body melts against mine, and the tension in my chest does the same.

Yeah.

I am so screwed.

"I'm just here to tell you I'm gonna take you home tonight," I say. Fast music plays around us, but we don't move to the beat. Instead, we sway slowly as I continue to hold her, and she clings to me, her face going confused.

"What? Why?"

"Because Jesse and Hallie want to get home and be alone together, and you'd be in the way of that." She looks over my shoulder, and as we move, I see Jesse and Hallie dancing slowly together, kissing more passionately than is appropriate for a bar, especially one owned by her brother. It makes Willa laugh, something I feel against me.

"Okay, yeah," she says. "That makes sense." Then the song moves to a slow one, and a wide, happy smile pulls on her full lips. "A slow song," she says, glee in the words.

"Willa—"

"One dance and then you can take me home," she says.

I can't fight it.

I'm starting to think I can't fight *her*.

So instead, I move with her, giving her an answer with my body. A light, happy sigh leaves her lips, and that, too, settles in my chest.

"Are you having fun?" she asks a minute in, her voice low, though her closeness lets me still hear her. I've been lost in the feel of her, so lost in the song and the way she hums to it with her eyes half shut, that the question startles me. I look down and smile at her soft expression. On instinct, my hand lifts, pushing back a chunk of messy hair that fell out of the braid and tucking it back behind her ear. She leans into my touch like a kitten desperate for affection, and again, something cracks my chest wide open, but this time, before I can close it back up and reinforce my walls, Willa somehow sneaks in and makes herself comfortable.

"I hope you're having fun. I don't think you have fun nearly enough." Her eyes are so hopeful, like it really matters to her that I am in fact having fun, so I nod, and as I do, I find I'm not lying.

"Yeah, honey. I'm having fun," I say, the nickname spilling from my lips without meaning to, but I can't find it in me to care. "Are you?"

"The most fun I've ever had," she says, and I know she means it. She's been to high-profile parties and awards shows and travelled the world, but he's never had more fun than right now, dancing in a small-town dive bar.

"I'm glad, Willa. You deserve to have fun."

Her eyes go somehow softer as her hands slide up the back of my neck, fingers moving to play with the hair there. Despite myself, despite needing and wanting to keep my distance, I find myself pulling her in a bit closer.

"Did I finally crack you?" she asks.

"Crack?"

"Yeah. You're a grumpy old man, but I know you can be fun. I just never get to see it." I stare at her, unspeaking, as she moves and her hand reaches up to rest on my cheek as she looks into my eyes. It's uncomfortable in a way, but so comforting in others, as she seems to read beyond my words, beyond what I'm showing her.

Eventually, her lips tip up with a soft, knowing smile.

"Yeah, I've cracked you."

FIFTEEN

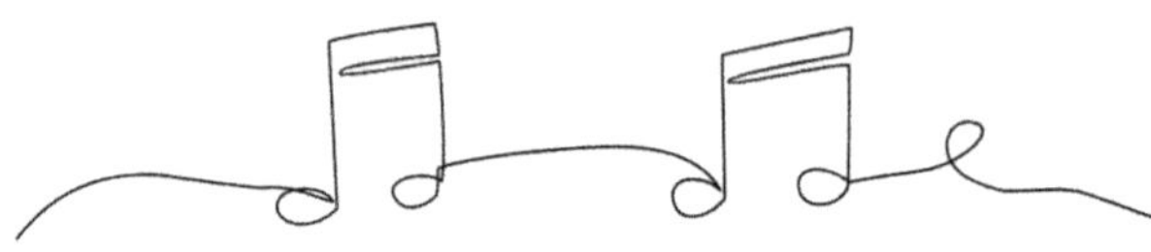

WILLA

"Bye, guys!" I shout, waving at the girls as they all get into their respective cars. "We need to do this again soon!" Leo helps me into his car after we exit the Mill. It's early summer, but compared to the warm bar we just left, it's chilly outside. Still, I barely feel it, my happy emotions running high.

Even more, I think Adam was right: I just needed a life in order to get inspired. In fact, if I weren't so drunk, I could probably write an entire album tonight. That's just how good I feel.

I can't say it would be a *good* album, but it would be an album all the same.

But I can't, because I am, in fact, very, very drunk.

Once the car is moving and Leo makes it clear he's not in the mood for chitchat, my mind moves happily over the night. Despite the bumpy beginning, it was the best night I can remember, and I feel like I even finally got past Leo's grumpy facade.

A successful night, if you ask me.

"That's my turn," I say a bit later, watching the entrance for Three Kings Farm pass by us without Lepo even slowing.

"I'm not taking you home," he says simply. I sit up a bit, my head swimming as I look at him, but his eyes are directed out the window, face neutral.

"What?"

"Willa, you're hammered. I can't in good conscience take you to your place to sleep alone."

"Because you're supposed to keep an eye on me and keep me out of trouble?" I ask, sounding petulant even to my own ears. He sighs and shakes his head.

"No, because despite you being a pain in my ass, I care about you."

"You do?" I ask, and his brow furrows. For a moment, his eyes leave the road to look at me, and that confusion is written across his face as well.

"Of course, Will," he says gently, and the words settle in my belly, sending a warmth through me that rivals the shots I took tonight. "I wouldn't be able to live with myself if something happened to you and I could have stopped it, Willa."

I stare at his profile, the moon casting shadows across it, and for a moment, I think about asking more questions, anything to better understand him, but I don't know where to start, so instead, I just rest my head against the cool glass, my eyes drifting shut as I do.

"I had fun tonight," I admit into the quiet cab of the car as we turn and make our way up Leo's bumpy, winding driveway.

"I can tell. I think the whole bar could tell."

I giggle, my heavy head shifting so I can look at him as he parks the car with effortless ease, backing into a spot on the gravel drive by doing that hot guy thing of putting his arm on the back of my seat. Finally, he turns off the car and opens the door. "Stay there," he says.

Even though I've made it my mission to do more of whatever Leo tells me *not* to do, I decide listening to him just this once might be for the best. He moves around the car, then opens my door and offers me a hand, which I take. He tugs me up, and when I stumble, he chuckles and wraps an arm around my waist before I fall. Then he pulls me into his side, and together, we make our way to the front door. Without meaning to, I melt into him, liking the feel of his strong body supporting me, aiding me, seemingly without judgment.

"You know, I don't think I've ever seen you drunk."

I lift a shoulder with the question as he unlocks the door, a basic, dark-stained wood with old-looking brass hardware, and pushes it open. Once inside, he steps away from me, and instantly, I feel cold.

An awkward silence fills the room for a moment; then he lifts a brow assessingly before explaining. "Can't very well fix reputations and clean up the bad boys if you're just as bad."

"I was always cool with it, child star and whatnot, so I don't need your pity. I've always had everything, never wanted anything at all." I bite my lip, but in my drunken state, I can't stop the words from tumbling out. "But I guess lately, I'm realizing I missed out on a lot of things."

"Like?"

"Like...dancing in a small-town bar. And girls' nights. And, and..." I smile at him. "Toilet papering houses. I haven't done any of that stuff before. It's always work and protecting the image and..." My head swims, and I close my eyes, taking a deep breath. "I had a s'more martini tonight. Wren said they were tasty, and she was *so* right. Have you ever had a s'more?" He looks at me, and the very edges of his lips tip up, entertained.

"Yeah, Will, I've had a s'mores."

"I haven't. I haven't done anything fun." I think about all of the things that the girls yapped about while we got ready, all of the fun Hallie had planned for Emma over summer break, and the strange, nostalgic yearning I felt for things I've never had. "I've never had a s'more, or gone to summer camp, or had a water balloon fight. I've never gone peach picking or shared lipstick with my friends or gone to a town fair or, or, or...anything fun." Feeling silly, I look down, picking at my nails. "I know. I know. It's stupid and selfish, but I like being...normal here."

"I don't think that's silly, Willa. I think it's normal to want to be normal." We stand in the entryway of his place for long moments, staring at one another until, eventually, he lifts a hand to the back of his neck and breaks eye contact. "Anyway. Let's get you something to sleep in." Then he walks off towards a room. I stand in his near-empty living room for a moment, feeling off-kilter in a way I know has nothing to do with how drunk I am, before following him. When I enter another bare room, I look around, but there's not much to see. The only furniture is a gorgeous antique dresser he's standing at, back to me, and a bed with dark green bedding. The walls are painted a pretty cream, and without meaning to, I start to picture ways to add pops of color, ways to fit the vision of Leo I have in my mind. All masculine lines, a classic style. Olive greens and mahogany to complement the wood of the dresser. With his back to me, I allow myself the small luxury of taking him in, his broad shoulders shifting as he digs through the drawers before turning to me.

"This should work," he says, tossing me a shirt.

"What's this for?"

"Don't think your shorts and shirt would be very comfy to sleep in," he says, a small smile on his lips as he crosses his arms on his chest.

"You know. you're much more handsome when you're not glaring at me," I murmur, and he lets out a quick bark of a laugh, seemingly against his will.

"I'll keep that in mind."

I smile at him as I throw his shirt over my clothes, then work to slowly remove my shirt underneath. Even drunk, I manage to take off both the bra and the top I borrowed from Hallie, tossing them in a small pile on the refinished hardwood floors with my bag. Then I undo the button of my shorts underneath the oversized tee and slide them down with a relieved sigh. Although the shorts are much more comfortable than the smoothing undergarments I usually wear, there are a few things in this world that feel better than sliding off stiff clothing at the end of the day. They pool at my feet, then get stuck on my sandals, so I bend to take them off, undoing the buckles, the effort requiring my full attention.

"Willa—" he starts, then fades off, but I barely notice as I undo one sandal and then the other. Finally, I stand and turn back to face him, seeing a strange look on his face before I slide into his bed and kick the covers down with my feet. The blankets and sheets smell like Dior Sauvage, the expensive cologne I know he wears because I send him a bottle every year for his birthday. It was a stupid whim, something I bought on an impulse after smelling it in a store once and thinking it would be perfect for him.

I was absolutely right.

"But you're still hot when you glare, so don't stop it all the time," I say, finishing my thought from earlier as I lie back in the bed, then shiver as my skin slides against the cold sheets. I look down my body, spot the comforter at my feet, and I kick it a few times, trying to hook it and pull it up my body. As I do, my shirt rides up my side, revealing the red lace of my thong high up on one hip. If I weren't so drunk, I'd probably be embarrassed, or maybe understand the look that was still plastered on Leo's face, but I am, so I don't. Instead, I say something that, again, if I were less drunk, I'd have the common sense to be embarrassed by. But the liquor is making me feel so good, so loose, and care so little, that I don't care at all.

Hell, the world has seen more of me in paparazzi photos on the beach, and the truth is, Leo Sinclaire could see me fully naked and not care in the least.

"Can you tuck me in?"

He stares at me, and I hold my breath before finally, his gruff voice fills the room.

"Yeah. Lay back," he whispers. I do as he asks, settling in as I try to ignore the stupid way my heart beats faster as he steps closer to me, then grips the ends of the blankets and slowly tugs them up, covering my body.

But he doesn't just drop them when he reaches my shoulders. Instead, gently, nearly reverently, he tucks in the downy comforter around me, settling it beneath my chin.

"Thank you," I whisper, holding his eyes with mine and hoping against all hope that he understands. "For taking care of me."

He stares at me for long moments, a soft smile on his lips, before he steps back.

"You look good in my bed, Will," he murmurs, taking me in. A flash of something comes over his face, as if he isn't sure why he said that, but he doesn't take it back.

"You could stay with me, you know," I murmur, and he smirks, then shakes his head.

"No, I don't think that would be a good idea."

I lift an eyebrow, tipping my head.

"But it could be a fun one." That smirk turns into a full-blown grin, and I categorize the rare event into the recesses of my mind for a rainy day.

"No, Willa. Tonight, the couch is calling my name."

"Killjoy," I murmur, snuggling in deeper to his ridiculously comfortable bed.

"Kind of my job. Sleep tight, Willa," he says. Then, shocking me, he shifts, bending down and pressing his lips softly to my forehead. They stay there for longer than I expect, long enough for me to close my eyes and breathe it in as I envision another world, another life where this could have been mine, where I really could have had it all. Finally, he steps back and away, moving towards the door before turning off the light and closing the door behind him without another word.

Lying in Leo's bed, I toss and turn, my mind racing as I try to fall asleep and fail horribly.

All I can think about is his hand on my jaw.

Or the way, his eyes dipped down to my lips more than once.

On how it felt to dance with him.

Old feelings I've long since buried are surfacing, and in my drunken state, surrounded by the smell of Leo on his sheets, I can't beat them back. He's everywhere and nowhere, and between the buzz I'm still feeling and the mix of emotions moving through me, I don't see sleep coming any time soon.

I need *something* to get this pent-up emotion out. I'm not home, so I can't write, which is always my first choice, and honestly, I don't know if I'm in a state to hold a pen, much less use my guitar, so that's out regardless.

The same goes for a workout: Pilates while inebriated sounds like a hospital visit waiting to happen.

But...the third option...the one that would also ease the throbbing between my legs...that one seems reasonable, right?

I'm still half weighing the ethical nature of what I already know I'm going to do as my hands skim down my body, sliding Leo's tee shirt up to expose my belly beneath the blankets.

Is it wrong to touch yourself in the bed of your publicist, for whom you've had a thing for eight years?

Maybe, but no one's ever going to find out, so there's no real reason to stop, right?

It's what I tell myself as my fingers continue to trail down, dipping beneath the lace edge of my panties, moving down to graze over the smooth skin there, always waxed because god forbid someone gets a glimpse of an ill-maintained bikini line.

But in my mind, it's not my soft fingers sliding down: it's Leo's, thick and rough and warm, the same ones that wrapped around my wrist at his place, the same ones that grazed along the bare skin where my shirt and shorts didn't reach when we danced.

When I brush over my clit, I find myself already wet, my hips shifting to get more, and I circle myself, pleasure spreading through my veins. My breathing hitches as I move down to my entrance, grabbing the wet there and dragging it up over my clit. The Leo in my mind groans when he feels just how wet I am, and a shaky breath leaves my lips.

After a few circuits of that, I need more and slide my hand down until a single finger slips inside.

A soft, needly mewl leaves my lips, and my breathing hitches and my body stills as I take in everything around me. My ears are on high alert, trying to listen for anything at all, but silence comes from the other side of the door, and I melt once more, my fingers sliding back out and over my clit.

Quiet.

I need to be quiet.

That's normally easy, but right now, as I slide two fingers in and pump them, I have to bite my lip. It feels *so fucking good*, and I know part of it is the visual I'm creating. Despite the precarious situation, my mind takes over, picturing what could have happened next if I were brave enough to ask for it.

Leo smiles when I ask him to climb into bed with me, then crawls up over me, a hand sliding up and under his tee as he cups my breast. His touch is rough, and it feels exquisite when his thumb and forefinger roll over my nipple, tugging as he goes. I bite my lip as my own hands follow that path, too soft to evoke the feeling of callouses, though. His lips move down my neck, licking and sucking, nipping at my skin as he goes. My hips lift as he settles between my legs, already naked in this drunken fantasy, before slowly sliding into me. I slide in three fingers, somehow knowing they won't fill me the way he would.

After a few slow thrusts, I begin to fuck myself hard and fast and wild, just like I think Leo would, untethered in a way I don't see him in his normal day-to-day life, and it builds fast. I could tell myself it's because it's been a while since I've felt the need to make myself come, since I've felt desire, but I know it's so much more than that.

It's Leo.

The temptation of him being around me all the time.

The bickering and bantering that feel more like foreplay than arguing.

The way, when he's around, his eyes burn into me just like the girls told me.

The way his hands feel when he's guiding me along, the way his hard body felt when we danced together, the way his eyes ate up the sight of me in his tee, like even though it would kill him to admit it, he can't get enough of it, the palpable sexual tension between us.

When my thumb grazes over my clit, I picture him thumbing it as he looks at where he's sliding into me and groaning deep. That's what sends me over the edge. I turn my head into the pillow and groan as it rolls through me, wracking my body with trembles as I come and come and come.

It feels like it takes an eternity to come down from that high, for my breathing to regulate, for my senses to return, and as my common sense returns, my ears become alert, trying to listen for any sign that I wasn't as quiet as I thought, but nothing but silence reaches my ears.

That was new.

Not just the speed or the intensity of the orgasm, but my own inability to bite back my reaction, the need to bury my face in his pillow as I came. I've always been quiet during sex and when taking care of myself, seeing it more as a necessary task to occasionally feel good and sate a human need. Making noise has never been appealing, and if anything, felt embarrassing. But just *thinking* of Leo, it was nearly impossible to hold it in.

I mull over that for a while, deciding it's probably due to my drunken state, lowered inhibitions, and all. After a while, my breathing evens out, and my eyes drift close. With the endorphins from a hard orgasm and the smell of Leo surrounding me, I fall into a deep, dreamless sleep.

SIXTEEN

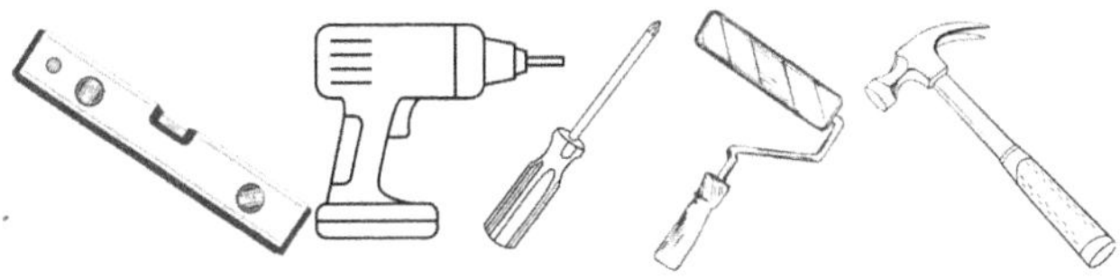

LEO

I hear it as I'm walking from the bathroom to the couch to sleep for the night.

The tiniest mewl.

A breathy sound I almost miss, but the house is dead quiet, so I don't.

I pause outside my bedroom door, behind which my client lies in my bed, and hear it again. Willa.

I should go to the couch.

I should go to the kitchen.

I should grab blankets and hunker down in the unfinished guest room.

I should sit outside and sleep in the patio chair.

I should do anything, really, but instead, I sit outside with my back to the door of my bedroom and listen to Willa Stone's muffled moan as she makes herself come in my bed.

And even though it goes against everything I know, even though I've spent years resisting Willa Stone's pull, I somehow know deep in my gut that I am so totally fucked.

SEVENTEEN

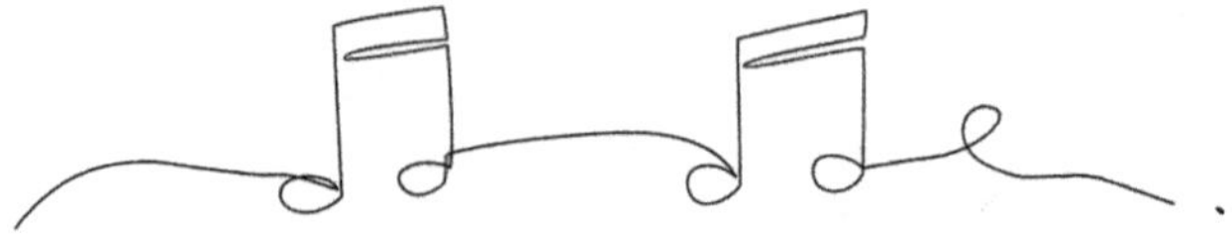

WILLA

Before I even open my eyes the next morning, I know something is wrong by the way my head throbs. When I do crack an eye open, the bright sunshine hits my vision, sending a sharp flare of pain through my head, and I groan and slam them shut.

Well, that's new.

Am I sick? I can't remember the last time I was sick, but this feels almost like the flu I had four or five years ago. Is that what it is?

I almost settle on yes when, slowly and painfully, memories slip into my subconscious.

Getting ready with the girls.

Heading to the Mill and sticking to a soda until Leo showed up and told me once again how to act.

Taking shots with Hallie, Wren, and Nat to prove a point.

Taking more shots because I was having fun.

Slowly, I attempt to open my eyes once more, squinting into the sun and finding myself in an unfamiliar bedroom, in an unfamiliar bed.

I look down my body to see I'm also in an unfamiliar, oversized shirt, and my shorts are gone, leaving me in just my underwear.

Suddenly, a second set of far more embarrassing memories flies through my mind.

Arguing with Leo in the hallway, and he surprisingly backed down.

Dancing with him, him taking me home, and jumping into his bed.

I cringe when I remember asking him to sleep with me, but it melts away when I remember the warm press of his lips to my forehead and the heated look he gave me before he left.

You look good in my bed, Will.

That part was a drunken dream, right?

Right.

It had to have been.

Slowly, I shift and roll over in the bed, forcing myself to stand before scanning the room for my things. My shorts are in a pile on the floor, and vaguely, I remember taking them off and trying to remember if, when I did, Leo was still in the room, but deep down knowing the answer.

I am never drinking again.

I don't care how annoyed I am or how convincing Hallie and Nat are.

Looking around the room, I spot my phone plugged into a charger on the nightstand, something I surely didn't do, and I wonder just when Leo did. The light is blinking, and I squint at it. There are a slew of new messages, one from each of the girls, but I ignore those when I see *two* are from Jackie. My pulse begins to pound a tattoo in my chest as I tap on the screen, sure that some kind of photo or video of me drinking and dancing last night was leaked.

She's going to kill me.

I'm never going to hear the end of it.

It will probably end my peaceful time away in Holly Ridge, that much is for sure, and even if I'm incredibly hungover and embarrassed from a night out, I don't *want* to leave Holly Ridge right now.

But relief washes through me when I read the actual message.

JACKIE

Good morning! Hope you're having a great time.

I know you're on break, but I spoke to New Hits Magazine, and they wanted to know if you could do a phone interview sometime next week. I think it would be a great branding opportunity! You could drop hints about the new album and possibly about being ready to start dating again!

I decide I don't want to reply while hungover, and mark it as unread before moving back to the girls' messages. Wren is double-checking that I got home okay, Hallie is telling me she had fun and insisting we do it again once she gets back from her week in Seaside Point, and Nat is asking how I feel and if anything interesting happened last night, accompanied by a line of emojis that has me questioning her sanity.

The final text is from my mom, which is a surprise, since she only really reaches out if she needs something, but with her gala coming up, I suppose it makes sense.

MOM

Hello, darling.

She does this, speaking as if she's some New England socialite instead of someone who was once borderline white trash and hit the lottery with a talented kid.

Now, where did that bitterness come from? I think to myself, brushing it off. This hangover is really something strong, it seems.

I haven't seen anything in the magazines lately, and wanted to check in. Is everything okay? I spoke with Jacqueline, and she says you're lying low from appearances — will you still be able to attend the gala in October? Lots of people are looking forward to seeing you.

I'm sure they are.

I don't think too hard about the fact that she didn't say *she* is excited to see me, or that she speaks to my manager more than she speaks to me. With a sigh, I decide that, too, can wait to be answered when I get home, long after I eat something and get about a gallon of coffee in my system and scrub every inch of my skin in the shower.

I reply to Wren, apologizing for not replying last night and thanking her for a fun night out, then tell Hallie I'm in, but I won't be drinking next time. I decide to also leave Nat's messages to answer when the pounding fades a bit more from my mind, then stand and reach for my pile of clothes. Staring at the small top from last night, I decide to just put on my bra and shorts, and claim Leo's shirt for my own before heading to the bathroom. When there, I contemplate using Leo's toothbrushes, but decide against it, instead doing three rounds of finger toothbrushing to get the gross taste out of my mouth. I borrow his face wash to get the makeup off my face, then use my fingers to brush out my hair a bit, undo the small braids at my temples, and grab a claw clip from my purse to pin up my blonde locks.

When I look in the mirror next, there's a human-adjacent being staring back at me, and I know I can't put off the inevitable any longer. Finally, I take in a deep breath and make my way out of Leo's bedroom. I don't find him in the living room, despite the rumpled pile of blankets there that makes guilt curl in my gut. The sound of a power tool comes from outside, so I follow the noise into his home. Clearly, he'd be in the middle of a bunch of different renovations, with various walls taped, others patched with drywall, and outlets removed and waiting to be replaced. When I'm on the road, I love watching home improvement shows and social media accounts, though I've never had the need or opportunity to do anything myself. Suddenly, I'm itching to explore this place, to see all of what he's doing and find out his plans for each and every room. It's a bit rough, but anyone can see that the potential is there.

I continue moving down the hall to the kitchen and step into a sunken living room, where a set of sliding glass doors is open to the outside, where Leo stands, working with some kind of loud power tool, the sound drilling into my mind. As I approach, I notice he has what looks like cabinet doors on a stand, and he's taking a sander to it. I lean in the doorway and watch, in awe of his ease with the tool and the way the wood slowly transforms beneath his clearly knowledge-able hands.

I don't know how long I stand there, but eventually I must move and catch his eye; his head lifts to look at me. Instantly, he turns off the tool, letting it sit there as he stands upright and steps in my direction.

"Ahh, she lives," he says, a smile in his voice, though I can't see his face because the sun is too glaringly bright. "How ya feeling, champ?"

"I don't think I'm going to drink again for a long, long time," I say through a groan, based more in embarrassment than illness, though I don't tell him that.

"Probably for the best." He stares at me for long moments, and another flash from the night before comes back to me: touching myself in his fucking *bed*.

While thinking of *him*.

For the first time this morning, my stomach roils, and I take in a deep breath, desperate to change the subject.

"What are you doing out here?"

"Making cabinets."

I blink at him, confused.

"*Making* them?" He nods but doesn't add anything. "You're *making cabinets?*" Finally, I step onto the sunny patio and take in the wood slab before him, a perfect recessed panel carved into it. I blink at him with awe, and an embarrassed look crosses his face before he lifts a shoulder.

"My dad was a carpenter. I spent all of my summers helping him. Turns out, you don't forget that kind of skill, even if you don't use it for a long time."

I blink at him, then look behind him at where four other finished doors lie.

Who would have known Leo knew how to work with his hands?

"Can I help?" I ask without thinking. He gives me a disbelieving and confused look before slowly shaking his head.

"Uh, no. These are power tools. I already sat by while you got drunk, I'm not handing you an industrial sander." My heart drops, and disappointment floods. Normally, I can keep up the facade, give everyone the reaction that causes the least amount of upset, but I'm too hungover, and my head is pounding just a bit too much to do that.

"That makes sense. Maybe another time," I say, trying to keep up my cheery facade but unsure if I succeeded. Thankfully, I have the perfect subject change. My stomach might not be roiling, but my head is killing me, and being out in the near-blinding sun isn't helping. "Uh, do you have any kind of painkiller? I might have kept everything down, but the little man in my head hammering at my eyes and temples is a near-constant reminder that I was very, very intoxicated last night."

Finally, it happens.

He smiles.

God, when he does that, he's too fucking handsome. He's hot when he's glowering at me, but smiling wide, entertained by some random bullshit I just said, he's panty-dropping hot.

"Yeah. I'll get you some water. You should probably drink a lot of it."

I nod, then follow him into the house. We step into the kitchen, where open cabinets with no faces fill the space. He grabs an unopened bottle of water from one, handing it to me before moving toward the hall bathroom. There, he opens a cabinet, grabs a bottle, shakes two pills into his hand, and offers them to me. I down the small white pills and chug about half of the drink, then awkwardly follow him out of the small room.

"What's this room?" I ask, tipping my chin towards an empty

room across the way. Blue tape lines the edges, and a tarp covers the floor, a tray with an unopened can of paint, and a roller beside it.

"It's going to be a guest room. It had three layers of wallpaper I had to take off, then spackle. I've got the primer done, now I just need color."

"What color are you thinking?" I ask, desperate to know anything I can about this project. I would do absolutely anything to have an old house of my own to fix up, but I know even now, Jackie would disapprove and insist on hiring a firm to handle the design and execution. He lifts a shoulder.

"Not sure. I have to go to the hardware store in town tomorrow, see if I can make a choice."

I nod, then speak without thinking. "A light blue would be nice, I think. Very calming and welcoming."

He lifts an eyebrow at me, and a nervous blush burns over my cheeks and down my chest.

"Welcoming and calming?"

"That's what they always say on those home shows," I explain quickly.

"Home shows? You watch those?"

"They're what I watch on the road. Easy to watch, no storyline I have to follow, and they don't require a ton of brain power." I shrug, suddenly feeling silly and picking at the edge of my shirt. Leo's shirt, I suppose.

"I wouldn't pin you for a home decor show kind of girl."

I lift my head, then tip my chin at him, unable to fight back the smile.

"What would you pin me for?"

"I don't know. Reality TV? Housewives of some random city?"

I shrug. "Too close to my real life, I suppose. I want to escape."

"Is that why you were drunk last night?"

"No, no," I say with a smile, shaking my head. I should keep it to myself, but I can't in this state, so I finally spill to him. "I'm here because I have writer's block. Adam told me I needed to get a life to fix it, so I came here," I explain.

"So you're not here to escape boredom after I told you that you have to hide away?"

I shake my head. "No, no. I'm actually very okay with being bored. I don't get the chance very often."

"So how's it going?"

"The boredom?"

He laughs, shaking his head, crossing his arms on his chest, and I fight not to stare at the way his biceps bulge as he does.

I fail miserably. My *god* who knew all this was hiding beneath those suits?

"No. Not the writing. The getting a life part."

"Oh, uh," I start, then bite my lip. "It's kind of a mixed bag. I wrote one song so far, but I keep getting stuck. I was hoping going out last night might have helped, stirred up some things to write about."

"And? Did it work?" He takes me in, assessing, and I feel naked beneath his gaze. Still, I force my breathing to remain steady. His look gives me the same light feeling as last night, and for a moment, I wonder if I'm still a bit drunk.

"Too soon to tell. But I think..." My mind travels, pulling at threads that I've sensed on the edge of my mind since I woke up. "I think I may have a little bit of something."

He reads me, and for a moment, panic sweeps through me, worried if maybe he knows what I'm thinking, if maybe he knows that the little bit of something might be tied to him in the smallest way.

We remain locked in that look for long minutes before he blinks, shakes his head, and then tips it towards the front door.

"Well, then I guess we should get you home, see if you can't get something onto paper."

And in my hungover state, I can't seem to assign any other name to the feeling in my chest than disappointment.

That night, I write.

I write, and I write, and I write, more inspired than ever before, the words and the chords flowing onto paper at an alarming speed as I ignore things like legibility, cohesiveness, or logic until, finally, late, late that night, I have a song.

A song so unlike anything I've ever written, ever produced.

A song about *yearning*.

Desire and need, and the uncertainty of it all.

Of fantasizing what it would be like to have someone all to myself, to feel their skin on mine. To toe past the line of traditional friendship into something far more satisfying. As I write, I pour all of the conflicted emotions into my words and the tension in my belly swirls and swirls, growing tighter and tighter until I'm nearly finished with the song. It's so far from what I normally write, so blatantly sexual and frustrated, that I can almost guarantee it won't make it to the album, but it feels good to get a song out regardless, to feel my muse once more.

And as I fall asleep, satisfied by the fact that I finally got a song out, I don't let my mind dwell on the fact that both times I've been able to write a song in the last six months have been after a night with Leo Sinclaire.

EIGHTEEN

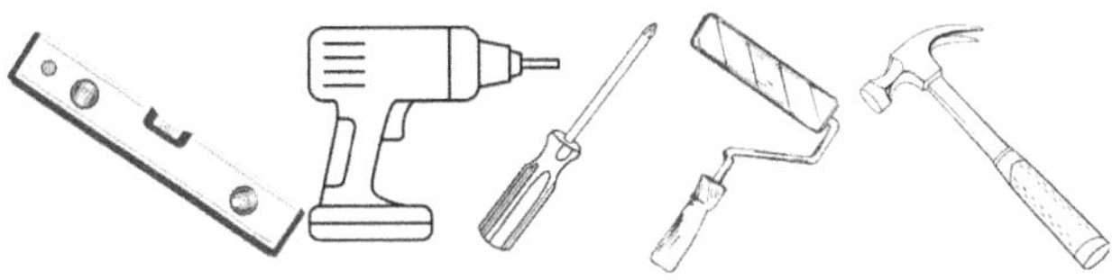

LEO

On Sunday, I head to the hardware store early, eager to miss the crowds, and head straight for the paint department, looking for paint for the guest room. I have no clue what color I'm looking for, but without thinking, I find myself navigating towards a specific section.

Blue.

Welcoming and calming.

Like the light blue shirt she wore Friday night. As soon as that thought enters my mind, I fight it, shaking my head, and reach for a yellow swatch. I don't like that one, so I grab a green one, then a cream color, determined not to choose blue. But none of them is right.

Without meaning to, my fingers graze over the blue paint chips again.

Fine. Blue it is.

It doesn't mean anything; it doesn't mean I'm doing what she said. It just means that blue is a good option, which it is. I would wager that it's probably the most popular color choice for a guest room. Maybe even just a room in general. Right?

Right.

Content with my choice and assuring myself that it has absolutely nothing to do with Willa Stone, I begin looking through the colors.

Powder blue.

Hydrangea blue.

Sky blue.

Ocean spray blue

Who the fuck knew there were so many shades of *blue*? Why isn't there just a *guest room light blue*? How on earth is someone supposed to pick out of the seemingly thousands of colors of blue, all of them almost identical?

Willa would know, a voice in my head says without my permission. I frown at the wall of paint chips, pretending I have no idea where that came from.

But I know. I know where it came from. It's the same place that almost handed her the sander when she asked to help with the cabinets, and I saw her sad face when I told her no. In my defense, I stand by that—the woman's barely ever held a hammer, I'm sure, and was hungover for what might have been the first time in her life. She shouldn't have been handling power tools.

But that part of me that always wants to give Willa exactly what she wants, who makes the most bizarre, specific requests for her career happen just to see that grateful grin light up a room, wanted to wipe that look off her face forever.

Stupid.

It's so fucking stupid.

Idiotic, stupid, absolutely foolish, and irresponsible.

Still, I find myself putting the paintbrushes I grabbed to paint the edges of the room back on the shelf.

Then I'm taking my cart to the front of the store and leaving at the cart return.

I find myself walking to my car and turning the key in the ignition. Driving back toward my house, but passing the turn for my driveway.

I shouldn't do it.

I should turn back to the store and get any old blue or maybe say fuck it and go for a green, but since moving here, the steely restraint I've built against Willa has melted away.

I know in the past, I've done the right thing, keeping a barrier between us, maintaining the professionalism I need. She's my client, and nothing else. I've never had any issue with keeping that divide between us until recently.

In the last week, I held her in my arms multiple times. In the last week, I've watched her stand her ground, argue with me, bring back that backbone that I thought was long gone and forgotten.

In the last week, I've contemplated crossing that very clear line in the sand more times than I should admit.

But I can't cross that line, not even if she's looked like she wanted me to cross it just as badly as I wanted to.

But what I *can* give her is a new experience.

She can't be mine, but we can be friends, right?

That's what I convince myself as I drive up a windy road, not on my property but on the Three Kings property past Jesse's place, and stop at a small cabin with a familiar truck out front. When I kill the engine, I take in a deep breath, dropping my head to the steering wheel, and try to convince myself to turn around. To leave and go back to the store, ask an employee to pick a color, any color, and move on with my life.

But I see her disappointed face every time I close my eyes. And I don't foresee that changing anytime soon.

So instead of being wise, I step out of my car and take the steps to her place before knocking on the front door. I don't have much more time to second-guess myself, thankfully, because in no time at all, the door opens, a sweaty Willa standing before me.

She's in a sport bra of some kind and a pair of tight shorts, both in a pale purple color that I've never seen her in before. Her hair is piled up on top of her head, her face free of makeup, making the freckles across the bridge of her nose visible. Her chest is heaving with breaths, and I have to fight everything in me not to look down and stare at the rise and fall like the sick fuck I am.

"Leo?" she asks, rightfully confused.

"Hey, Willa." Then I stand there at her front door at ten in the morning, staring at her and not saying a word.

Like a fucking creep.

Words move through my mind, but none of them make sense, and none of them are something that ever should fall from my lips, so I just stand there, quietly.

Staring.

"What are you doing here?" she asks, hesitantly, the words throwing me out of my daze.

What am I doing here?

What am *I* doing here?

What *am* I doing here?

"I—" I start, then I remember, and before I can think better of it, words fall from my lips. "Do you want to help me pick out paint?"

"Paint?" The confusion on her face deepens, leaking into her voice now.

"For my guest room. And maybe a couple of others, so I don't have to bug you next time."

"You want me to help you pick out paint colors for your house?"

"You said you liked to watch those shows, and while I don't need my place to look like it was from one of those shows or a magazine or anything, I would like it to be...nice. And I went to the store to buy paint today, and did you know there are a billion colors of blue?" Her lips tip at the edges, her arms cross over her chest, and once again, I fight everything in me to stay looking straight ahead.

Eyes up, Sinclaire. Be a gentleman. Be a goddamn human.

"I did," she says.

"Yeah, well, I didn't, so imagine my surprise when I tried to find one, but there's at least a thousand just for light blue, and they all kind of looked the same to me, so I wasn't sure what I should go with. I don't really want to repaint it if I don't have to, and you said you saw those shows, so I thought maybe..." My words trail off, and I look at her face. That's when I realize that she's entertained by this. By me.

This was a terrible idea.

"This was stupid," I say, shaking my head. "I'm an adult. I can pick out paint colors–"

"No, no!" she says as I step back, arms uncrossing and one reaching out to grab my forearm, bare beneath a T-shirt I threw on this morning. Her touch is warm and soft, something new I desperately have to fight not to catalogue for later. "Don't go. I would love to help you." My eyes move from where she's touching me to her eyes, brown again, something that, for some reason, brings me a spark of joy.

"Really?"

"Yeah. I'm bored. Nat's working, and Hallie and Jesse are packing to head to Seaside Point for the week. Adam and Wren are going away, and I'm kind of..." She shakes her head. "I have nothing to do."

"Will you help me pick it out?" She nods.

"Under one condition," she says, and I sigh. I should have known there would be a catch. "You have to let me help you paint."

"So we just dump the paint in here and start going at it?" she asks, staring at the can, then the tray on the floor at her feet, and I can't help but smile.

We spent an hour at the hardware store, picking up three gallons of paint and more supplies than I probably needed, but watching Willa in the store was so thoroughly entertaining that I couldn't resist adding the things she pointed out.

"They used this for edging on one show!" she said, showing a foam edger that I *know* my dad would absolutely have said was a piece of overpriced bullshit that no one actually needs.

I added it to the cart.

"Did you see this?" she asked excitedly. "It starts out pink, then turns white when it's dry! How smart is that?" I had enough spackle and had patched most of the holes already, but I instantly tried to think of where in the house she could try it out. I added the biggest tub and a palette knife to the cart.

"For keeping your feet clean! It's like you're a surgeon!" she said, showing me the little booties that go over your shoes. I'd laughed and thrown them in, for some reason eager to see her in the ugly things.

It took three trips to bring all of the new gadgets and tools into the house and twenty minutes to settle in, and now we're in the guest room I had already primed, ready to fulfill her apparent life-long dream of painting a room.

"Basically," I say, grabbing a paint key and gently opening it before reaching for a stirring stick.

"Oh my god, can I do that?" she asks, wide eyes on the wooden stick in my hand.

"Sure." I hand it off, feeling that familiar fire when her fingers graze mine as she grabs it. I watch with fascination as she looks over the stick before dipping it into the can. Too quickly, she stirs the paint, a wave cresting the edge and dripping down the side in a moment.

"Oh, shit!" she says, letting go of the stick, then staring wide-eyed at the drip. I shake my head, reach for a rag, and wipe the side clean.

"You've gotta go slower," I instruct, taking her hand in mine and moving it to the stick, showing her how to hold it. "Like this." Then I slowly stir the goo into the can. "Scrape the bottom and keep going until it's totally mixed."

"Oh. That makes sense," she says, her voice a bit off as I let go and step away, needing the distance. We both watch the paint turn a uniform light blue before I tell her it's good, pour a generous amount into the tray, and hand her a roller.

"Go to town," I say.

"I am so excited!" she says in a squeal, and I shake my head.

Who the hell is excited about *painting*?

Willa Stone, it seems.

"God, you're bad at this," I say with a laugh after a few moments, watching as Willa puts way too much paint on the roller then slaps it on the wall, paint splattering as she does. There's so much paint on it that it starts to drip before she can start moving, and as she does, she barely covers a three-foot section.

"It's my first time! I'm a virgin!" she says, then blushes at her choice of words. "I mean—"

"Like this," I say, unwilling to think about Willa being a virgin or anything related to that. Instead, I take the roller from her hands, being careful not to bruise her hands with mine. I remove some of the paint by spreading it on the tray, then make long, sure strokes on the wall. With a practiced ease, something that came back quicker than I expected, I move the roller up, then down again cleanly, getting close but not touching the trim or the ceiling. When I hand the roller back to Willa, her eyes are wide. "You try." She takes it, then slowly copies my moves, dipping the roller, then rolling it off on the tray. I give her a few tips as she moves, and she does a decent job on her second attempt.

"How do you know all of this stuff? You don't even watch the shows," she says as if that's the main place to find out that information. "And you're...*Leo*."

"What's that mean?" I ask with a laugh and a skeptical look in her direction as I start to unwrap a paintbrush to do the edging.

"It means you're designer suits and expensive Italian loafers, not work boots and jeans, and knowing how to refinish cabinets."

I shrug a shoulder,

"In Holly Ridge I am," I say, then look over her. "Just like how in Holly Ridge, you let go of those crazy ponytails and your contacts."

A blush moves down her chest, and I watch it creep along her skin, endeared by it before I force myself to look away. I need to stop it, put the professional wall back between us, and most importantly, remember it exists.

I need to remember it exists and why.

"My dad was a contractor," I explain as I dip the brush into the paint and move to the corner where the roller won't reach. "He built a business with his brother and did everything. Carpentry was his specialty, but he knew how to do it all. I worked for him during summers, so I also kind of learned to do it all." There's silence as I work, the blue spreading over the walls smoothly. When I go to dip my paintbrush again, I finally look at her to find she's staring at me, taking me in as if seeing me for the first time.

"I never would have thought that."

"I don't really talk about it."

"And your dad. Does he still have the business?"

An ache forms in my chest, though this time it doesn't make me want to call the hospital. This time, it's an all-too-familiar grief. I shake my head, eyes averted back to the wall as I spread the paint.

"The business still exists. My uncle and cousins run it. My dad..." My mouth goes dry, and I realize I haven't really talked about this to anyone but doctors and my therapist. But for some reason, I continue spreading the paint. "My dad had a heart attack when I was twenty. He didn't make it."

"Oh my god, I'm so sorry," she says, eyes wide, her hand pausing as she rolls the paint off on the tray. "Leo—"

"It's fine, really. No need to apologize." Her eyes go wider. "Not like in an 'I'm glad my dad's dead' way, but in an 'it happened a long time ago' way." She blinks as if that doesn't make it better, and I guess, she's right: it doesn't. "I'm okay. Really." A moment passes, a long one, before she speaks, and when she does, she seems to shock herself.

"I haven't spoken to my mom in nine months," she says. I blink at her.

"What?"

"Well, that's not true. We've talked about getting her tickets to my concert, to the auction she's hosting, and to a signed guitar. And we texted to confirm that I was going to her gala in October. And she insisted she talk to me when I turned down that TV docuseries."

I roll my lips, remembering that. It was probably five or six months ago when Jackie called to ask for my opinion on a docuseries Catherine Stone had been approached to work on about the early life of Willa. Catherine was very excited, saying it would be a great opportunity for Willa, but it was clearly something to get herself some exposure, and, I'm sure, some money, even though she doesn't need more.

The woman could live off her earnings from Willa's childhood career for the rest of her life and still leave a healthy trust to donate to some museum that would put her name on a plaque, forever immortalizing her.

When she called, I told Jackie it felt cheap and wouldn't benefit Willa's current career in any way. It felt like the kind of choice someone who is fading away would make, not someone at the top of their career. Sure, her diehard fans would eat it up, but they'd eat it up in ten, fifteen, or twenty years just as much. To my surprise, Jackie agreed, and I didn't hear about it again, but it doesn't surprise me that Catherine wanted to try to convince Willa personally. Even Jackie complains about that woman and her ill intentions toward her daughter.

"She only ever wants to talk about my career or how it can help her," she murmurs, eyes locked on the wall as she spreads more paint across it.

"Willa," I start, unsure of what to say, but she shakes her head and gives me a smile. It's the one the cameras love, all dimples, but not too wide to show the one crooked tooth on the bottom row that I know she and Jackie argue about often. I never noticed until just now, but it's a blank smile.

Stunning and angelic but absolutely blank.

"Can you fill the tray with more paint?" she asks, changing the subject as she tips her chin to the can of paint.

I want to tell her that the tray absolutely doesn't need paint, to call her out for her change of subject, but I don't.

Instead, I let her have it and pour the paint.

"We did it," she says excitedly an hour later. "I can't believe it. I painted a room."

"You painted the first coat of a room," I say to her. "This color will need at least two."

Her grin drops, but then she shrugs. "I'll call it a win regardless. I painted a room! And it was fun!"

"You're a nut, you know that?" She shrugs as if it doesn't even faze her before she steps over to me, demolishing the gap I have been very intentionally keeping between us all day and wrapping her arms around my waist. I hesitate for a moment, but her head settles on my shoulder, and I can't stop myself: I return the hold, draping my arms around her waist.

"Thank you, Leo. Thanks for letting me help you. This is exactly what I needed."

That night, those words are what I use to justify my actions when I wonder why I spent an entire afternoon with Willa, even though I had decided to avoid her.

Because I will always give Willa Stone everything she needs.

NINETEEN

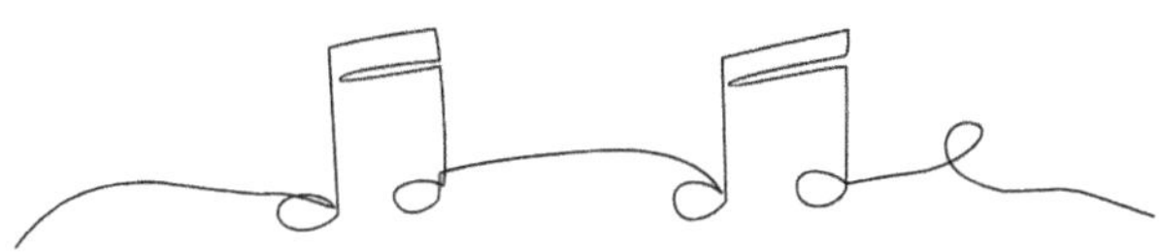

WILLA

The next morning, I wake up energized. I take my Pilates class, shower, make myself a quick breakfast, put on a comfy yet cute tennis dress in a pretty lavender, and nervously sit down to inspect what I wrote the night before after painting with Leo.

Relief washes through me when I realize it's not just decent: it's exactly what I wanted from this song. It perfectly captures the excitement of feeling butterflies after a long time without, the joy of a new crush, and that nervous energy that seems to linger about. I make a few small changes, then set it aside to start on the next track. Nervously, I stare at a new blank piece of paper, dread creeping in at the thought that nothing will come, that my routine will once again fail me.

Except my routine *hasn't* worked for this album.

In fact, the opposite seems to be happening: the more I stick to my routine, the more my creativity fails me.

Which leads me to believe that maybe that's my problem. Maybe I need to tire myself out all day, then try writing at night. I've never been one to write at night, preferring to do it earlier when my mind is fresh, but I also have never had writer's block that feels this immovable.

Maybe I need a *new* routine. That thought would normally would bring panic, but as soon as it crosses my mind, I find myself smiling, because I know exactly where to start.

Fifteen minutes later, I'm pulling the key from my ignition after I park in Leo's driveway just as he steps out onto his front porch.

"What are you doing here?" he asks, crossing his arms on his chest, and once more, I can't help but watch his muscles move and ripple beneath the tight tee. He's in a pair of light-wash, paint-speckled jeans, and his wavy dark hair is messy, no product keeping it contained.

Blue-collar Leo is *way* hotter than expensive suits Leo.

"Here to work, of course," I say with a grin as I slide my sunglasses on top of my head, pushing my hair back. I have a claw clip in my bag to keep it contained later, but I drove here with it down and loose, the windows down and blowing it about. I don't miss how Leo does a top-to-toe of me as I step towards him. This morning, I'm in a ribbed white tank top, a pair of old blue-jean shorts I found at the back of my closet that are definitely not Jackie-approved, and flip-flops. I tossed a pair of sneakers in my car too, unsure of what I'd be assigned to today.

"Work?" he asks, and I nod before explaining.

"Yup. Yesterday, you earned yourself an assistant, like it or not." He looks at me, then sighs, but his face is missing his signature irritation.

"Aren't you here to write?"

"Adam and Wren are away for two weeks now that she's off work for the summer. I'm just...here. So now it's your job to keep me entertained." He lifts one thick eyebrow at me, and I suddenly have the strangest urge to close the gap between us and rub my thumb along it.

"It is?" he asks, and I push the intrusive thought away and nod stoically, then lift a shoulder in a half-shrug.

"Or else I might get bored. You did tell me to stay out of trouble, didn't you?"

"And then I believe the very next day you toilet-papered my house."

I nod as if we're on the same page and bite back a grin.

"Exactly. So put me to work. Keep me busy so I can't find any trouble."

He stares at me, and I wonder for a moment if he's going to get mad. I half expect him to snap at me and tell me that I'm not his responsibility to entertain and keep out of trouble, but he doesn't. Instead, he sighs, then steps aside and opens the door for me.

"Come on. We've got another coat of paint to do."

We spend the day painting another coat in Leo's guest room, then he adds the trim. I help when needed, and when I'm not, I start taping the edges of his living room. We work in silence most of the day, talking occasionally, but mostly we listen to music. A lot of oldies and some new stuff, some Atlas Oaks. Anytime one of my songs comes on, I hurry to change it, something that Leo seems to find increasingly entertaining, but I *hate* listening to my own music casually. I hear the mistakes, the small things that, with time and bettering my craft, I would change if I were recording it now, and it always makes me self-conscious.

We pause midday for a quick lunch of peanut butter and jelly sandwiches, something I haven't had in years, but considering Leo's kitchen is relatively empty, it is one of our only options. I've eaten at some of the most highly regarded restaurants in the world, but it's the best meal I've had in years. At around four, we decide to call it quits, and when he walks me out to my car, my body aches with the same kind of satisfied exhaustion I feel after a day of practicing for tour or a performance.

"So, what's next? Another room?" I ask, turning toward him once I'm at the driver's side door. He stares at me, and I expect him to argue, but he doesn't. Instead, he seems to accept this new fate of his with a sigh.

"It's going to be nice out for the next week, so I'm thinking about tackling outside tasks. Next time it rains, I'll go back to indoor things, but there's enough outside to keep us busy for a month." My heart flips a bit at the word "us," but I push it down and clap instead.

"Fun! Landscaping!" With my excitement, he grins.

"You know, if you told me that Willa Stone would say the word *landscaping* and *fun* in the same sentence last month, I'd tell you you were out of your mind."

"Then you didn't really know me at all," I say, lifting a shoulder and smiling at him over it, opening the door.

"I'm starting to see the truth in that," he says. We lock eyes for a long moment before he nods, as if to himself, then puts a hand on the frame of my car door as I slide in, start the truck, and roll down the windows. Once I'm buckled in, he slams it, then gives me a wave before I drive off.

That night, I follow the same routine as the day before: make a salad for a quick dinner, shower, slip into my comfy clothes, pick up my guitar, and try to write.

Once again, words hit the page, and once again, relief washes through me. I don't get a ton done, just some lines and a couple of melodies before I decide to go lie in bed and read a book, but I fall asleep exhausted, excited, and satisfied for the first time in a long, long time.

• • •

"Can we go look at the flowers?" I ask a few days later as we move through the parking lot of the home improvement store and past a huge outdoor display of flowers. I've come to Leo's house every day since I helped him paint, and this morning he didn't even question me when I showed up, instead asking if we could take my SUV to the home improvement store in order to get some pavers to fix up his front walkway.

"Flowers?" he asks over his shoulder as he grabs a giant flat cart. I nod, then explain.

"There are a few pots outside of Hallie's place. I was thinking about filing them."

"Do you know how to grow things?"

I shake my head.

"No. But I've watched videos," I say.

He smiles at me, the real one that he seems to be giving me more and more of when I say something that thoroughly entertains him.

"You seem to watch a lot of home improvement videos for a woman who painted a room for the first time this week."

"I keep my feeds very, very well regulated, so I don't see anything about myself that might ruin my day. It's a relatively safe niche for me to watch, and I like watching them."

"You're a strange woman, you know that?" he asks with a laugh. Instead of moving in through the main door, though, he guides the cart to the right of the store where the nursery is, and I smile as I follow him.

"Oh, these are pretty!" I say, running my fingers over the colorful flowers of the hydrangea bush. "I love hydrangea." Then I step over to touch the petal of a rose. "Oh, and these roses are gorgeous. And these coneflowers!" I sigh reverently. "They're all so pretty."

"Get them," Leo suggests, and I shake my head.

"They're perennials, so they come back every year. I don't want to plant something Hallie will have to do upkeep for in the future." I sigh, stepping away and moving back towards the annuals I came for, but his voice stops me.

"I could use some bushes. Pick some out." I turn back towards him, but his face is impassive.

"What?"

"Pick some out. The front gardens are a mess. You can fill them up." My heart skips a beat as excitement floods me.

"Really?" I ask hesitantly, trying to play is cool.

"I don't see why not. I want it to look nice, but I don't see myself prioritizing flowers anytime soon, much less even knowing which ones to plant." He looks beyond me at the garden center. "You'd actually be doing me a favor. I figured I'd have to hire a landscaping firm to do it, but you can try your hand at it if you'd like."

"Oh my god!" I say, then, without thinking, I lean in, wrapping my arms around his neck, hugging him tight. He's still for a moment, then relaxes, an arm moving loosely around my waist in a sideways hug. When I step back, I clap excitedly, nearly unable to contain myself before I get it in check, but when I look back at him, his eyes are soft, his lips tipped up in a way I've never seen on him, but in a way that looks really, really good on him. I take it in for long moments, trying to calm the haphazard beating of my chest before I finally look away and start loading up on flowers.

"Those flowers match your shirt almost perfectly," he says, looking over at me an hour later as we walk out into the parking lot with our haul: what I have to think is a literal ton of paver stones and a big bag of setting sand, four different hydrangea bushes, two roses, and a flat of cone flowers in various colors. I'm going to research more flowers that would do well in this area before we have to make another trip here, but this should keep me busy for a while.

Today I'm in one of the two colorful sports tank tops that I bought, this one a pretty, vibrant pink. When I look down, I realize he's right: the coneflowers I've picked out are almost the same color, nearly blending into my top.

"You're right," I say with a laugh. He continues to navigate the heavy cart with minimal effort, eyes taking me in as he does.

"You know, I don't think I've ever seen you in anything colorful outside of events and tour."

An unexpected thrill runs through me at the idea of him noticing things about me, the thought of him taking note of what I wear and when. Quickly, as I've taught myself to do with Leo, I tamp it down and look at it from a logical standpoint: he's my publicist. He's probably seen, inspected, and approved more photos of me than anyone else. He's seen every tabloid photo, perfectly curated by Jackie with my cool-girl outfits, complimentary neutrals, and cool colors. Of course, he would notice if I started wearing brighter colors outside of that normal brand.

"My streetwear is curated to be trendy. Neutrals and whites and blacks are trendy and the most flattering, so it's what I wear."

"Where'd you get that one?" I hope that the blush burning on my cheeks can be explained away by the summer heat emanating off the blacktop.

"I bought a few things a few weeks ago myself, trying to reflect the album vibes so I could get inspired." I lick my lips, trying not to overthink and overspeak instead. "Jackie would very much not approve, but no one is hounding me here, so I figured..." Nerves rush through me as I try to interpret his words, to see if he means that he prefers the other aesthetic, or if he's just taking note of things and making small talk. He doesn't speak when my words fade out, just reaches into his pocket for the keys to his car, clicking the locks and popping the trunk. Then, he starts moving things in quickly and efficiently. But when he reaches for the flowers I'm still awkwardly holding, he holds my eyes.

"It looks good on you. Color. You look nice, Willa." Then, completely unaware of how my pulse is pounding, he starts loading up the car before handing me the keys and telling me to start it and get the AC going.

And when I go home and place a new clothing order filled with pinks, purples, and blues, I tell myself it's just because I want more color in my life.

Definitely not because Leo Sinclaire said they looked nice on me.

On Friday, Leo is watering a patch of grass seed he laid down with a hose, and I walk towards him with my watering can. He mentioned eventually adding an automatic watering system, but for now, I don't mind watering the plants I added to his landscaping.

"Need some?" he asks, tipping his chin towards the bucket in my hands, and I nod. Today, he's in a light blue tee that, once again, hugs every single inch and a pair of dark gray loose shorts. His sneakers are stained green from mowing the lawn, and there's a dark blue Atlas Oaks hat shielding his eyes from the beating sun. He hands me the hose, and I drop the end into the bucket, waiting for it to fill.

"How's that going?" I ask, tipping my chin to the patch of hay lying over the grass he put down. He reaches up, takes off his hat, and pushes his hair back once more before setting it on his head.

"We'll see in a few weeks, I guess. I should have put it down a lot earlier, but it wasn't my priority. Hoping that if I keep it watered, the seeds will sprout and I'll be in business." I nod as if I know exactly what he's talking about, but I'm far too distracted by the way he's lifting the bottom hem of his shirt up to his face to wipe off the sweat. I catch the bottom of his toned stomach, the light dusting of hair that leads down below his waist.

A laugh breaks me out of my daze, and my eyes shoot up to his face, entertained and pleased.

"You good?"

"Huh?"

"You were staring," he says, that grin widening.

"No, I wasn't," I lie, rolling my eyes and looking back down to the half-full watering can. My *god*, could it go any slower? I desperately need to get out of here.

"You absolutely were."

I look back up at him.

"If I was, which I absolutely was not, but if I was, it was because you were flashing the whole world."

"Flashing the world?" he asks with a laugh, and I can't help but smile. Leo laughing feels sacred, rare, and something I strive to hear more often.

"I think you were just stunned by my killer abs."

Without even really thinking, I bend, putting my finger over the opening of the hose, then lift it in Leo's direction, spraying him with it. I divert the hose's direction back to the watering can, the long stream loudly filling the watering can as he stands there with a shocked look on his face.

His T-shirt turns a darker color where the water hits him, and I can't help but watch it spread and cling to him as he stares at me, his mouth open.

"What the hell?" he asks, a smile on his face.

"My bad," I say with absolutely no apology in the words, something that is made even clearer when I hit him with the water again. He looks down at the shirt, now drenched, and back at me.

"You brat," he says.

I aim it at him again, and while he once more gets wet, he also takes a step towards me. My eyes widen, and I take a step back, but not quick enough as he reaches forward and takes the hose from my hands. Then he directs it towards me, spraying me with the cold water.

"Oh my god!" I shriek, because it's colder than I expected.

"My bad," he says mockingly, then directs at me again. I let out a loud laugh, then start to move, turning away from him and trying to escape the stream. He chases me, spraying me as I yell and laugh, getting soaked as I go. The hose is long, and I run in circles, but never fully out of reach, enjoying this game.

"I give up!" I shout, throwing one hand up after a minute, my hand going to my aching side, a stitch from running and laughing stabbing my side. When I look up at him, he has a similar entertained look, and I realize either I got him a bit more wet than I thought, or his wild spraying of me got him just as wet as it got me.

Either way, despite the stitch in my side and the cold water making my clothes stick to my skin, this is the most fun I've had in...a long time.

With a sigh, I move to the ground, stretching out to wait for the stitch to resolve itself as I lie in the warm grass. Pulling my sunglasses that somehow stayed on my face off, I use the one, somehow dry corner of my shorts to dry them off, slip them on, and let out a deep sigh as the sun's rays warm me through. After a moment, a shadow crosses, and water drips onto me. I look up at a smiling Leo, his soaked hair dripping down on me.

"Stop it! I said I give in!" I say with a giggle, shielding my face.

"You started it," he says, but lies down beside me. I turn my head to him.

"Sorry, it just always looked so fun in the movies."

"Dousing me in water?"

I laugh, but shake my head.

"No, although I'm seeing the benefits." I look him over in a way that makes a blush burn on his cheeks. Just like his laughs, Leo getting shy or embarrassed is happening more and more often, and I'm realizing it's fun. *Flirting* is fun.

I can see why people do it so much.

I never thought I liked flirting. It always felt unnatural, scripted, and awkward, but I'm realizing it was. The only time I've flirted in recent memory was for a fake relationship, for the cameras.

But flirting with Leo feels...natural.

"No, I meant a water fight." His brow furrows as he takes me in, clearly confused. "Like, hoses and water guns and water balloons. It always looks so fun."

"You've never done that?"

"Not a lot of time for water balloon fights and water guns when you're a child star. Plus, scraped knees make more work for the makeup crew, so it was mostly activities that were gentle or helped me improve in some way." I stare at the sky, fluffy white clouds floating overhead, and smile. "That's why I got into playing guitar. That's a safe activity."

"Wow, Willa, I'm sorry, I didn't—" he starts, and an all-too-familiar embarrassment swirls in my stomach. I shake my head, then turn to face him once more. I see it there, that pity that I didn't have what he deems to be normalcy, a normal, healthy childhood.

I do what I always do: fake it.

"I'm not. It was a sacrifice I made that gave me all of this," I say.

I've seen that look before. A pitying look, and I don't deserve it, I don't deserve people's pity, their empathy. That's for people who have had hard lives and rough times, not for pop princesses who were always handed everything.

Well, mostly everything.

"You can't have it all in life. I chose my career, and I'm okay with that. I had some of the most amazing experiences, and I've never had to face any true hardships. What do I have to complain about?" He stares at me, assessing, trying to read past my shield, but I keep my smile on my lips, making sure it's part friendly, part sweet, all airy and carefree before I turn back to the sky.

"Willa—"

"What do you see?" I ask, gently, desperate to change the topic.

"What?"

"What do you see? In the clouds?"

He's silent, and when I turn to him, he's not looking at the clouds at all, but at me, confused. "People do that, right? Look at the clouds and find shapes?" An embarrassed blush burns over my cheeks now. "Or is that just a movie thing, too?"

"No, no, it is." From the sound of his voice, I know he's looking at me, but I refuse to turn my head and return the gaze, to see if he still has that pity on his face, if he's still trying to read and understand me.

After a long, near-painful moment, he speaks again. "A cat," he says. "Right there." His hand comes into my line of sight, pointing at the clouds to one that has two peaks, and I grin.

"I see it," I agree. "There's a dolphin jumping out of a hamburger," I say, pointing elsewhere. A loud laugh leaves his lips, filling the sky, and it settles that icky feeling in my chest.

"You're a nut," he murmurs.

"You like it," I say without thinking.

"Yeah. I do," he says, low, but I don't look at him.

I don't know what I'll see, and the fear that whatever I'm picturing in my mind won't be the reality is far too terrifying. Because

I'm picturing something sweet and impossible, and for once, I want to let myself live in that fairy tale.

So, instead, we lie like that for a long time, pointing out shapes occasionally, and it's the most at peace I've been in years, if I'm being honest.

And despite every ounce of logic screaming to keep that hopeless romantic locked where I've kept her for eight years, she smiles.

TWENTY

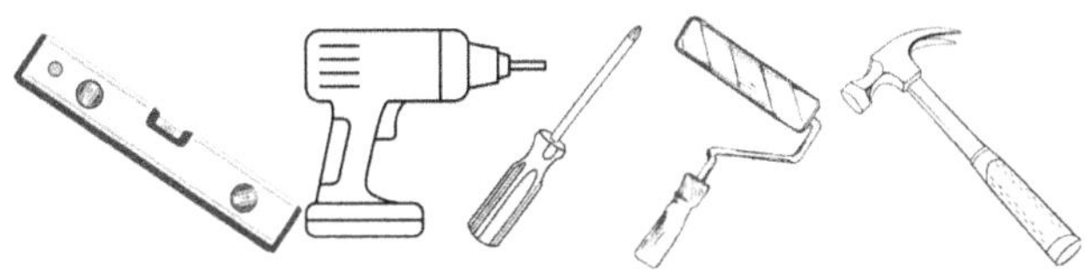

LEO

I'm having my morning coffee on the back patio, the pavers now weeded, and at least half of them moved, reset, and leveled with the help of Willa. It's been almost two weeks since she started coming to help me out with house projects, and even though she originally said it was because everyone else was out of town, both Adam and Wren and Hallie and Jesse have returned from their own summer trips, and she's still here every day to help out.

For the most part, I've managed to keep us outside and keep my distance while she's here. After painting the walls inside for two days in a row, I realized being indoors was a terrible, terrible fucking idea. I would consider myself to have pretty good willpower, but in close quarters where I couldn't ignore her, where I could smell her sweet perfume lingering long after she left for the night, there are too many opportunities to brush an arm against her, and too many opportunities to envision her sharing this space with me in a very, very different way.

An inappropriate way.

A way that never, ever could happen, even if with each passing day, I find myself wondering *why not?*

For that reason, outside is safer. So much safer, especially when I can take intentional steps to be on the opposite side of the yard from her, or when I use loud power tools like the lawn mower or the weed whacker, making conversation impossible. It helps that Willa seems to enjoy being outside, clearing out the garden beds and planting the dozens of plants she's helped me pick out. Two days ago, she moved on to one of the overgrown areas along the fence line, weeding and clearing what was once a garden, but looked like nothing of the sort. She told me she had a vision for a flower wall, naming some flower that would creep up the fence, though the name went in one ear and out the other as soon as she said it.

I agreed instantly because when she spoke of white, fragrant flowers and green vines along the fence, her entire face lit up with excitement, and there was no way I was going to say no and wipe that look from her face.

Unfortunately, as I sit outside, I watch a dark cloud roll in from the west and realize today might be the day the plan fails. I'm lost in that thought and trying to think of what to do if we're stuck inside, where I can stay as far from her as possible, when my phone rings. My stomach tenses at the instant worry that it's a call from Jefferson. It's been this way for weeks, and the mere fact that this is my instinct each time my phone rings—fearing it will lead to another conversation with Jefferson—is further confirmation that my exit plan is a necessary thing.

But more concerning, as of last week, every time I get any kind of communication from Jefferson, a brand-new worry sets in—worry that it will be the call confirming the start date for Willa's next relationship.

At first, I convinced myself that the gnawing pit in my stomach was a signal that my peaceful retreat was ending. But more and more, I realize it's because it will also signal the end of *Willa's* peaceful retreat, and with the way the color and joy that's slowly been leaving her over the years has returned to her face, I want to draw it out as long as I can.

Relief racks through me when I see that it's my mom.

"Hey, Mom," I say when I answer, and an exaggerated gasp comes over the line.

"Is that *Leo?* Leo, is it really you? I thought you were lost at sea, gone forever!" she says. "My baby boy is alive! I should call the papers!" My mom has always had a flair for dramatics, something my dad was both annoyed by and deeply adored.

"Okay, okay, I get it," I say with a shake of my head.

"I'm sorry, I just never thought I would ever actually hear your voice again. I was preparing to send a carrier pigeon, but I wouldn't even know where to send it since you haven't given me your new address," she says, accusation in the tone. Despite that, I close my eyes, shaking my head and smiling.

This is my mom in all her chaos, and even though she drives me up a wall, I know she loves me more than anything, and there's something familiar and nostalgic about her pestering. For a moment, I wonder if maybe that's why I've been enjoying someone else's brand of pestering lately. Maybe it's a sick and twisted family trait.

"I haven't given you my address because the place I bought is a dump. I knew if I gave you the address, there was a not-small chance you'd show up at my front door randomly one day, and I don't even have anywhere for you to stay yet. I want you to see it when it's done."

"Or maybe you just hate your dear mom," she says, but I ignore that, continuing on with my explanation, a smile on my lips.

"And even more, I am sure you *do* know where I live, since I guarantee you had Uncle Tino check the MLS when I bought the place, and he gave you the listing. I'm sure you and Aunt Kate were combing through the online listing, hemming and hawing about all of the problems."

Silence fills the line before she sighs.

"I was just curious!"

I laugh and shake my head. Although I've been out of the house for years and years, some things never change, and my mom's need to be in my business is one of them. Thankfully, these days she does it from afar. "So what you're telling me is you're never gonna let me see this place for yours?"

'There's no guest room yet, Mom. But I'm working on it. I'm thinking you could come here for the holidays."

"The holidays? Like these holidays? The photos I saw looked like at least a year of work, if you were doing it alone." And she would know, since she still works for my dad's company, scheduling the jobs. She never liked to get her hands dirty with the work, no matter how much my dad teased her about it, but she was always great with the business side. I hesitate to answer, knowing that if I say what I want, it means she will never be off my ass.

For some reason, I find myself saying it anyway.

"I've had some help," I say. "So I might be able to get things moving a bit faster. Some of the guys who live up here have been pitching in, and one of my clients is actually here for the summer, so she's been helping a lot."

"She?" Mom says, picking up on only one word, inevitably.

"Mom," I say, though I know the warning falls on deaf ears.

"Please tell me it's Willa," she says.

"What? Why?"

"Because you two have been toeing around one another every single time I go to one of those events with you."

I let out a loud laugh, shaking my head.

"No, we have not," I say, though she's been to enough events as my date, always so excited to see the glitz and glam, that she's seen Willa and me in the same room more than enough times over the years.

"You have! Every time she's there, you always have an eye on her, know what she's doing, anticipating what she might need."

"I do that for all of my clients," I argue, something I've always argued internally, but something that, lately, I'm wondering if it was really some kind of justification, some excuse I didn't want to look too closely at.

"You don't do it for those boys of yours," she says, and I know she means the members of Atlas Oaks. A classic suburban mom to her core, Mom treats anyone she deems a friend of mine as if they're just a neighborhood kid, even if they're multi-platinum rock stars.

"It's not the same, and you know it. The media is harder and far less forgiving on her than they are on the band," I say, though the excuse feels hollow. "Anyway, yes, it's Willa, but don't get your hopes up. We have a strictly professional relationship."

"Sure, you do," she says, and that single word tells me all I need to know. I open my mouth to argue, to continue to tell her that it's not the case, that she needs to nip whatever idea she's stirred up in her mind, but before I can, she's speaking again and throwing me back when she does. "You sound happy," she says. "You sound...at peace."

I don't miss the surprise or the relief in her voice.

I tip my head back to take in the trees of my yard, and I sink into the chair once more, bringing my coffee to my lips for a small sip. "I am."

Time passes, though it's not uncomfortable, before she speaks again.

"I worried, you know. About you. Heading down the path you were. I'd seen it once before, and I've been worried." She doesn't know about my health scare, doesn't know that for a moment, I also thought that I was headed down that path, and it's what pulled me back, and right now, I'm glad she doesn't. I'm glad I didn't add any more stress to her plate. "But you seem better. Healthier. You sound like you're balancing better. I hope you can hold onto that."

"I'm...I'm trying," I admit. "I'm well aware that dad worked like crazy when I was a kid, and we both know how that ended."

"Stubborn man just like you, worked himself to the grave." I smile at her familiar refrain, still annoyed by my dad in death, as was their way. "He wouldn't want you to make that same mistake. He'd want you to choose happiness." That knife twists in my chest, but before I can respond, she continues. "I'm proud of you and all you've accomplished with your career, Leo, but it's not all there is in life. You can have all the success in the world, but what does it matter if you don't have anyone to share it with?" Her words echo the ones I thought that day in the ambulance, but again, I keep that to myself.

"Mom, I'm happy with the way things are for now," I say, even if the lie tastes sour on my tongue. Six months ago, it was true, or at least, I had told myself it was. And even three months ago, it was true. Once I had my plan in place, once I started taking steps towards finding my peace, towards restructuring my priorities, I was happy with what I allowed myself to have. But in the last month, I don't know if I believe it anymore, if I believe I'm happy with the way things are, especially when it comes to my relationship with a particular sunny blonde.

We're friends now, but is that enough?

Eight years ago, a month ago, a week ago, I told myself it was the only way for us to both have what we wanted, but maybe I was wrong all along.

As if responding to my thoughts of her, I hear the familiar sound of tires on gravel out front and stand, walking into the house and setting my cup in the sink.

"I know that. But I know better than anyone that you only have right now. If you wait until everything is perfect to get what you want, or, *who* you want, you might never get there. Tomorrow is never promised, Leo."

Her words settle in my chest, as does the light hint of grief that hangs in the words. It's been years since my dad died, and she will never get over it, will never move on, something I find both sad and beautiful.

But her words settle differently right now, the truth of them weighing on me in a way I don't expect, and when I move through my house to the front door and see a smiling Willa in her front seat, waving at me, I can't help but wonder that if this was all gone, would I regret things I didn't do?

"I know. But I gotta go," I say, opening the door and stepping out. "My help is here."

I wonder if she can hear the smile in my voice, the same way I can when she responds. "Okay, Leo. Just keep what I have in mind, okay?"

"I will. Love you."

"Love you, too. And get that guest room done for me—I'm coming for the holidays whether you're ready or not."

I think we might make it through the entire day outside, since Willa normally leaves around four, but the sky gets dark faster than I anticipated, clouds rolling in quickly around two. We're finishing up installing a swing on my front porch, something Willa insisted would make the front of my home look absolutely perfect when we were at the home improvement store earlier this week. I faltered for only a moment before I realized I'm highly receptive to her charms and can't seem to not give in to any of her wants. I slid the heavy thing onto our flat and headed to the hardware aisle to figure out how to install it.

We were only there for mulch and grass seed, and my current project list is already a mile long, but it didn't matter.

The clouds rolled in that morning, and Willa asked if we could add it, saying she'd love to watch the storm from the covered porch. Again, I couldn't do anything but agree. We're barely finished, and I'm adjusting the chains so the swing hangs evenly, when suddenly, the sky opens up, and a downpour begins. Willa stands up from where she was cleaning up cardboard, instructions, and plastic, and moves to the very edge of the steps. Today she's in a loose purple T-shirt and a pair of jean shorts, and as I watch her, standing under the cover of the porch still, the wind blows a few drops of rain towards her, making darker spots appear on her top.

"It's pouring," she says, stating the obvious.

I smirk at her back despite myself.

"I can see that," I say, standing and moving to rest my arms on the railing beside where she's standing. The raindrops are warm as they hit my forearms, not the chilly fall downpour that I expected.

"We should go play in the rain."

I stare at her, but she has that far-off look in her eyes, barely noticing I'm beside her. I've seen it a few times, often when she sees or thinks about something that I'd never thought twice about, but clearly, she sees it as a memory she never got. Water fights and watching clouds and getting an ice cream from an ice cream truck, something we did on Tuesday when we drove past one stopped on our way back from the store.

All things I've done countless times over my life, simple memories I never thought twice about, memories that, now that I've made them with her, mean a fuck of a lot more to me.

"Play in the rain?" I ask.

She doesn't answer, not verbally. Instead, she just grins and nods and runs into the rain. I shift, stepping towards the edge of the steps, and open my mouth to call her name, but the word dies on my tongue as I take her in.

She's smiling, head tipped back, arms out like some character in a movie or a cliche stock photo. Her top is already soaked to a dark purple, clinging to her curves, and her hair is drenched and stringy, but it flares out behind her as she begins to twirl in the rain.

She's the most gorgeous thing I've ever seen in my life.

It's a moment of pure joy, beauty in its most basic form, something that is so deeply Willa in a way I can't quite explain.

I'm still in awe when she stops, turning to me with a bright, beaming grin and waving her hand towards me.

"Come on!" she shouts, spinning in a circle as water continues to fall, dripping down her skin, her hair sticking to her face. She kicks off the flip flops she's wearing, and I'm suddenly also grateful that the grass is soft and lush where she's playing.

"What are you doing?"

"Dancing in the rain!" she yells back as if I'm not ten feet away from her, as if the excitement in her chest can't maintain normal volumes. I can't help it. I smile back at her, and she waves her hands at me once more. "Come on, Leo! Dance with me!"

She's beautiful, smiling and spinning, and even though common sense tells me to drag her inside, get her out of the rain, I can't find it in me to do it. I can't find it in me to dampen this example of pure, unmitigated joy.

So instead, I step off the porch, the rain warm as it instantly soaks my skin through my shirt. I run a hand through my hair, and the rain slicks in back, and she squeals as I approach. With each step I take, her smile somehow grows brighter, and when I am a few feet from her, she closes the gap, wrapping her arms around my neck and tipping her head back, her body pressed to mine.

She is so blissfully happy, and even though it's because she's giving herself an experience she's never had, for a moment, I let myself imagine it's for me, that she's smiling because I came over here.

That she's happy we're here, together.

"Dance with me, Leo," she whispers, and just like in the bar, we start to sway.

Just like in the bar, her fingers move to the hair at the back of my neck, gently twirling the strands, caressing the skin there and sending a shiver through me. Water drops off my nose and off her lashes and trails down her cheeks to her lips. I watch in utter fascination as her tongue dips out, licking the water from them.

My breathing grows heavier as we move into the rain, and despite my best efforts, my eyes keep tracking her lips, moving from her eyes to her lips, then back to her eyes, but never anywhere else.

And hers do the same.

And for the first time, common sense takes a back seat.

Would it really be that bad, kissing her?

Would it really be that detrimental to give in just this once, to take what I want? To, as is quickly becoming my favorite thing, give Willa what she clearly wants?

If anything, it would be rude *not* to. Why not make this moment even more memorable?

Fuck it.

My arm tightens on her lower back, pulling her wet body closer to mine, and my head starts to dip. Her breath hitches, eyes going wide as her chin tips up a bit more in a moment of acquiescence as she prepares to meet me halfway.

That's when the lightning strikes, not anywhere too close, but close enough that the thunder follows instantly, deafening. It shocks both of us and jolts me back into reality.

The moment is broken, and it feels like the universe is reminding me of all the reasons that I can't do this. Despite that, my chest drops with disappointment. Still unable not to steal the smallest moment, I brush my thumb along her soaking-wet cheek before I force my better judgment to take the wheel once more.

"I should get you inside," I whisper. She licks her lips, and god, I want to taste the rain on her lips.

"Probably," she says, and I don't miss the hint of disappointment that's mirrored in my own chest. I almost say fuck it, but then another crack of lightning lights up the sky, and logic wins.

While I'd do just about anything to keep her happy, right now that need is battling with my other need to keep her safe.

With a sigh, I release my hold on her and step away, then tip my head to the house. "Come on. Let's get you dry. You can borrow something of mine."

She nods with a soft, sad smile, and I lead her into the house. We move silently as I grab a towel for her, then lead her to my room, where I grab a dry outfit for myself before handing her a pair of shorts she can tighten at the waist and a T-shirt.

"It's better than nothing," I say with an apologetic laugh. "Change in here and bring your wet stuff out—I'll toss it into the dryer." She accepts the clothes from me as her hair drips water onto her shoulder, and I force myself not to watch the way the rain glides down her skin. I don't say anything else, afraid to open my mouth because I have no idea what would come out, instead moving out of the room and closing the door behind me.

Quickly, I change in the bathroom, bring my wet clothes to the laundry room, and toss them into the wash, making sure the dryer is empty for her. Then I stand in the kitchen, unsure of what to do with myself and, more importantly, Willa, until the rain lets up, since I don't want her driving in this.

After the night at the Mill, once I got past my frustration with her and realized she wasn't here to cause me a headache but was instead looking for the same thing I was, I thought it would all be okay. I thought I'd been able to pull myself together, to pull that shield back up that I've kept between myself and Willa Stone for nearly eight years, but clearly, I was wrong. So fucking wrong.

The wall of professionalism I've erected between us is crumbling from all of the moments I've spent with her over the last few weeks, from laughing with her and watching her learn new things, and catching moments of precious vulnerability that I cherish. It's like with each inch her own shield lowered, with each sliver of the real Willa I'm shown, she took a brick out of the fortress I'd built until all that's left is a shaky, hole-filled wall that's doing nothing for my restraint.

Needing to keep myself busy, I start moving around the kitchen and decide to make coffee. When the bedroom door opens, I keep my back to her while asking, "Do you want coffee? I'm making some."

"Do you have creamer, or are you boring and only take it black?" Willa's musical voice asks behind me. I take in a deep, fortifying breath before turning to face her.

"I have half and half or whole milk," I say, smiling at her as she steps into the kitchen. I needed that fortifying breath because her damp hair is pulled into a messy bun at the top of her head, her face wiped free of the little makeup she was wearing, and worst of all, she's in my clothes, the shirt hanging off her narrow shoulders, her smile a bit nervous as she shuffles in.

Once again, as I find happening every day, my chest tightens.

"Thank god," she mumbles, then turns out of the kitchen towards the laundry room, already knowing the layout of my house as if she herself lives there, just another tiny moment that tugs at my chest.

"Are you going to steal this one, too?" I ask,

"Maybe. The other T-shirt is very comfy. Perfect for sleeping in." I'm sure she means the night she spent here, but I can't help but envision her sleeping in my tee at her place. That momentary daydream must be why I ask my next question.

"And the sweatshirt?" Her brows furrow, creating the perfect soft crease between her brows, but there's something on her face, the tiniest hint of panic.

"What?"

I should drop it, but I don't.

"The sweatshirt. My sweatshirt."

"I—" She hesitates, the words dying on her lips as she blinks at me, shock written on her face.

"You were wearing it the day you toilet-papered my house," I remind her, trying to sound casual when I feel anything but.

"Do you know how I got it?" she asks, voice low and soft, and my brows furrow, not understanding the question.

"How you got it?"

"Yeah. Do you...do you remember that?" Despite her clarifying the question, I still don't understand what she's asking.

Because, *of course,* I remember.

I remember stripping my sweatshirt off when I completely drenched her, because I couldn't make her walk home in a tank top in that cold weather.

I remember talking with her for nearly an hour, feeling as if the world made sense, as if everything was finally falling into place for me, as if it was all *working out.*

I remember her leaving before I could get her number, and I remember every moment after that proved to me that the universe had a very twisted sense of humor.

Of course, I remember. It's a moment in my life that's haunted me for years.

"Why don't you ask me what you really want to know?" I say, setting down the coffee pot, and turning to face her, crossing my arms over my chest. Her eyes follow the shift, pausing momentarily on where the cuffs of my tee hug my biceps. I fight back the surge of pride at that. She does it a lot, whether she realizes it or not, and with my walls all but decimated, I'd decided that occasionally flexing just to get a reaction is totally fine and not a violation of the boundaries I have to live by.

Further proof of just how far gone I am.

"It's just....you...I..." I smirk at her flustered behavior, and she closes her eyes, taking in a deep breath. "You didn't recognize me after I walked into the office that day. When did you realize it was me?" My head moves back, unsure of what she's saying.

"You thought I didn't recognize you?" She looks at me like I've lost my mind.

"Well...yeah. I walked into that room, and you looked right through me."

"Will, honey. You don't look *that* different when you're out of your shield."

"Yes, I—" she starts to argue, but I shake my head, answering before she can finish.

"Not to someone who's looking." It's the truth: with a hat and her signature hair tied up, makeup free, and without the blue contacts, she *could* be passed off as not Willa, but I have never been confused about who I met that day, fake name and low-key look or not.

"And were you? Looking?" Her voice is soft and nervous, and it pangs in my chest.

"I've been looking at you and for you since that day in the coffee shop." Her eyes widen, as do her lips, and I sigh, running a hand through my slowly drying hair and pushing a loose lock back.

What does it matter anymore? What do these secrets and the walls matter when she's here?

"That day I met you in the coffee shop," I start, unsure of what I'm doing. I know this is stupid. Something I should take to the grave if I want to salvage any bit of the professional relationship I'm clinging to with her, but that look in her eyes is the only thing I'm processing right now. "That day, you left, and I realized I hadn't gotten your number. I stepped out of the coffee shop, tried to catch you once I realized, but you were gone, already out of sight. I went to the barista and asked if she knew you and if you came in regularly. She told me you came in on Mondays, and I made a plan to haunt that place every Monday until I bumped into you again."

My mind travels to those moments after I watched her walk off, a cheery smile and an irritated look on her face, as if she were annoyed that her prior plans overlapped with our impromptu date.

"That woman," I said, tipping my head towards the table I sat with her at for nearly an hour. "Does she come here often?" The barista looked to where we had been sitting, then to me, with an uncomfortable look on her face.

"I—"

"I swear I'm not trying to be a creep. I just had the best forty-five minutes of my life, and she had to leave before I got her number. I just want to know if she comes here often and if I have a shot of finding her again, or if I totally just fucked up and missed out on my chance." The woman's eyes softened, a tiny smile tilting her lips before she nodded.

"Normally comes Monday mornings around seven or eight like clockwork." I grinned widely, thanking her and shoving a hundred into the tip jar before walking off, feeling like the world was finally working out for me. I had a career-changing meeting coming up, I'd met my dream woman, and I had a plan to find her again.

"But then I went to that meeting, and you walked in, and it all clicked into place. Who you were, what we were about to do, and what it meant."

"What did it mean?" she asks, her voice shaky. There's barely a foot between us, but it feels like an ocean, so I move, closing that gap until the space between us is closer, but we're still not touching.

"It meant I couldn't have you, Willa. I'm not allowed to be with clients. It's against my contract." I reach out and push a wet tendril of hair behind her ear.

"Couldn't?"

Of course, she would take note of the exact words I used. She steps closer until we're close enough to touch, but neither of us seems to want to be the one to cross that line, waiting for the other to break first. I wonder if her heart feels like it's about to break out of her chest, too.

"I still can't have you now, Willa." The glimmer of hope melts from her face in an instant, making my heart pang. Even though I had already decided to go for it, that look would have changed my mind if I hadn't. "But I don't really care about what I can and can't have anymore, Willa. Eight years ago, I had to choose between my career and my heart, and I've regretted it ever since, but I'm not making that mistake again. Not if it means I have to pretend that you aren't everything to me for a fucking minute longer."

Her breath catches, and I lean in, catching the gasp between my lips, my hand sliding to her neck to pull her to me as my other arm moves around her waist.

There's no going back now, and even if I could, I know I wouldn't want to.

TWENTY-ONE

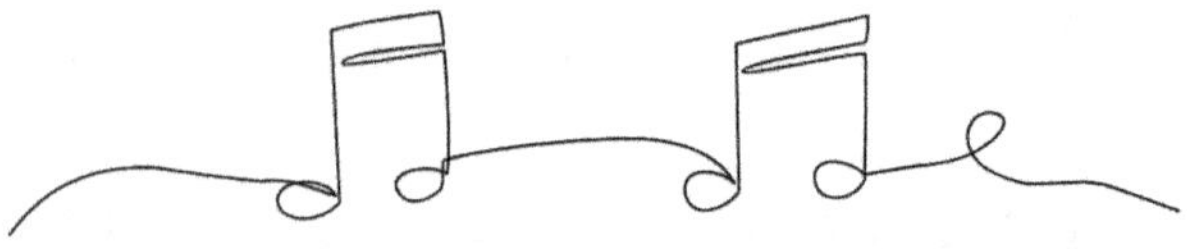

WILLA

Leo Sinclaire is kissing me.

Leo is killing me.

No, he's not just kissing me: he's consuming me. Devouring me.

One of his warm hands is buried in my hair, and his lips are moving on mine, and the world around us doesn't exist as I lift my own hands to cup his cheeks, desperate to feel him, to ensure this isn't some kind of fucked dream, some manifestation of my desperate mind.

I hold his face, shifting in an effort to get closer to him. He groans, the arm on my waist pulling me in even tighter, gluing his body to mine as if he, too, is worried this moment will disappear.

My mind could never conjure something this beautiful.

"Leo," I murmur when he breaks the kiss, pressing his forehead to mine and looking down at me with dazed eyes, fighting to hold on to whatever thread of control he still has.

I want it to snap.

"Willa," he says, breathing heavy, his hand on my chin, tipping it to keep me looking at him. "Will, honey, please tell me you want this. Please tell me I haven't completely fucked this up."

I shake my head, a smile spreading over my lips as I look at him in awe, my heart ready to combust as all of the pieces fall into place.

He always knew it was me.

He kept his distance because he wanted me, but couldn't let himself have me.

Like I've done a million times before, he chose his career over chasing what his heart wanted, and right now he wants to set that right.

I have no idea what this means. I have no idea what will happen tomorrow, no idea what this will mean for our working relationship or my career or his, but for the first time in my life, I don't care. For the first time in my life, I'm unsure of what I should do, so instead, I take what I desperately want.

"Took you long enough," I murmur.

He smiles, wide and genuine and blinding, before pulling my face to his. This kiss isn't sweet and hesitant; it's fiery. Filled with need that we've both carried for years, desire and pent-up tension that are finally being released, he kisses me with all of the passion I've been seeing in his eyes for weeks, and I give it back to him, my hands moving to the back of his neck to pull him into me. His knees bend, his hands slide to my hips, then down to my ass before he cups it, then lifts me. On instinct, my legs wrap his hips. I giggle as he lifts me up until we're face-to-face, but it quickly turns into a different sound altogether when he presses into me, his hips grinding into mine.

That's when I find him already hard and let out a heavy breath.

"Leo," I whimper, but can't get any more out because his lips fall to mine once more, kissing hot and deep with a passion I've only ever read about. My hands move, trying to touch every inch of him I can, as if this is my one chance to commit it all to memory.

"Fuck, I don't wanna take this off," he grumbles, hands sliding under the shirt as his hips keep me pinned to the wall. "Like seeing you in it far too much."

"I'll put it back on later," I promise, and this time he groans, hips pressing deeper into mine. I groan at the contact, at the scrape of him against my clit, and then gasp when his hand cups my bare breast. His head pulls back, and instantly, I miss his hot breath at my neck.

"No bra?" I bite my lip.

"It was wet. I didn't want to put it back on."

"You were just going to walk around my place in my shirt, no fucking bra on, and not even make a move?" His voice is incredulous. "And now you expect me to just take it off, not getting to see that beauty?" I let out a disbelieving laugh, then shift my hips forward again, trying to get some kind of friction against the throbbing between my legs.

"If you fuck me, I'll put it back on after, and this time I'll leave the shorts off too."

"Fuck," he groans, low and long, and it makes my core tighten.

"Leo," I whisper, and his lips drop again to my neck, peppering kisses to the skin there. My chin tips, trying to give him more room to work, and my hands reach for his shirt. "Please. I want you."

That, thankfully, seems to do the trick.

"Whatever you want, honey, I'm going to give to you."

He steps away from the wall, carrying me down the hall to his bedroom before tossing me on his bed. Reaching behind himself, he pulls his tee off, and I hold my breath as finally, all of those delectable muscles that have been tempting me for weeks are revealed.

He's fucking magnificent.

It's actually illegal that he hides those broad shoulders beneath business suits, that his chest, speckled with the perfect amount of chest hair, leading to and disappearing beneath his shorts, isn't on billboards. For a moment, I contemplate starting a petition to make him an honorary firefighter so he can be on one of those hot firefighter calendars.

I'd buy every damn copy.

But those thoughts are gone as soon as they come when he steps towards the bed, a determined look on his face as he puts a knee to the mattress and starts to crawl up my body, hooking his thumbs in the bottom of the tee and pushing it up as he goes.

My breath freezes in my lungs when I feel his hot lips against my belly, placing a gentle kiss on each inch of skin he exposes.

Oh. My. Fucking. God.

I get one right beneath, then one right above my belly button, another at the side of my rib cage, and then another on the underside of my breast. When he reveals a nipple, he groans, a sound that seems involuntary before he presses his lips there, then to the other, as if he wants every inch of my body to know just how much he appreciates it.

I have never felt so wanted in my life.

"Leo," I breathe as he pulls the tee over my head and throws it into the corner before dropping his lips to mine once more. His tongue slides against mine, and one of my hands rests on his chest, feeling the firm flex of muscles there before attempting to slide lower, to get to his shorts, to move things along because the need in me is unprecedented.

Before I can, though, his lips move again as he reverses his trail of kisses, this time adding tongue, tasting me as he moves back down. I watch with bated breath, gasping and arching when he moves to my nipple once more, laving each one like he'd be happy doing it all night long before continuing down, down, down.

Finally, he hooks his fingers into the waistband of his too-big shorts and slides them down, groaning when he sees I also didn't put my underwear back on, but this time he doesn't question it. Instead, he removes them and slides his body down until he's nearly face-to-face with my pussy. Without meaning to, I tighten, something I think he catches if the moan that leaves his lips is anything to go by.

That's when I realize what his intention is, and nerves fill me. "Leo, you don't have to," I say, shaking my head.

"I know that," he says, not even bothering to look up at me as he continues to move, pressing a gentle kiss right on my center. something soft and almost reverent.

"Leo, it's—" I start, but my words cut off as his head dips, as he flattens his tongue against me and drags his tongue up along my center in one long, slow lick.

Holy. Fucking. Shit.

I force myself to stay focused.

"Leo, really. I don't want..." My breath hitches as he uses his thumbs to spread me and groans at what he sees there. Holy fuck. That noise alone could sustain me for the rest of my life, I think. I take in a deep breath to focus.

"Leo," I say, fingers moving through his hair and tugging so he looks up my body at him.

Stay focused, Willa, I tell myself, because the visual of looking down my naked body at a half-naked Leo lying between my legs, looking like he's settling in to have a good old time, is almost enough to distract me. Almost.

"Leo, you don't have to do that. I can't...you know, like that."

His brows furrow, confusion crossing his face for the first time.

"You can't what?"

A blush burns on my cheeks, and I bite my lip, something his eyes track with precision.

"I can't come," I admit, the words tight with embarrassment. "You'll be down there forever, and we'll both be frustrated. Just come fuck me." It's happened a couple of times, partners meaning well, determined to be the first and failing miserably, and it's always embarrassing.

I thought that by being straightforward, I would get him to do what I asked.

But instead, he smiles widely.

Devious.

Excited, even.

He holds my eyes as his head dips, as his lips come together, and he presses a soft kiss to my clit, then flicks his tongue out to taste it. I suck in a breath and tighten at the sharp need that cracks through me, and he grins.

"I don't mind," he says.

I've heard that before, before I wrote off sex with other people because it wasn't worth the headache of having to find someone and coordinate a low-key hookup only to leave unsatisfied. I've been told that before, and lay there while a man did his best work, never taking me anywhere close to where I needed to be. I've had to fake it to end the uncomfortable show and get fucked the way I asked.

I do not want to fake it with Leo.

Something tells me this isn't just a one-time thing, and I don't want to start something that could be beautiful by faking it.

"Leo—"

"I like playing, Willa. Even if you don't come on my tongue, I promise you, we're both going to enjoy the ride."

I'm speechless, and he smiles before he dips his head, and all thoughts of convincing him to stop are long gone when his tongue starts to move on me.

He moves from center to clit, dipping inside to taste me and groaning as he does, then moving up to flick at my clit with the tip of his tongue, and I suck in a sharp breath. His eyes move up my body, and even though I can't see it, the smile I know is on his lips shines in his eyes. When he moves back to my entrance, his tongue slides into me, and he moves his head left and right, his nose pressing against my clit.

I bite back the moan that climbs up my throat, releasing a heavy breath as his eyes stay watching me, reading me. He does it again, sliding his tongue in a bit deeper this time and groaning as he does. Need curls in my belly, and my breathing quickens, but it's not until he slides two thick fingers inside me, his lips wrapping around my clit, that another moan slips from my lips. I stop it halfway through, my back arching as pleasure courses through me, but then his fingers stop, his head snaps up to look at me over my body.

"None of that," he says, voice firm, almost *angry*.

"What?"

"You and me, we're done pretending, and that includes pretending you're not completely into what I'm doing to your body, Willa. I want to hear it all, honey. Every noise you make, every sigh, every moan. They're mine. Don't withhold them from me." His fingers start to move again, slowly sliding in and out of me, slowly fucking me, and I gasp. When he crooks them, his thumb moving to brush over my clit, a small moan leaves my lips without my permission, but when his eyes are still on mine, they light up, and I can't find it in me to be embarrassed like normal. "No more making yourself smaller, Willa. No more of it. When you're with me, you're you. You're loud. You don't hide if you're enjoying something I'm doing."

I watch him and speak before I can even think. "Okay, Leo," I murmur, and he groans at my acquiescence. It starts a chain reaction, my pussy tightening around his fingers, and another groan leaves his lips. I smile at him, and he returns it, but it's gone from my lips as soon as his head drops again.

Then he starts to eat me again, his mouth and tongue moving on my clit, and his fingers start to fuck me, crooking and hitting a spot that even I've never touched, and my hips lift. Even though I want to tip my head back and slam my eyes shut as the pleasure moves through me, I don't. Instead, I keep my eyes locked on Leo as the wave moves through me, and I moan loudly.

And I am so fucking glad I did when I get to watch a satisfied smile spread across his lips.

"That's my girl," he murmurs. Then his head drops, and his lips circle my clit, sucking deep as his fingers move inside of me. My hips buck to get more, and another sound comes out, something I couldn't control if I wanted to, but it's almost as if the dam has broken, and I can't contain my sounds any longer.

I rock on his face as he eats me, as he finger fucks me, moaning his name, writhing with need as the pleasure twists, coiling into itself in my belly, growing warmer and warmer and seeping into my veins.

"That's it, baby," he says when he lifts his head. His lips are wet with me, and I moan again, tightening around his fingers as he slides a third in and starts to fuck me hard and fast.

"Please, Leo. Oh god, please." His thumb swipes over my swollen, needy clit, and I groan. "Fuck me."

"No, no, I'm having far too much fun down here, baby. Whenever you're ready to come on my tongue, I'll be waiting."

And then he drops his head again and continues to devour me.

And for the first time in my life, that doesn't feel like a threat or a challenge. Instead, it feels empowering.

And to my surprise, after what feels like no time at all, I can feel it coming, the orgasm to end all orgasms approaching as he sucks and fucks me, groaning his own appreciation as he does. His own hips move, grinding into the bed like he genuinely is getting just as much out of this as I am. My breathing halts, stuttering as my hips try to move. A firm, rough hand moves to my hip, pinning me down, and I mewl. He looks up my body, his hair a mess, his eyes hot and wild, and without thinking, I slide my hand down, pushing his hair over his forehead to get a better view.

His eyelids lower as he groans into my pussy, clearly liking that I want to watch, and it tips me closer to the edge.

I just need a little more. A little more pressure, something rougher, something...

As if he can sense it, he nods, and my fingers tighten in his hair, pressing his head into me.

I've never done anything like it, tell a man what I need, much less guide him to give it to me. But when he moans deep into me, the vibrations colliding with the added pressure of his mouth on me, and his fingers sinking in deep, curving to hit my G-spot, I come.

I come, and I come, and I come, screaming his name, my body quaking with the most intense relief and pleasure rolling through me in waves until I'm panting.

"Holy shit," I moan, my hips still moving, shifting, and searching for more, even as my body comes back down from the high he just gave me. "Holy shit."

"I know," Leo says, hungry eyes roving over me, taking in my body, my heavying chest, his fingers still inside of me, moving slower now. His thumb grazes over my clit, and my hips jerk, still sensitive.

"I've never...no one has ever..."

He pauses, then, staring at me.

"No one has ever?" I shake my head. "You've never been eaten out?" His eyes are wider now, a hint of something close to nervousness in them. I smile and shake my head.

"No, I've been eaten out, my god. I'm not *that* sheltered."

"Have you..." I roll my eyes.

"Yes, I've had sex. Not in a while, but... yes." He licks his lips, and despite just coming harder than ever before, I tighten around the fingers still inside of me. "I just meant no one has ever been able to make me..." My words trail off as the last of the orgasm fades away, and with it, the confidence I had moments before. His fingers are still inside of me, though they're no longer moving, as if he needs to be completely focused on this conversation. Note to self, keep all thoughts to myself until after his fingers leave me.

"Are you telling me no one has ever made you come, Willa?" The blush creeps down my neck and spreads to my chest, but I answer, because I know he wants me to.

"I've come from sex," I murmur, but then continue to explain. "But only if I was on top and basically...doing it myself." I don't know what to expect, but the wide smile that spreads across his still-wet lips is not it.

"Oh, I'm going to enjoy this," he says, voice rasping and low, before he dips his head down, five o'clock shadow scraping at my skin as he takes a nipple between his lips and sucks. His fingers continue to move, gently playing with me, grazing over my clit, circling and tweaking before sliding back inside. He fucks me slowly, languorously, and his lips move on my nipple, sucking and nipping until my breathing is labored again. He pulls back to blow cool air on the taut skin, and a breathy moan leaves my lips.

"Leo," I moan, my back arching, and my hips lifting. "I don't think I can—" I lick my lips and catch my breath. Leo's eyes move from my center to where his fingers are deep inside of me, to my stomach, to my breasts, before stopping at my face. "I don't think I can come again. We should just—" He shakes his head, cutting me off.

"I can do this all fucking day, baby. All day."

"That doesn't sound very fun for you."

"Are you kidding me? I've been daydreaming about this for years." I tighten around his fingers again, and my breathing goes just a bit heavier.

"For years?" I ask, eyes wide. His fingers move more slowly but go deeper as a smile spreads on his lips.

"Years, baby." His fingers start to speed, and a hand moves to my belly, his thumb swiping over my clit and making my hips buck. "Years, I've wondered what you would look like with my fingers deep inside of you. What you'd sound like coming on my tongue, on my fingers, on my cock. I wondered what you'd look like, writhing beneath me, panting my name. I have about a thousand fantasies of you, and I'm determined to make every one happen. Now," he says, fingers his sliding out and rubbing them flat against my clit. The stimulation is so sudden, so different, it pulls a groan from me. "Now you're going to come again. You're going to gush for me like the good girl you are, and then I'm going to fuck you hard and fast, watching your face as I fill you."

"Okay," I say, because really, what do you say to a proposal like that? He grins.

Wide.

And then his fingers slide back into me.

"That's my good girl," he murmurs, moving to his knees between my legs, his cock hard beneath his shorts. His fingers shift, fucking me deeper, pressing harder just above my G-spot, and I moan, loud and uncontrollably, hips shifting without reserve as it starts to build again, but this time it's different. It feels just as good as the last orgasm when it crept up, but it's different, bigger, deeper, in a way.

"Leo, I..." I pant, a strange, foreign feeling building in my belly. It's not unpleasant, but it sends a surge of panic through me at its newness. His fingers fuck me hard, curling to brush against my G-spot with each move.

"God, Willa. You should see yourself."

"Leo, I—"

"Just let it go," he says, nearly panting now, his muscles flexing with each thrust of his fingers, an erotic show just for me as he fucks me, pumping hard and fast. His lips are parted, his eyes locked between my legs as he breathes heavily, clearly very into what he's seeing.

"Leo—" That pressure is building, and despite knowing some foreign, intense pleasure will soon hit, panic fills me.

And it escalates when his fingers leave my body, his free hand pressing on my lower belly, and his fingers of the wet hand flattening and quickly rubbing over my swollen, needy clit. I shriek as it builds and starts to crest.

"You're good, honey, come on. Come for me." He's so insistent, so hot, his voice so needy, it sends me higher.

"Leo—" I try to warn once more, but then it happens.

I scream.

I scream as pleasure wracks my body, almost sobbing at the relief as liquid gushes from me, and I come, my body quaking, unintelligible sounds leaving my lips.

"Oh, my fucking god," he groans, his fingers still moving against my over-sensitized clit, and it sends another wave through me, more wet coming from me.

"Leo," I whine, my hips bucking, away or toward his hand, I can't even tell. I both want and need more, and can't handle another moment of his touch.

"I am so fucking hard watching you right now, Willa. Holy fuck. That was the most magnificent thing I've ever seen."

"I think I—"

"You squirted, honey. You made a big fucking mess, and it was fucking glorious," he says, then proceeds to lay wet kisses to my body: my stomach, my wet inner thighs, the dip between my hips and my thigh, my center, my clit.

Despite the now numerous intense orgasms that have wrung me dry, when Leo speaks, I moan. He gives me one last lick from the entrance to clit, groaning before he stands and slides his shorts off. His cock bobs free, and despite the dazed state I'm still in, I make sure to catalog my first glimpse at the glory of a naked Leo. His cock is hard and thick, his thighs muscled, hips narrow, and instantly, I want him inside of me,

"Now I'm going to fuck you," he says, and I nod eagerly, watching as he strokes his cock, standing between my legs. His fingers are soaked in my wet, and I watch as he coats his long, thick cock with it, another moan leaving my lips. "Do you like that?" I can't focus, my body still humming, my mind still lost, my eyes still locked on the visual of him stroking himself. "Do you like seeing yourself all over me?"

I nod, though still, my attention never leaves the sight before me. I burn it to the back of my eyes. Save it for a rainy day.

He moves then, kneeling between my legs on the bed, continuing to stroke himself.

A groan leaves his lips, and his hand moves between my legs, swiping there, and I catch my breath, but then he moves back to himself, stroking the new wet all over. "I could come like this," he says, voice low, sending pleasure ricocheting through me. "Looking at you, spread before me, bed soaked, your cum all over my cock."

"Do it," I whisper, then, without thinking, I slide my hand between my legs and touch my clit gently. It's so over-sensitized, so swollen, that I jolt when I do, sucking a sharp breath. A rough, deep groan leaves Leo's lips as I so, and it makes me moan.

"Maybe next time," he says, then shifts away. "Keep playing while I get a condom."

I don't know what happens.

I don't know what happens, because if there is one thing that has been hammered in my head, it's to use a condom.

If America's sweetheart can't get drunk, she surely can't get pregnant.

But I haven't had a hook-up in nearly two years, and I've been on birth control to control my acne since I was fifteen.

So I reach out and grab Leo's wrist, stopping his retreat.

"I'm on the pill," I whisper. His hand on his cock pauses, and his jaw slackens.

"What?"

"I'm on the pill. And I haven't been anyone in a long time. I've been tested since, and it's all clear. When he still doesn't speak, nerves enter. "But we don't have to. That was silly, I—"

"Are you telling me I can fuck you bare?"

"If you want?" I ask, unsure now. "But it's not—" My words stop when he moves again, this time shifting off the bed.

"Keep fucking playing with your clit while I slide into you," he says, shifting his body so he's over me, a hand between us as my knees cock out to give him room to slide in between my legs.

"I—" I start, unsure, but then he's between my legs, the thick head of him sliding up and down my pussy before stopping at my entrance, and two thick inches slide into me. My head falls back as he stretches me, and I groan, hips lifting to get another inch, but his hand moves from his cock to my hips, stopping me. "Leo," I mewl.

"Fucking years," he groans, holding me, moving to the inside of my thighs, spreading me wider. He pulls out an inch, then gives it back, and the stretch of him pins me right to the edge already. "Fucking years I've told myself I couldn't have this. Thought I never would, my dream woman." He groans, deep and visceral as he slides in all the way, filling me in a way I've never felt before. I moan his name. When I do, his hips buck a bit, sliding just a bit deeper.

"I need you," I whisper.

"And we have an eternity to get whatever we want, Willa.

Because I'm telling you right now, now that I've had you, I'm never fucking letting you go."

It should scare me.

It should terrify me.

There are so many reasons this shouldn't work.

So many reasons it can't work.

I'm his client.

I'm about to start dating someone for PR, a relationship that had a dozen different contracts that are seemingly unbreakable—something he set up.

If this goes bad, it would be so messy.

Even if it goes well, it will be so damn messy.

But for the first time, I don't think about the what-ifs.

I don't think about the people I might disappoint.

I don't think about what might happen in a week or a month or a year, because, just like Leo, I think I've known all along that this was always going to happen. And more importantly, this was always meant to work.

It just took a lot fucking longer than we anticipated.

He continues this torture, one inch in then one out, and I beg and plead, but when he bends, pressing his lips to mine and swallowing my moans, I stop complaining. I let him take over.

I let him fill me slowly, and it turns into something completely different in a moment. It turns into something sweet, something I've never had before in my life. His thrusts go deeper and longer and harder, and his breathing starts to match mine, going heavy, our groans and moans mingling around us. When he fills me completely, my fingers dig into his shoulders, and his fingers dig into my hips. When he starts to fuck me in earnest, his head drops to my neck, pressing soft kisses and whispering sweet words, telling me how long he's wanted this, how he's never letting me go, how he's never had anything so precious in his life.

And when I come, he follows right behind.

I've had a lot of beauty in my life.

I've been given some of the most gorgeous jewelry, dresses, and shoes.

I've gone to some of the most beautiful places on earth.

I've stood in front of tens of thousands of people, listening to them repeat the words of songs I wrote with nothing but love and joy in their voices.

But I've never had anything as beautiful as this moment.

And in that moment, I know I have it all.

TWENTY-TWO

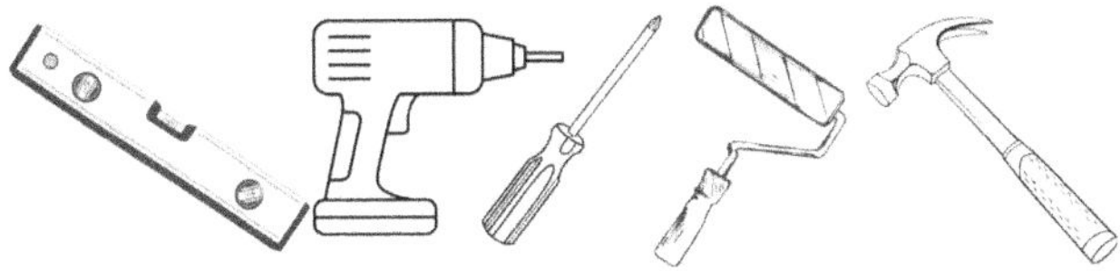

LEO

When I wake the next morning, Willa is curled into my side, and every muscle is relaxed as I take a deep breath, basking in this moment I've barely even let myself daydream about.

If I were being rational, I would do the opposite. I would probably be concerned. Actually, I would be full-out panicking. The repercussions of Willa and me being together go far and wide, affecting both our careers if this turns into a worst-case scenario. She's supposed to start dating someone in less than two months, a relationship I set up, and I'm strictly forbidden from hooking up with clients. My boss is looking for any excuse to get rid of and blacklist me, and if he found out about this, it would play directly into his hands.

But then, Willa murmurs a sleepy, "Morning," into my neck, and whatever remaining nerves melt away.

Because this. *This* is what I was always meant to have: Willa in my arms, her voice sleepy, her body slack from sleep and from being fucked the night before.

And most importantly, mine.

And because of that realization, I decide not to care about the *shoulds* or *woulds*. I don't care about the repercussions because, deep in my gut, I know we can overcome anything. The road before us is rocky, and I have no idea what the next year will look like, but the only thing I know for sure is that at the end of this, Willa is going to be mine.

"Morning, honey," I say, and she sighs, then burrows deeper into my chest.

"Love that," she says, something I feel more than hear, though I still catch her sleepy voice.

My hand lifts, brushing her hair back so I can see her soft face better.

"Love what?"

"You're calling me that. Honey."

I smile, instantly bringing it higher up on my list for Willa. She lets out a small yawn before continuing. "Everyone else says it in a bad way. Like I'm dumb or simply childish. You say it like you think I'm sweet."

"You are." We lie like that for a bit longer, and I watch her peaceful face, watch her shift in and out of sleep as I gently move my hand through her hair. After what could be two minutes or twenty, her eyes drift open, her warm brown eyes lock on me, and that sweetness she's talking about moves through me, slow and sticky, like warm honey.

I think in that moment, I fall in love with Willa Marie Stone. Or, at least, I stop denying I've always been in love with her.

"How do you feel?" I ask, biting back a confession of my undying love, knowing it's far too soon and neither of us is ready for *that* much honesty. We barely just got past the fact that we're both into one another, and that this inevitability is something that's been brewing between us for years.

She smiles.

"I found out that you haven't hated me all this time, and that you did, in fact, recognize me out of my glam all those years ago; you just needed to set a boundary. My dream man fucked me all night after years of wanting him. I feel pretty fucking good."

"Your dream man, huh?" I ask, smiling, and she gives me an eyeroll and a deadpan look. I have to fight back a laugh, instinctively knowing she would not appreciate it right now.

"Leo, I met you in a coffee shop, and by the time I left, I was daydreaming about white picket fences and wedding bells. You're hot, you're smart, and you're funny in a dry way that I find incredibly entertaining. You understand the complexities of my life and my career. You know how to work with your hands, in more than one way, I've learned, and I've never met anyone more determined to take care of me than you are. Yeah, I'd say you're my dream man."

Her words catch me off guard, both for their honesty and for the words themselves. I stare at her for long moments, taking in her early morning beauty and wondering how the fuck we finally managed to make it here. Her eyes roam my face, as well, trying to read me, and a small furrow forms between her brows as she does. I use my thumb to smooth it over before drifting my fingers down her cheek and dipping to press a soft kiss to the top of her head.

"I fucked up," I say, looking down at her. Her eyes go wide, and I see it, those big brown eyes that only a select few get to see, the golden flecks shining in the early morning light.

"You did?"

I nod, continuing to take her in, and shake my head with a heavy sigh.

"I did this all wrong," I say. Nerves take over her face, and I shift, moving her to her back beneath me and hovering over her, my forearms supporting me on either side of her face, caging her in. Then I dip a bit, pressing my lips to hers softly. She melts beneath me, a soft hand coming up to cup my cheek, the five o'clock shadow scratching at her palm, I'm sure. "You deserve it all. The perfect first date before I take you to bed. If I did this right, I would have wined and dined you properly."

Her nerves visibly melt away with my words, and a sated smile slides onto her face.

Willa deserves the whole nine, the big, well-planned date, a huge bouquet of flowers when I meet her at the door, a fancy dinner, an activity, and then a sweet kiss at the door.

"Well, you definitely dined," she says, and I let out a laugh, press my lips to hers again, then shake my head.

"Mmm, I did," I mumble against her neck, smiling when a shiver moves through her before I pull my head back. "I just wish I had given you everything you deserve." She opens her mouth, probably to argue, to convince me she doesn't need what I want her to have, to say something along those lines, but I speak before she can. "Tomorrow night." Ideas are already pinging around in my mind.

"Tomorrow?"

"You and I, we're going out. A proper date."

"Really?" I smile, loving that look on her face, and I nod. Her white teeth sink into her full lower lip. "I don't think I've actually ever done that."

"Gone on a date?" I ask teasingly. "I know for a fact that's not true."

I regret the words instantly when an embarrassed blush burns on her cheeks.

"I mean like, a proper date. A normal date." I smile softly at her.

"Well, then I'm honored I get to be the first one to give that to you."

"You're giving me a lot of firsts lately, Leo."

"I don't plan to stop anytime soon." Her face changes, almost unconsciously, and I hesitate. "What?"

"What exactly..." She licks her lips. "What is this now?" I roll us again until I'm on my back, her body lying on top of mine, chest to chest, and slowly, I stroke her back, soft and gentle.

"This is me and you finally doing what we were supposed to eight years ago."

"By fucking?" she asks, her voice frail, trying to hide her nervousness with a joke. I don't let her have that; instead shaking my head.

"By you becoming mine and me becoming yours."

"So what are you, then? My boyfriend?"

"I don't care what you call me, so long as when I try to take care of you, you don't argue, and when you start to get under my skin, I get to throw you over my shoulder and take you to bed until you see my way. So long as you sleep in my shirt every night, and I give you all of the firsts you want." As promised, she took my shirt off after the first round and wore it while I made us a quick dinner of grilled cheese sandwiches and tomato soup, then took her back to bed and continued making up for lost time.

"I'm whatever you want to call me, honey, so long as, at the end of the day, you call me yours."

My hand slips up that same shirt, skimming over soft skin and feeling her stomach hollow as she sucks in a breath.

Yeah, lots of benefits to Willa sleeping in my bed.

"But when you come, I want you to call me Leo," I murmur, cupping her breast, a thumb brushing over her nipple.

"Leo," she whispers, voice breathy and needy.

"Yeah, just like that," I groan, pressing my hips into hers and running my tongue over her neck.

An hour later, Willa's getting ready for the day and apparently responding to a dozen texts from girls. Apparently, yesterday Hallie noticed Willa's car hadn't come back last night and grew worried. That is, until she sent Jesse over to my place, and he reported that her car was still there. It seems that the nosy woman has put two and two together and is trying to get the full details from her. She explained it with a deep blush, but the smile on her lips told me that, while she was a bit embarrassed to be called out, she is enjoying this new form of friendship.

While she does that, I go into the kitchen to make us breakfast, starting with the coffee, then move to the pantry. There's nothing in there, since I haven't gone to the grocery store in a bit—too busy with Willa and getting work done in the small pockets of time I steal while I'm not working on the house. I've been doing a lot of takeout and cereal, but I used the last of the latter yesterday, and with last night's activities, I didn't make it to the store after Willa left, as I had planned.

With a sigh, I move to the fridge, hoping there's something in there, but find it mostly empty, other than the milk and half-and-half that I bought last week on a whim, knowing Willa likes it in her coffee.

It seems I've been a goner longer than I was willing to admit.

But a light shines when I open the freezer, and I grab a familiar blue box with a smile before placing two pastries into the toaster. I'm plating our five-star luxury breakfast when she steps out in one of my tees, the hem tucked into the now-dry shorts she wore yesterday. Her hair is in a mess on top of her head, and there's a nervous look on her face, but she's never looked more beautiful to me.

"I borrowed your toothbrush," she murmurs, breaking the silence and stepping further into the kitchen. "I hope you don't mind."

"My mouth was between your legs last night. I think I'm okay with sharing a toothbrush." A blush burns, but I keep going. "I'll get you one for here tomorrow. When you come here tonight, bring some things to keep here for the days you don't feel like going home after working on the house." The nervousness or hesitation leaves her face instantly.

"Really?" I move then, stepping into her space and pulling her into mine before pressing a soft kiss to her lips.

"Let me make this very, very clear, Willa. Last night changed everything for me. I plan on recreating it many, many times, from making you moan out my name to sleeping wrapped around you. So yeah, I want you to keep your things here."

She smiles then, the full one I love most of all.

"Okay, good," she whispers then. Two words, so simple, so insignificant, and yet they mean everything to me. After a moment, she glances over my shoulder to the counter where the plates still sit. "What's that?" I grin, remembering my find, then step away and toward the counter to grab both plates. She follows me as I move to the kitchen table, where I set them down at two catty-corner seats.

"The greatest luxury ever to grace the frozen foods aisle," I say, then return to the counter where our coffees are, hers made with far too much cream and sugar.

"Oh?" she asks with a laugh, accepting the cup I offer her as we both sit down.

"It's a toaster strudel. Still never had one?"

There's a moment where she's still, then she looks down at the little rectangle on her plate, and she bites her lip before looking up at me, with awe on her face.

"You really remember that?"

Clearly, she still doesn't understand.

"I remember every single moment I've ever spent with you, Willa, but I definitely remember the first time I met you." She stares at me, awe written across her face, before she shakes her head and looks at the plate again.

"Still haven't had one. This will be another first," she whispers, and I sit down.

"I told you, I'm going to give you all of the ones you want, honey." Her face goes soft, but she doesn't say anything else, instead picking up the pastry before her and taking a small bite. I watch with anticipation, strangely hoping she enjoys it.

"Okay, I've definitely been missing out."

I grin, then sit back and enjoy her company. We sit for a few minutes, sipping our coffee. I can tell she's itching to ask something, and though I don't know exactly what, I do know there is very little unknown in Willa's life, and that what small amount there is always makes her uneasy.

She confirms my thoughts when she finally breaks the silence. "So...how does this work?"

"Work?" I ask, knowing what she's asking, but wanting her to say it.

"You and me. I mean...we're...."

"We're together, Willa."

That makes her smile, a look she hides with another small bite and some thoughtful chewing.

"Okay, we're together. But I'm assuming no one can know?" The decision weighs heavily on me, something I mulled over and over in my mind while she was getting ready, but each time I came to the same conclusion.

"No one in our professional life can know," I agree. At first, I thought of telling her we could tell anyone we wholeheartedly trusted, since I'm sure Riggins and the rest of the Atlas Oaks guys will get a kick out of this finally happening, and I know they would never tell a soul if I asked them not to. Still, I wasn't sure where Jackie would fall on that spectrum, and I am not ready to have that talk with Willa yet, the talk where I admit that I don't trust her manager, or her intentions with Willa. So, for now, I keep things simple. "At least, not for a while."

"What about outside of our professional life, like here in Holly Ridge? The girls—"

God, I love that. I love that she has this now, a group of women she wants to share things with, because looking back, I know she's never had that. It's also very telling that she doesn't instantly think of Jackie when she thinks of someone to confide something in.

"I'll talk with the guys; you talk with the girls. We tell them what we are to each other. We keep PDA low when out and about, but I think we should be okay here." She scrunches her nose when I say minimal PDA, and I smile. "Not non-existent PDA, especially where we're comfortable, like the Mill, but in places we don't know everybody, like, say, the home improvement store, I won't be pinning you to a shelf and making out with you."

"Okay," she agrees. "That makes sense." I watch as she takes another bite, chewing for a moment before a thought rises in her mind and makes her face sour. My stomach drops as I wait for her next argument.

"My relationship with Chris starts in September," she reminds me gently, as if I wasn't the main contact for settling that up. I reach over and push her hair back, forcing her to look at me instead of her nearly empty plate.

"I know."

"I can't...I can't bail on it. Contracts have been signed, and too many people are involved. If we canceled, it would cause way too many headaches, and Jackie would lose her mind if we went off the pre-determined plan."

I nod, knowing this as well.

I mulled over this this morning before she woke up, and I fell asleep with it on my mind.

Contemplating what would happen if, now that Willa and I were making a go of it, despite her current career expectations and responsibilities. I laid out a dozen different options, and each time, I came up with the same answer: I will never get in the way of her career.

"Absolutely. If you back out at this point, there would be too high a chance of rumors flying or the truth slipping out, ruining a decade of brand building." I don't miss the slight twinge of irritation that moves across her face with those words, but it's gone almost as quick as I see it. "The media is forgiving with you, but if everyone finds out all of your relationships have been fake to trick people into becoming invested in you, it would be an uphill battle."

She nods, a hint of relief on her face as she realizes I'm not going to fight her on that.

I wonder for a moment if there have been others over the years who couldn't see past her obligations, her drive, her career, but the thought of any other man with Willa sours my stomach, so I brush it off as quickly as it comes.

"I'm going to have to date Chris for six months," she says. I reach out when I notice her nervousness, grabbing her hand and twining my fingers with hers. For a single, unhinged moment, my eyes linger on her ring finger, always empty, the one line she's always held. Once, two years ago, Jackie suggested a fake marriage or engagement, but Willa instantly shot that down, one of the only times I've seen her say no to something Jackie suggested.

"If I ever get married one day," she said, her voice strong, *"It will be for real. I'll never fake that, Jackie."* Jackie was unhappy, but she must have seen the fire in her eyes that I spotted, and never mentioned it again. But I never forgot the way she said *if I ever* instead of *I will never.*

"I know," I say. "And during that time, we'll have to be even more careful, because there's a pretty solid cheating clause in those contracts. I'd say that unless you're in Holly Ridge, there's absolutely no PDA, even if it will certainly kill me to be in the same room as you and not even touch you, but we can figure that out when the time comes."

Her brows furrow.

"So we're going to...stay together?"

My head jerks back in confusion.

"What?"

"I can't...." Her cheeks flare with a blush. "I can't expect you to just hold tight for me for six months, Leo. Longer, once we calculate a rational breakup time. I—"

"Six months in the grand scheme of a lifetime with you doesn't really matter to me, honey," I say, the words spilling without even thinking, but once they leave my lips, I don't have any regret, even if her eyes go wide with surprise.

"I can't tell the future, but I know that I've spent eight years regretting not taking that jump with you. Eight years regretting suggesting you fake date Riggins, which in turn meant I spent eight years watching you be with men who didn't deserve to breathe the same air as you, much less date you. Much less *kiss* you. It's only been one night, but for me, it's been eight years and then two weeks of being tempted by you, of realizing it's always been you, of realizing you've always been perfect for me. I work a lot. That's been an issue for women in the past, but I like knowing you won't hold it against me, just as I will never hold it against you. I understand it's not just a job for you: it's who you are, to your core. I would never try to tell you how to navigate that." I reach up with both hands, combing her hair back and holding her face in my hands before bending to press my lips to her knuckles. "Plus, it's not just your work getting in the way; my contract with Perfect Image has about a year more on it."

"Okay…" she says, hesitantly.

"It's not just your relationship with Chris; we're going to have to wait out. It's my contract." Her brows furrow deeper, but she waits for me to explain. "My contract with Perfect Image has a little over a year left on it. There's a non-fraternization clause: I can't be with anyone who is my client, or it's grounds for termination."

"So you'd be leaving Perfect Image because of me?" she asks, and I can hear the unwarranted guilt in her words, so quickly I shake my head and clarify.

"No. I've been planning to leave once my contract is up for a while. I want to start my own small boutique firm." She widens her eyes with surprise. "I'm not happy there. I hate working with Jefferson, and our styles are far too different." She nods, probably already knowing that herself. "I'd leave now, but if I quit or I'm fired with merit, I can't represent any of my current clients until their term expires, which would mean they all—Atlas Oaks, Harper, and even you—would have to work with Jefferson or someone else until that period expires, and not for nothing, everyone in this industry is a piece of shit."

She nods, ideas and thoughts moving through her mind before finally nodding.

"Okay," she finally says, some decision made up already. "Okay, so a year? A year and then we can be open?"

I nod, never mind what she's going to think, but she smiles. "I can handle a year of being secret if it means at the end, I get you."

And that time, when I kiss her, it ends with her moaning my name as I seat her on the edge of the kitchen counter and show her just how grateful I am we're on the same page.

TWENTY-THREE

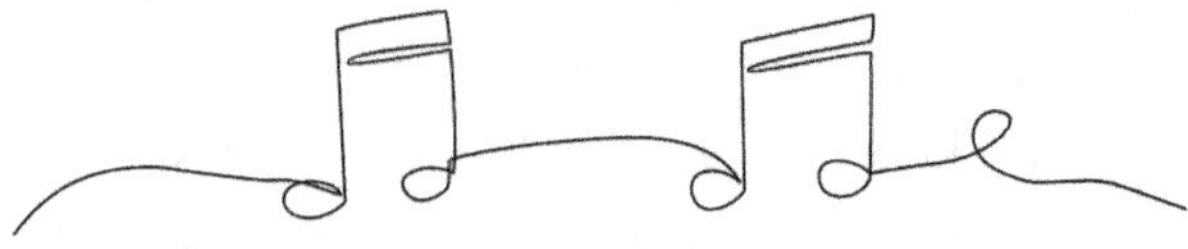

WILLA

The second—well, third, I suppose—morning I wake up in Leo's bed, I'm not awoken by the sun creeping in or an alarm or even the feeling of Leo's eyes as he watches me sleep, like the day before.

No, I'm awoken by a banging outside.

I jolt upright, my mind racing to catch up, to wake up and understand what is happening. Looking around the room, I'm confused for a moment. Although I've woken up in this room before, it's still unfamiliar, and it takes me a moment to figure out what's happening with the added stress of the loud noises outside.

Until a rough hand slides over my skin to my hip, squeezing me there, gently.

My eyes drift down to see a sleepy, rumpled Leo beside me. Like this, he looks five years younger, without the pressure or stress of work, his hair a mess, his eyes squinting up at me, and with the look, the past two days come back to me.

I'm in Leo's bed because I'm now *Leo's*.

I smile down at him as he looks up at me, but when the sound comes again, his brow furrows with a mix of irritation and confusion. "What the hell is that?" he asks. My attention moves back to the sound, which I now realize is someone knocking on Leo's front door. Nerves flood my system, worry, and panic so strong, nerves I haven't felt since I stepped foot into Holly Ridge. Nerves that my real life has found me here in my fairytale one.

"Someone's at your door, I think."

"My door?" he asks, sitting up next to me and turning towards the sound. The knocking comes again, more insistent this time. Leo bends, pressing a soft kiss to my bare shoulder, and a shiver rolls through me. Despite the chaos infiltrating our peaceful morning, he gives me a wicked smile. "You stay here, I'll go figure it out. It's probably a telemarketer." I don't necessarily buy that, but I nod all the same, watching as he shifts out of bed, then slides on a pair of loose shorts before padding towards the door. "Don't leave this bed, I'll be right back." There's a glint in his eye, and I can't help but smile, shaking my head. Once he's gone, I flop back onto the bed and smile at the ceiling, this new feeling bursting from my chest.

A thought enters my mind, one about feeling sunshine inside and outside after a perfect lazy night, and that feeling grows inside me as I realize it's a lyric. I reach for my phone to get it down, but before I touch my fingers to it, I hear a familiar voice.

"Out of the way, pretty boy, we have work to do." I sit up quickly, looking towards the door, my brows coming together is confusion, because I think I *know* that voice, but there's no reason for it to be in Leo's house.

"What the hell?" Leo asks, but his voice is more annoyed than concerned.

"We've been summoned," another familiar voice says.

"Hey, Leo, how's it going?" a third voice asks, soft and lilting, and with it, I whip the blankets back, stumbling to the ground and reaching around on the ground for something—anything—to throw on. I find my panties and Leo's shirt, sliding both on just in time.

"You decent?" Nat asks, the door to Leo's bedroom creaking open before the brunette walks in without even bothering to wait for my answer.

"What is happening?" I ask, confused, looking around the room for my shorts. When I spot them, I slide them on, hoping I don't show Nat my ass, but pretty sure she doesn't care one way or another.

"An intervention," Nat says.

"I tried to stop her!" Wren calls, though I can't see her.

"I didn't!" Hallie calls, but she pokes her head in through the door. "Oh, she'd been fucked *good*." Then she steps in further, the door hitting the doorstop loudly. "Please tell me he's good in bed. It would be criminal for that man to look like that and be bad in bed."

"I—"

"You don't have to answer any of her questions," Wren says, a smile on her lips as she follows Hallie inside and, even better, a coffee in her hand.

I sigh with appreciation as she hands it to me, and when I check the side, I realize it's an iced latte from the cafe in town.

Leo smiles at me, and I see he has his own coffee in his hand, his own name on the side.

So very Wren.

"Yes, you do, but we can wait until we're not in the presence of the man in question," Hallie says, directing her beaming grin to Leo.

He lifts a shoulder, unfazed, and it becomes glaringly clear he will not be jumping in to protect me on this topic.

"What are you guys doing here?" I ask after I take a long, fortifying sip of my coffee.

"Girl's day," Nat says, and my eyes move to Leo. He simply continues to smile, the asshole.

"I have plans today," I murmur, remembering my date with Leo tonight.

"You have a date *tonight*. We're here to help you get ready," Hallie says with a knowing grin.

"What?"

"Leo told me it's at three."

I blink at her, then look to Leo, who suddenly is looking

anywhere but at me. Hallie continues to explain. "You texted us to tell you you weren't murdered by a serial killer—"

My eyes widen, and Wren steps in.

"No one thought you were murdered by a serial killer; Hallie just has an overactive imagination."

Hallie glares at her best friend and soon-to-be sister-in-law before continuing.

"And then told us you *finally* got with Leo. So *I* texted him on the side to ask when he would be taking you out on a date and making an honest woman out of you, and what do you know, he already had plans. So I called up the gang, and here we are, ready to make your first date perfect."

I blink, first at Hallie, then at Nat, then at Wren, and finally, at Leo.

"Did you know he planned a whole date for you two? *By himself?* Dinner, an activity, other fun stuff I'm not allowed to talk about. All by himself! I called to ask if he needed help, and he was all, *no thanks, I've got it covered,*" Nat says, looking both baffled and put off by this news.

"Uh," I start, both intrigued by this potentially Nat-approved date and trying to figure out when he had time to plan it *and* when he could have possibly texted the girls about it, but Wren cuts in, eyes shifting between her friends and Leo.

"Nat, I don't think that's for you to share just yet."

Leo doesn't look annoyed, though; he's leaning in the doorway, smiling at the chaos in his bedroom.

"Fine, I can't tell you that part, but I *can* tell you that *then* he told me to get the girls together and come here to help you get ready for your date, that you'd like that."

My heart skips a beat, and not for the first time, I'm struck with the thought that he gets it. He gets it, and more importantly, he gets *me*. He gets the small moments of normalcy I've missed out on, and he told me he wanted me to have it all.

And here he is, once again, giving it all to me.

"I don't think I said to come at nine a.m., though," he says, but Nat ignores that, instead, continuing to ramble on.

"And really, Willa, I hope you know just how much you hit the jackpot with this one. He knows how to fuck, *and* he's a gentleman? May this kind of love find me one day," she says, clasping her hands together and lifting them up in a plea to the heavens.

"Nat!" I say, giving her wide eyes, but she just grins at me. "You don't even *know* if he knows how to...you know."

Nat gives me a deadpan look, then turns to gesture at Leo, still leaning in the doorway, arms crossed on his chest like he's the hot male lead in a romcom movie poster.

"Willa, look at him. He knows how to fuck."

Hallie shrugs as if she can't disagree, and even Wren remains silent at that. I decide it's not a topic worth arguing, so instead, I turn back to Leo to argue with him.

"I don't need to go on any kind of fancy date, Leo."

"I know that," he says. "I'm going to do it anyway."

"Leo," I say. "I don't want you going out of your way, I—"

"Jesus, Willa, I know you're like a bajillionaire, but if a man offers to take you on a fancy date, you just nod and say *thank you, daddy*," Nat says.

"Nat!" I say, snapping towards her, embarrassment burning on my face.

"For the record, I am *not* into the daddy thing," Leo says.

"Please, do tell what you *are* into," Nat says, grinning.

"Do not dare," I say without thinking, giving Leo a stern look, and Nat and Hallie start laughing instantly. That's when Leo pushes off the wall and steps towards me.

"Oh, I cannot *wait* to get all the details of *that*," Hallie says.

"And on that note, I'm going to head out. I'm gonna go get ready to head out in the other room and then run a few errands before tonight."

"Errands?" I ask, and he smiles wider before pulling me into his arms.

"Yes. Now have fun with your girls, honey."

I don't know if it's the thought of having girls and the joy that brings me, or the soft way he says *honey*, or maybe the way he dips his head in front of a room full of women to press his lips to mine, but I don't argue any longer. Instead, I kiss him back until he ends it, it's far too soon.

"Tonight," he says against my lips, then steps away, before waving to the room at large.

"Later, girls."

There's a chorus of *Bye Leo!s* before he leaves the room. After a moment, I hear the bathroom door click behind him, then three sets of eyes land on me. I groan, needing way more caffeine to handle what I already know will be the third degree that, at the very least, Hallie and Nat are going to subject me to.

"Can I shower first at least?" I ask, and Nat grins.

"Yes, but at your place. I don't trust that one letting you shower alone," she says, tipping her head towards where Leo went.

"Natalie!" Wren says, eyes wide. "My goodness, give the girl a break!"

"It's fine, I haven't brought my shower stuff here yet," I say, with a sigh, moving to where my bag is in the corner. Last night we went to my place to grab some essentials, but I didn't bring everything I would need, realizing I should probably get doubles so I wouldn't have to lug things back and forth. Leo agreed, and instead of writing that night, I sat at my laptop and placed an order for delivery to his house, which should arrive tomorrow afternoon.

"Yet," Hallie says with a knowing smile, but I just roll my eyes before hefting my bag over my shoulder and making my way towards the front door.

⚜ ⚜ ⚜ ⚜

An hour later, we're at my house on Three Kings property, and I'm sitting on my bed after getting ready for the day while Nat goes through my closet. They hung out nearby while I showered and dressed, chatting the entire time, and even though it should feel a bit intrusive, I strangely find it doesn't at all. During this time, I've filled the girls in on most of the important details, though it took a while to explain the coffee shop mess from years ago, the drama with Leo's boss, and why we have to keep things low-key until my next relationship and Leo's contract are up. I swore the girls to utter secrecy until we were ready to announce it to the world, and I didn't even second-guess that decision. Normally, with something like this, I would make people sign an NDA, but somehow, just getting a couple of pinky swears from women I genuinely trust felt more binding than any contract ever has.

"So, we're having a full girls' day today before your date. We're going to the salon to get your hair done–lucky you, Nat's schedule is clear for the day because she hates working on Sundays. Then nails," Hallie explains.

"We need to pick out your outfit now so we know what color to paint them," Wren says with a gentle smile.

"This is your casual stuff. Where's your going out stuff?" she asks, looking over her shoulder at me. I bite my lip, then stand. She steps aside as I move hangers over until the outfits I brought with me are revealed. I haven't touched any of them in weeks, realizing pretty quickly that I didn't need much more than a couple of shorts, a tee or two, and mostly, comfortable workout clothes. It's strange seeing the things I brought, knowing the expensive labels are sought after, but suddenly hating them and the boring, colorless version of me they represent.

"Do you have anything that isn't...neutral?" she asks.

"I'm sorry?"

"All of your clothes are neutrals. Like, browns, blacks, and beiges. And don't get me wrong, they all look absolutely killer on you, I'm sure." She pulls out a tan mini dress, then holds it up to herself. "This is hot, for sure. But it's still sad girl beige."

"It's not sad girl beige, it's…cool girl beige," I say, suddenly feeling self-conscious.

"Says who?" Nat says, crinkling her nose.

"Uh, my stylist? The media? The world?"

"Well, the world is a sad, colorless place these days, so that tracks," Hallie says, and Wren nods in agreement.

"They don't seem very…you," Wren says. "They're all very nice, they're just…"

"They're boring," Hallie says, bluntly.

"And you're not boring," Nat says with a shrug of her shoulder. "Unless that's what you like, of course."

"I…I don't think so," I say with a cringe. I'd noticed that, of course, and have been wearing the colorful workout clothes I bought on rotation, but I figured it was that they were the better choice for doing work around Leo's house. But maybe I was really just happy that they felt more… me.

"I just don't think it *fits* you, you know? I mean, your stylist is great on your tour stuff—" Nat starts, but I shake my head.

"That's Harper," I correct quickly. "Tour costumes and red carpets are all Harper Holden. She designs and custom-makes everything for them for me. I have a different stylist for my streetwear and interview looks."

"Well, that explains that. Harper has good taste. Your stylist does not," Nat says, retreating from the closet with a disappointed sigh.

"Nat!" Wren chides.

"Oh, come on, it's true! None of this says Willa Stone! It says… basic boring bitch. It says someone who wants to fit in and follow trends, not set them."

"I don't necessarily *want* to set trends," I say, biting my lips. "I have more than enough eyes on me at all times." Nat gives me a deadpan look, as if she's over me.

"Yeah, well, unfortunately, you do it regardless. But right now, you're setting *boring* trends." She has a point, I suppose. "You know, you should spend your time here experimenting."

"I think she's going to get plenty of experimentation time with Leo," Hallie says, and once again, Wren groans. I just laugh, somehow becoming numb to this strange behavior.

"I mean with clothes, but yes, absolutely with Leo. We can circle back to that later today and make a list of everything to try. I'm sure he has a lot to teach a woman." She fans at her face, and Wren grabs a pillow, tossing it at her with a laugh.

"Stay focused, Nat. Clothes. What is she going to wear on her date tonight?" Wren asks, laughing. Nat nods, then pinches at her face as if trying to center herself.

I laugh, shaking my head, deeply enjoying my time with these unhinged women. "I'm sorry my options are limited. I didn't exactly expect, well, any of this."

"Do you think we have enough time to go shopping after the salon?" Hallie asks Nat, whose eyes light up. "It's only a block from the salon."

"Oh, definitely," she says. "We can get her something there. They should be open now, and if we're out of there by, say, 10:30, we should be golden."

I look from Nat, contemplating her adjusted timeline, to the admittedly boring closet behind her, and speak without thinking.

"I think...I think I need a new wardrobe," I say. "Do you think we have time to get a few extra things?" Silence lingers before Nat speaks.

"Oh my god, I think I just came," Nat says, and I look to her, part concerned, part entertained.

"Ignore her. She's gross," Hallie says.

"And has a shopping addiction," Wren adds.

Nat ignores them, moving to me and falling to her knees before me.

"Willa Stone, goddess of pop music, queen of tabloids, please, please, please let me help you pick out your new wardrobe. Summer stuff that you can wear around town. Casual things. Colors! Patterns!"

She's lighting up with each addition, and I watch in fascination, giggling a bit.

"Put her out of her misery," Hallie murmurs. "She won't stop until she passes out."

"Oh, uh, well, yeah," I say with a laugh. "That would actually be so great—" I can't finish my sentence because Nat is standing, pulling me up and into her, and hugging me tight.

"Oh my god, this is so exciting! Next week. I'm off on Wednesday?" she says, pulling back to look at me. "There are a few cute boutiques in town, and we can do some online shopping if you have a store you love."

I shrug, and she finally releases me, stepping back,

"Honestly, I don't. I haven't gone shopping in a long time."

Nat's eyes close, and she takes in a deep breath.

"I think you broke her," Wren whispers. "Okay, so shopping first, quick, and then next week on my next day off, we'll do some real damage." Nat ignores her, grabbing a strand of my hair. "Then we'll head right to the salon to do your hair."

"Do my hair?"

"I mean, I can do the norm, wash, blow out, *or* we could touch up your roots," she says, a bit hopeful. I don't have to look at my hair to know that my darker blonde roots are showing, and I know that in a week or two, they'll start to drive me crazy. I'm creeping up on my normally needed eight-week update.

The mere idea of a random small-town hair stylist doing my hair would probably put Jackie into a heart attack, but I trust Nat more than most stylists I've worked with and have seen her work enough to know she's amazing at what she does.

I picture how I looked in the mirror earlier and remember thinking that my brown eyes clash with the bright shade of blonde my hair is now. With the blue contacts, it works. I look icy, unapproachable, too cool for everyone in the room, but here in Holly Ridge, I don't want to be the fake, expensive version of myself. Touching the ends of my hair, I shrug.

"We can go a bit darker? Closer to what you think my natural color would be?" Silence fills the room for a moment before I look up at Nat and see her eyes are wide with excitement.

"Better cover your ears," Hallie mutters.

"Oh. My. God," Nat says, then starts jumping up and down. "Oh, my GOD! Yes! Yes, yes, yes. I didn't want to pressure you because that's rude—"

"Oh, now you're worried about manners," Hallie murmurs with a smile, fully entertained.

"But this color washes you out so much. This is going to be so fun! Ah!" I blink a few times, her excited shrieks causing me to flinch.

"Yeah, definitely broke her," Wren says with a smile, but Nat is already grabbing my things, snagging a pair of white tennis sneakers from my closet and some socks before tossing them into a bag.

"Come on. We have *so* much to do," she says, then heads out the door, leaving the rest of us no other option but to follow.

TWENTY-FOUR

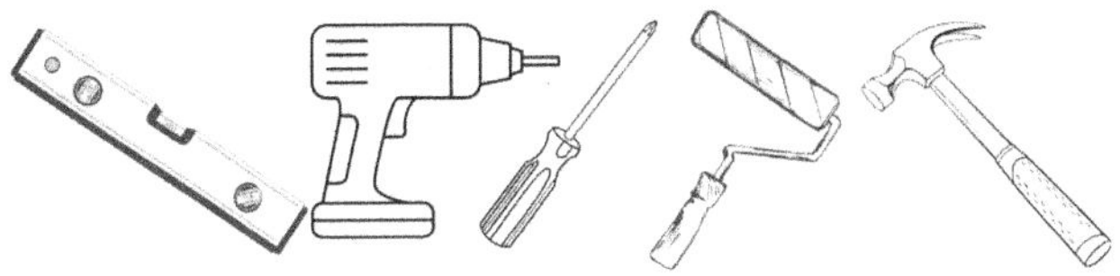

LEO

The text comes through hours later, at 2:45, and relief moves through me. I don't regret asking Hallie to come with the girls to help Willa get ready for our date, since I know that she hasn't had much of that in her life. When she smiled at me when she realized why they were there, I realized that I had made the right choice, even if I secretly wanted to keep her to myself for just a bit longer.

That being said, I'm more than happy that it's time to get her and get on our way. Without a pause, I step outside and into my car, then make the drive down my driveway and up Willa's. The whole time I'm driving, I wonder just how long this will stick—us having separate places—before I can convince her to just move into my house with me.

The thought is fleeting, though, as I park out front and walk up to the front door and knock. To my surprise, butterflies are in my chest, something I've never felt before a night out with a woman. But this isn't just any woman I'm taking out. This is Willa.

Wren opens the door with a kind smile on her lips. "Leo's here!" she calls over her shoulder, then opens the door fully and gestures for me to step in. As the door closes behind me, I can vaguely hear a quiet argument behind the bedroom door.

"I don't need to be presented, Hallie. It's just Leo," Willa mutters. I smile, and Wren returns it, rolling her eyes and shaking her head.

"She'll learn," Wren says. "It's always easier to just let them do their thing than it is to argue with them." I smile and shake my head, but don't argue. I can see how that would be the case, for sure.

"Can you just let me have this?" Hallie says, then opens the door to Willa's bedroom and pokes her head out, giving me a grin. "He looks hot."

"Oh my god," Willa whines. "Can you guys be normal?"

"No. Now come on, let's go!" Nat says, then pushes Hallie out of the room. She tries to close the door behind her, but Willa's hand moves out, a fire-red nail polish on her fingers. I stare at them, blinking and trying to remember if she's ever worn anything but nude polish as long as I've known her.

"You guys are being ridiculous. I have a date to go on!"

"I know; we've spent the whole day preparing you," Nat says, but steps aside so Willa can step out of the bedroom, and all thoughts of her nails leave my mind.

I get, then, why she wanted to present her...Nat completed a full transformation. Not in a bad way, and not in an unrecognizable way, but it's almost as if the shield is not just temporarily lowered, as I've seen more and more over the weeks, but it's gone altogether.

Her hair is down in loose curls, with bright makeup applied with a light hand on her face, a pretty pink blush across her cheeks and nose. And her hair isn't just down: it's changed. Instead of her icy blonde locks that Jackie insists fit the brand, it's a softer, slightly deeper shade of blonde that, in an instant, I can see suits her so much better. It's a few inches shorter, though her hair was so long before that it's still long, the ends brushing past her breasts.

She's wearing a reddish-orange dress that skims her knees, held up by thin straps at the shoulders, and a pair of white sneakers. I've never seen her in the color, but it looks absolutely perfect on her.

She looks nothing like Willa Stone, the pop star, but everything like *my Willa*.

"Wow," I whisper, taking her in.

"Oh, we did well," Nat murmurs, a smile in her voice, but I don't break my gaze from Willa as I continue to take in every beautiful inch of her.

"Hell yeah," Hallie says.

"Yeah," Wren murmurs, a hopeless romantic sigh in her voice.

"Do I look okay?" Willa asks nervously, white teeth biting into a full, pink bottom lip, and I finally step forward, three long strides until I'm in her space and pulling her into me.

"You've never looked more gorgeous," I whisper.

I watch her lips part before a million arguments cross her face. She wants to tell me that I've seen her in designer gowns, one-of-a-kind masterpieces made only for her, winning awards and playing arenas for tens of thousands of people, but I stop her before she can speak her objections aloud. "Never, Willa."

"Wow," Nat whispers, a quiet awe I don't think she experiences often in her tone.

"Well, we'll just be leaving," Wren says, pulling my attention from Willa for a moment. She gives her friends a pointed look, then tips her head to the side before grabbing Hallie's arm.

"Right. But I want an update tomorrow!" Hallie says, waving at us as she moves out the door.

"And we're going shopping next week! I don't care if you two are fucking like bunnies, take a minute away. Your vagina will need a break!" Nat calls, narrowing her eyes as she walks backward.

"Dear god, Nat," Wren murmurs.

Willa laughs, shaking her head, and the prettiest blush burns over her cheeks. "Bye, guys!"

"Use protection!" Hallie yells.

"Don't do anything I wouldn't do!" Nat calls, and then the door slams behind them.

I turn back to my girl. She still has a soft, happy smile on her lips. Finally, I dip my head and press my lips to hers, soft and sweet, forcing myself to leave it at that, knowing we have plans for the evening. She melts into my hold, and I smile into the kiss before breaking it.

"You good?" I ask. "If they were too much—"

"No, no. I'm good. They're intense, but they're good people. They feel... genuine, which I haven't had much of in my life." I know exactly what she means, because it seems like everyone in Holly Ridge is that way.

"Ready to go?" Her eyes are a bit dazed, but her pink lips tip, and she nods.

"Yeah."

She grabs an overnight bag with a grin, and I lead her out the door and to my car.

Thirty minutes later, we're pulling up to a large property. She squints at the sign.

"A farm?" she asks, unsure.

"It's a farm-to-table restaurant," I say, trying not to reveal too much as I move into a parking spot in the empty gravel parking lot before parking the car and turning it off. "Stay."

She smiles, and I know it's a shot in the dark of whether or not she'll listen, but when I get to the passenger side, she's still waiting patiently. I put out a hand to her, and she takes it, letting me help her out of the car. I give her one quick press of my lips to hers, unable not to, before twining my fingers with hers and moving to the small building to the left I was told to go to.

"What are we doing here?" she asks, walking at my side, eyes scanning the area, excitement clear in her words.

I grin as we approach the building, the sign becoming clear. She squeals, reading *Peach picking—Please check in here!* on a small building, but I answer regardless.

"We're going peach picking, then going to look at some animals, then we're having dinner at the restaurant."

"Peach picking?" she asks, looking up at me, eyes wide and hopeful. "We're going peach picking?"

"You've never been, right?" I ask, as if I haven't had her drunken rant from weeks ago playing in a loop on my mind since that night, reminding me of all the things she's never done. As if I haven't been slowly categorizing any other additional mentions in passing. There's a sweet older woman at the stand who smiles at Willa and me before handing us a basket and a map to show us which orchards are ripe before Willa and I set off. She holds the basket, I hold the small stepstool we were given, and Willa nearly gallops through the fields, excitedly pointing out cute signs or different fruits.

"We should come in the fall for apples!" she says, pointing to a sign for the fruit. I smile and nod, instantly trying to think of how to make that happen, knowing that the fall will be much busier than the summer, but determined to do it regardless.

Eventually, we find the peach trees, and Willa sets the basket down, grabs a low-hanging fruit, and gently places it in the bin. I set the stool down, unfolding it and locking it in place beneath the tree. She grins at me before standing on the top step. Her legs are smooth and at eye level, and I can't resist the urge to place my hand on the side of her knee, then up, just an inch beneath the flowy hem of her dress, still filled with my desire to have my skin on hers at every viable moment. She looks down at me over her shoulder, a mock-glare on her face that doesn't meet her eyes. It melts away in a moment when she rolls her eyes and then grabs the fruit, twisting to pull it off.

She hands it to me, and I accept, that familiar jolt moving through me when her fingers brush mine before I set it into the basket. We move like that for an hour or so, moving from tree to tree as Willa finds the perfect fruits and hands them off to me until the basket is nearly overflowing. I have absolutely no idea what we're going to do with all of these peaches, but I don't argue.

Afterward, we bring the basket to the front for safekeeping, and I tug her towards our next destination, a small area with animals for us to feed. She squeals with excitement, cooing at each animal, snapping pictures, and chatting with each one. Warmth spreads in my chest as I realize this was clearly the right call. She's feeding a horse a carrot when she looks around as if realizing something.

"Why is there no one here?" she asks, brows furrowed. I'm surprised that she didn't notice earlier, but I bite back a smile.

"They're normally closed in the afternoon on Sundays," I tell her.

"Normally?"

"I may have made a couple of calls yesterday, pulled some strings."

She turns to me, her eyes wide.

"You pulled some strings?"

I lift a shoulder, suddenly wondering if it was the wrong call.

"I want our first day to be for us. Perfect. You're lying low right now, and, for a while, you and I are going to have to lie low as well. I wanted your first real date to be perfect." Her eyes soften.

"Our first date," she whispers. "And it is perfect. But you didn't have to do all of this, Leo. Really. It's...it's too much." I stop our movement and tug her into me. My hand slides into the hair at the back of her head, the strands silky soft.

"I see you're still not getting it, Willa. I'll give you everything." Her eyes water with the words, her breath hitching. "No, no. Willa. No. What's wrong?"

"I always thought it was a myth," she whispers, and I can hear the tears scratching at her throat, but I continue to stare at her, confused and worried. "I thought it was a myth, some lie we're told as kids so we don't just give up and get comfortable."

My brows furrow. I don't know what the hell she's going on about.

"What was?"

"Having it all."

My heart begins to beat faster, and the hand not in her hair slides down her back, pulling her in closer to me.

"I thought I had to choose. I thought I could have one or the other. My career or love. I was happy with my decision, I knew I was one in a million and that I should be grateful and I was—I swear, I was," she says that last part quickly, as if she's afraid that I'll accuse her of not appreciating what she has, but she forgets that I've watched her career over the last eight years, watched it grow, watched her work her ass off, watched her do everything she could to make sure her fans were always put first, even if it meant meet and greets and extra tour dates that pulled her past her physical capabilities. I've watched her sacrifice so many things, such as her own comfort and her own happiness, to make this career happen. If there's anyone on this earth who knows that Willa Stone deserves the fame, that she's *earned* it, it's me.

"But I felt it in my soul. That deep gnawing, a hollow loneliness, I tried to ignore. Sometimes, late at night, I'd lie in my bed alone and wonder if I had chosen wrong." Her tongue comes out to lick her lips, but she never breaks eye contact with me. "If I should have given it all up, settled down, found someone I liked well enough, and gone in a different direction. And when I did, I felt a different pain, knowing that if I did, I couldn't have what I already had: performing and making music and sharing it with the world. I told myself I could have only one of the others. And I was okay with it, until recently." She licks her lips, looking at me, eyes glimmering as her lips tip up in a small smile. "Until recently, when I realized that maybe, just maybe, I could have both." My heart breaks and heals all at once, and I lift my hand, putting it to her cheek and tipping it up before pressing my lips to hers, unable to express myself with words, but hoping that my touch could say it all for me.

That I'm promising to do everything in my power to make sure that Willa Stone gets to have it all, forever.

<h1 style="text-align:center">TWENTY-FIVE</h1>

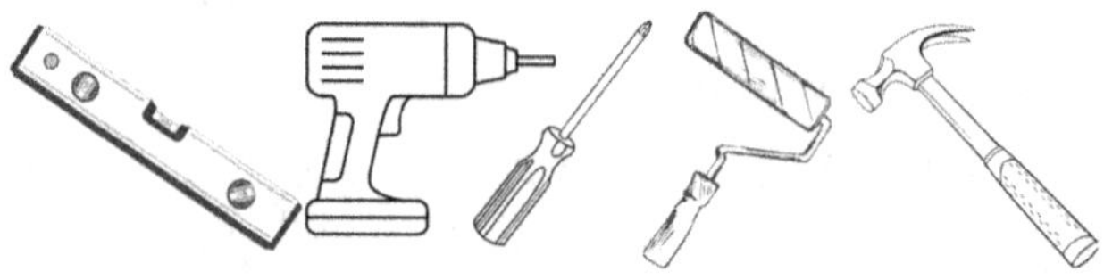

LEO

"Can we sit outside for a bit?" Willa asks as we walk up the front porch steps of my house later that night. After letting Willa pet the animals to her heart's content, we washed up and ate at the restaurant on the property, the two of us the only ones there. I surprised Willa by moving her to a bonfire near the edge of the property and making s'mores. We laughed, ate, and kissed until it was time for us to leave. Her voice is soft, and I turn to her, putting a hand to her chin and tipping it toward me. Staring down into her warm brown eyes, I speak words that hold so much honestly, they ache.

"Whatever you want, Willa." Her lips tip up a bit, and I bend, pressing mine to hers in a soft, sweet press before breaking apart and resting my forehead to hers. "I'm gonna get a beer—want anything?"

"Can I have a glass of that peach wine?" she asks with a little smile, speaking of one of the many goodies we bought at the farm, most of which are in an oversized bag in my hand. I nod, then gesture towards the swing we put together the other day.

"Go sit, I'll get it for you." She eagerly settles on the swing, kicking off her sneakers and tucking her feet beneath her. She looks perfect on the porch she helped me repaint and decorate, sitting on the swing she insisted I needed. I am once again reminded she is meant to be here.

With me.

Moving through the house quickly, I grab a beer and pour her a glass of wine before stepping outside and handing it to her. She takes it before I sit, then lifts her legs and drapes them over my lap. When she settles into my side, that same, familiar feeling of peace moves through me, and I realize I could do this every single night, sit out here with Willa and just...be.

"Thank you," she murmurs a little while later. "For today. It was...it was perfect."

"There's no need. Thank you for coming with me. I hope it was a good first date."

"A lot of firsts today," she says, pressing her lips into the side of my neck. "Getting ready for a date with my girls. Peach picking, going to a petting zoo. S'mores." I smile, remembering all of those and the joy on her face with each moment.

"I want to give you all of the firsts I can, Willa. You tell me what you want, and I'm going to make it happen." I hope she realizes just how much I mean it, how I really would give her anything, so long as it made her happy.

"We could have another first, you know," she murmurs, her voice low, somehow changed. When I look down at her, she's already looking up at me, mischief written across her features. She reaches down, setting her wine glass to the floor before grabbing my beer and doing the same.

"Oh?" I ask with a raised eyebrow, but instead of responding, she moves, rearranging her body until she's straddling my lap, her dress pooling around her hips. Between her closeness and the mischievous tilt of her lips, my cock goes hard. "Willa—" I start, but I don't know where the warning is headed. There's no way I would stop whatever direction she wants to take this.

"I've never...you know...outside," she says, her voice a low murmur as those perfect white teeth bite into her lower lip.

"I sure as fuck hope not," I reply, and with a mind of their own, my hands move to rest on her knees before sliding up and down her soft skin. Her breathing hitches as I repeat the movement, stroking casually from her knees up her thighs. Each time, my thumbs go just a bit higher on her inner thigh.

I love this most of all, teasing her. Constantly teasing her.

"We could..." she starts, her words trailing off as a flush spreads across her skin.

"We could what?"

Her tongue dips out, wetting her lips, and this time, my thumbs move up, grazing along her panties. I bite back a groan when I find they're already damp.

"We could... You know... out here. On the swing." My eyes drift shut at the mere idea, at this sweet woman before me, asking me to once again give her everything and knowing damn well I can't say no.

I can never say no to Willa.

"We could what?"

"You know," she murmurs, hips shifting.

"We could...kiss?" I guess, knowing it's the wrong answer, but pressing my lips to hers all the same in a heated touch. My tongue slides along hers, her hands moving to behind my neck. When I break the kiss, we're both breathing heavily, her hips continuing to shift to try to get something from me.

"More than that," she breaths. My cock twitches at the need in her voice, and on their next circuit of my hands on her thighs, I graze more intentionally over her center.

"Or I could finger you out here, right on this swing." I drop my head to press kisses to her neck, and she tips it to give me more room to taste her skin.

"More," she whines, hips seeking, and I don't know if she means more than what I said, or if she means she needs more in this moment.

Probably both.

My thumb presses on her clit over her panties, then down,

pressing the fabric into her wet center. "Or do you want me to slide these over, fuck you right here on this swing?"

"Yes," she says quickly, nodding, shifting to try to get my fingers inside of her. I slide her panties to the side, then slowly, torturously for both of us, slide two fingers into her center. She tightens, already drenched, and I groan as her wet heat envelops my fingers, knowing intimately what it feels like on my cock.

"Ride those, baby," I murmur, and she does as I ask without hesitation. I watch in utter awe of her beauty as she shifts, lifting, then drops onto my fingers. The first time, a heavy breath leaves her lips. Then again…rise, fall…but this time, her head tips back, and a pleased sigh escapes. Rise, fall, a swivel of her hips as she tries to catch my thumb, to get some pressure on her clit, and she bites her lips, muffling a moan. I press my thumb to her clit, giving her what she wants for just a moment.

"Loud," I say, voice firm.

"Leo—"

"Loud, Willa. You don't hide that from me. I get everything from you," I remind her of what I told her that very first night we were together.

'Oh god," she moans, the sound filling the night air, as I crook my fingers.

"There's my girl."

"Leo," she mutters, breathing hard. My thumb swipes over her clit, and her fingers tighten around me, and I drop my head, groan into her neck at the mere feel of it. "I won't…"

"Won't what, baby?" I ask, lifting once more to take in her face, flushed, parted lips, heavy lids.

"I need you. I won't last," she mewls, rocking her hips despite the warning, trying to take herself there. The swing shifts with each of her movements, and I already anticipate what fucking her will be like.

"That's good, baby, because I don't want you to."

Her head snaps up to glare at me, a spitfire even when I have her like this.

"Leo!"

"Because you're going to come on my fingers just like this, fucking yourself, taking yourself there, and then when you're still coming, you're going to slide onto my cock and take me there."

"Oh god," she moans, and again, her body tells me just how much she likes it. I grin at her.

"Take me out," I say, groaning as her hips move against me, brushing over my hard cock.

"What?"

"My hands are a bit busy, honey. Take me out, get ready to take me when you come."

I don't need to tell her again, and her body shifts once more, hips never stopping their undulation on my fingers, before her fingers fumble with my belt.

"Why the fuck are you wearing a belt?" she murmurs, desperation clear in her words, and I bite back a laugh.

"Next time you plan to fuck me on the porch, give me a heads up. I'll make sure it's easy access."

"I was easy access for you. You should have known." I grin then, wide, but the humor fades into a deep, uncontrollable groan when she finally pulls me out, her small hand tugging at my cock. Yeah, I'm gonna need this to speed up.

"Fuck, WIlla. I need you to get there quicker."

"Just, just..." she says, panting, her hips moving quickly, now grinding insistently against my palm that is resting on her clit. "Just fuck me."

"Hell no," I say. She stares at me, and I shift my hand, giving her more pressure, and that glare melts away, turning into a low, keening moan. "You're far too pretty like this." I'm tempted to tug the top of her dress down, since I noticed long ago she isn't wearing a bra, and with the way she's moving, it's even more obvious. But I'm worried that if I let go of my grip on her, she might fall. And, even though we're far off the beaten path, I wouldn't put it past any of our crew to show up unannounced. Her floaty sundress covers most of what I'd be worried about, but any further, I feel like I should just take her inside.

"Leo," she moans, hips rocking, and I put my hand to the back of her neck, pulling her in close. Her hand moves on my cock still, unable to keep a rhythm, but I don't care, as always, she feels like fucking heaven.

"Come on, baby, I know you like this, being my bad girl, riding my fingers outside. Anyone could come up the drive, you know," I murmur into her ear, nipping at the lobe and smiling when her breath hitches, when she tightens around me. "You like that, don't you? You like knowing that anyone could find us out here?"

Her breaths come faster, and I know she's teetering on the edge. I may not have had her a million times yet, but I've spent so many years pretending I'm not watching her, training to read every change in her body, voice, and face. Training for this moment, it seems.

"You can be a good girl to everyone else, but I think with me, you want to be my bad girl, don't you? My little slut, pushing your panties aside and begging me to take you out here." She tightens further, and her hips stutter. I groan into her neck.

"Leo, I—"

"Come for me, Willa. Right fucking now. Come for me, and then slide your tight pussy onto my cock." The demand is clear in my voice, and relief and a thrill move through me when she obeys. Head snapping back, body tightening as she moans out my name, sinking a bit deeper onto my fingers. I watched in awe, watching her body shake, her hips rocking, squeezing every drop of pleasure from the moment. I think I'll have to remind her of my instructions, but then her eyes open, hazy with a small smile on her lips as she grips my cock, stroking and lifting her hips with slow, shaky movements. Finally, I drag my fingers out of her, making sure to press along her clit as I do, then use my wet fingers to pull her panties again. A sigh of dismay leaves her lips as I do.

"Line me up, baby." There's no hesitation as she does what I ask, lining the tip of me up with her, then sliding down and filling herself. A moan leaves her lips, and I groan at the feeling of filling her completely, her cunt still tight with her orgasm.

"Oh, fuck, you feel good," she groans loudly. She slides her hips forward and back, once again grinding her clit against me. Then she puts pressure on her knees, lifting, then sinking again, and a hot breath coasts along my neck. "Leo."

"Yeah," I groan in appreciation. My hand moves from where it was pushing her panties aside to her hips, holding her there and helping her move, up and down, back and forth. It's torturous pleasure, watching her take her own time, watching her fill herself, tackle what she needed, but my god, I would chase it to the ends of the earth.

"I'm gonna fill you, Willa. I'm gonna fill you, and then I'm going to slide you off me and put your panties back on. We're going to stay out here until you finish your drink, my cum dripping out of you, pressed right against your pretty pussy," I murmur after a few minutes of this, as her pussy starts to tighten once more, her hips growing jerkier with each movement.

"Oh my god," she groans, shifting faster and faster, her pants becoming breathier, her movements less controlled. She's not rising and falling anymore, instead rocking back and forth, my cock buried deep, her clit grinding on me with each move, and I fucking love it. I love how she is taking what she wants, and even more, how she knows she's going to get what she wants. After our first time, she explained that she's only ever been able to come while on top, taking what she needs, and in this moment, even though I hate any fucker who puts his hands on her, I can see why a man would let her do it.

She's fucking magnificent.

And with my filthy words, she tightens further.

My Willa, my sweet girl, America's sweetheart, likes it when I talk her through it. A dozen ways I can and will use that knowledge to my advantage in the future flit through my mind, before I focus on the task at hand: making her come again and then following her over the edge.

"Do you want that, honey?" I moan, my fingers digging into her hips to help her along. The swing shifts with my motions, furthering the movements.

"Yes, yes," she chants, eyes glazing before she dips to take my lips in a quick, heated kiss. Neither of us can handle more right now.

"Not until you come. You're going to ride my cock until you finish and then take me with you." Her hair falls back, blonde curls falling down her back, and one hand moves to her breast, palming and pinching the nipple beneath her dress.

"Leo."

"That's it, baby. Ride me like my little whore. Everyone gets the sweet version of you, but I get this, don't I?

"Only you." I groan loudly, lifting my hips to get deeper because I like that a fuck of a lot. "Yes!" she calls out. "Like that!" I grit my teeth and buck my hips up to give my girl what she needs. "Fuck, fuck, fuck," she mutters. "I'm gonna—"

She doesn't finish her sentence; instead, groaning out my name long and low, tightening around me like a vise, and her body trembles before me. I'm barely able to concentrate, to take in how fucking pretty she looks coming on my cock as I pull her down onto me forcefully, probably bruising her hips in the process, and spill into her. We sit like that for long, long moments, both of us catching our breath, before I finally pull out and do what I said, sliding her panties back in place. When I do, I brush my fingers over the soaked fabric, pressing on her clit and pulling a soft moan from her lips that makes me smile. Then I settle her back into the swing, legs in my lap, reaching down to grab our drinks and hand hers back to her.

"Another first," she mutters, and I can't help but laugh, shaking my head and pressing a kiss to her temple.

Twenty minutes later, we head into the house, and Willa goes to my bedroom to clean up. She returns in comfy clothes, her hair in a bun, her face clear of makeup. She looks a bit nervous, biting her lip.

"What's wrong?" I ask, pulling her into me.

"Do you mind..." she bites her lip, looking away before looking back at me. "Do you mind if I write for a bit?"

I blink at her, confused for a moment because of the way she looks so anxious about this simple question.

"Of course I don't. Do you want me to leave you alone?"

Her brows furrow. "What?"

"Do you want me to leave you alone while you write? I'm not sure what your process looks like. If you want, I could also go to your place, get your guitar, and anything else you might need."

That furrow erases, and her eyes go soft, a look that I'm seeing more and more on her face. Each time I see it, a bit of joy enters my chest, followed by sadness that she doesn't just expect people to treat her with kindness and understanding.

Something to work towards.

"You really wouldn't mind if I wanted to be alone?"

I hesitate for a moment before shaking my head and placing a hand to her jaw, tipping her head up so she's looking into my eyes when I speak next.

"Willa. You're a once-in-a-generation musical genius. Do you really think I'd tie myself to you and not know that would be a part of my life?" Her eyes go wide, and her bottom lip quivers. "Do you really think I would ever stop you from chasing that, from doing something that so clearly makes you the most magical, talented person I've ever met in my life? I told you before, and I'm telling you again, I will never—and I mean ever, Willa—get in the way of the career you were born to follow."

"You're tied to me?" she murmurs, clearly still stuck on the beginning of what I said. I grin down at her.

"Knotted so tight, I don't think I can ever undo it," I say before pressing my lips to hers, tipping my head. "Go pick a spot. I'll go get your guitar and anything else you might need. Just text me what you want and where it is, then I'll bring it to you. I'll sit outside and answer some emails while you work. Just let me know when you're done, but no rush. I've got things to do." She stares at me, long moments passing as her eyes glisten.

"I might be up late," she warns.

"I have nowhere to be in the morning."

Another beat passes before she speaks again, eyes glistening. 'You're perfect for me."

"We're perfect together," I reply, then step away to grab my keys.

That night, Willa writes "Tied to You," the second single for her next album.

TWENTY-SIX

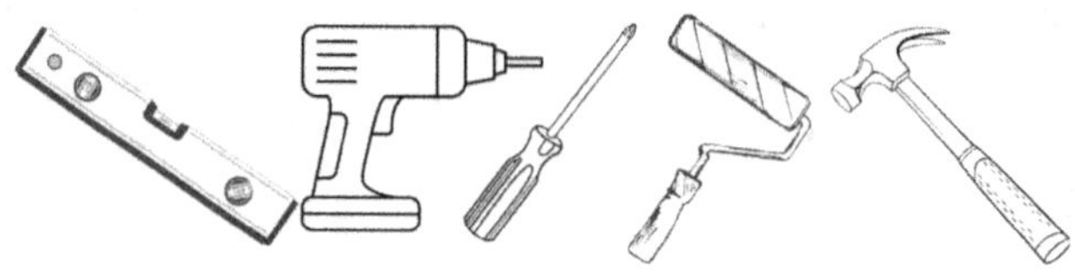

LEO

After the rainstorm, I don't spend a single night without Willa in my bed. While we haven't had a formal *moving-in* conversation, I think we both can feel the clock ticking before our private little bubble pops, and neither of us wants to waste any more time than we already have. In September, things will change when she starts her next marketing cycle, and during that time, we'll have to keep things under wraps for both my job and her career. Until then, I want her as close as possible.

When I think of the future, my gut clenches at the conversations we're going to have to have, the fact that I'm going to have to watch her pretend to be in love with another man and stand back as she does, but that's a hurdle I'll have to tackle later. At the end of the day, I would never do anything to stop Willa from having what she wants, and I'll do everything in my power to give it to her. If she wants another number one album and the kind of media storm that captures the entire world's interest, then I'll make sure she has it.

In the past two weeks, during quiet moments in bed, on the back patio, or on her porch swing, we've had many conversations, and she's mentioned here and there that the few relationships she's attempted outside of her fake ones have crashed and burned because the man didn't understand her need for success, her need to follow her dreams. After a while, she stopped trying and just gave herself to the fake relationship, deciding that her career was the more important aspect of her life and that the disappointment from others wasn't worth the headache.

I refuse to fall into that category for her.

Our days grow routine, waking slowly and, more often than not, making love in the early-morning light. After Willa does some kind of workout, sometimes a video of Pilates, where I have to leave or else get too tempted to interrupt, and sometimes we go for a hike around the property. We have breakfast together, and she writes while I work before we start on the house for the better part of the day. Most nights, we have dinner at home before Willa gets some more writing in, and we spend the evening out on the back patio.

Some nights, we end up working later than others and fall into bed exhausted, but we always end the night with me inside of her. After one of those long days, when we spend the day in the pounding sun finishing up the front walkway, I'm too exhausted to cook.

"Fast food, fucking you hard, then sleeping with you in my bed," I grumble as we step into the house. In this moment, I've never been more grateful that the air conditioning works, because the sharp hit of it is a relief against my heated skin.

"My dream day," Willa grumbles, and I look over at her with a smile. "But I need a shower too." I lift my eyebrows in suggestion, and she glowers at me, making me smirk. "You can join, but I'm not fucking you until I'm clean, rested, and fed."

"Okay, then, a quick dinner it is. Junk food," I say. "What's your favorite fast food? We'll grab that." There's a moment of hesitation before she responds.

"I... I don't know."

Turning fully towards her, I attempt to read her face, confused. "What?"

"I don't know my favorite fast food." Her eyes drop to pick at her nails, the red polish replaced by a pretty yellow that Nat picked out during girls' night last week at Wren's house, while I went to Jesse's place for poker night.

"You don't..."

"I've never really had fast food." I blink at her for a moment before a blush reddens her cheeks. "I just...you know. I've always had things that fit into my nutrition plan. Chicken nuggets and French fries weren't really in that typically. And if they were, they weren't fast food."

Understanding hits, and with her discomfort, a newly familiar feeling moves through me: the excitement of knowing I'm going to get to give Willa another first.

"Okay," I say, moving to grab my wallet and the keys to Willa's SUV, an idea brewing quick. "Let's go. We'll figure out what you like." She moves, following me out the door. I open the passenger side door, letting her slide in before jogging around the driver's side and driving off.

I drive to the main highway on the outskirts of Holly Ridge, where, along a half-mile stretch, there are four different fast-food joints. "Fries?" I ask at the first stop, and she gives me a soft smile.

"I do know I love French fries."

"Onion rings?" I ask as the car before us moves ahead, and she shrugs.

"Never had them." I grin then, excited to once again give her something basic that I've taken for granted. I order an array, get it from the window, and then move back onto the highway for only a moment before turning into the parking lot of the next fast-food restaurant.

"Leo—"

"We've gotta figure out what you like," I say. "Ever had popcorn chicken?" I ask, pulling up to the speaker, then ordering another feast.

"Leo," she murmurs once we pull out, and she realizes I'm repeating the same process. "Leo, this is nuts."

I stop behind the car ordering, and turn to her to see that soft look on her face, the one she gives me when she's excited and thrilled by something basic, but feels like she should protest because she feels a bit silly.

"Yeah, but who's gonna stop us?" I ask. She grins.

After we have our huge fast-food feast, I drive a minute or two to a county park I've noticed in passing, then drive another minute before we find a lookout, like some kind of kismet. I back her SUV into it, then moved quickly to open the trunk and lay the rear seats flat before we carried the food to the back and climbed in. Willa has the widest smile on her face as I open bags, ripping the paper and laying them out like some five-course meal.

"I think this is my new favorite food," she says, stealing another fry from one of the bags twenty minutes later, and I laugh.

"Sorry, it's not fancier, but that would kind of defeat the purpose. You gotta eat fast food like this quick. It's not as good cold." She shrugs as if it doesn't faze her at all, reaching for the chicken nuggets she deemed to be her favorite, and sliding them through barbecue sauce.

"This is the best meal I've ever had," she says, and the grin on her face tells me she means it.

"I'm glad I could give you another first." I look at the bags around us. "Or ten." She laughs, then, head tipping back, happy and free in a way I've only ever seen on her here in Holly Ridge.

My phone chooses that moment to ping with a new email, and at the same time, Willa's does. Neither of us reaches for our devices immediately; instead, we look to one another, somehow knowing. The only reason we'd both have a message at the same time would be if it were about her and the timeline. She puts a hand out, grabbing my hand and twining our fingers before grabbing her phone and tapping a bit.

"August 20," she says, her voice low, looking at the screen, and my stomach drops. "The relationship starts August 20."

Her head lifts, eyes locking on mine before she gives me a soft, sad smile. I see it there, clear as day: the internal battle of wanting to extend this further, but also excited to record her next album, to get the ball rolling towards being able to share it with the world, with her fans. I've heard a few of the songs, and each one is the best thing I've heard her create. With each one, she tells me about how she thinks her fans will love it, which one will be their new favorite, and ideas for music videos.

She loves that life, or at least parts of it.

And once again, I know I will make it all happen for her, so Willa Stone gets the career and the life we're building in Holly Ridge.

"It just means I have four weeks." I lift her hand and scoot closer, pressing my lips to her fingers, and watching her shield go up for a moment before I clarify. "I have four weeks to make magic for you, to make sure we both have all the memories we need to tide us over."

"Leo—" she starts, and I know where this conversation is going, too, because we haven't fully ignored the future since we've gotten together. There have been a few moments when she's caved to her worry, tried to convince me she can't expect me to just sit around while she off dating someone else (her words, not mine) and each time I've done what I can to reassure her that I've already been sitting around and waiting for years now—but those years, I didn't know she was mine. That I can handle another six months, another year of that, if it means I know that at the end of it all, I get to have her, free and clear.

"We're going to live the next month like nothing is going to change because other than the location and the inability to be open, nothing *will* change, Willa. We're going to do our *jobs*. And we are going to be together."

'Yeah, but we can't—"

"Not being able to touch and kiss you anytime I want is going to cut deep. I won't pretend it will be sunshine and roses. But we'll make it through just fine. We'll have the occasional weekend in Holly Ridge, and we'll see each other often, even if we'll be guarded. And there are phones. And here are video calls," I say, a smile moving on my lips as I shift her, pulling her into my lap. "I might not be able to touch you every night, but we can do other things. We can be creative."

"I like creative," she whispers against my lips.

"I know that." I kiss her, soft and sweet and reassuring, I hope, and after a moment, when she pulls back and rests her forehead against mine, I know I did my job.

"We're going to be okay, aren't we?"

'We're going to be okay, Willa. I'm going to make sure of it."

A week later, on Saturday afternoon, Willa walks into the bedroom where I am sorting through clean clothes, phone in hand and smiling. We've fallen into a rhythm that feels so natural, sometimes I forget we haven't always been this, Willa and I together.

"We're going out tonight," she says, throwing her phone on top of the dress, then stepping over to the closet that, without any kind of real conversation, has become *her* closet. She still keeps some things at Hallie's old place, but the trips there to grab them have become less and less frequent, with most of her essentials finding a new home here. In my mind, I'm already thinking of ways to make her feel more at home here, things she might need, like turning the smaller closet into a larger walk-in style and talking to Adam about what she might need for an office-slash-music room here.

I want this to be her home, and to make that happen, she needs her own space. She's not necessarily ready for all of those conversations just yet, though, so I mostly just plot and plan in my own mind.

I stand then, reaching for and snagging her around the waist before she makes it to the closet, and pulling her into me.

"We are?" I ask, my head tipping to press my lips to hers. She smiles into the kiss, then nods when it breaks.

'Yeah, that was Hallie. We're all going to the Mill. I think it's about time we finally have our first night out in Holly Ridge together."

I couldn't agree more.

This time, we walk into the Mill together, and when all eyes move to us, there are smiles instead of intrigue; our friends' warm faces welcome us in rather than watching me enter alone and wondering just what might happen next. Once the door closes behind us, Willa drops my hand and moves quickly to the girls, hugging each one of them and instantly falling into a quick, excited conversation. The sight of it settles in my chest, warm.

This is the same woman who, despite being one of the most popular stars in the media, still walks into every room nervously, as if she doesn't know quite where she belongs. The woman who, to my knowledge, has never had a night out, a lunch, or a shopping trip with another person that wasn't preplanned for optimum exposure and who confessed to me recently that she thought girls' nights and getting ready together were just a cinematic theme, not a real, everyday occurrence.

And now she's running over to a group of women as if they're her lifelong friends.

I'm reminded once more just how magical Holly Ridge is.

"Hey, man," Jesse says as I approach the group, slower than Willa, veering toward the men instead. "You got wrangled into this, too?"

"Your fiancé's hard to argue with."

"You're telling me," he says, but there's a look on his face that tells me he deals with that on a daily basis. From what I hear, his daughter is more like Hallie than she is her own father, so I'm sure his house is chaotic at all times.

"You drinking tonight?" Madden asks.

"I'll have a beer, but I'll grab it once Will's done gabbing and tells me what she wants." She still mentions the s'mores martini she had here last time, but I wonder if there's some other drink she's never had but always wondered about. I look to the bar to see if there's a line and should order sooner rather than later, and I'm surprised to see someone other than just Colton standing behind it.

"Who's the woman?" I ask, my brows furrowed at the pretty brunette standing behind the bar and glaring at Colton.

His arms are crossed over his chest as she talks to him, clearly agitated, but he doesn't exactly seem fazed, either by the woman or the fact that she's behind the bar with him. Hallie moves over to Jesse's side, tucking in under his arm and grinning deviously.

"Oh, that's the love of Colton's life," she says.

I blink my eyes, looking from her to the woman, who is now throwing her hands up in the air, clearly annoyed. To Hallie's credit, though, Colton is smiling.

"Uh, she kind of looks like she hates him?" I say.

"That's how he likes his women."

I raise an eyebrow, unsure of what to do with that, but get momentarily distracted when it seems Willa has done her rounds and comes to my side, sliding an arm around my waist. I return the favor, holding her tight but looking back to Hallie.

"He likes women who hate him?"

"No, no, he likes the chase. And Sloane is most *definitely* making him chase her."

"She looks kind of scary," Adam mutters, and Wren slaps him in the chest chidingly.

"Again, that's how he likes 'em," Hallie says with a shrug.

"I get it. Mean girls are kind of hot," Madden says, and I wonder if anyone else sees his gaze lock across the way on Nat.

"Okay, enough. I've given you guys enough canoodling time. It's time for shots!" Nat shouts, averting her eyes from Madden almost before I catch that it was there in the first place.

"Shots!" Willa shouts, excitedly, and I laugh, something that even I have to admit is hilariously ironic. If you had told me that I would be watching Willa Stone cheer to take shots with a smile on my face, I would have called you out of your goddamn mind.

But here we are.

She hesitates before stepping out of my arm, though, looking over at me and biting her lips, then looking back at Nat. "Actually, I should probably take it slow tonight."

My hand tightens on her hip, and she looks at me as I shake my head, then tip my head to Nat, who is watching us like a hawk.

"Go on, honey. You're good."

"*Honey!*" Wren says in an excited hush.

"I know, isn't it so cute?" Hallie murmurs.

"You all make me sick," Nat grumbles, but Willa ignores them.

"You should be allowed to get drunk this time," she whines, and I bite back a laugh, because I intuitively know laughing at her will not go well. Instead, I pull her in close and lower my voice.

"I have to be sober to do what I want to do to you tonight." Her eyes go wide, and her lips drop open. "Because I've been thinking about fucking a drunk Willa for a while now. Tonight's my night." I lower my voice and lean in until I'm barely whispering into her ear for only her to hear. "Don't know if you know this, but the night you touched yourself in my bed, I sat outside and listened. Been looking to recreate that but make it much more enjoyable for both of us, honey."

When I pull back, her lips are parted, her eyes wide, completely speechless.

That is, until she turns to Nat. "Shots. Lots of them."

"Oh my god, that was hot," Nat says. "I need to get laid."

"I'm here whenever you're ready, baby," Madden says in his normal, joking, *Playboy* way, and when she gives him a look of utter disgust, then turns on her heel and tugs Willa to the bar, Wren and Hallie in tow, I can't help but let out a bark of a laugh. Once the hilarity dies down, I notice Adam is watching me.

"I don't know if I've ever seen you laugh out loud like that. Seems like Holly Ridge has been good for you," Adam says, grinning at me. I look from him to the bar where Willa is throwing back a shot like a champ and find myself smiling.

"Yeah, I guess it is."

But I know that it's really the blonde carrying a beer in one hand and a cocktail glass in the other as she walks the way that's been good for me.

✦✦✦✦✦✦

"There's no way the pop princess can shake her ass," Hallie says a couple of hours later. There are a few appetizers on the table, decimated, but despite all of our efforts to get the girls to eat and combat their drunkenness, they're all long gone. And even though it's happening from the other side of the table, I can tell that Hallie is baiting her.

"Are you joking me?" Willa asks, eyes wide and disbelieving. "Have you ever seen my sets? I very much know how to shake ass."

"You know how to pop star dance. You never had to go to a homecoming dance in a high school gym and grind in the darkest corner so a teacher doesn't come in and separate you."

I think for a moment this will go poorly, Nat reminding her of things she never had, but Willa just rolls her eyes.

"Just because I was very much lacking in childhood experiences does not mean I don't know how to throw ass, Nat."

"*I think this calls for a competition!*" Madden yells, clear excitement in his voice.

"Oh fuck," I groan, because Willa might be soft and sweet, but if there's one thing I've learned in the past few weeks, it's that she cannot, for the life of her, step down from a challenge.

"Yes!" Willa yells, then grabs Hallie's hand and tugs her to the jukebox, flipping until they find some song. Eventually, the familiar sound of "Low" comes over the speakers, and I close my eyes and sigh. On the other hand, Adam starts laughing loudly beside me.

"Oh, this is going to be good," he says, not even watching the women, instead, watching me.

It's going fine, the girls dancing and cheering, grinding on one another drunkenly and laughing until about two-thirds of the way through. I watch as Hallie stumbles and is caught by Willa, both of them bursting into a fit of giggles before Willa pauses and says something to Nat, whose eyes go wide.

"Do it!" Nat says, loud enough to be heard over the music. Willa laughs and shakes her head, but Nat says something else, clearly challenging my stubborn girl.

Then it happens.

Willa pulls out a chair from one of the lower tables and puts her foot on it.

Then she steps up.

Then she steps up again until she's on top of the table, and she starts to dance, Nat, Hallie, and even Wren hooting and hollering, encouraging her as she gets more confident on top of the table.

"No way," Adam says, but I continue to watch in shock as, with the beat of the song, Willa drops it low. I've never been more grateful that she's wearing shorts instead of a skirt.

"Holy shit," Jesse says.

"Okay, that's my cue," I say, shaking my head, grabbing her bag, and standing, hearing a chorus of men's laughter behind me as I move to where Willa is dancing, standing before her with my arms crossed on my chest.

"Come on, honey. Time to get you home."

She gives me the sweetest glare, still in a squat, and I try my best not to laugh.

"I'm not ready to go."

"Remember what I told you before?" I ask, stepping closer and putting my lips to her ear. "You're good and drunk, baby. I don't need you tipping into the blackout zone before I get my fill of you." Her breath hitches.

"Okay. We can go," she murmurs, and I smile.

I shift, putting my hands on her waist, then bend and slide her over my shoulder. She giggles, and I wave goodbye to our friends as they laugh while I turn to the door, Willa over my shoulder.

"Told you it would happen," Adam calls across the bar, and it reminds me of what he said that first night here, something I didn't understand but do now. At the memory, I smile.

"Later," I say.

"Bye, guys!" Willa calls.

"Girls' night Tuesday!" Nat calls. "I want all the details!"

"Deal!"

Willa giggles from over my shoulder as I take her outside, then I take her home and make the night memorable, so she has something to share with the girls.

TWENTY-SEVEN

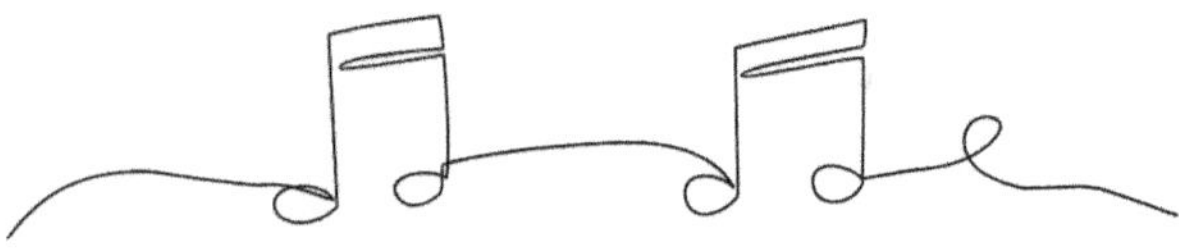

WILLA

In the final weeks I get to spend in Holly Ridge before I'm tossed back into reality, Leo and I fall into a routine, but it looks a lot different than it did months ago. I still wake up early, but I do it more often than not with Leo pressing kisses to my face. I still work out, but once I'm done, Leo waits to take a shower with me.

I still don't drink the green juice.

Most days, we work on the house together, and almost every night, we sit out on the back patio or the porch swing after dinner. Most nights, Leo answers more emails, reads, or works in the garage on some kind of woodworking project, while I continue writing for the next album.

And I write *so much.*

My muse is back with a vengeance, as if she's making up for the time she was missing with song after song after song. I've never been so inspired in my life, and even though I know the source, I can't help but feel in awe of it. After breakfast, I've gotten into the habit of playing whatever I worked on the night before with Leo there, something I've never done, but I like watching the awe on his face, like him finding little crumbs of our relationship in each song, and the way they make his face soft. And I love the way he kisses me after, filled with so much love and adoration, it takes my breath away.

I'm cherishing each and every one of these mornings while I can, saving them up, as Leo told me to, to hold me over on the mornings I can't have this.

Some mornings, we have coffee at home, but others we get it at the coffee shop down the way from the salon where Nat works, and that's where we are in the morning. He orders for us while I look at the mugs and accessories for sale, eventually wandering to the community board in the corner. It usually has advertisements for tutoring, swim lessons, and fundraisers, but pinned dead center is a sign that catches my eye and reminds me of something I nearly forgot.

"Oh! Look! Wren was telling me about this," I say as Leo moves up behind me, resting a hand on my hip.

"A fair?" he says with a skeptical tone. I lean my back into his chest, and he rests his chin on the top of my head before wrapping an arm around my waist. For a moment, I almost forget what I was talking about, melting into him and this moment instead. "When is it?"

"It starts tomorrow. According to Wren, they're going to have food trucks, rides, and games." Something clicks, and then I turn in Leo's arms, giving him a wide-eyed look. "Do you think they'll have a Ferris wheel?"

"A Ferris wheel?" he asks, face looking confused.

"Yeah, the thing with the seats that goes round and round."

I use my free hand to imitate the motion of the ride in question, and he gives me a smile. One hand reaches up to brush hair back from my face.

"Willa, honey, I know what a Ferris wheel is. Why are you talking about it like it's an alien spaceship?" I bite my lip, looking away and feeling that all-too-familiar embarrassment move through me. His hand, rough from working over the past few months, captures my chin and tips it up until I have no choice but to look into his eyes. "Willa?" His eyes are soft, all humor gone as he takes me in.

"I've never been," I say low, trying to remind myself that this is stupid, that there's no reason to be embarrassed.

"On a Ferris wheel?"

I lift one shoulder. "Yeah. Or to a fair."

"Really?" he asks, disbelief in the single word. "You've never been to a fair? That's, like, an American tradition."

I tip my head ot the side, sifting through memories before shaking my head.

"No, actually, I sang at one when I was nine or ten. But then we went home."

Annoyance moves over Leo's face, not directed at me, but once again directed at the people in my life that he believes wronged me.

"Let's go," he says, simple as that.

"Go?"

"To the fair tomorrow. Let's go. It'll be fun."

I bite back an excited smile, trying to be normal, since he didn't exactly sound excited about it earlier.

"Oh, there's no need. We don't have to go just because I said—"

"It would be for me," he says, and I give him a look that tells him I don't believe his lie at all. "I'm serious. A new experience. I've never taken a woman to the fair. I've surely never kissed her on top of the Ferris wheel. It'll be a new experience for both of us."

I love that about Leo. How he not only wants to give me new experiences but also never makes me feel silly or ungrateful, and how he makes it something new for both of us.

"Really?' I ask, hope filling my chest.

"You want to go?" I bite my lip, feeling silly, but— "Honest answer, Will."

I nod.

"Then we'll go."

"Can we, like, do stuff on the Ferris wheel?" I ask the following night as we stand in line to board the Ferris wheel at the town fair. It's not a big one at the ones I've seen in pictures, but considering it surely wasn't in the middle of town this time last week, I'm still impressed that such a big ride has made its way to Holly Ridge.

We arrived an hour ago and hit up four different food trucks, even though there was no way two people could eat that much food. Leo decided I needed to try all of the fair food, so we got a little bit of something from everywhere: a place that did meat on a stick, a deep-fried spiral potato, a gyro, and a corn dog. I'm already eyeing up the other trucks for desserts, but right now we have wristbands to ride as many rides as possible.

"No," he responds quickly and fiercely. I sigh and roll my eyes.

"You're such a party pooper."

"Will, I'll bend a lot of rules to make you happy, and if you want me to finger you or eat you out or fuck you hard, I'll happily get right back in that truck and head home to do it. But I am not doing that in a crowded town fair in front of hundreds of people."

"Party pooper," I pout, and he shakes his head, letting out a laugh.

"You're a nut," he murmurs, pulling me into his side and pressing his lips to my hair.

"Next!" the man at the front says, and I almost squeal with excitement as we move forward and are ushered onto a small cart, then locked inside. We go around and around, moving as others are let on. Leo holds me close and laughs as I point out all of the sights from the wheel.

Finally, the wheel stops at the top, and I stare out across this tiny town I've begun to feel like I belong in. People mill around; laughter dances through the night air, with cheers, music, and the sounds of people winning games. Leo's arm is around my waist, and he tugs me in close to his side, the tiny cart rocking a bit as he does. I look up at him, and his head dips as he presses his lips to mine and kisses me at the top of the Ferris wheel. And in that moment, I realize I am head over heels in love with Leo Sinclaire.

And it's not just the kiss, or the Ferris wheel, or the fair. It's the way he's gentle with me and the way he pushes me. The way he wants to protect my soft parts, but also pull out the rough ones, the way he draws out what he calls my backbone. It's the way he's patient with me when he's teaching me something I should already know, and the way he understands when I need my space. It's the look on his face when I sing to him, and the one on his face when I get excited. It's the way he holds me at night and the way when we're out and about, even if it's just in the front yard, his eyes are always on me, he always has tabs on me.

It's the way he shows me *he* loves me every single day, not in grand gestures or expensive outings or gifts, but in small moments that mean more to me than anything else in this world.

It's the way that I realize right here, right now, that I would give it all up if it meant I got a lifetime for small moments like this, but also, that I know he would never make me do that.

My heart is pounding when he breaks the kiss and rests his forehead against mine, closing his blue eyes and taking in a deep breath like he's trying to savor this moment. But when he opens his eyes, I'm given another reason why I'm completely gone for him: because we're on the same page.

"I love you, Willa," he whispers, the words echoed by a scream of kids on a roller coaster. The lump in my throat swells along with my heart in my chest. It's simple, basic, almost as if he already says it a million times a day, and I realize it's because he does, just not with words.

With actions.

"I love you, Leo Sinclaire," I say through a watery smile, and before he can say anything else, I lean up, laying my hand on the back of his neck and pulling him back down to me to kiss the love of my life again, with an awkward, toothy kiss because we're both smiling wide when we do.

At the top of a Ferris wheel in a tiny town I've learned to call home, I finally have it all.

***

"Oh my *god!*" I squeal, pointing to the giant otter hanging from a clip at one of the game vendors. It's so cute!" My fingers are twined with Leo's, as they have been the entire night, and even though I'm sure it's more than just the locals here at the fair, in the dark, neither of us felt like we had to keep the PDA to a minimum, because this version of me doesn't scream *Willa Stone*. For the first time in my life, I'm incredibly grateful for the strict brand that I've stuck to for the past ten years, because it makes the real me almost unrecognizable.

I'm wearing a worn Three Kings Tree Farm hat, I think I stole from Wren, or maybe Hallie, and my darker hair is in a low bun at the back of my neck. I'm wearing a red tank top and a pair of jean shorts with beat-up sneakers I've been doing housework in, and I've never felt more like I fit in somewhere. Occasionally, someone gives a double take, as if they think they see someone of importance, but each time, they shake their head, an embarrassed look on their face when they realize it's "not" me.

But right now, I'm not focused on the people around me. Instead, my full attention is on one of the game stands. My steps falter as we approach it, Leo's steps slowing as my hand tightens in his. The man manning the game smiles widely at customers approaching.

"Step right up! Win a prize for the lovely lady," he says.

"Oh my god, Leo, can we?" I ask, jumping up and down. "I want that one!" I say, pointing to the giant purple otter hanging at the top.

"Just gotta knock down all six milk bottles and it's yours," the man says. "Win the lady a prize, and you'll win her affections."

Leo glares at the man.

"Yes! Win me a prize!"

"It's a scam, Will. They're all scams," Leo grumbles.

"You're just afraid you won't be able to do it."

He pulls me into him, his lips tipping up, though he's already pulled his wallet out.

"What do I get if I win?"

'The joy of giving me a prize?" I ask with a light-hearted laugh, but he pulls me in closer, his lips moving along mine as he speaks in a near whisper.

"Whatever I want. You at my mercy, all night..."

My body stills. "What?"

"I get an entire night, doing everything and anything I want."

"Are you—" I ask my eyes wide, my lips parted, my breathing suddenly coming heavy. "Are you bartering for sex?" I ask under my breath.

"Are you against it?" he asks, face sobering. I bite my lip, and when his lips tip, I know he sees the intrigue on my face. His hand slides into the hair at the back of my head, gripping it and angling my head. He does that a lot, burying his hands in my hair, and there are a lot of ways I like it, especially when we're alone and naked, but I like it like this the most, when he grips my hair to get my head where he wants it to kiss me.

He does that just then, dropping his head and pressing his lips to mine gently. He kisses me, something that from afar would look soft and sweet, but the way his body is pressed into mine, the way his fingers feel in my hair, I know it's anything but.

"You're into it," he murmurs, against my lips. I'm still breathless and lost when he steps back, hand sliding out of my hair and down my arm to grab my hand before tugging me closer to the stand.

"Five balls, five dollars," the man says, a wide grin on his face as if he saw the whole show we put on. "Win something for the little lady."

"Hey, guys!" a familiar voice calls, and when I look over, Hallie, Jesse, and Jesse's daughter Emma are approaching us. I've chatted with Emma, Hallie's soon-to-be stepdaughter, a few times since I did a FaceTime with her at her birthday party earlier this year, and although she's a big fan, she's incredibly chill, mostly because, according to Hallie, she thinks she and I are best friends now.

I am totally okay with that, since Emma is possibly the coolest twelve-year-old I've ever met.

"Hey!" I say, moving over to give them each a hug before Leo does the same, giving Emma a fist bump and Jesse a bro-hug of sorts that I never thought I'd ever see uptight Leo Sinclaire give anyone.

"You got wrangled into this money suck?" Jesse asks, tipping is chin towards the game before us, Leo's five balls lined up.

"He told me it was a scam, and I told him he was just scared he'd lose."

"Ah, yes, my favorite tactic. Works every time," Hallie says, face looking stoic. "Come on, businessman. Let's see if those muscles are all for show, or what." Leo glares at her, and I bite back a laugh.

"Hallie," Jesse says, but Hallie ignores it, lifting an eyebrow at Leo. With a sigh and a roll of his eyes, Leo grabs a ball, winds his arm up, and throws it, hitting the top bottle off, though the rest stay perfect. Emma lets out a hiss, but Hallie laughs.

"Oof, god, Leo, you suck at this."

He looks over his shoulder and glares at her.

"Hallie," Jesse repeats his warning, but his own lips are tipped in a smile.

"You've got this, babe!" I encourage, pressing a kiss to his cheek. He looks down at me, a hint of exasperation on his face. He throws and misses the next one, which makes Hallie hoot with laughter. On the third throw, he hits another, leaving four still standing.

"It's a scam," Leo grumbles, glaring at the bottles. It's clear there is some kind of product keeping them from all tumbling easily.

"Willa's got a great arm," Hallei says with a smile. "She should try."

"Oh, yes!" I say, clapping. "Let me try!" Leo sighs, shaking his head, and handing me the ball. I grip it, tossing it once in the air before throwing, no real hope that it will work.

But somehow I hit the bottom-center bottle. I watch, holding my breath as they shake, and then...all of the bottles fall.

"Yes!" Hallie yells.

"You did it!" Emma calls.

"Oh my god!" I say, jumping up and down, locking my arms around Leo's neck. He smiles down at me, shaking his head.

"I can't believe you just did that," he grumbles, but he does it with a smile, one that stays as he points to which toy I want. Once we have it, all five of us walk off towards the zeppole tent for Hallie. She found out I'd never had one and insisted she fix that immediately. We're standing off to the side while the little King family waits in line.

"It was rigged for sure," Leo says, an irritated groan, but still, he carries the giant otter for me. I step into his space, putting my arms around his neck.

"I know, baby. But don't worry: I'll still let you do whatever you want with me tonight," I murmur into his ear, then press a soft kiss to his neck, let my tongue dip out to taste him as I do. His body stills, and for a moment, I wonder if I said the wrong thing, but then his head turns, and he looks down at me, fire in his eyes.

"After you eat this zeppole, anything else you want to do here?"

"What?" I ask, confused.

"Did you get your fill of a town fair, or am I good to drag you home and get my prize?"

I let out a loud laugh before pressing my lips to his.

We don't spend much longer at the fair.

TWENTY-EIGHT

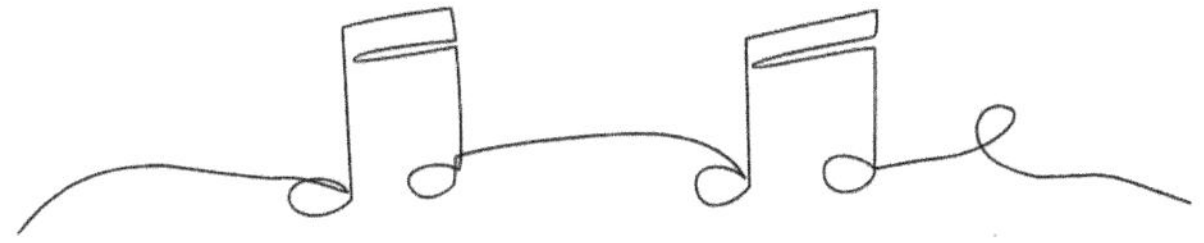

WILLA

We get one more week of peace.

One more week of laughing and working on Leo's house together.

Another night at the Mill with the crew. One evening, I get wrangled into a girls' night, which turns out to be just helping Wren organize and prepare her fall decorations. That night, I get my first glimpse at how chaotic Wren gets with holidays, something Adam has warned me about, and excitement floods me at the mere idea of spending a Christmas in Holly Ridge.

But on Sunday night, I lie in Leo's bed in his arms and wrestle with the understanding that tomorrow, it all ends. Tomorrow, I go back to the city, back to being Willa StoneTM. Tomorrow, I leave *Just Willa* and Holly Ridge and nights at the Mill and chaotic girls' nights and everything I've come to love about this place, even if it's only for a little while.

But most of all, I lose Leo.

I, of course, have taken breaks before, though they've never been this extensive in degree of visibility or in length. As far as I can remember, the longest I've ever lain low like this was for a month, and at the end of it, I was absolutely *itching* to get back to work. To get back to the appearances, the smiling, the performing, the building of my brand.

For the first time in my life, I'm not overly eager to go to work. For the first time, I'm not seeing it as a return to my real life, but to a fake one, curated to benefit my career, not necessarily myself. Three months ago, that thought alone would have sent overwhelming guilt moving through me, guilt from feeling like I didn't appreciate all that I have, the life people would kill to experience, but now, I'm realizing it's okay to want more out of life, that it doesn't make me ungrateful or spoiled to wish for balance.

"I don't want to go back," I whisper into the dark room, my head on Leo's chest, his fingers moving through my hair. I didn't mean to say that aloud, but the thoughts have been moving through my head over and over and over until eventually, they slipped out past my lips.

But now that the confession is out in the room, a weight lifts from my shoulders, as if the confession alone released some of the tension that was haunting me.

"What?" His hand stills in my hair for a moment before continuing, sliding down before repeating the movement.

"I don't want to go back." This time, my voice is shaky, and I close my eyes tightly. It's strange to speak it aloud, these words I never ever imagined myself saying, but I also never thought I'd find myself falling deeply in love in a small town. I never imagined I'd see my responsibilities and career as something that's getting in the way of my happiness.

"You have to give me more, honey," he says low, the words patient as he always is with me. I realize now that he always has been this way with me, even when I was driving him crazy, even when I first showed up, and he wanted me to walk the straight and narrow. He's always been patient and understanding in his own way, keeping a pulse on what I was happy to do and what I wasn't, adjusting plans and expectations accordingly. It drives Jackie crazy, since she sometimes sees it as him playing things too safely, but I understand now he's always had my best interests in mind. Me, Willa Stone, the girl, not Willa Stone, the brand.

"I don't want to go back to real life." Silence takes over, Leo giving me time before I break it again. "I don't want to go back to the city or to being followed around or pretending I'm this person I don't think I really am anymore."

Leo is quiet for a few moments, and my heart races before he finally speaks.

"Do you want to quit?" There isn't judgment or shock or fear in the words, and that gives me the room I need to be honest, both with him and myself.

Do I want to quit?

This is the last album I have on my contract. I could record it, go on tour, and then fade into oblivion. I could live a normal life here in Holly Ridge, put my old life behind me, and never look back. It's not like I work because I need the money, after all.

But the mere thought of not continuing to make music, not performing, or recording or writing sends a bolt of dismay through me, answering my question quickly.

"No," I say, because it's the truth. I can't imagine a life without music. It's what I love most of all. I want to sing, perform, and meet fans. I want to keep selling out stadiums and touring the circuits, but on my terms. "I love my career. I love the fans, and I love performing, but I don't like...the rest of it. I don't love the interviews, the events, the paparazzi, and the pressure of it all."

He continues to lie beside me quietly, his hand making reassuring movements against my hair as I process what I'm feeling.

"I never thought I could have the kind of peace I've found here, but I did, and now that I have it, I don't want to let it go. Being here made me realize I want a life where I can have that and what I have here."

"And you'll have it," he murmurs in his soft voice. Normally, it appeases me, especially when paired with his closeness and his fingers moving through my hair, but I can't deny it anymore—the panic and nervous energy that's been creeping in from the sidelines for weeks now, lying in wait to strike.

"How? How are we going to do this?" I whisper, my throat aching. "How am I supposed to just...leave all of this? How am I going to just leave you?"

"You're not leaving me, Willa," he says.

"But everything is going to be different," I say, the words spilling out quickly. "What if it all falls apart? What if you see that version of me again and—"

"Hey, hey, hey," he says, cutting me off. "What's going on?" My lower lip wobbles. "Honey, how long have you been worried about this?" I lift a shoulder, trying not to look at him, embarrassed. "Willa, you have to talk to me about this kind of thing, or else it's going to eat at you."

"I didn't exactly want to remind you that I was going to date another man, Leo." He smiles at my attitude, and something about that eases the vise in my chest just a fraction. "How are you so okay with all of this? If you were dating some other chick in front of me, I'd lose my mind, Leo. And you're so...calm."

"That's because you're not dating another man in front of me, Willa. You're going to be doing your job. I'm man enough, confident enough in what we have, to separate the two. Am I pleased that I'm going to see photos of you on some asshole's arm? Not exactly, but that's your job, and I told you before: I will never get in the way of that. It's no different than acting for a movie or a show, and if you wanted to go back to that, I would be just fine with it. I'm okay with it, because he's not actually getting you, Willa," Leo says, voice firm and reassuring as he sits up and then pulls me into his lap so my legs wrap around his hips, our faces close, his forehead to mine.

"Here's how it's going to go. Tomorrow, I'm driving both of us to the city, and we're going to walk into the building together, because I've already agreed to take you. Then we're going to sit in that meeting and let Jefferson think he's cowed me, you're going to meet another asshole who doesn't deserve you, and he's going to schmooze you because we all know that no matter what Jefferson does or says, if he is an ass to you in front of Jackie or me, he's done." Nerves move through me, remembering that it's not just me who has something on the line here: Leo does, too.

"Leo, I don't want you to get into trouble, I–"

"I won't be any more protective of you than I always have been, and we both know I've always been a little protective of you, if not a little standoffish."

"I guess…I guess that makes sense," I agree, because it does. Looking back, Leo *has* always been protective of me.

"Then you're going to go back to your place. Not your home, because we both know your home is here, with me, in Holly Ridge." A tear falls at his blunt words, and he swipes it away quickly with his thumb. "You're going to get ready, and then you're going to go on your date. It's going to suck, knowing you're out with him, but when you're done, and you're home, you're going to call me and tell me all about it, and honestly, Willa? That's all that matters. All that matters is that at the end of the night, you're mine. You can go play pretend, be the fake version of yourself for everybody else, but every night, I go to bed knowing I get the version that dances in the rain and on tables and who toilet papers houses. I get the version who eats chicken nuggets in my truck and calls it the best meal ever. And every night, I'm going to get the version that whispers *I love you* in the sweetest, softest voice, and I get to know I'm the only one who gets that." Another tear falls, and he swipes that one away, too. "And we'll do that every fucking night, Willa. Every night until you're done. Next month, you'll come home for Hallie and Jesse's wedding, and we'll have our normalcy for a weekend, and then you'll be home again for Christmas, and you'll meet my mom." My eyes widen with his declaration, which is news to me. In the past few weeks, I've been around while he spoke to his mom on the phone and asked him to say hello for me, but we've never actually had the *meet the parents* talk.

"What?" I say, my voice squeaky with a different kind of nervous energy, and his lips tip up with a smile. "Your mom?"

"She's going to love you, Will. She already loves you because she knows that you've changed me for the better."

"I—"

He keeps talking, forcing me to move past that momentary shock, if only just for now.

"And then in February, your relationship will end, and in July, my contract will be up. I'll be free to quit and start my own firm; we'll make it official; and then we'll *never do this again*." He says the words like a vow, his hands on my face pulling me closer for a soft press of his lips to mine before he speaks against them. "We are never going to be apart again unless we have to."

That familiar pit swirls in my stomach, knowing that with a new album will come a new tour.

"I have tour–"

"And I will come to every one I can."

My brows furrow, and I shake my head.

"I can't expect you—"

Leo rolls his eyes and sighs, and from the sound, I know he thinks I'm being stubborn.

"I'm your publicist, Willa. It's not like you're asking me to do anything outside of my job description."

He does, in fact, have a point there. Mentally, I picture Leo and Jackie battling the entire tour, Jackie trying to cater to Willa Stone, the pop star and performer, and Leo determined to keep his Willa, *Just Willa*, happy, healthy, and sane. The idea actually makes me smile a bit.

"And then we'll spend every free minute down here, being us. You'll be Just Willa, and I'll be relaxed Leo, and we'll have nights at the Mill and summer days working on your garden, and you'll decorate this place until it's exactly what you want."

The way he says it all makes sense, and it's the knowledge that settles inside of me, the knowledge that not only are we both on the same page, but we're both determined to make it work. That the next year might be one of growing pains as we wrap up one era of our lives in order to start the new one, but we're both okay with that because we have our eyes on the prize: our future together.

"We're really going to make this work, aren't we?" I ask in a whisper, an uncontrollable grin spreading across my face with the realization. He presses his lips to mine once more before settling his forehead to mine.

"We're going to have it all, honey. Always."

Those are the words that tide me over the rest of the night as I fall asleep in his arms and as I get ready the following morning. They move through my mind as, for the first time in months, I put my Willa Stone shield on, realizing that it no longer fits perfectly, the facade feeling a bit like a shirt that shrank a bit in the wash after months of growing into the louder, more colorful version of myself. When I stare in the mirror, despite my hair being a bit darker, I see Willa Stone, the pop star, staring back, and despite spending nearly ten years as her, she's no longer as familiar as she once was. The dress I'm wearing today is not the one Jackie sent me, but a slight twist on my normal color palette that Nat helped me pick out last week, a subtle hint at the colors that will be on the next album. A fun easter egg for fans on my first sighting in months.

Because, despite what I need to present to the world today, I am not the same girl who fled to Holly Ridge three months ago.

"Ready?" Leo asks from beside the bedroom, and I turn to look at him over my shoulder. He, too, is different from the man I'm used to seeing, hair combed neatly back instead of mussed, one of his hot as fuck suits on, expensive leather shoes instead of work boots. But now, there's a soft look in his eyes and a smile I know he saves just for me.

"Yeah, give me a sec," I say, then reach for a lipstick on the counter, one of the brighter pink ones Nat helped me pick out, one far off the Willa Stone color palette, but I swipe it on anyway. And when I smile at the mirror, remembering the beauty I've lived since I've been here, I smile—the real one, the wonky one, and I find comfort in seeing it.

TWENTY-NINE

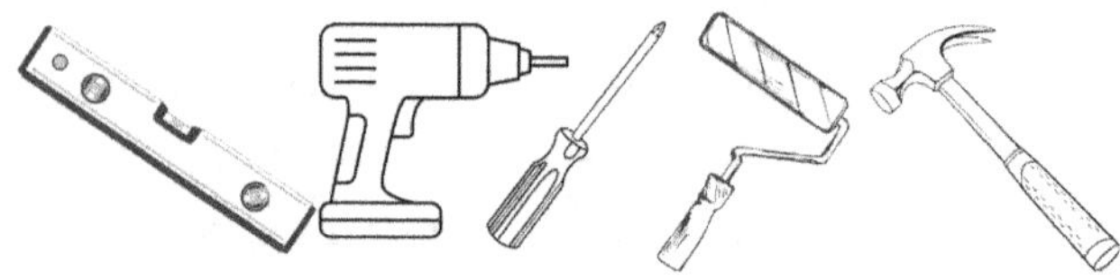

LEO

The next morning, Willa gets ready before we drive to the city together. During the drive, I hold her hand and savor these last quiet moments. We're both silent, lost in our thoughts. Last night, I saw the panic on her face, and not for the first time, realized there haven't been many people by her side—people who wanted to make sure she got what she wanted in life, even if it meant temporary discomfort for themselves.

Like so many times in these past three months, I'm determined and excited to give her that first. I'm not eager to watch her flirt with someone I've found—through investigation—to be a genuine asshole, though any reputation could be fixed by someone as sweet as Willa. But Willa is committed to honoring her promises, staying reliable and easy to work with, so I know this relationship is strictly business for her. For me, it's another chance to show I'll always support her.

It takes us about an hour to get to the city, and when I stop outside of the building, there's a decent-sized crowd waiting. I realize that Jackie or maybe Jefferson must have leaked that Willa would be here today to start her reappearance with a bang. Irritation moves through me, since no one ran this decision past me, and from Willa's wide eyes, I can tell no one gave her a heads-up either. I give her one last squeeze of her hand before finally, regretfully, letting go and putting the car in park. Gabe is already walking towards Willa's door, and I step out, key in hand, to hand over to Willa's bodyguard as planned.

"Good to see you, Willa," Gabe says, offering a genuine smile as he helps her out. I fight the urge to intervene. I like Gabe—a detail assigned by Jaime, and I reviewed his resume before approving the swap, so I know he's qualified. He and Willa have a good rapport, but a new possessiveness tugs at me as she takes his hand to get out of the car.

That should be me.

As quickly as it comes, I stuff that thought down. It's not helpful right now, and I have to stay focused on the task at hand: getting Willa inside with Gabe's help. The crowd starts cheering, thankfully keeping the path to the door clear, and I watch as Willa's shoulders straighten and Gabe leads her towards the door. I've seen this a hundred times before, every time there is a group of paparazzi waiting for her. She's a pro, stopping and moving slowly, constantly aware of her face and making sure each paparazzi gets the photo they came for.

Except that's not what happens.

Instead, she freezes.

Her body stiffens, and she stands for a moment, a smile on her lips that looks glowing but is actually hesitant. She shifts, her body freezing in the slightest way before she turns to Gabe, who is a step or two behind her. He steps forward instantly, and Gabe whispers something I can't hear, but when his face transforms a bit and nods, something grows cold inside of me.

Something happened.

Something is wrong.

Gabe moves so he's close behind her, blocking her as best as he can. Cameras snap. Their flashes are blinding. People waiting call Willa's name, trying to get her attention, but I drown it out. I watch

Gabe guide her along, faster than normal. Willa's shoulders are tight. Her head turns just a bit, her smile stiff for the cameras, as if she can't bear to give them anything. The light has left her eyes. My steps speed. Panic spills into my stomach as I try to school my face and get inside with her.

"Leo! Come on, a few more photos!" a paparazzi I recognize calls. "She's been gone for months!" I give him a grin, wide and mischievous, playing into the role of all-knowing publicist with a plan.

"We've got to keep you guessing," I say, winking to make this seem strategic, though it's anything but. They laugh and jeer, granting us time to get Willa inside, but before more questions come, I slip through the doors, rushing to catch up with Gabe guiding Willa. I'm keenly aware of the large windows exposing us to the still-shouting paparazzi as I hurry after them.

"What's going on?" I ask, panic coursing through me freely now. Something is not right.

"She wanted to skip the press line," Gabe says, trying to mask the confusion and hint of worry in his words and failing. My eyes move to Willa, who looks pale and small as she stands in the luxurious hallway. Her shoulders curve inward, and her chest rises and falls quickly with short, shallow breaths. Her eyes are glazed and wide, her lips parted, and her pointer finger is scratching at the edge of her thumb rhythmically.

"Willa, what's going on?" I ask, trying to keep my voice calm.

"I—" she says, but can't seem to get the words out, her breathing growing quicker as her eyes shift towards the windows. She needs to get behind closed doors, somewhere she feels safe, to come down from her panic.

"I have to move the car," Gabe says nervously, glancing at the door and back to Willa. The plan was always for him to get her inside safely, then move the car to the parking garage—a safety measure Jaime enacts since a valet could plant a tracker if alone with her car. "But I can't leave her."

"I've got it," I say, handing the keys to him and moving Willa to a nearby room without another word. The meeting room is usually empty, but when I see a cleaning woman inside, I nod toward the door.

"Get out," I say firmly. The woman, Fran, looks at me wide-eyed. I'll send her flowers and a gift card later, but I don't have the luxury of niceties now. "Get out now." She nods frantically, pulling her small cart out behind her. I lock the door and move a now-shaking Willa to a chair.

"Willa, honey," I say, my voice much calmer than it was a moment before, squatting a bit to get on her level as she stands there, dazed and breathing heavy. "What's going on?"

"It's nothing," she says, but it's obviously not the case. In fact, she's lost even more color now. The side of her finger is turning an angry red from her nail scratching at it. Then she shifts her head to look at me fully, and my heart falls further. Panic is written clearly across her face, now mixed with guilt. "I'm so sorry, Leo. I'm sure you guys wanted me to take pictures. This was my shot after not seeing me for so long. I think I forgot what it was like. It was so much. It was so loud and—"

"Hey, hey, hey, Will. Don't apologize. I do not care. What I care about right now is you. Are you okay?" Her eyes are starting to water, but that only seems to make things worse.

"This is why I need my stupid routines!" she says, making absolutely no sense at this point. "Now everyone's going to be so mad at me. I'm going to let them down. Jackie and you and Mom and Jefferson and...Jackie—oh my god, Jackie's going to kill me. I'm, I'm, I'm..." Her breathing becomes choppy and more irregular as the panic consumes her.

I do the only thing I can think of, sitting next to her and pulling her into my lap, her legs draping over mine. But with our closeness, her breathing slows a bit, easing the pressure in my own chest.

"What do you need, Willa?"

She closes her eyes and takes a shaky breath, holding it for measured moments, then releasing it slowly before speaking.

"I just need to get it together. I just need…" Her voice is breathy, not her own, "I need to get myself in check."

"I'll be fine," she says, her voice anything but. I'll be fine. This is —" She's still shaking, but her mind is trying to convince herself she's okay. "I'll be fine. It's just that I haven't done that in a while. I didn't prepare." She takes a deep breath. She starts to calm, and my own pulse slows with hers.

It's all going to be fine.

That is, until a familiar voice can be heard through the door, Willa's head snapping in the direction, and that look on her face going panicked once more.

"Where's Willa?" we hear called from the other side of the door, and without thinking, I put my hands to her cheeks, pulling her face to look at me once more. Her eyes are haunted, but that dazed look is gone, at least.

The fear isn't, though. The fear and panic are still there, stark, and I hate seeing it on my sweet girl's face.

"I need to go, Leo," she says, trying to stand, but I hold her steady. "I have to go see her. She's going to be so mad I messed up the paparazzi walk. She's going to freak. She's going to, she's going to—" her breathing gets more and more frantic, and I know that bringing Jackie in right now will only make things worse.

She doesn't need Jackie right now. What she needs is a distraction, and I'm going to be the one to give it to her.

And when her head snaps to mine, a bit of the light returning as I confuse her just enough to distract her a bit, I know I need to continue.

Right now, I am not Leo Sinclair, Willa Stone's publicist.

Right now, I am Leo, and she is my Willa, and I need to do what I have to do to calm her down.

My mind runs through a dozen ideas and solutions, things doctors and therapists taught me for managing a panic attack, ways to quickly overcome one, and landing on a single idea that is just as stupid as it is effective.

I shift my hand on her face and pull her into me, pressing my lips to hers.

Instantly, her body melts, and relief moves through me.

Her hands lift, though I can still feel them shaking as they move to the back of my neck.

More.

She needs more. She needs something to counter the panic, something to snap her out of it quickly.

Without thinking, I shift her, settling her on my lap until she's straddling me. I slide a hand up beneath the hem of her dress, my hand moving over the smooth skin of her thigh, and her body stills again. When she pulls back, her pupils are still blown, still hazy with the panic attack lingering, but hopefully, I can make them hazy in a different way soon.

"Leo, what are—" she asks.

"Do you trust me?" A moment passes, a single moment in time before my heart explodes with her nod.

"Of course," she says, and I press my lips to her in favor of biting back the groan that wants to leave my lips at her sweet trust in me. As I kiss her, I slide my hand up, shifting until I press my thumb against her clit over her panties. I'm not sure what her reaction will be or whether she'll go with my plan. Her system is already on high alert, cortisol running through her body, but when her hips tip towards me, I can't help but smile as I drop my head to her neck. "What are you doing?" she whispers, and the panic in my own chest eases when the words sound less panicked.

"You're having a panic attack. You need a hit of dopamine and endorphins, and I'm going to make it happen." My thumb moves in circles over her slit, and she lets out a heavy breath. "You're gonna have to make this quick, but I know you can come for me fast, can't you?" I murmur. I'm pleased when she doesn't argue like she did that first night, telling me she can't do that.

She knows that she can.

"I think so," she breaths, her hips shifting. I read about this once, that you can trick your brain out of the fight or flight that comes with an orgasm, but obviously never had a need to test it out.

Until now.

"That's my good girl." My thumb continues to move over her clit, and my middle finger presses into her panties over her entrance, teasing her. I note when the stiffness of her panic attack leaves her body and a new tightening enters as I press her clit in hard, rough circles, which I know from a lot of testing that she likes most of all, her hips bucking as it builds, fast and quick. I desperately want to sink into her, but we don't have time.

We don't even have time for this, but I'm making time for it.

"Leo," she whispers, and when I look up at her, her face is dazed but in a much better way now.

"I know, honey. Let go. Let me take care of you."

She bucks again, a breath, leaving her lips, her eyes fluttering shut.

"You look so fucking pretty like this, all done up as your pretty princess version, but being my little slut."

"Yes, yes," she whispers, head nodding. I feel her clench along the tip of my middle finger and decide to give her a little more, to tip the scale. My middle finger moves, sliding along the seam of her underwear and then sliding under. She's soaked, and I bite back a rough groan.

"You like that, don't you? You like it when I call you my little slut?" I murmur, my forehead to hers, and she nods, breath hitching as I slide my middle finger into her, my thumb still roughly circling her clit. "That's because you were made for me, Willa Stone," I breath, and that's what does it.

That's what has her teeth sinking into her lips. Her head tipping back as her body quakes over me, tightening around my finger as she comes silently in my lap. I hate that she's swallowing her sounds, but it just means I'll have to make sure she's even louder next time. I wait until she comes down from her orgasm before sliding my hand out from between her legs and rearranging her. I brush her hair back and rub a finger over her lips, but her makeup is still perfect.

The light is also back in her eyes, which is the real relief.

"What was that?" she asks with a small laugh. I grin wide.

What it was, was risk. Stupid, and idiotic.

But I don't care about that right now. I couldn't care about it when that blank look was on her face, and I can't care about it now.

"How do you feel?" I ask, and I'm pleased when instead of brushing me off, she takes a moment, seeming to take stock of her body and her feelings before grinning at me.

"Amazing. But what was that for?" she asks, a goofy smile on her lips.

"Are you calm?" Her eyes widen in disbelief.

"That was to calm me down?"

"You were having a panic attack. You needed a distraction, and orgasms release endorphins and dopamine to counter the cortisol from panic."

"How do you know that?" she asks, furrowing her brows.

I press my lips to hers, softly. "I'll tell you all about it later. Right now we have places to be." She scrunches up her nose, and I smile, shaking my head before my hands move ot her hips. Lifting her and setting her to her feet. I stand after, rearranging my hard cock to make it less noticeable, but also removing my suit jacket and draping it over my hand, just in case. She watches with an amused smile on her lips, and I roll my eyes.

I stare down at Willa, then dip to give her one last kiss before swiping my thumb over her lip.

"Still perfect." She smiles sweetly, and I'm tempted to stay in here forever with her. Unfortunately, the sound of Jackie's voice filters in through the door, and I sigh. "But we've gotta go."

"Jackie's going to be mad that you wouldn't make me take more pictures," she says, nervousness returning to her face, and I hate that this is the kind of reaction her manager pulls from her. I don't think she's ready for that conversation any time soon, but one day, we're going to have to have the very uncomfortable conversation about how poorly Jackie treats her.

For now, I put my hands on her face and force Willa to look at me.

"They can go fuck themselves. I'm your publicist. I know what I'm doing."

"And what are you doing, Leo?"

"Putting you first. Always." That pulls a smile onto her face.

"I love you," she whispers, and whatever remaining tension bleeds from my chest because of *that*. That is why I will jump through hoops for as long as she needs me to. Because at the end of the day, that's what I get.

"I love you, Willa. Now let's go meet your new boyfriend," I say, and despite where we're headed and the fact that she just had a full-blown panic attack, she lets out a loud laugh, and I know to my soul we're going to make it through this just fine.

"What the hell is going on?" Jackie asks when we step out of the room together, though I leave a good amount of space between us, forcing myself to fall back into *publicist who is taking care of his client on a professional level*. Jackie looks the same as always, if not a bit angrier, though with all the work she gets done, she might be a lot more frustrated than her frozen face lets on. Willa walks right up to her manager, and I expect to see her a bit frazzled still, but instead, I see her shield is locked in place.

Now, she's the world-wide pop star. America's sweetheart.

She's officially on.

"We had an incident," I say, before Willa can speak. "And I brought her in here to collect herself." I rack my brain trying to think of some kind of excuse for why I pulled her into a room for any stretch of time, but Willa speaks before I can think of one.

"I had a panic attack," she says clearly, and for a moment, Jackie's face softens. I might despise the woman and believe she doesn't have Willa's full interests at heart, but I can't say she doesn't care for her in some way, shape, or form.

"Are you okay?"

Willa nods, and then Jackie tips her head towards the elevator. We all pile in, headed to the floor where the Perfect Image offices are, and finally, Jackie looks her over.

"That is not what I sent you, Willa," Jackie says, jaw tight, though her face shows a smile. I don't have to look her over to know she looks beautiful: a light, almost-white-purple dress with a high neck and long sleeves that flare out a bit, the short skirt doing the same, hitting at her mid-thigh. It's paired with a pair of high black boots that stop right over her knees. She looks beautiful, the perfect mix of my Willa and the one she normally shows the fans, and I wonder if this is her way of bringing the color she found in Holly Ridge into her Willa Stone world.

"I know, but I saw this the other day and thought it was gorgeous. It's one of the colors for the new album, so I thought it would be a fun hint for fans to catch."

"We haven't discussed the new album yet. The dress you were sent was specifically curated for you and your brand," Jackie says, and the way she says it with a hint of frustration in her words rubs me wrong, but the way she bosses around Willa *always* rubs me wrong.

In the past, Willa would have apologized profusely, but she doesn't. Instead, she lifts a shoulder and holds Jackie's gaze.

"I decided the colors for the album months ago. I talked to Harper about it, and she's working on the wardrobe already for it."

"You didn't talk to me about it," Jackie accuses, and Wila gives her one of her sweet smiles, but beneath it is a thin layer of disappointment. I'm not sure if it's for Jackie's own frustration or something else.

"You didn't ask," Willa says, and I decide that's where that disappointment is coming from. Willa poured her heart into this album, and I know she created a full mood board for its vision months ago.

"I think it's smart," I say, trying to ease the tension that's brewing in the small elevator. "The fans are excited about a new album, and we can add some color to her outfits before we announce the cover. They love piecing together hints Willa leaves after the fact."

Jackie's jaw is tight, and she stares at me, a flash of utter dislike on her face. It's gone as soon as I catch it, replaced with a pleasant, if not a bit annoyed look before she smiles.

"Well, what's done is done; they already have photos with you in this piece," Jackie says with a sigh as the elevator doors slide open. "Come on. Chris is in the office—we snuck him in through the back so as not to seem obvious, but I wanted you two to meet before your first date." She steps out, expecting us to follow, and Willa turns to me, giving me a small smile and wide eyes. I roll mine, then gesture for her to go first.

And then I follow her, like I know I always will, and watch her ass sway with each step.

THIRTY

WILLA

"I still can't believe you dyed your hair," Jackie says, touching a strand of my hair as we drive to the restaurant where I'll go on my first public date. It looks seamless, just like my old hair, and the hairdresser who styled it this afternoon agreed it was a good-quality piece.

So good, that Jackie didn't realize I was wearing a wig until we came back to my place to chat and go over my calendar for the next month after the meeting with Chris Klein. As expected, the actor was a complete gentleman, charming and kind, complimenting me and accepting the basic terms we always lay out for each relationship before the first appearance: boundaries I hold, such as no extreme PDA, and the contractual rules, like no external relationships for the next six months. I made sure not to look at Leo when that was spoken; instead, I doodled on paper, a couple of words and lines for another song that's been swirling in my mind.

The meeting ended, and then Leo stayed in the building while I left with Jackie, making sure to follow my usual routine before stepping out this time and leaving without a panic attack.

I still felt like I was leaving half of my heart behind when I stepped out of the doors, though.

"I've got something on the calendar for tomorrow to fix it," Jackie continues, scrolling on her phone.

"No," I say firmly.

"No?" Jackie asks, lifting her eyes to look at me, confused, a hint of shock on her face. I've seen that expression more today than I have in the entire time I've worked with her, and I'm sure it's because I've never been one to argue with what she's saying.

But I'm not the same girl I was three months ago, and even more, I don't *want to be her* anymore.

"I'm not dyeing it," I clarify firmly. Jackie stares at me in horror. "It's not healthy for your hair to be that light, and honestly, it washes me out. I don't like it. I like my new color." Despite my confidence, a hint of nervousness settles in my gut. "I'm going to wear a wig when I'm on."

"You can't wear a wig all the time, Willa. What are you, Hannah Montana?"

I smile at her words, though she clearly isn't amused.

"It's fine, Jackie. I already wear contacts. What's some fake hair, too?"

She stares at me, then must realize it isn't worth the argument because she sighs and shakes her head.

"We'll revisit in two weeks. Putting on a wig every day is going to get annoying," she says, but I shrug, knowing I'd rather maintain a level of anonymity outside my career. The wigs are just another small way I'll be able to have it all.

My phone vibrates in my hand, and when I look at the screen, it's a text from Leo, a reply to the photo I sent him this afternoon while getting ready. It was before I put on the boring black dress Jackie picked out for me, and my arm was covering my breasts.

Miss you already, I had said. It seems he only just saw it, or at least only now found the time to respond.

Fuck, honey.

You can't do this to me, not if you don't
want me to crash your date.

It makes a smile spread across my lips, even though we both know he wouldn't crash the date. It's a fun image of him throwing me over his shoulder as he did at the Mill and claiming me in front of everyone.

"What are you smiling about?" she asks, giving me a skeptical look, and I fight not to let the blush burn across my cheeks.

"One of my friends from Holly Ridge just texted me," I say, deciding the fewer details the better. Leo *is* one of my friends from Holly Ridge, after all, so it's not a total lie.

181 days left.

Counting down every single one.

Me too

After I send that, I check my other messages and see I've been added to a group chat with Nat, Wren, and Hallie, and another smile comes to my face as I watch them go back and forth. Hallie sent a paparazzi pic of me from this morning, from me leaving, thankfully.

HALLIE

I am so borrowing this dress, Willa.

WREN

You look so pretty! I hope you have a great
time today!

NAT

The wig looks SO good! Look at me, styling
a celebrity!

You've been styling me for months, Nat.

NAT

Yeah, but not for everyone and their mom
to see.

Mentally, I try to figure out whether I could bring Nat on as my actual stylist and how to convince Jackie of it. They would definitely butt heads, but Nat understands the industry and my vision for my brand, and I think she would be an amazing asset.

Another message comes through, this one from Leo. I fight back a smile when I see he sent me a photo of a beaten-up wooden vanity with chipping paint. It's sitting on the side of the road near what I think might be Adam and Wren's house.

Should I bring this home?

Home.
God, I love that.
Instantly, my mind goes to ideas for it, where we could put it, and how I could style it. I saw a video on stripping paint, and I've been dying to try it. It looks like the wood might have been really pretty before the owner painted it a distressed white.

Yes, please! She's gorgeous!

Got it. Adam's grabbing it, and I'll pick it up
when I get home later.

Since he drove my car up here today, he's taking a rideshare on the hour-long drive home, and knowing that distance is already between us aches in my chest.

Will you be awake for me to call you
tonight?

Yes. There's a gift in your room waiting
for you.

My eyes widen, and instantly I'm desperate to know what kind of present he could have left me and how he got it into my room. I ask, and he avoids answering, as usual. We text back and forth for a few minutes, Jackie occasionally asking me questions about interviews or lunches with other celebrities, but we're close to the restaurant when she throws me back.

"We're aiming for an engagement, this time," she says, and it's so casual, so offhanded, that I think I must have missed something important. Setting my phone aside, I give her my full attention.

"What?"

"An engagement with Chris. We're still deciding whether it would be best to make it a quick, exciting whirlwind soon or in a few months. Jefferson said that around Christmastime could be fun, and we could use it to promote your holiday album." I blink at her, realizing I didn't miss anything at all.

"No," I say, shaking my head. "No. No engagement." Where the *hell* is this coming from? I've been on board with the fake relationships for years now, but I've always made my stance on anything further very clear.

"Willa—" Jackie starts, voice low and soft, the kind you might give a child who doesn't want to take a bath, rather than an adult who doesn't want to *marry* someone else.

"No. I told you from the very beginning that fake relationships were fine. Engagements, marriages, absolutely not. I'm only doing that once, and I'm not doing it for the cameras." It was the one condition I set when we started doing these relationships regularly. Even though my hopeless romantic went into hiding when I thought I couldn't have a relationship and a career, she wouldn't let me cross that line. It would have felt like a betrayal to the little girl who daydreamed about Prince Charming, and now that I've found mine, I'm glad I always stayed firm on that.

"Willa, please, be practical. How many high-profile relationships can you be in before people start to question you? Eventually, you have to stop being so stubborn and accept that this is clearly the next step in your career."

Frustration is etched across her face, and it sets me back, leaving my voice firm when I respond.

"My career and my personal life are not the same," I say, telling her something I thought we both understood, but when she rolls her eyes, I wonder if maybe I was wrong all along.

Over the years, Jackie and I have often disagreed about something related to my career, whether it's outfits, timing, or which song should be a single, but I've never felt this pure irritation and, honestly, sense of betrayal toward her.

It settles in my chest in a way I very much do not like, though I push it back as just not being around her for a long time, losing some of the buffer that I've built over the years to handle her cutthroat desire for success.

"Willa—"

I lick my lips and take in a deep breath, speaking over her before she can continue.

I hadn't meant to have this conversation right now. I'd planned to bring it up with a strategy for countering each and every one of the arguments I'm sure Jackie will have, but it seems we have to have this talk now. I take a deep breath and say what I should have said years ago but never felt brave enough to.

"I'm not getting engaged, and even more, I'm not doing any more fake relationships after this one." I force my voice to come out firm and without any room for argument, and Jackie's entire body goes still. "I hate them, the fake relationships. I hate how they make me feel."

The nervousness leaves her face, and she waves a hand as if my concerns hold no bounds. "You just have first date jitters."

"It's not a first date, Jackie. It's...it's the first episode. It's acting," I say, shaking my head and trying not to let the frustration I'm feeling leak into my words. "I'm tired of faking it. I'm tired of creating this entire illusion. I get that some of it is necessary, but I'm done with the rest." Jackie is silent, and I continue to explain, desperate to get her to understand what I'm saying. "No more fake relationships after this. The last few months have shown me I need to restructure my priorities. After this relationship, after this album, I want to slow things down. I want to live my life, find balance."

"Willa—" Jackie says, a softness on her face that suddenly feels disingenuous. It's no different from the one I've seen a million times over the years, but after three months with people who genuinely care for me, I can see the difference clearly. It makes my stomach cold. "We can revisit this—"

"No. I'm telling you right now I'm not doing this again, Jackie."

She stares at me, trying to decide what to say, but before she can, the car stops. When I look out the window, a group of paparazzi is waiting outside a five-star restaurant I've been to before. Cheering starts, and through the tinted glass, I see my date approaching, a grin on his face as he waves to the fans waiting.

"Now, I have a date to get to," I say, then close my eyes and take a deep breath, pushing the irritated Willa aside and putting my shield on just as the door opens, letting in the noise from outside.

"Hello, gorgeous," Chris says, loud enough for the cameras to hear, and I smile wide, then let him help me out of the car and into the restaurant.

And with that, the show begins.

THIRTY-ONE

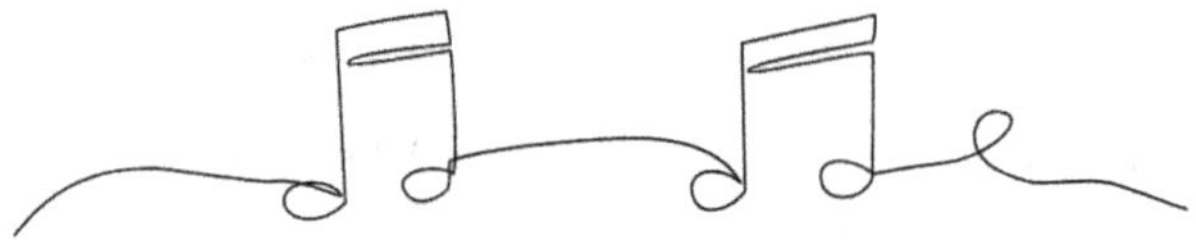

WILLA

Dinner is a misery.

Chris orders for himself before ordering for *me*, and he gets me a salad I absolutely hate. I end up pushing it around the entire meal while he devours a plate of steak and potatoes that look fantastic. I contemplate asking the kitchen to make me what he has, but after just forty minutes with this man, I'm already desperate for this date to end.

He spends the entire time smiling, showing off alarmingly white veneers, and talking about himself. His accomplishments, his projects, his notable movies. With each one, he asks me if I've seen it, and if I say no, he gives me a rundown of the entire plot. Unfortunately, I learned early not to lie; if I say I've seen it, he asks me for my favorite scene, which, obviously, is difficult. Having been in this industry for most of my life, I'm very used to self-absorbed celebrities who only want to talk about themselves, but this situation definitely takes the cake.

As the night goes on, I find myself desperately hoping this is simply his nerves showing. He was kind and charming at the meeting this morning, so I thought it wouldn't be too much of a hassle. For a bit, I even thought that maybe, when it ended, I'd have another friend in the industry, as had happened a few times before.

Instead, I find myself wondering just how the hell I'm going to manage *six entire months* of this.

When the server comes to ask us about dessert, Chris answers before I can. "Have to watch your waistline, am I right?" he asks with a grin. When I smile back, I can taste blood from biting my tongue so hard, but I figure that enduring his douchebaggery is better than staying here longer than absolutely necessary.

After I pay the bill (yes, *I* pay the bill), Chris leads me into the entryway, where we wait for Gabe to give the all-clear before we leave. I'm almost home free, just needing to take a small walk around the pond in the nearby park, giving paparazzi a chance to take shots of our magical first date before I can go home, curl up in some sweats, and call Leo.

"One thing," I say quietly, looking around to make sure there are no listening ears around. "Before we head outside."

"Yeah?" he asks, his attention to his wrist, adjusting his cufflink. I force myself not to make a face at his inability to even *pretend* he cares about what I have to say.

"No kissing tonight." His head snaps up, finally giving me attention, and his brow furrows.

"Excuse me?"

"No kissing," I start, then take in a deep breath. "Not for the first date. I'd like to spread it out." I know rationally I'll have to kiss him at some point, have to give the cameras and the media what they want, but the idea of doing it so soon after leaving Leo makes my stomach turn. I'm relieved when, after a moment of hesitation, Chris nods.

"Okay, that's fine," he says with a smile, and I return it with a genuine one for the first time all night. My phone buzzes with a text from Gabe, and I look up at Chris.

"Thank you for understanding," I say.

"Of course. Now let's go stun the cameras, shall we?" he asks, giving me his elbow. I take it and smile again as he leads us out of the restaurant, the camera's flashing and paparazzi calling our names.

We walk along the pond, lit by the moonlight, and chat some more. He asks me a few questions about myself, and I find myself almost enjoying the evening. I decide he must have just been nervous earlier in the dimly lit romantic restaurant, feeling the all too familiar pressure of the strange situation. As we walk and chat, I realize Jackie did a great job, as always: from the outside looking in, this is a romantic first date.

A far-off thought in my mind recalls an interview where someone asked what my dream date would be, and I said a moonlit walk along the water after a great dinner, and I know that this date is intentional.

The problem is, this isn't my dream date, not anymore.

These days, my dream date is a day of housework, then being too tired to make dinner, ordering a dozen different chicken nuggets from different fast-food restaurants, eating them in the trunk of my car, and then fucking in the shower.

Or going to a cheesy town fair, riding the Ferris wheel, and winning a silly prize.

It's going to a local dive bar with all our friends, and just...being.

"Paparazzi to the left," Chris murmurs, his voice low, breaking into my thoughts. His hand drops mine and slides along my waist. "Let's get one more shot, and then we can head to your car." I look over and nod, seeing the paparazzi standing near my car. Gabe is also there, watching like a hawk. Relief washes over me, knowing the night is almost over. It's way more exhausting keeping my act up than I remember. We agreed this morning that leaving in my car and dropping Chris off at his place would make the most sense and avoid a media-fueled romantic goodbye.

We make our way toward the paparazzi and Gabe, smiling and

chatting when I see them: not paparazzi, but a couple of sweet-looking girls, grinning wide and barely containing their excitement.

"This way," Chris says in a low voice, moving toward the car and the cameras, but I veer to the side. My name grows louder from the cameras, but I do my best to block it out, smiling at the young girls. Even though my nerves are on edge and I'm desperate to get some quiet and decompress, I can't walk past these girls, clearly waiting to see and talk to me. They're the reason I'm even where I am, after all, the fans.

Not to mention, the paparazzi always love to capture a fan interaction, so really, it's two birds with one stone.

"Hey, there," I saw, turning towards them. One is probably nine, the other eleven, and they have the widest, giddiest smiles spread across their faces.

"Ohmigod," the older one squeals. Her mother, behind her, has a phone at the ready, recording the interaction with a hesitant grin.

"Mom! She said hi!" the younger one says, looking over her shoulder. Her mother laughs, shakes her head, then looks to me.

"We were out for dinner nearby and walking past when we saw the crowd. They overheard someone mention you might be nearby, so I told them we could wait, but not to expect you to have the time to say hi."

I nod, understanding, then turn to them. "I always have time for my fans."

"My sister is your *biggest* fan," the younger girl says, clearly the more talkative of the two. "And I'm your second."

"Is that right?" I ask, and the older one, eyes still wide with shock, nods. I try not to laugh at the adorable look. "What's your name?"

"Ruby," she whispers. "Ruby Finch."

I nod, then turn to her younger sister.

"And I'm Harper," she says, not even waiting for me to ask, and I let a little laugh out.

"Harper! I have a friend named Harper. She makes dresses," I say.

"No way!" the girl says, eyes wide, and I nod, then open my mouth to say something more, but I'm stopped by my date.

"We have to go, Willa," Chris says, putting a hand to my waist. I look up at him with a smile that hides my irritation.

"We're not in a rush," I say, trying to keep my voice soft and neutral before turning back to the girls.

"I wish I had something for you to sign," Ruby says in a still awed whisper. I bite my lip, knowing I don't have anything in my car, but wanting to surprise these two with something.

"Well, I can fix that," I say with a grin, digging into my small bag for my phone. Then I open a new note and hand it to the girls' mom. "Would you be okay with giving me an address to send something to?"

"No way," the older one says in an awed whisper.

"MOM!" the younger yells, jumping up and down. "PLEASE PLEASE PLEASE!" Their mom laughs, then nods and takes the phone. I don't miss how her eyes go wide and watery as she types in the information.

This.

This is my favorite part of my job, behind performing. Being a part of tiny, magical moments like this.

"Can we take a picture?" the older one asks softly, and I nod.

"Of course!" I say, as if that was never even a question, then squat between the two girls and smile at their mom's phone. "Okay, now I really do gotta get going, but it was so great to meet you two! Can I give you girls a hug?" They nod enthusiastically, and I watch to make sure their mom nods as well before bending to give each girl a tight hug. When I back off, Chris is standing beside me, jaw tight, and his hand moves to my elbow, pulling me toward him.

It takes everything in me not to snap at him.

"Are you two together?" Ruby asks, clearly the curious one of the two.

"Ruby!" her mom chides. I laugh, then open my mouth to answer in my normal, vague way, but get interrupted.

"We sure are," Chris says with a dazzling smile, pulling me into his side. I stumble a bit, and my hand lands on his chest to catch myself. As I do, I notice that the paparazzi have gotten closer, clearly seeing an opportunity.

"Kiss!" one calls, and I roll my eyes, jokingly shaking my head in the negative. But before I can step away toward the car, Chris moves, pulling me in closer, my hand still on his chest as he drops his face to mine.

My entire body stills.

I try not to give in to the urge to push him away and do it *hard*, instead forcing myself to do what I've always been good at: acting.

I let Chris kiss me, a soft, delicate touch of lips, almost sweet and considerate. It's the kind of kiss that, at a different time, when we hadn't just agreed *not* to do this tonight, I would have been fine with.

But it's not that.

So instead, fury bubbles in my veins, and with the crowd watching, cheering, and awing, I'm fighting everything in me not to flip out on him.

Finally, after what feels like an eternity but is probably closer to a few seconds, Chris pulls back, giving me a wide, satisfied grin. I force myself to reflect on it, reminding myself that I am supposed to be into this, before turning back to the two little girls.

"Okay, well, it was nice meeting you girls," I say through a tight jaw. "I'm sure I'll see you again soon." They squeal and say goodbyes, and their mother mouths a heartfelt *thank you*, before Chris and I stiffly make our way to my car. Gabe opens the door, and I slide in, taking deep breaths to center myself.

"What was that?" I snap as Chris closes the door behind himself. He took an extra minute, waving at the additional fans who began to gather—*my fans,* I should add—before coming in, and it's only given me more time to stew on my anger.

"What was what?" He has a shit-eating grin on his lips, the cocky boyish look I'm sure gets him everything and anything he's ever wanted and out of trouble more than a couple times over his career.

Unfortunately for him, I am immune to it.

"That kiss?" I say, voice cracking in the small vehicle. "What the fuck was that kiss?"

"Playing it up for the cameras." My jaw tightens, and I've never in my life wanted to hit someone, but right now, my fingers itch to slap that annoying smile off his face.

"I said I didn't want to kiss tonight, for the cameras or otherwise," I remind him, trying to keep my voice neutral.

"I did what I had to do to give the people what they wanted. In that moment, what you wanted didn't matter."

Horror rolls through me at his words.

"Excuse me?"

He shrugs as if this entire exchange isn't unhinged.

"You're like me: you'll do what needs to be done for the press."

I force myself to take in deep breaths, and as I do, I remind myself why I'm here.

The marketing plan that Jackie has put a lot of work into.

The contract's already in place.

He could out all of my previous fake relationships if this falls apart.

Leo's career very well could hinge on this, what with Jefferson just *looking* for a reason to fire him.

And just as Leo would never do anything to get between me and my career, I have to make sure I do the same for him. I can't let my own discomfort, the same discomfort I've tackled time and time again over the years, be the reason Leo loses everything he's built.

"Never do that again. Ever. If I explicity say no kissing, no touching, *anything*, you will respect my wishes." Despite my focus being solely on the obnoxious man before me, from the corner of my eye, Gabe stiffens as if he's understanding what is happening. I know if I wanted him to, he would step in, but I've got this handled.

"Oh, come on, it was a good kiss," he says, trying to make light of it and giving me what I assume is meant to be a swoony look.

"I am not an idiot you need to seduce, Chris. I am your colleague, that is all. We have a purely business partnership, but if you want to continue this, you absolutely have to respect my wishes," I say, my voice firm. "You do not kiss me when I specifically told you not to. That violates my consent, my safety, and my personal space. "

"Jackie told me I was to kiss you if given the opportunity," he says.

"Then fucking kiss Jackie. I am not Jackie. And while we're at it, you do not rush me when I am interacting with fans. Ever." A moment passes, and we stare at one another, and the look on his face changes in an instant, the charm turning off instantly. It makes a shiver run down my spine, and not the good kind Leo gives me.

"What are you going to do?" he says. "You're as locked into this as I am."

And whether I like it or not, he's not completely wrong. For the first time in a long time, I feel trapped, and he must recognize it, because his lips tip up, that cruel smile growing more confident.

And in that moment, I know the next six months are going to be longer than I ever expected.

THIRTY-TWO

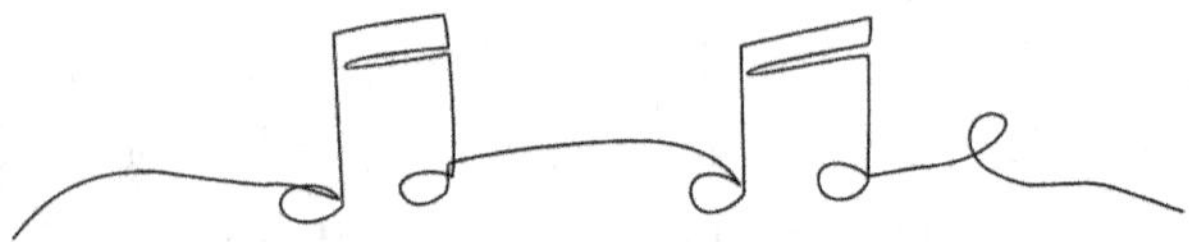

WILLA

I stay silent for the rest of the drive to drop Chris off, then sit the rest of the drive back to my place, stuck in my thoughts, desperately trying to center myself and organize my mind. But when my phone rings in my hand, Leo's name on the screen, I answer without thinking.

"Hi," I say low, reaching up to the wig and pulling out the pins that keep it in place. I'm increasingly grateful for it and the anonymity it gives me, but after a full day as Willa Stone, I'm eager to just be *Willa*.

"Hey, honey. How are you?" he says, and with it, a sense of relief moves through me.

"Good, I'm in the car on the way back." Before he can ask me how the date went, since I'm not sure how to respond just yet, I slide the wig off and take a deep breath. "Trying to get this wig off."

"How'd that go?" he asks with a laugh, bedding moving behind him quietly as he seems to settle in. In my mind, he's in bed already, tired and mussed, and I try to shelve the disappointment that I'm not there, too.

"'Jackie's annoyed, but I like it. It's an added layer separating my lives."

"Easier to transition from Willa Stone to Holly Ridge Willa," he says, and I grin as I remove the wig cap, then the pins holding my hair in place, shaking it out with a relieved sigh.

"Exactly. So how was your day?"

"Fine, the cab back to Holly Ridge was easy. Adam was able to grab that piece of furniture for you, so I'll get it tomorrow."

I squeal with excitement.

"Don't strip it without me," I beg, and he chuckles.

"Of course not."

"I'm bummed you're going to even be working on the house without me," I grumble, and that laugh sounds again, free and happy in a way I hadn't heard before Holly Ridge, and with it, warmth fills me.

"You would hate refinishing the floors, will, trust me. Sanding and stripping are a pain."

"I think stripping could be kind of fun."

When he hesitates for a moment, I can't help it. I laugh again. "The floors, you sicko," I explain. We continue to chat as Gabe takes me home, and I sink deeper into the chair, feeling comfortable. "What's this gift?" I ask, and there's a smile in his voice.

"Are you home yet?"

"Pulling into my garage now," I say.

"Then you'll see soon. Call me once you open it."

"What—" But I can't ask because he's hanging up and leaving me holding a silent phone. Before I can call him back, though, the car stops, and Gabe opens the door, helping me out before seeing me into my place and heading out. Once he's gone, I head to my room, where my suitcases wait to be unpacked. I open the largest one, hoping I picked right, and when I unzip it, there's a white bag tied with a bright red bow sitting on top of my things, a bag I very much did *not* bag up. I grab it eagerly, then move to sit on the edge of the bed. My hands reach for one of the ends of the bow, but my phone dings before I can tug on it.

> Did you open it yet?

> Not yet. Impatient much?

> Unbearably.

That intrigues me, the idea of whatever lies in this box making Leo so eager, so I move back to the bow, tugging at the ends and watching the fine ribbon fall to the sides. My pulse pounds with excitement as I open the lid and look inside, then gasp at what I see.

It's...a sex toy.

Not a simple vibrator, either. A fucking dildo lies in the box, in a box of its own. *Ribbed for her pleasure*, the box reads, alongside a ridiculously lifelike photo of a fake dick. Delicately, I take it out and inspect each side with curiosity. My phone rings beside me, and when I glance at it, Leo's name flashes there.

"What the hell is going on?" I ask, answering without any introduction.

"Did you open it?" There's a clear grin in his words, and despite the absurdity of the situation, I find it to be contagious.

"Did you get me a sex toy?"

"I can't touch you right now, Willa, even if it's all I want to do. But we're going to find workarounds. I know how much you like it when I talk you through it." A warm roll of pleasure moves through my body, and my voice catches in my throat.

"I—"

"Open the box, clean it off, then get your laptop and transfer this call to it," he continues. My eyes remain fixed on the toy in its brand-new box.

"My laptop?" My brain is muddled now, unable to piece things together.

"Just do what I asked, honey," he says, voice low now, almost a whisper. Without even thinking, I shift, cradling my phone between my ear and shoulder, then begin unboxing the toy until it's in my hand.

"It's kind of heavy," I muse, standing and taking it to the bathroom. His deep laugh fills my ear.

"I didn't buy the cheap one."

"Only the best for America's Sweetheart," I say as I wash it in the sink, then dry it off before slowly padding towards the bedroom once more. My pulse is picking up, nerves and adrenaline rushing through me.

"Exactly. I can't wait to watch you take it," he murmurs, and my hands hesitate as I unlock and open my computer.

"Watch?"

"Transfer the call, honey." His voice is smooth and easy, and I start to understand. My breathing quickens as he speaks, but I do as he asks, switching the FaceTime call seamlessly to my laptop. I set it on the bed, and my heart aches when a rumpled-looking Leo sitting in his own bed—our bed—without a shirt on fills the screen.

"You look beautiful," he murmurs. I step back, giving him a full view of the tight black dress I'm wearing, and I twirl a bit to show him the 360. "Jackie picked it out. Kind of boring, but even I have to admit I look hot as hell in it."

"Yeah, you do," he agrees. "Now take it off."

My sass piques, my eyebrow lifting as I look at him.

"Excuse me?"

"Undress, Willa. Now." The teasing is out of his voice, and the firm, hot Leo is in his place, making my pulse jump. My tongue darts out to wet my lips before, without further argument, I move my hand behind me and start to tug at the zipper. Leo's eyes are locked on me through the screen as I slowly reveal inches of skin to him. When I'm finally standing in just my bra and underwear, my shoes already kicked off, he tips his chin.

"Now the bra." I grin.

"Bossy, aren't you?"

"You like me, bossy, Willa. Now do as I say and take off your bra. Underwear, too," he instructs.

I undo the clasp of my bra, and his lips part as the bra slides down my arms, revealing my breasts, nipples hard. I'm already turned on, and the reality of what we're about to do suddenly becomes crystal clear. He mentioned this, that calls and cameras existed to bridge the gap while we were separated, but I guess I hadn't really thought it would be *this* fast.

And with the way he's looking at me as I slide my underwear down and then stand before the camera naked, I am more than happy with this sequence of events.

"On the bed, Will. In front of the laptop." My pulse pounds as I follow his instructions, sitting before the camera and tucking my feet beneath me. On the screen, he shifts the blankets down, revealing his already hard cock.

"Oh," I whisper, eyes wide and locked on his hand as he wraps thick fingers around himself and strokes.

"Cup your breasts," he murmurs, voice low. "Roll the nipples for me." Eagerly, I do as he asks, cupping a breast in each hand and letting out a breathy sound when I use my thumb and forefinger on each nipple, rolling and tugging a bit.

"So fucking pretty," he murmurs. "Keep one hand moving, but slowly move down your belly with the other." Again, I do what he asked, my center tightening already at the thought of what we're about to do: what *I'm* about to do.

If I've never come during sex, I surely haven't masturbated in front of anyone before.

But I *am* loving all of these firsts with Leo Sinclaire.

My hand hesitates right above where I want my fingers most, and my hips shift a bit, widening to give myself some room, but I don't move until I'm told to. When Leo notices my hesitation, a grin spreads across his lips.

"That's my good girl," he murmurs. "Waiting until I tell her she's allowed to touch what's mine."

That should absolutely not be hot.

A man telling me my clit, pussy, *my pleasure* is not my own? It should not be hot.

But it's not just any man saying it. It's Leo, and with the reverence he says it with, I am so very okay with it.

"Leo," I whisper, and he smiles.

"Circle your clit, baby." A relieved breath leaves my lips, and my head tips back, a low moan falling from them as I circle my needy clit. I'm already panting from the pure eroticism of this moment, from the tone of Leo's voice, the promise in his eyes, and the way his hand tightens when he watches my hand dip. "Lower. Tell me if you're wet yet." Eagerly, I move, sliding down and finding that I am, in fact, soaked. I can't help but slide the tip of a finger into myself. My body tightens around it, and I groan.

"Show me," he murmurs, and I lift my wet fingers to the camera to show him. A moan comes through the line, and more wet forms between my legs at the sound. "Fucking soaked. Now go get your toy, baby."

I move quickly, grabbing the dildo, and any hesitation I felt earlier about using it is gone. I'm empty, desperate, and needy. If I can't have Leo, this will have to do, and if I get to watch him take himself there as I do, it really isn't a sacrifice at all.

"Get up on your knees, and spread your legs," he instructs, and I do, shifting the cameras as needed. "Yeah, just like that," His voice is low with desire and sends another rush of heat through me. "Slide the tip between your legs, get it nice and wet." My breathing grows heavy as I do, not sliding it in like I really want, rubbing the tip along my center before sliding it up. I give Leo a show, letting him see me rub the smooth head of the toy over my clit, and he growls. "Fuck yeah. Now, put the base on the bed, between your legs.' I position it, then hover over, holding my breath with anticipation, desperate to slam it down as I did on the swing all those weeks ago. It won't be nearly as satisfying without his fingers digging into my hips, but it will have to do.

"Slide on to it slowly, just an inch," he says.

"Leo—" I protest

"Just the tip. That's what I would do. Tease you for teasing me. I've been thinking about that picture all day, honey."

"Oh god," I whimper as I do as he asks. His eyes are locked on me, but I'm fascinated by his hand slowly stroking himself. I watch as he moves it up and down the shaft, twisting a bit at the tip, his breath going light each time he does. Mentally, I catalog it, filing that away as something he likes for the future.

"Just like that," he says. "Now out. Then back in. Fuck yourself with just the tip, baby." My hips lift and fall just a bit, a tease as he watches with utter fascination. My body screams, desperate for more, but despite it, I feel the pleasure curling in my belly, need almost suffocating.

In this moment, I realize I have been so completely and totally changed by Leo that I could probably come just like this. Minimal stimulation, but having the erotic privilege of watching him bring himself utter pleasure at the sight of me doing what he asks.

But still, I want more.

And he knows it.

That becomes clear when he speaks next.

"All the way down, baby. Take it all." I don't hesitate, and on my next drop, I fill myself, my hand moving up as my hips move down and I moan, loud. "Fuck," he groans. "Fuck, look at you." I can't respond, not as I slide the dildo out and then back in, as I fuck myself, trying to get relief from the need spiraling in my belly.

"How does it feel, Willa?" he asks.

"So good," I groan, hips rocking, hand moving. "So good. Not as good as you, but fuck."

"I know, honey," he murmurs, "I wish I were there, fucking you as you need. But this is good too." His hand is moving fast, and after a moment, I realize he's moving at the same rhythm as I am, like I'm riding him, and I moan before speeding up. I'm riding it now, uncaring what I might look like, moaning as it fills me each and every time, the curved tip grazing along my g-spot with precision that has my breath stuttering, as the pleasure swirling in my stomach has me tipping towards the edge and doing it quickly.

"Stop," he says, his voice low and gravelly, his own breath panting like mine. Without hesitation, I do as he asks, my hand stopping with the toy deep inside of me. My pussy throbs around it, and I desperately want to move, to take myself higher, to get myself there, but the desire to do what Leo asks is stronger. "Pull it out." I groan, already dreading the lack of fullness, but I do he asks regardless. "On your ass, pussy facing the camera, let me see you." I fumble, adjusting quickly until I'm sitting on the bed and angling the camera so it's focused on my cunt, my head just barely making it on screen. I spread my legs, feet on the bed on either side of the laptop.

"Wider." I don't ask what he means, simply spreading my legs wider, and I'm rewarded with a guttural sound. "God, you look so fucking pretty like this, your cunt glistening, legs spread, your nipples tight. Pinch one, baby." I do, and it sends a bolt of pleasure through me, centering on my clit that is desperate for attention.

"Fuck me," he breathes, eyes locked on the screen, his hand moving faster, which, I have to admit, feels unfair. "The way you tighten is fucking fantastic."

"Leo," I whimper.

"What do you want, baby? What does my Willa need?"

"I want to fucking come," I groan, my hips shifting with a mind of their own, trying to get something that isn't even there. A deep chuckle fills the room.

"Okay, honey. Slide it back inside, then," he acquiesces, and I nearly drop the toy in my effort to do as he asks. I moan loudly as it slides inside, filling me deep and stretching me. "Fuck, you taking that is almost as pretty as watching you take me." I move the toy in and out, but it doesn't touch the need in my belly.

"I want to rub my clit," I whine, desperation in the words.

"Do what you want, baby. Make yourself come for me." Relief glides through me as I move, one hand fucking myself hard and fast as the other rubs my clit. A deep, guttural moan leaves Leo's lips, and even though I want to close my eyes and give in to the pleasure swirling around me, I watch in utter fascination as he strokes himself hard and fast, tugging with much firmer strokes that I would use if I were there, low grunts leaving his lips with each movement.

I decide I'm going to hold out, then. I want the pleasure to wash over me as I watch him spill onto his belly.

"I want you to come, saying my name," I whimper, hands moving feverishly as I watch, enraptured by the show he's putting on for me.

"*Fuck*," he groans, hips bucking into his hand, and I moan again. "You look so pretty fucking yourself. You want to watch me come, don't you?"

"Yes, yes, yes," I breathe, my eyes locked to the screen.

"Fuck, Willa," he says, and then it happens, cum spilling from the tip of his cock, hitting his stomach, dripping over his hand as he moans loudly, continuing to stroke himself through his release.

With the visual, I follow, screaming his name, my body quaking as I fall back onto the bed, my hands still moving between my legs, but unable to hold myself up anymore as wave after wave of need and satisfaction roll through me. When I return to reality, my hands move slower, and I catch Leo speaking.

Gorgeous. So fucking pretty. Perfect. Love you.

Eventually, I sit up, sliding the dildo out with a hiss, and Leo has some tissues, cleaning himself up. He smiles at me, almost sheepish, before tipping his head to the side. "Go clean up, honey, do what you gotta do to get to bed, but don't get dressed. Then go back into your suitcase and beneath your clothes, there's a pink bag. Grab it, but don't open it up. Bring it here." I smile, eager for another prize, and follow his instructions without another word. In record time, I clean myself up, wash my face, and brush my teeth before grabbing the pink bag that was also in my suitcase and bringing it back to the bed, sitting cross-legged, naked before the camera. He's settled himself into the bed, the screen in his lap, I think, the lights off now, only the glow of the screen lighting him up. It makes my chest ache, knowing I'm not there to cuddle into his side.

"Open it," he murmurs, and I do, and then my eyes water when I see what's inside.

Shirts.

At least three of them. Leos' oversized shirts, the ones I like to sleep in. I had stolen one, plus the other one I'd claimed as mine after my first night at the Mill, but I was already trying to figure out how to rotate them to sleep in them every night.

But it seems, as always, Leo thought ahead, giving me exactly what I need and want.

"Put it on, honey," he murmurs, and I try not to cry, suddenly missing him so deeply, I don't know how the hell I'm going to make it a full four weeks before I get to be with him for real again.

"I can't believe you did this," I murmur.

"We've got four weeks until you're back here, and I'm going to make them as easy as we can. You can't sleep here with me, but I want to be there with you, however I can."

"And the dildo?" I ask with a laugh, sliding the shirt over my head and then shifting to grab my phone. When I see him again, a wide white grin is spread across his face.

"That was for me. I can't last four weeks without hearing you mention my name." I shake my head, then quickly transfer the call back to my cell before moving through the house to close things up for the night. Finally, I snuggle into bed, the lights off, and set the phone on the pillow beside me. If I try hard enough, I can almost pretend he's here with me.

Almost.

"All right, baby, tell me about your day," he says, and I do, telling him about heading home after the meeting, Jackie coming over to catch me up on my schedule for the next week or so, and the argument we had about the wig. I *don't* tell him about the strange conversation in the car. Leo already isn't Jackie's biggest fan, and I don't want him to have any other reason to butt heads with her once we're out in the open. I need them both to be on the same page, since I don't see either of them going anywhere for a long time.

"How was the date?" he asks, and I fight to keep my face neutral, since he can always read me so easily.

"Fine."

He lifts an eyebrow.

"Fine?" I can hear him becoming more alert, and I force myself to take in a deep breath, to settle that uneasy feeling in my chest. It's just that I have someone now, and because of it, it now feels icky. I've always dated assholes and idiots, though I do think this one takes the cake. At the very least, they usually have some kind of shame or appreciation for my help, knowing that, without me, their career is ruined.

Instead, Chris seems almost like he knows his reputation fix is already a done deal, and that we're inexplicably linked together.

But if I tell Leo that, he's going to lose it. He's always been protective of his clients, and I don't think with our relationship changing, that's going to lessen. If I tell him what a miserable time I had and how he pushed boundaries, he's going to rush over here, figure out a way to get me out of this thing, even if it means getting fired and ruining his entire career.

And the truth is, Leo won't do anything to put my career at risk, and I won't do that for him, either. We both worked incredibly hard to get where we are.

"Well, it was no peach picking, then private farm to table dinner, or chicken nuggets in the trunk of my car, or a night at the Mill. It was..." I try to find the right word for what it was. "It was work." I yawn then, cuddling into the bed with the phone perched in front of me,

"You're tired. I should let you go."

"No, I'm fine."

"You had a long day, between this morning and your date."

If I'm being honest, the day does feel like it was a week long. I can't actually believe that just this morning, I was still in Holly Ridge.

As I think over everything that happened today, though, I pause, remembering the panic attack I had this morning. Normally, I'd be embarrassed if someone caught me in the middle of one, but I don't with Leo, not only because of the way he handled it or the care he showed me, but the way he somehow seemed not only to know what was happening but how to handle it instantly.

It's something I've been wondering about all day, and now that I'm settled in bed, the question spills from my lips. "How did you know what to do today?"

He lifts an eyebrow.

"I think I've proven myself more than capable of knowing what you need to come, Willa," he says, voice low, and a blush burns across my cheeks.

"No, I mean this morning. When I had a panic attack," I clarify, and some of the humor fades from his face. "How did you know what was happening and what to do?" A moment passes and, just like it has happened a dozen times over the years, I half expect him to avoid the question, to change the subject.

But that is the Leo of a few months ago. Not Holly Ridge Leo. Not *my* Leo.

"Because I've been there," he says simply. "I've had panic attacks in the past."

"Really?" I ask, somewhat shocked because I've never met anyone more self-assured or put together than Leo Sinclaire. He nods.

"Yeah. It's why I came to Holly Ridge." I stay silent, watching and reading his face and giving him the space to elaborate if he wants, and warmth fills me after a moment when he expands. "In October, I had a panic attack. A bad one. It was the first one I ever really had, and I thought I was having a heart attack. I went to the hospital in an ambulance, and honestly, I thought I was going to die." My eyes widen at this news, and how that must have felt, especially with my knowing that his father died from a heart attack. He's told me a dozen stories by now about his dad, both from his childhood and working with him, stories about how his dad was with his mom, and how twelve years after his death, she still hasn't moved on, and he is pretty sure she never will.

"Oh my god, Leo," I whisper. "I had no idea."

"Once I found out it was just a panic attack, I didn't really want to publicize it," he says with a self-deprecating laugh, and more than ever, I wish he were here with me so I could hold him.

"October...that's when you stepped back from clients," I say, trying to make a mental timeline. He nods.

"I thought I was going to die, and all I could think about when I was in that ambulance was that I didn't leave anything of note behind. That my dad would be so disappointed I didn't do more with the time I was given. Of course, he would be proud of my career, but he'd be so pissed that I dedicated everything to it, that I spent so much time at work, and I wasn't even really happy. Before then, I kept telling myself I just had to hit the next milestone, then I could slow down and focus on my life, but there was always another one to hit, and having a personal life, living for anything but work, would just slow me down. But when you're faced with the reality of life, it makes you wonder if it's worth it. If you couldn't have made another choice and had more, had balance. Had it all."

"Leo," I whisper, unsure of what to say because I know exactly what he means. Wasn't I just there? In a way, aren't I still there, desperately trying to figure out how I can balance my career and my personal life?

"The thought of dying alone, with no one to really care about me, is what made me make the change, what made me move to Holly Ridge. I realized I had nothing memorable. No one to miss me, and I wanted to change that." A moment passes before I speak, a small smile on my lips.

"Is it weird to be thankful for a panic attack?"

"Probably," he says with a laugh.

"Well, weirder things have happened in my life," I murmur. "And now?"

"Now?"

"You moved to Holly Ridge because you didn't like where your life was headed. And now?"

He stares at me for long moments before he speaks.

"I've never been happier, Willa. Now I know what I want from life, and I have found peace, knowing to my soul I am not going to be living that life alone."

"Yeah, Hallie would never let you be alone for long," I say, trying to keep it casual, swallowing the lump in my throat.

'No, Willa," he says, clearly not wanting to let me brush this off. "It's because I have you. Because I could be in the city, or LA, or Hollywood, and if we still had what we have right now, I would have the same settled feeling. You could be miles away, but at the end of the day, I know you and me? We're not going anywhere. We can't be together right now, but that doesn't mean you aren't mine, and that's what I need. That's all I'll ever need. My career could go to shit, and I could lose all of my clients, and I would be just fine," he murmurs. "Because with you, Willa, I already have it all. The rest is just a bonus."

THIRTY-THREE

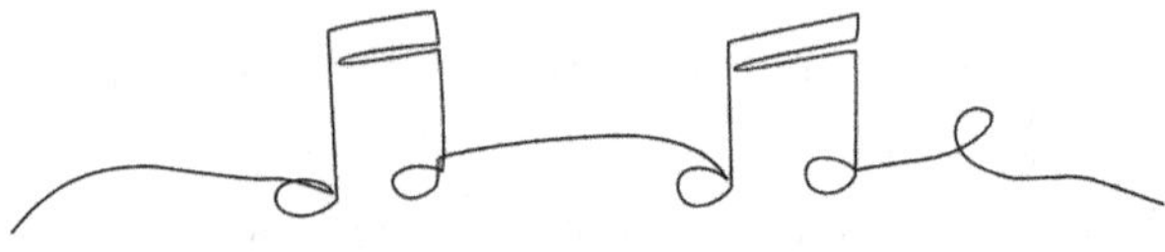

WILLA

Over the next few weeks, I go on six more highly public dates with Chris. None of them is any less annoying. Still, as with every other fake relationship I've had, I figure out how to avoid issues and frustration.

Jackie and I thankfully fall back into our normal groove, part playful ribbing and part maternal, though there is definitely a learning curve for both of us as we try to navigate how my new backbone fits into our working relationship. Thankfully, she doesn't try to push my boundaries any further, and I make life a bit easier on her by wearing whatever outfit she suggests and smiling at each and every event she asks me to attend.

I drop hints left and right about the next album, and we bump up the recording to October, something I am incredibly pleased with since it will mean that the second and probably third month of my fake relationship, I will be busy with work, and I won't have as much 'free' time for appearances with Chris.

During these weeks, Leo is also wildly busy, making sure my album promo is falling into place for early next year, helping Adam with a slew of new deals, and working on the rollout for Atlas Oaks' new album, all while diligently finishing the guest room for his mom's visit. Every day, he sends me a handful of different decor pieces, asking for my opinion on everything from wallpaper to decorations to wood finishes. I know he's mostly doing it because I miss being home and working on the house with him, but I appreciate more than he knows that he continues to include me in the small, ordinary moments as he works on what I've begun to think of as *our* home.

Despite our busy schedules, we somehow fall into a reliable routine.

Every morning, I call Leo, and we chat before we get on with our days.

Throughout each day, we send each other texts, little moments of *this made me think of you,* or *love you,* or *here's something that just happened to me.*

Every day, I miss him a little more.

Every night, he reminds me of just how many days until I'll be back in Holly Ridge for Hallie and Jesse's wedding when we talk on the phone until we fall asleep.

In a way, it's another first, another moment I didn't have, that teenage feeling of being so obsessed with someone you have to talk to them every night, late into the night, and just like every other first, I cherish it.

Although I find I have yet again fallen into a routine, it's much different than the bland, lifeless one I was living before Holly Ridge.

I don't get up at the ass crack of dawn, mostly because I'm up late talking to Leo. I don't roll right out of bed and start getting ready. Instead, when I wake up the morning of my mom's charity gala, I go about my new routine. I reach across the bed to my bedside table, where my phone is plugged in. I find Leo's number and hit video call before snuggling back into bed, setting it before my face.

"Morning, honey," he murmurs, his own voice raspy and rough, and it makes that ache in my chest throb. It's been three weeks living this new routine, and some days, I think those *morning, honeys* are one of the only things that keep me going.

That, and the promise that in about ten months, we'll be in a position for me to hear it every morning, whispered into my neck instead of across a phone line.

"Morning," I yawn, turning to my side and curling into a ball. I'm wearing Leo's old Midnight Ash tee. I still rotate his tees for sleep, though they've lost his scent. I'm so far gone that I bought his cologne and spray it on my things before bed, just to feel less homesick.

It's not working perfectly, but it eases it a bit.

"What do you have on for the day?" Leo asks a few minutes into our morning murmurings. Sometimes, I have to rack my brain to remember my schedule. But not today. I've been eagerly awaiting this morning's activity all week.

"This morning I'm going to All That Jazz," I say of the dance studio I try to visit when I'm in town. It's one of the few secrets I've managed to keep from the public. Any time I spend there always brings me utter joy. I donate regularly, quietly funding scholarships for dancers who can't afford the expensive tuition. I love taking a private lesson from the owner, a sweet, older woman named Margo, whenever I can.

"Just remember to go in through the back," Leo reminds me, making me smile. "With everyone on alert for your mom's event today, they're going to be on the lookout for you." I smile, loving that he knows this is just for me. Over the years, Jackie has tried to convince me to publicize the good I do, and sometimes I give in. In others, I prefer to keep it quiet. Margo likes things at her studio to be quiet and understated. She doesn't want extra publicity. I like having a few places where I can just *be*.

"I will. Gabe's already got it covered. Then, after, I have to head back here to get ready for the gala. Harper designed the dress—it's so pretty. I can't wait to wear it. It's cream, which makes Jackie happy, but it's covered in pastel butterflies."

"An easter egg," he murmurs, and I grin at his knowledge of all of the small moments I'm trying to hint at. After Adam, he was the *first* person to hear the rough recording of it in its entirety. When I miss him the most, I close my eyes and pull up the soft look he gave me when he realized that each and every track, other than "Are You Mine?" and "Good Trouble," was about him.

"Send me pictures," he says. "I'm sure you're going to be dazzling."

"Okay," I whisper with a smile on my lips.

"And more tonight." Now his voice is a bit gruff, low, and gravelly in a way that makes liquid heat pool in my belly.

"You want pictures tonight?" I ask, a smile tipping my lips. "You'll be long asleep by the time I get home." We already had the argument about him staying up late, with him trying to convince me it was fine, but I didn't want him to burden himself, so I know he'll be long asleep by the time I roll in around midnight.

"That's why I said pictures, and not a video. Give me something good to wake up to," he murmurs, his voice husky now. I swallow. I lick my lips, deciding he will get a video tonight, too.

"Will you do the same?" My breathing goes a bit shallow despite the early hour, despite the fact that I'm barely awake.

"Whatever you want, honey," he murmurs.

"I want that."

He grins then, a wide thing.

"Then you'll get it." He looks off, and instinctively, I know it's the alarm clock beside his bed. He sighs, confirming my thoughts. "I should let you go. I gotta get ready. Jesse and Madden will be here at 8:30, and I have some work to do before they arrive."

"Headed to the furniture store today?" I ask, and he nods. He's almost done with the guest room; he's furnishing it today. I told him to wait for me, but he reminded me we'd have better things to do during my short visits to Holly Ridge. Even though it was disappointing, he was right. "Send me pictures of that, too," I say. "I made a Pinterest board for the second guest room. I'll show you my vision when I come home next weekend."

When I talk about our future, his eyes soften.

"I can't wait."

"Me, neither." We sit there for a moment before he sighs and sits up.

"Okay. I'll let you go get ready for the day. I love you, honey," he says, soft. He always says it that way, like he thinks it's precious and gentle, and it never fails to feel that way each time he says it.

"Love you, too. Bye, Leo."

Another moment passes before he smiles and hangs up, knowing I'll never be the first to do it.

Then, finally, I go on about my daily routine.

But I still skip the green juice.

Hours later, I'm packing my things after a couple of hours dancing with Margo. Even though I've danced on hundreds of stages for tens of thousands of people, she never fails to have me an exhausted mess at the end of one of our lessons, giving me a laundry list of things to work on to improve my form.

"Thank you, Margo. This was exactly what I needed," I say, because it is: a few hours of turning my brain off, moving my body, and most importantly, laughing with one of the few people I consider an old friend.

"Thank me when you get those turns perfect. You're getting lazy," she says, smiling. She adds, "Thank *you* for the extra scholarship. Things have been tough, and some of my best girls' families are struggling. I help when I can, but rent here isn't cheap."

I've offered to cover it more than once, knowing the good she does for the dance community. She always declines. Scholarships are the best I can do.

"Of course," I say, reaching out and holding her hand, my eyes sincere. "And if you *ever* want some extra eyes on the place, media or advertising or anything like that, you know to just let me know."

"Oh, hell no. I don't need all those snobs thinking they'll be your next backup dancer if they take lessons here. If word gets out about that, it's over for me. You know I'm not guilty for the press."

I smile, thinking about when Leo had to clean up a mess after a reporter came to the studio about one of the graduates. She cursed them out in very colorful terms, and the reporter took it poorly.

"Yeah, yeah, well, you let me know if you need anything." She rolls her eyes and opens her mouth to say something, but is stopped by a loud cheer.

And then my moment of peace shatters.

The front doors open, and in walks Chris, a man holding a video camera, another handheld camera following him, his eyes brightening and a wide smile spreading across his face as he walks toward me.

"Willa! Baby!" he says, arm out to grab me, but my entire body is stiff, and I'm frozen in place. He looks over his shoulder at the cameras behind him, then tilts his head towards me, that wide smile on his lips, looking so unnatural and fake as they all start moving towards us. I turn to Margo, who looks concerned, unsure of the interlopers, and in an effort to fix this, I step away from her, making my way towards Chris.

"Chris," I say, my voice tight but my Willa Stone smile in place. I take in deep breaths, trying to center myself, but my pulse races as I move towards him. I scan the room, seeing the cameras and panic a bit, wondering if they caught anything that I could get picked apart for, but then calm moves through me, knowing that if they did, Leo will bury it.

He always protects me.

"What are you doing here?" I ask with a tight smile as he pulls me in for a hug, thankfully no kiss, before tucking me into his side. His cologne is strong, and I force myself not to cough or make a face.

"I heard you were going to be here, and I wanted to give props to the amazing things the love of my life does."

Giving Margo one last apologetic look, I put my hand on Chris's back and try to usher him to the door.

"Unfortunately, this area hasn't been cleared for filming, and I know Margo is not interested in something like that, so in order to respect her wishes, we do have to leave," I say, my professional face glued on.

"I'm sure—" Chris starts, preparing to argue.

"Now, Chris, sweetie," I say, hoping the venom in my veins doesn't leak into my words. "We need to be respectful of others." My tone is chiding, the kind you'd use on a child who wants a cookie before dinner, and for a moment, his face flashes with not just irritation, but utter hatred.

How the fuck are we supposed to last another five months like this? I have no idea, but I'm tired of playing nice with him. He continues to push past my wishes and boundaries, and I've allowed it so as not to rock the boat.

I am Willa fucking Stone, and *he* is the one who needs *my* help.

"Let's go," I say, and after a moment, he nods, letting me lead him and the paparazzi he invited onto private property outside. When we get out there, there's a lot more out on the sidewalk, and I fight to keep my shield up high.

"So what are you doing here?" I ask, trying to keep lightness in my voice. Gabe is just ahead of us, and his face is hiding much less of the irritation.

"I wanted to come see you before you get ready for tonight. I can't stand being away from you for long," he says, and I fight my lip lifting in disgust. "I was kind of hoping I could hang with you while you danced. You know how much I love to watch you move." My stomach churns at the innuendo and the way the press lets out a small laugh at his words.

"I wish you had told me ahead of time, but I have to get home to get ready. If I had known, I could have wrapped things up faster and gone to lunch. I'm sorry."

"That's what I get for trying to surprise you." He looks over his shoulder at a male paparazzo. "Women, am I right?" When the paparazzo laughs, I mentally catalog his name and face to share with Leo. I don't mind working with the paparazzi, but if they're going to be misogynistic assholes, I won't be giving them *anything*. "Anyway, go get beautified for tonight's event," he says, turning back to me. "I know how much work that all takes; you don't have to feel bad." The crowd laughs at the dig, and I try not to react before nodding.

He pulls me in close, and I place a hand at the back of his neck, fingers sliding into his hair, and smile up at him. There's a soft whoosh of air from the paparazzi around us, an awed coo as if they think this is the sweetest, most romantic moment in time. Anyone who has ever told me I'm not a good actress can suck it because I am selling this. Despite him being possibly the biggest tool in Hollywood right now and the biggest pain in my ass ever, I know I look like a lovesick idiot.

"See you later?" I ask, a small smile tipping the corners of my lips. Chris grins down at me, a cocky look that makes me want to grimace, though I don't.

"Definitely," he says, too loud to be natural, so the paparazzi and cameras can catch it.

It's clear *he* was never an actor.

"Good," I say, trying not to turn green when he dips and brushes his lips to mine. He holds it for a moment longer than necessary for the cameras. I fight the urge to argue, to push at his chest, to get him away from me. Instead, I let him take the lead. He pulls back finally, pressing his forehead to mine, and the flash of cameras glints along the lip piercing that sends the teenage girls feral, but he looks far too much like a thirty-year-old trying to be cool.

"Love you," he says, and for a moment, I freeze, unsure. We've never done this. I've never done this, an open, out-loud confession of love in front of cameras, for a fake relationship. I'd mention it in songs and talk about love in a general sense, but not...not like this.

I never wanted to toe this line, feeling that if, in some universe, I actually got the real thing, I wouldn't want my previous lies to be on the same stage as the real thing.

It's also a boundary of mine, Jackie knows, another one that I laid out before this charade started.

"You too," I murmur. I know it's not what he wants me to say when his lips shift to the corners, almost infinitesimally down, and irritation flares in his eyes. Clearly, he wanted the big moment for the cameras, but I'm not giving in to his bullshit. Instead, I step away, and his hands tighten just a bit before releasing me. I quickly spot Gabe, who nods at me. "Bye," he says, then gives a pleasant smile and wave to the crowd before Gabe leads me into the car.

I wait until the doors are all shut and he's driving away to ask.

"Did you know?" My voice is shaking.

"Absolutely not," he says quickly, eyes meeting mine in the rear-view mirror. "No clue they were going to do that, or, at the very least, I would have warned you. I was parked out back when he pulled in with his crew. When I figured out what was happening, I drove around so I wouldn't leave you alone for long." He turns onto the highway before he asks the question that's been brewing in my own mind, sour and nervous because part of me already knows the answer.

"Does Jackie know?"

"I don't know, but I'm about to find out," I say, then place a call on my phone, listening to it to my ear and waiting for her to pick up.

"Willa, how are—"

"Where are you?" I ask, not in the mood for niceties. There's a moment of hesitation, shock, probably from my quick and sharp response.

"What? Why?" Jackie asks.

"Did you know Chris was coming to All That Jazz today? Because I sure as fuck didn't. Who told him where I was going to be? You know I don't put that in the media."

There's a moment, a beat before she sighs, then answers.

"I'm at the Perfect Image offices." Something about that settles in my chest. Uncomfortably, but like I've done with very uncomfortable exchanges with Jackie over the past six months, longer, if I'm willing to be truly honest with myself, I push it down. Right now, I need to focus on the issue at hand.

"I'll be there in ten," I say, then hang up and tell Gabe about our change of plans.

When we arrive out front, I'm relieved to see there are no paparazzi, and Gabe quickly gets me inside the building without any issue. My foot taps as I move up the elevator, my pulse racing as I try to keep the tentative grasp I have on my temper. In some recess of my mind, disappointment that Leo won't be here when I walk in lingers, knowing he's back in Holly Ridge, but in a way, I'm happy.

If I'm angry, he would be furious and probably do or say something impulsive that he can't take back.

I give a tight smile to the secretary, who opens her mouth, but I just move towards where I instinctively know Jackie is, finding her in Jefferson's office, sitting on the edge of his desk. Their familiarity, especially with the knowledge of the sketchy shit he's done over the years and the way he treats Leo, makes me uneasy, but that, too, I ignore.

"What the fuck was that?" I ask, irritated. Jackie's head snaps up, eyes wide as she looks at me. "What was that, Jackie? What just happened at the dance studio?"

"It was...press?" she asks, and the way she's trying to play it off and play dumb makes that anger swell.

"We don't do press there. How did Chris even know I was there? Who set that up? Was it you?" I ask, each question escalating in frustration and volume as I try to understand what just happened.

I won't be able to go there again, at least not for a long time, not until the press starts to forget, and even then, if they know I'm in town, they'll have someone camped out there.

Just another moment of relative normalcy that's gone for me.

This goes against everything we've ever agreed to, goes against the clear lines I've drawn in the sand on what the press can have.

They can have my relationships, they can have my day-to-day moments, they can have every personal moment crafted for the brand.

That's it.

They don't get to see my process.

They don't get music before it's done.

They don't get any kind of charity work, I do, since no matter the intention, it always gets spun to look bad.

Except she brought them right into it.

"You know, I think Leo did it." Jefferson says with a lift of a shoulder. "He probably saw what a goldmine for Chris this was and knew it would be good for your charity work to be publicized as well."

I snap to him, then shake my head.

"Leo wouldn't do that. We've worked together long enough that he knows my boundaries. The work I do there is never made public, something he knows."

"Why not?" Jefferson asks, clearly not understanding. I take in a deep breath, trying to remind myself that his entire business is PR, that there's a reason he is this way, that it's because he sees every member as an opportunity for PR.

"Because I don't do it for the *brand*," I say, trying to center myself. "I don't donate to the studio because I want people to think I'm a good person... I do it because I want to bring a little joy to the kids at the dance school, and to be able to dance in peace once in a while. I won't ever be able to go there without it being splashed everywhere now," I say, that all too familiar grief moving through me. I've always loved coming here, but now it's ruined by Jefferson and Chris.

"So who did it? Who told Chris and all of those paparazzi where I was going to be?" I ask, getting angry the longer I think about it. Jefferson blinks at me, not expecting this, but when Jackie speaks, all attention moves to her.

"I did," Jackie says, looking confused, sliding her phone into her bag. "It was a good opportunity. What does it matter?"

"Because I don't do this for the media, Jackie. You know that."

"Yeah, yeah, yeah, goodwill, performative, I know. But it's really going to help Chris."

That one twists, frustration building as she speaks.

"You're *my* talent agent, Jackie. Not his. You'd do well to remember that. If you pull something like this again, I'll also have to."

Something flashes on her face before she stifles it down.

"Jefferson, would you mind leaving us for a moment?"

"Of course not. The room is all yours."

Jackie gives him a soft, pleasant smile before she walks him to the door as if he owns the place, sitting behind him, resting her ass on the edge of the table, and giving me a soft smile.

"What is this really about, Willa?"

"It's about you not respecting my wishes. What is going *on*, Jackie?"

"Willa, please, you're throwing a temper tantrum like a child. I can't believe you embarrassed me in front of everyone like that!"

I stare at her, trying to find the woman who helped raise me.

I can't find her.

I don't know if it's just because my own shield is forever changed, or if the way I see things, people, and understand their expectations of me has changed so much that I can't understand what or why she's talking like this, but I'm lost.

"I just don't understand where your priorities are, lately. In the past, if I told you it was a good idea, you were fine with it. If it were for the brand, you would be okay with it. You're acting different, and I'm concerned."

"You're *concerned?* Were you concerned when Chris kept blatantly pushing boundaries? Or when the press keeps coming when I don't expect it, priming me for a public panic attack?"

"You're being dramatic, Willa. You know, I've been talking to your mom, and she agrees—"

"My *mom?* I haven't talked to her in months! She has nothing to do with this."

"She understands the brand we've been building for decades now. More than you do, recently."

"Because I'm not trying to build a legacy! I'm trying to work my job and then *live my life*."

"Right now, your *job* is to help rebuild Chris's reputation, and we're all working toward that except for you."

That's what it always boils down to, I suppose.

"That. That right there. That is why I'm done with this shit. Why this is the last one," I say, my voice firm. Her face goes chiding, like a parent whose child is demanding dessert every night, here until eternity. "I'm done with the fake relationships and with using my personal life to build my brand when I'm already the biggest pop star on earth. I'm tired of bringing myself down to build up people I don't know, much less even *like*."

"We'll see," she says, and for the first time since I can remember, true, pure irritation and anger at Jackie flares to life. I wonder, though, if I've felt it before, if I've always felt it, I've just also always buried it beneath duty and gratitude. "You're very emotional right now, so we won't be making any rash decisions."

"No, Jackie. This is the last one. That wasn't a request: it was me telling you this as a fact. I'm telling you right now, this is the last fake relationship. I'm not doing this forever, Jackie."

"This isn't the time, we—"

"It is the time because I say so. I am telling you now, not as a request, but as a courtesy. I am not having any more fake relationships."

"Is this because of Leo?"

"Excuse me?"

She looks around, then sighs like a disappointed mother before giving me soft, disappointed eyes.

"I know you're fucking him, Willa."

I blanch, panicked.

"I—"

She rolls her eyes before I can explain, deny, or choose some other option I haven't yet processed.

"I know everything about you, Willa. I manage your life, I have access to everything." Panic runs through me at her words, unsure of just how much she means by them. What exactly does she mean by *everything?* "I allowed it because you weren't writing and then you were, and I have to admit, the album is exactly what I was hoping for." She slides off the table, taking two delicate strides towards me before grabbing my hand. "But you should know he's using you, Willa."

"Jackie—"

"I know, I know you don't want to believe it. This is your first real relationship since you were a teenager, and you've worked closely with him for years. Add in that he's had months with you alone, able to twist your head up in knots, and it's hard to see through his games. But you'll see, Willa. He doesn't have your best interests at heart."

"Jackie…"

My words trail off as my heart beats loudly in my ears.

"But I have always had your career and the brand's best interests in mind. Always. You'll see that, at the end of the day, it has always been and always will be me. I'm the one who always wants what's right for you. He's only doing this with you because he is planning to leave Perfect Image and wants to ensure you'll go with him."

She reaches out, grabs my hand, and holds it. "I don't mind you having a fling with him or anyone. You know how to do it and keep it under wraps, but I'm worried about you. He's messing with your head, manipulating you, and soon it's going to blow up in your face. He's going to hurt you." She stands then and looks at her phone. "And when he does, I'll be here, like I always have been. I'm the one who's always here, Willa. But I do have to get to another meeting. I'll see you later."

And then she walks out, leaving me stunned with my thoughts.

THIRTY-FOUR

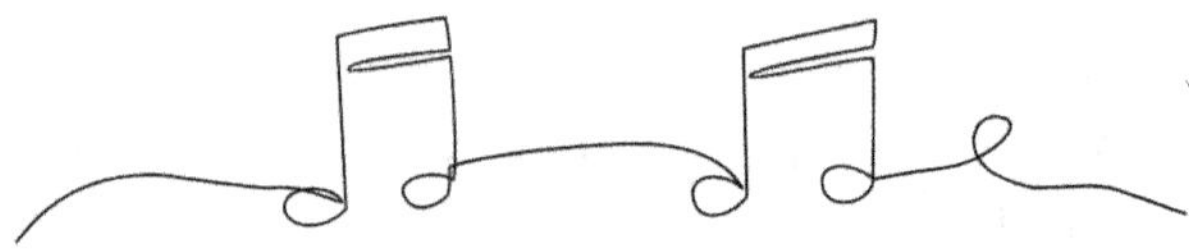

WILLA

I sit in silence as Gabe drives me home. Everything inside me is stirred up, confused, and strange, as emotions ricochet through my mind. I'm unable to sort through them logically or make sense of them, and I desperately want to call Leo. I need to talk it out with someone who knows me and whom I can trust, but I know I need to take my time. I need to be patient and not rush into this.

Leo already dislikes Jefferson and, in his own way, Jackie. Still, I had convinced myself that when things are less busy, when Leo is free from Perfect Image, I would be able to convince them to work together relatively amicably. I've had a rapidly increasing reluctance to tell Leo about just how miserable things have been with Chris, for fear he might step in and, in turn, jeopardize his own career.

Up until now, I thought I could make it through the next six months with a bit of a headache and inconvenience, and then, years down the road, when there is no risk of Leo's concern and protective-ness of me causing him to implode the career he loves, I would tell him the whole mess, and we'd laugh about it. It would be a funny story, the dumb shit we both had to deal with in order to get to where we are today.

But each day, it seems less and less funny.

Thankfully, by the time Gabe gets me home and into my house. I've begun to formulate a plan. First things first, I realize now I'm going to have to tell Leo at least a bit of what happened today. Even if I could hold it in, because he's going to find out through the media, and I need him to step in and help me avoid any backlash for Margo. After that, I'll move right into prepping for my mom's charity auction tonight, and tomorrow, Leo and I will have to have a much bigger talk about what's been going on around here.

And, most importantly, Jackie and I are going to have to get on the same page very soon regarding my future, my career, and my life as a whole. This working relationship was fine before I decided I wanted more from life, but now her vision and my needs are clashing in a way I can't live with for long.

Once I'm home, I quickly take a shower to clean off the workout grime. During that time, I move through what I am going to say, practicing so as not to alarm him, before, with a nervous belly, I call Leo. I have about thirty minutes before hair and makeup start to arrive, though, and I need to do this before listening ears arrive.

"Hey, honey," he greets after picking up on the second ring, surprise in his words. He didn't expect me to call this afternoon.

"Hey, babe," I say, trying to keep my voice neutral and clearly failing. Something about hearing him has the emotions and confusion I just managed to bury popping up already, my carefully laid plan falling apart.

"What's going on?" Instantly, his voice is concerned, and it tugs at the strands in my chest, both loosening and tightening the nerves and emotions in different ways.

"Nothing," I lie quickly, but the silence that follows make its clear I am not selling that in the least. "I need," I start, then take in a deep breath, trying to steady myself. "I need you to take down any mentions of All That Jazz from the press. It's going to come out that I was there."

"What happened?" he asks, his tone changing instantly, moving from my Leo to work Leo, and if I weren't still shaking, I'd find it funny. "I thought Gabe had it covered. Did they corner you?" I shake my head, then remember that he can't see me.

"No, no. I uh," I bite my lip, wondering if maybe I should have held off on this, if I should have tried to manage this myself, put some distance from it so I could think clearly, but with something like this, time is of the essence. "Chris showed up today when I was about to leave. With the press."

"He what?"

There's anger in his words, and I try to quell it quickly.

"It's really not a huge deal. I guess Jackie slipped it to him here, and he thought it would be good press for both of us. It was a..." I swallow back the feeling of lying. "It was a misunderstanding." Silence lingers on the line before he speaks with an alarming level of calm.

"Jackie let it slip?"

"I guess. I don't know. It wasn't a big deal, I—"

"It is a big deal, Willa. You've held that boundary for years." Sometimes it *really* sucks that he knows me so well. "You give her plenty of opportunities to exploit your good deeds. This one has always been for you and off-limits. She knows that. What was she thinking?"

"I don't think—"

"Fuck it, I'm going to call her," he says, and I shake my head.

"No, no, Leo. You can't do that. It's fine, really, I just need—"

"It's not fine, Willa. I can hear your voice from here. It's not fine, and you are not fine, so I'm going to speak with the people who are responsible for that. I won't sit by when people are fucking terrible to you, Willa."

God, but I love this man. Still, I force myself to attempt to talk him off the ledge.

"They're not terrible," I murmur, shaking my head. "They're just... misguided."

"They're taking advantage of you," he states bluntly.

"If you're going to be with me, you're going to have to learn to deal with that. I don't need you coming in and fighting my battles for me."

A moment passes before he speaks, his voice suddenly low and calm.

"A battle implies you're fighting back, honey." My entire body stills, but when I don't respond, he continues. "I'm happy to let you fight your own battles, but fighting your own battle implies that you're standing up for yourself, and you're not. I know that's not easy, Willa, because of your history with Jackie: you're close and you've known her for longer than you haven't. So it's my job, not just as your man, but as your publicist, to step in for you. Because, until you tell them no, they aren't going to stop."

I close my eyes and take in a deep breath, a confusing mix of emotions battling in my chest. On one hand, I feel warmth and joy that, finally, finally, I have someone in my corner whose sole priority is *me*. On the other hand, I know I have my own responsibility to take care of Leo and his own interests, the same way he does mine. If he goes off on Jackie and Jefferson now, things could go terribly.

"I have. I did," I say. "I told Jackie that she crossed a line today, and I did so clearly. I think she got the message." I leave out that she knows about Leo and me, deciding that neither of us has time to brainstorm what to do about it right now. "Look, I know there's a bigger conversation that has to be had here, but right now isn't the time. I'm coming home earlier. I'm not waiting until Thursday, I'm coming back tomorrow morning. While I'm home, we'll talk about it all, figure things out."

"Come now. Skip the next event. It's not that vital, pretend you're sick."

My shoulder drops, and my voice goes soft despite the fact that I'm about to deny him.

"I can't, Leo. People are relying on me."

"Who? Who is relying on you?"

"Jackie, for one. And my mom. And in his own way, because

Chris is my date, Jefferson, and you and I both know that we have to keep him content for the next year until you're free of your contract."

"I don't care about that anymore, I—" his voice is strained, and it tugs at my chest, but I stop him. He's speaking from a place of impulse and protectiveness, not from common sense. Right now, it's my turn to be the rational one.

"I do, Leo. I'm not letting you risk your career for me," I say, my voice soft. "Just like I know you would do the same to me."

A heavy pause takes over, and my heart pounds before he lets out a frustrated sigh.

"Willa, you know I wouldn't."

Relief moves through me, quickly followed by dismay that I have to say what I have to next.

"Then you know I have to go today. I'll be home soon."

He groans, the sound deep, and I can picture him running his hand through his hair.

"Yeah. I know, honey." Another moment passes before he speaks again. "I'm sorry. I wasn't being fair. I know you have to do what you have to do for your job, and you're right: we have to keep them happy, especially if Jefferson is in Jackie's ear, trying to get her to stay with Perfect Image. I don't trust him with your career at all, and if I am out of there, you'll be stuck being led by him." If I hadn't already had the gut feeling against Jefferson, today would have cemented that, but that, too, can hold on until I go home.

"There's more we need to talk about," I whisper, thinking about how Jefferson tried to throw Leo under the bus and how Jackie seemingly knows about Leo and me. Despite my best intentions, Leo is right: we might need to be working on plan B earlier than later. An unhappy laugh leaves his lips.

"I'm sure we do." The words make a dread spiral in my belly, but just then a text comes through, Gabe informing me he's sending the hair and makeup team in.

"Shit. I have to go," I whisper into the phone. "Hair and makeup are here."

"Okay," he says, the words curt and final feeling, making my heart pound with nervous energy, unsure of where we stand.

"Are you mad at me?" I ask without thinking.

"Fuck," he says, voice low. "*Fuck.*"

"Leo—"

"I need you to know right now that if I, for any reason, am ever pissed at you, Willa, I will always tell you. I will never be a dick and bury that. You and I are a team now, which means I get you out of situations you're uncomfortable with, not because I work for you, but because I love you, and I hate to see you unhappy. I hate that no one else in your team or in your life does that, and that's what I'm pissed about. I'm furious that Jackie is only ever worried about your fucking brand, as if you aren't the fucking brand. As if you couldn't show up in sweatpants and your hair in that messy bun you wear around your house and not think you're the most beautiful, interesting person in the room. And I hate that you want to let her have that, because you feel like you owe her something, as if she made you when you've always been *you.*"

"She did—" I start to argue, but I stop when he continues.

"Willa, I've seen videos of you as a kid. I've seen you acting, and I've seen you singing, and I've seen you dancing. Jackie did not make you. Jackie found you, saw that no matter what, you were going to be something big, and saw that your mom was so desperate for you to have fame, she could make herself absolutely indispensable. That she could live the rest of her life off of your talent. Then, as you grew older, she saw the sweet, kind person you are and found ways to manipulate that, too, to benefit her. I'm not mad at you, Willa. I'm mad at the world, and the way it has learned to take advantage of a sweet, kind woman like you." Despite myself, I find myself smiling. "But don't worry. We'll work on that, too. We're a team now."

"I kind of like this team, Leo."

"Good. You're stuck with it." I grin then, full out, something I didn't think I'd do after my shit day. "Now go let everyone think that they're going to make you somehow even more beautiful than you already are, and make sure you send me photos." That smile spreads wider, and I don't miss the way his words are so different from those of Chris.

"Okay, Leo," I say.

"Love you, honey."

I'm relieved when I hear the same smile on my lips in his voice.

"Love you too." And then I go off to get ready, one last task before I can go home.

THIRTY-FIVE

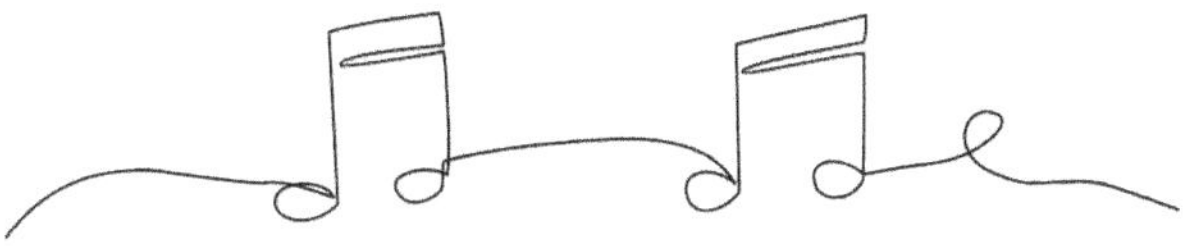

WILLA

Four hours later, and I'm in full Willa Stone regalia, my hair and makeup impeccable. I'm wearing a tight, cream-colored, floor-length gown with clear gems all over, adding flash and glam, and a cascade of pastel-colored butterflies moving over one shoulder and down to the floor, all the colors of my next album from the vision board I sent Harper represented. When I unzipped it from the bag, I gasped to see she had also added a few other small Easter eggs, like a paintbrush, a tiny peach, and even a little Ferris wheel. They're not just personal moments, but now ones forever tied into the lyrics of my new album. Harper got a copy of the rough recording to help with her designs, and she completely understood the assignment. It's almost as if Leo is here with me, and when I see the final product, my throat tightens with emotion. In addition to the photos Leo requested of me in the dress, I sent him a handful of shots of the individual icons on the dress.

You're here with me in spirit

Always. You look phenomenal. Have fun tonight.

> I love you, Willa. We'll figure all of this out
> when you get home.

I also sent the girls' group chat a photo, which resulted in a lot of caps and exclamation marks, and everyone agreed Harper absolutely killed it. Once again, I was reminded how nice it is to have a group of friends who I can send thigns to without having some form of underhanded comment or jealousy leaking in.

I'm still smiling at Leo's message as we walk into the venue for my mom's charity event before everyone arrives, through the back. In about an hour, I'll make my grand entrance on the red carpet, something Mom requested since the press will absolutely eat it up. But until the perfectly timed moment, while everyone else starts to arrive, I will sit in a room in the back, waiting. Gabe decided this would be the easiest, safest way to get me into the building.

"Willa! Darling!" my mom calls, nearly floating toward me with a soft smile on her lips. She looks beautiful as always, with her dark blonde hair pinned up elegantly and in a navy dress, the color of the vague charity she's sponsoring, though I couldn't tell you what it actually benefits, clinging to the curves I inherited from her. There's not a single strand of gray, and her face is flawless, just enough work to keep her youthful, but not too much to make her look like she's trying too hard—her words, not mine. She's wearing jewelry with large gems on her neck, bracelets, earrings, and a ring, and the entryway lighting glints off them as she moves towards me. There's another, slightly younger, woman beside her, an excited look on her face.

"Hey, Mom," I say with a smile. "How are you?"

"You know, busy as a bee, but eager to get tonight moving along." She gives me a quick kiss on each cheek before stepping back, and I fight the urge to pull her in for a big hug, the way I've seen Mrs. King do to Hallie and Wren, even if she hasn't seen them in just twelve hours.

I don't know when I last actually *saw* my mom, but I remind myself that my mom and Mrs. King are different, and that's okay.

"This is my co-chair for the event, Catherine. Catherine, this is my daughter, Willa Stone." The way she says my full name rubs me funny, as it always does, a reminder of which version of me holds more weight for her. "She's been dying to meet you."

"Oh, gosh, Willa, I am *such* a big fan. Can I get a photo?"

I nod, then take a selfie and have Gabe take a full-length shot with the kind woman. We chat a bit while Mom watches, occasionally smiling at people passing. Eventually, Catherine gets pulled away, leaving just Mom and me.

"How are you?" I ask, smiling at her. "How is the event going? It all looks so beautiful."

She gives me a distracted smile and nods.

"It's taken so much of my time, but I'm pleased with the exposure." A beat passes before she adds, "For such a good cause, of course."

"Of course," I say with a small smile before her eyes narrow on me.

"You were out of the press for a while. Where have you been? Jackie said you ran off to some little town?"

"Yeah, I've been lying low before the next album is announced." Unease fills my chest, but I push it aside, smiling widely. "It's such a great little town. You should come visit! I can take you to the Mill; it's this bar that's so fun, and they have the cutest little coffee shop, and I can show you the Christmas tree farm I'm staying at—"

"You're staying at a farm?" she asks, her lip raising in disgust. I should have expected that; she may have grown up in a small, rural town, but that was never the life she wanted, not for herself, nor for me.

"I know, it sounds crazy, but it's so gorgeous out there. I'd love for you to come. We could spend a weekend together. We haven't done that in a long time, probably since I've been on tour, when you stayed with me on my stop in Paris." We went shopping together and dined in fancy restaurants, but this could be a fun contrast to that, showing my mom the other side of my new life. "The holidays are huge there, lots of lights and a big festival. Maybe you could come then and—"

My mom cuts me off with a sigh and a wave of her perfectly manicured hand.

"I don't think I could make that work, Willa. I have a lot going on over the next few months."

"Oh, yeah, of course," I say with an easy smile, but disappointment moves through me.

Thankfully, she doesn't notice, not with my shield up high and tight, not with my being *on,* my face perfectly trained to be sweet and serene at all times when I'm Willa *Stone.* I just guess I never realized that the shield wasn't just hiding a lonely, scared woman, unsure of who she is or what she really, truly wanted.

It also hid a girl who had never felt like enough.

"Maybe—" I start, but her eyes are already locked on something in the distance, her focus no longer on me.

"I have to go, I think I see the event coordinator, and I have some questions for her. But have Jackie call me, will you? We need to have lunch soon."

"I'd like that, I—"

"Tell her that I'm free on Wednesday, will you? I can't wait to catch up and hear about her new client. Chris, I think his name is?" My stomach churns as I realize she doesn't want Jackie to schedule a lunch with *me.* "And I think my assistant will be reaching out soon, with your new album coming out, we'd love backstage passes for an auction."

Even with the shield, I know my smile is brittle.

"Of course," I say with a nod, my voice weak even to my own ears, but she doesn't notice.

She never does.

"Kisses!" Then she's off, following someone else and arguing about place settings or timing or something else...I don't know, as I'm left here, baffled.

It's another reminder, sharp and cruel, of things I've long ignored.

Slights that ached for years, but I never had any reason to question, not when they always fit into what I thought I was allowed to have, the expectations that I had created for my life.

I had my career, and that was enough. Asking for anything more was selfish. Ungrateful.

Tonight, though, everything seems a little less easy to brush off.

Because Leo and Hallie and Nat and Wren and all of Holly Ridge showed me that it was okay to want—no, *demand*—more from my life and not feel bad when I do.

Wren, Hallie, and Nat, who dropped everything on a moment's notice more than once for silly things like helping me move or getting me ready for my first date, never expecting anything in exchange. They just did it because we were friends and they're kind. On the other hand, here I am, dropping everything to help out my mom, who can't seem to find it in her to spend more than two minutes talking to me.

That now-familiar heartache, that longing for a home I have only known for three months, scores deep inside me again, the pain throbbing, raw, and persistent. It's another reminder that I desperately need to restructure my priorities.

As I contemplate that, Gabe leads me to a room where I am supposed to relax until it's time for me to walk the red carpet. To kill time, I reply to a text from Leo about thoughts on the kind of cabinets we should look at for the kitchen redo, then wade into the group chat where Nat and Hallie are arguing about whether a garter toss is tacky. Hallie is strongly opposed, citing that *Jesse's daughter will be present,* while Nat says it's a tradition that cannot be ignored. Wren and I try to find a compromise, and somehow we're headed towards Nat picking a lucky single guy to take off *her* garter, when I'm interrupted by the door opening. I begin to stand, but then sit down with an eyeroll when Chris pops his head in.

"What are you doing here?" I ask, irritated. I'd been able to push away my frustration with Chris after some space, a conversation with Leo, and chatting with my friends, but it seems the mere *look* of the man brings my irritation right back to the surface in an instant.

"What, you're not going to let your boyfriend in?"

"You're not my boyfriend, Chris," I say, but he ignores that, stepping fully into the room and closing the door behind him. I watch with utter irritation as he moves through the room like he owns the place, then pulls a chair up across from me and sits in it. He's in a perfectly fitted black tux, his hair tamed and his face cleanly shaven. I can see the appeal, of course; he might be an asshole, but I can't say the man isn't good-looking.

Still, having him here makes me uneasy, especially with the way he's smiling at me.

"You're right. I'm not your boyfriend," he says, sitting back, legs spread, and looking me over like he has some kind of claim to my body. He nods with approval at what he sees, and an uneasy chill moves through me. "Because I'm about to be your fiancé."

A beat passes.

Two, even as I take in his face, the smug grin on his lips, the way he is sprawled in the chair like he's on a photo shoot.

Finally, I let out a laugh. A loud one, because what he's saying is, in fact, funny.

Unfortunately, he isn't smiling.

Instead, he expands. "At dinner tonight, right before the auction begins, I'm going to stand up to toast your mother's charity work. Then, I'm going to propose to you," he says.

I raise an eyebrow at him.

"And you're going to be blasted on every single tabloid and social media channel when I say no. That will be pretty embarrassing for you. I don't know how that actually works in your favor, breaking up this early. I don't think that we've really done all the work to rehab your image just yet."

"I won't be embarrassed," he says.

"That's very brave of you. Are you going to work on the love-sick schmuck angle?"

Honestly, I would be okay with that, since it would mean this relationship ended sooner rather than later. In fact, a hint of hesitant excitement creeps in.

"I won't be embarrassed, because you won't say no."

I give him a pitying look.

"I love the delusion, really, but—" All joking leaves his face as he sits up and leans in, causing me to lean back a bit to avoid getting too close to him. He reaches into his pocket, grabs his phone, and taps it a few times before turning it to face me.

"You won't say no, because if you do, these photos are going to be spread to a dozen different news outlets along with the headline that America's Sweetheart broke her beau's heart by cheating on him."

My heart sinks to the floor when I see what is on the screen. My hand shakes as I reach for the device, and carefully scroll through the album, each one making me more and more nauseous.

"Don't bother trying to delete them; these are just my copies." My first instinct is, in fact, to delete them, because on the screen before me are photos. Photos of me in various states of undress, mirror selfies with soft smiles or daring glances, lowered lashes, and teasing grins. Dozens of photos of me.

Photos I sent to Leo, one for each day I've been gone from Holly Ridge. None are fully naked, but some of them are close enough to make my head swim, to make that familiar panic tighten my chest, but I force it back.

This is not the time for a panic attack. Not when I am unsafe, not when I am being threatened. Blackmailed, even. I've never actually experienced it before, but I think that is exactly what is happening here: I am being blackmailed.

"Where did you get those?" I ask, my voice faint. He grins, taking his phone and sliding it back into his pocket before crossing his arms on his chest.

"Leo Sinclaire gave them to Jefferson, figured they might be useful. Your team wants this engagement as much as mine does, and everyone is aware you'll need some extra pushing." My breathing goes heavy.

"Leo gave them to Jefferson?" My mind is spinning with this news, trying to piece things together, understand, and make sense of reality. He nods, looking like he already knows he won.

"So here's what's going to happen. You and I are going to get engaged. We'll be engaged for some time, then after your next album, we'll get married."

"Married?" I stutter, and he rolls his eyes, clearly over me and my drama.

"Yes, Willa. That's what happens. Jackie says she talked to you about it, how you can't be single forever, and dating around. Eventually, you'll seem like a washed-up has-been who can't keep a man. You need to keep the magic of your music alive, make people believe happily-ever-after exists."

"And that happily-ever-after is you?"

"In public, yes," he states. "Now, I don't mind if you want to fuck around while we're together; just be quiet about it, and I'll do the same. You can keep up your little thing with your publicist, I don't care." His lips tip up. "Though something tells me you won't really be feeling the love there any longer."

I stare at him, at his cruel face, and realize he, too, has a shield, but he holds his evil, terrible side back. Where I have a shield to protect my soft spots, his is to keep others from learning who he *really* is.

"So? Do we have a deal?" he asks, interrupting my thoughts. I stare at the wall behind him blankly, then shift my focus back to him, my heart racing, my stomach twisting. A thousand things move through my mind at once.

I think about a lifetime of work, of sacrifice, of missing out in order to build my reputation, to build my career.

I think about the brand I have painstakingly built to reflect women's empowerment, hard work, love, and laughter.

I think of the dozens of relationships built over the years, based solely on what I could do for them; some of them I'm just now realizing weren't as genuine as I thought they were.

I think about my months in Holly Ridge and everything I learned about myself while I stayed there.

I think about Leo, the man I fell for, who promised I could have it all.

And then I say the only thing I can, even if it kills me to speak the words aloud.

"Okay. I'll do it."

THIRTY-SIX

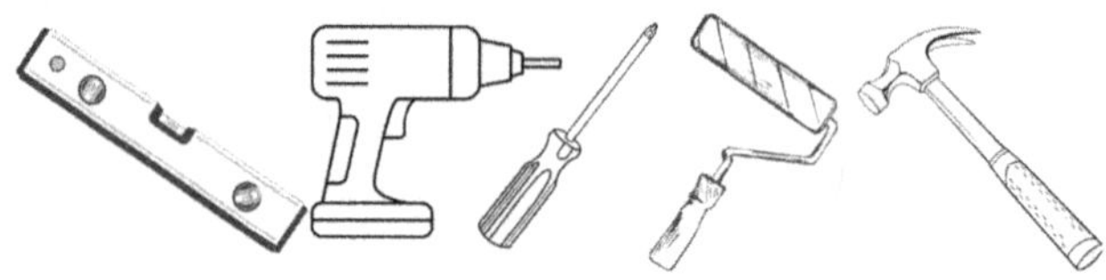

LEO

Something isn't right; my gut tells me something is brewing, made worse by Willa not being close, and it's rarely wrong, And I have to fight the urge to drive to the city right now and be by her side.

But Willa is right: she has to attend the event she agreed to, and I can't stop her. If I show up, our relationship will be questioned, which will add more stress. She doesn't need that, so I pace the house, keeping busy with small tasks. While she gets ready, we text a few times. She sends a photo of a dress, revealing Harper's hidden details. I'm considering assembling furniture with Jesse and Madden, but since Willa will arrive early tomorrow, I leave it for us to do together.

As expected, around 4:30, she stops replying to my texts. The event is about to start. Still, her silence, no matter how anticipated, settles in my chest.

I keep refreshing social media, waiting for Willa's photos, but see nothing. I check my phone and the emailed schedule, confirming her back entrance at 3:30 and red-carpet appearance at 4:45.

I check the charity's, Willa's, Jackie's, and her mother's feeds—

still no photos. At 5:30, I send Willa a quick text, but she doesn't answer.

Just before six, my phone rings. I grab it, almost dropping it, but my worry only grows when I see Jefferson's name, not Willa's.

"Hello?"

"Do you know where Willa is?" Jefferson asks without any introduction, and with his words, everything in my world stills. A voice calls Jefferson's name from the background, and he mumbles something I don't catch.

"No, why would I?" I ask, hesitantly, just in case it's some kind of trick.

"She's missing. No one knows where she is." Cold washes over me. "She was waiting in the backroom for the red carpet, but when Jackie went to get her, she was gone. Her smashed phone was left, but her bag is missing."

"What about Gabe?"

"Can't find him either."

I'm not sure whether Gabe's absence is good or bad. Best case, he's with her. Worst, something happened to both.

"Have you called the police?" I ask the obvious question.

"No, we don't want to make a big deal out of it."

"A woman is missing, and you *don't want to make a big deal of it?*" Anger replaces my fear, and I welcome it.

"Jackie thinks she's throwing a temper tantrum because Chris met her at the dance studio she was at."

My jaw goes tight, and I fight to remain calm,

"Being frustrated and disappointed for bringing press to a location she has repeatedly told everyone on her team she does not want press to follow her is not throwing a temper tantrum. Demanding answers from the people who made those decisions without her approval is good business, not a temper tantrum."

He sighs as if he's exasperated by me. "It's good for the brand; Jackie agreed."

'Willa isn't a brand, she's a person. She's allowed to have personal things."

"Not when she's part of a couple."

I shake my head; it's not worth debating now.

"What about Chris? Is he missing?"

"No."

The word is so simple, so little explanation is needed, that it sets off an alarm.

"Has he seen her?"

There's a moment of silence before he answers.

"He says he spoke to her shortly before she went missing."

Everything freezes.

"About what?"

"I don't know," he lies.

That's when something inside me snaps.

Fuck this job. Fuck pretending, fuck clinging to remaining amicable with Jefferson.

Fuck the non-compete.

Fuck everything except keeping Willa safe.

"We both know you're covering for him, though your reason is a mystery. When I find her, she'll tell me everything—exactly what you did, Jefferson. If you hurt her or made Chris do something to hurt her, know this: I'll find out soon. Get ready for that, and get ready for me—because when the truth comes out, nothing will stop me from destroying you."

"Are you threatening me?" Jefferson asks, voice low.

"It's only a threat if you did something to her. Get off the phone and go find my girl." I don't wait to hear more; I hang up. My mind races. I hesitate for just a moment, trying to decide who to call first, but the answer is obvious.

"Hey, man, what's—" Jesse greets me.

"Willa's missing," I say, heart pounding as I reach for socks, then stop—why do I need socks? Shoes barely matter. I just need to get in the car and *find her*.

"What?"

"Willa's missing. She was in the city, supposed to be going to her mom's event, and she's gone. No one knows where she is. Her phone was left behind, smashed."

"Oh fuck," he breathes.

"What?" a familiar voice calls from behind him, and then there's a tussle before Hallie's voice comes on the line. "Leo?"

"Hallie," I say, relieved. If anyone can assemble a team, it's her. "Call everyone. Ask if they know anything about Willa or when they last spoke to her."

There's a beat before she responds.

"What's going on, Leo?"

"I just got a call from my boss. She's missing. She was in a dressing room, waiting to go to her mother's auction. When they went to get her, she was gone."

"Oh, my god." I grab my keys and wallet from the counter. "We were just texting her hours ago. I—"

"Call Wren, Adam, and Nat, then anyone else who might have heard from her. See if they've spoken with her, if they know anything."

"Leo—"

"Can you do that? Hallie?"

"Yes," she says definitively. "Of course." I head to the door, open it, and slam it behind me, about to say goodbye when I hear tires on the drive.

"What—" I start, squinting as an unfamiliar car pulls into the drive.

"Leo?" Hallie asks, but I don't respond, tipping my head to try and see who is in my driveway. "What's going on?"

"I...I don't know. Someone's here," I murmur, stepping off the porch toward the car. It's a newer sedan, but not one I recognize.

"Is it her?"

"No, I don't recognize the car."

"Her location still says she's in the city," Hallie says. Normally,

I'd smile that she trusts these women enough to share her location with them, but right now, I have no words.

Because a tall blond is stepping out of the backseat of the car, then waving goodbye happily at the driver before the car starts to back up. Then she's moving toward me, quick and sure, lips tipping up.

" Leo?" the voice in my ear calls. "Leo, what's going on?"

"I found her," I murmur as adrenaline drains. Willa smiles, clutch and blonde wig in hand, wearing her cream gown. Her makeup is perfect; her blue eyes meet mine.

I've never known beauty like this—because she's here, breathing, alive, real.

Safe. The word cracks through me, sharper than air.

Alive. My lungs finally fill.

"You found her? What the hell?"

"She's at my place. I don't know why, but she looks safe."

"Oh, thank god."

"I'll call you back," I say and hang up. My phone rings again, but Willa jumps into my arms and kisses me.

I'm home.

I've been in this house for weeks without Willa. It's felt empty— like I was somewhere else.

But once more, it feels like home. I'm here, and Willa is here with me.

"You're here," I breathe out, burying frantic kisses across her face, desperate to taste her skin, to know she's real. "You're okay."

"What?"

"You were missing. Jefferson just called me. No one knows where you are. You left your phone behind. I've never been more worried in my life," I pull back, putting my hands to her cheeks, looking over her face for anything wrong.

"You didn't call Gabe?" she asks, a bit confused. I shake my head and watch as she bites her lip.

"Oh. I figured you'd call Gabe, and he'll tell you what happened."

"Gabe knows?"

"Yeah. He helped me get into a town car he approved. I should probably text him. Can I borrow your phone? I left mine behind."

I stare at her, still unsure of what is happening; it's all like some bizarre dream at this point.

"Well, I actually smashed it, but that's because I think Jackie has been accessing it." Cold moves through me, and she reaches out for my phone. "Can I?" I nod without even thinking. I hold her as she unlocks my phone, knowing the passcode already, then tells Gabe she made it home okay and will call him soon.

"You're cold," I murmur as she shivers, sweeping her up the stairs and into warmth, rubbing her arms, heart pounding with fierce gratitude. She looks up at me, sweet and soft. With her here, I finally believe she's safe.

And that's when a new feeling filters in.

Because Willa is safe, and in my place before me, her eyes soft, and I haven't held her in weeks.

Without hesitation, I pull her in close, wrapping my arm around her waist and dipping my head to kiss her. Her hands move up to my neck, holding me right, the same need moving through her as she returns the kiss.

"You're here," I murmur against her lips.

"I am," she smiles.

"Never do that again," I say, breathing heavily as my head rests against hers.

"What?"

"Never do that again, Will. That was dangerous. You could have been hurt. What were you thinking? Why didn't you call me?" The panic that I felt veers into something altogether different, verging on frustration that battles with the relief that she's here and safe.

"I had to escape. Chris cornered me in my dressing room, blackmailing me to accept his proposal tonight."

I blink at her.

"What?"

"I know, it's crazy. It's...I don't know. It's a lot. I didn't know what to do, except I knew I needed to get here, to you, so we could try to figure out the next steps together."

"You couldn't have called anyone? Told me?"

She lifts a single shoulder.

"The only person I knew I could trust is you, Leo. It's only you. Gabe helped me get into the car, but I didn't tell him why. I couldn't bring my phone because I think Jackie had been accessing it, and I didn't want her to know where I was until I knew for sure what my plan was."

"Did you have to smash the phone?" I ask. "You could have texted me, then turned it off. I didn't know what was happening until Jefferson called not long before you got here." She bites her lip, looking at me nervously.

"I admit, I was a bit rash when I threw my phone." My phone rings, still in her hand. "Why is Hallie calling you?" I look down at my phone where Hallie's name is flashing on the screen, and despite the chaos, I can't help but smile.

"Because I called Jesse and told him you were missing. Hallie heard, and I was on the phone with her trying to get the cavalry together to try and find you when you showed up here." She smiles, eyes going soft, before she lifts my phone and taps the *accept* button.

"Hey, Hal, it's me. Yeah, I know. I know. I promise, I will fill you in on everything. I'm sorry I stressed you out, but I haven't seen Leo in a few weeks, and he's about to show me just how much he missed me." There's a moment of silence from Willa, but there's *not* silence on the other end while Hallie laughs loudly. Without a goodbye, Willa hangs up, then tosses my phone to the couch, followed by her clutch, before her hands wrap around my neck again.

"Ready to show me just how much you missed me, or are you still mad I disappeared for all of an hour and a half?" She's light as air, smiling wide despite what I already know was a long and emotional afternoon, and it makes me fall for her just a little bit more.

"If you even *think* about doing that again, I'm taking you into my room and putting you over my knee until you see reason."

Her eyes flare, and she lets me go before stepping back from me.

"Not exactly the threat you think it is, bud," she whispers. "Maybe I should get a preview of just that."

"Willa—" I start, but she keeps stepping backward down the hall towards the bedroom.

"Come on, Leo. It's been a long three weeks. I need you."

Who am I to argue with that?

So I follow her towards our room. She grins then, turning to face the hallway, but her steps falter when she sees a light on in the room that, up until recently, I hadn't started renovating. She looks over her shoulder at me, eyes intrigued.

"What is that?"

My heart races.

"It's not ready," I warn, trying to beat her there, but I know it's no use, something she proves when she ignores me, moving more quickly to the room I've been working on while she was going. The guest room was finished just a few days after she headed back to the city, though I made it seem like it was taking me a long time. With my need to keep myself busy while she was gone, I moved on to something else.

My days without her felt so damn long, the house empty without her wide smiles and her gentle teasing, and I needed something—anything—to keep myself busy while she was gone. She calls this place home, but I wanted to make it *her home*, and I knew for that to happen, she needed her own space. Somewhere to escape to, to write, to feel inspired, to work. Over the summer, she enjoyed writing a bit outside, on the back patio or on the porch swing, but when inspiration hit hard, she wanted to be alone while she created her art, something I always tried my best to give her. But with the house still under construction, there weren't many options.

I knew that if we were designing this space together, she would choose things that she thought I would also appreciate, paints and accents and decor that would not fit her girlish heart, things she thought *I* would enjoy. While I couldn't anticipate all of her dreams for her ideal music and room, I had an ace in my pocket to help me plan. Hallie helped me figure out Pinterest and find Willa's home decor boards, specifically the ones labeled "music/office."

There, she saved spaces that were filled with light yellows, blues, and greens. Each one gave the same vibe of sunshine and spring and summer and things that felt so purely Willa from the moment I saw them, and I knew those were the spaces she wanted, the ones that made her feel inspired.

The ones she needed.

The kind I needed to create for her.

I used those as the starting point, with Hallie, Nat, and Wren helping where they could, and the guys helping with any of the hard stuff, like installing bookshelves, redoing the lighting, or adding an additional window for extra light. Still, everything, whether she realized it or not, is something she chose: wall paint and accents, lighting and runs, wall decor, even the wallpaper on the back wall was something she picked out.

But of course, the most important part is the light wood desk in the center of the room, my first fully custom piece of furniture, something that my dad showed me how to do, but I never actually did myself. I thought about buying her something cool and vintage, but for some reason, I decided to try to do it myself. I'm glad I did, because it fits the room so perfectly, and I can't help but feel like some ghost of my father helped me finish it. It's all curves and heavy wood, the grain of the wood popping beneath the stain she chose when I texted her last week, pretending I was stripping and refinishing the dining room table, and even I have to admit it looks absolutely perfect in this room.

"What is this?" she asks, looking around, voice soft.

"It's yours," I murmur, a confession of sorts. She turns to me in shock, and I smile before explaining further. "It's your office. For when you're home. You need a space that's yours, to be free and write and make music."

"But this..." she starts, stepping in further, her eyes wide as she continues to take in the room.

"That's the wallpaper Hallie showed me," she whispers, stepping toward it before reaching out and sliding her fingers along the perfectly laid wallpaper. Hallie did show it to her, since I sent her three different options, one of them from her Pinterest board, asking which she liked best, pretending it was for Emma's room, and she was getting votes on everyone's favorite option.

"I needed some help," I explain, watching her with anticipation, still unsure how she feels about it. Does she like it? Does she hate it? Is it too much, too soon, too presumptive? She's normally so loud with her emotions and her thoughts, telling you how it is and how she feels right from the jump, but right now, she's anything but.

"And the paint color," she whispers. Last week I asked her which color would be best for an office. I think she thought I meant mine, but when she said *green or a pretty yellow, something inspiring and calming,* then compared to her dream office board, I knew what to pick.

Over the last three weeks, I've asked her opinion in one way or another, be it through myself or Nat or Hallie or Wren, on each and every aspect of this place, slowly building up this dream room for her.

She continues to move through the room, fingers ghosting over a comfy love seat Nat picked out, her eyes shimmering as they pass over the wall mounts for her guitars. The bookshelves behind the chair are empty, but with the way she runs her fingers over the wood, I already know she's envisioning decorating and filling them. In the corner, there is a lamp she had pinned, with butterflies on it, that I instantly knew she absolutely needed.

"Where did you find this?"

"Your Pinterest board," I say, slightly embarrassed, but she smiles.

"My Leo, always giving me everything I could ever want."

"Always, Willa."

She doesn't speak, instead smiling at me over her shoulder before moving to the desk, running her fingers over the top almost reverently.

"Where did you get this? it's absolutely stunning," Her words trail off as she looks to me. She must see something on my face because her eyes go wide before I nod.

"I made it," I answer. "I'm not sure if you actually needed or wanted a desk, but if not, I can move it to any other room, or—" my words die on my lips when the tears well in her eyes, when she hiccups and puts her hands over her face, crying in earnest.

"No, no," I murmur, moving to her quickly and pulling her into my arms, desperately hating to see her like this. "No, honey. No tears."

"Leo, you can't tell me not to cry over this," she says, slapping my chest half-heartedly. "This...this is the most amazing thing anyone has ever done for me. This is the most beautiful gift I've ever received. All of it. I..." I use a hand to tip her face up to me, forcing her to look at me instead of around the room.

"You needed a space to write, Willa. It's not just my place." My fingers move, pushing hair behind her ear, and she gives me a watery smile.

"So I guess this means you're in this for the long haul, huh?" she asks. She loops her hands around my neck, her fingers moving through my hair at the nape of my neck.

"I see you're still not getting it," I say, pushing hair back from her neck with the back of my hand and dipping my head down to press my lips to the pulse there. Her breath hitches, and I smile against her skin.

"Hmm?" she asks, slightly distracted, and I lift my head to look in her eyes.

"You're still not getting it: I'm not in this for the long haul, Will. I'm in this forever. This isn't about some grand gesture or me giving you what you wanted for fun: it's about what you *need* to stay here with me. You *need* a place here where you can work. One day, it'll probably make more sense to build you a small building that has soundproofing out back, but for now, this works. But as we grow, as we expand, start a family," I wonder for a moment if this is too much too soon, but when her eyes go even softer, I know it's not, not when we've been building to this for years. "We'll adjust so you can continue to have it all. So *we* can have it all. And I'm open to discussion, baby, but I want this to be our home. Not just this house, but Holly Ridge. I think we both found what we need here, including each other."

Her eyes are watery when she looks at me, but this time, I don't tell her not to cry; instead dropping my head as a tear falls to kiss her, letting it mingle on our lips. She pulls me closer as our lips touch, as I pour everything I want and need and envision for us into the kiss before it shifts and transforms into something altogether different. Filled with the passion and love and desire that's been tamed for weeks, but never sated. Soon, we're a tangle of limbs, clashing teeth and heavy breaths, my hands in her hair to hold her where I want her, hers in mine as if holding on for dear life.

"I need you," she murmurs, as it spirals through me like fire, burning everywhere she touches. I need her out of this dress, in our bed, moaning beneath me right this minute.

"I know, let's—" I try to step away, but she stops me with one word.

"No," she says, shaking her head, then she steps back, her hands reaching back to the zipper. She fumbles for a moment, and I watch in utter fascination, unable to do anything else and knowing I should probably stop her, but as the dress loosens, I'm frozen. Then she slides the straps off her shoulders until the dress pools at her feet.

For a mere moment, reality and common sense appear.

"Will, we have a lot to talk about. People think you're missing. Clearly something happened, maybe we should—"

She smiles and shakes her head.

"All those problems will be there in twenty minutes, in an hour. Tomorrow. They aren't going anywhere, but right now, I haven't had you inside for me in weeks, and you're standing in front of me, in a room that you created for me, telling me in no uncertain terms that you want me here, with you, forever, and I *need* you, Leo."

I shake my head, brows furrowing, but I still dip my head, pressing my lips to hers for a brief moment.

"I already told you I wanted you here for the long term, Willa."

"But now you showed me, and that means even more." She smiles as her hands move behind her once more, undoing the strapless bra and releasing her breasts. Without thinking, my hand moves up her bare waist, sliding until I cup her breasts, basking in the feel of her skin beneath mine once more.

It feels like it's been a lifetime without this.

"Honey," I breathe, but it's not a protestation; it's a prayer.

"Leo," she whispers, her hands moving as I brush a rough thumb over her nipple and watch it peak. My gaze drifts down to where she's sliding her thumbs into her underwear and pushing them down until she's naked before me.

"Fuck," I groan. "Willa—" She moves, stepping back and away from me. Her hands move to the desk behind her, pressing and lifting her body until she's sliding her ass on the edge of it.

I wish I had the presence of mind to take a photo, her naked on something I built, looking at me like she desperately *needs* me the same way I need her.

But I have bigger priorities.

"Come on. Let's go to the bedroom." She lifts an eyebrow at me, a challenge as she settles herself onto the desk.

"What, are you worried it's not sturdy enough?" I tip my head back, a full-bellied laugh escaping my lips, and I feel like I'm floating on air. My Willa is back, and everything is good again. Everything is right.

"Willa, don't insult me," I say, stepping closer.

"Then prove it, Sinclaire." I move then, closing the gap and standing between her spread legs. My hand slides up into her hair, tugging it to angle her head where I want her, using the other to pull her close to me and kissing her wild, senseless, until we're both breathing heavy. Her hands move to my hair, pulling and twisting in a way I missed so desperately.

I need to taste every inch of her skin, and I start on that journey as my lips move down her neck. Her fingers tighten in my hair as I move to her neck, sucking and biting, sure I'll be leaving a mark, but unable to have the presence of mind to care. Not when her legs are spreading wider, hips shifting, breathy pleas falling from her lips.

Mine move lower, over her shoulder, down her collarbone, sucking a nipple into my mouth. As I do, my hand moves down her side and over her hips to grab her leg, lift it, and set the heel of the shoe she hasn't taken off onto the edge of the desk. I hope the stiletto leaves marks in the wood, a permanent reminder of tonight. My lips continue down, pressing against her stomach as I move to my knees. Suddenly, she must catch on to my goal, because she shakes her head.

"No, no," she mutters, eyes glassy and hooded. "I want you to fuck me."

I smile up at her. "I will. But I haven't tasted you in too long, Willa. Let me eat."

Her lips part before her tongue comes out to wet them, a dazed look on her face. I dip my head once more on a mission.

She doesn't hesitate this time, unlike the very first time I did this. Instead, now, her fingers move through my hair, using the strands to grip and tug me where she wants me, tightening when she needs more and loosening when I'm right where she needs me. I groan into her cunt, and her hips move, bucking and shifting to ride my face.

"Fingers," she moans, and I oblige, sliding two thick fingers inside her. Her hips buck up, and she tightens as I crook them, stroking along her front wall. I continue working her, and her fingers hold my face to her pussy as I devour her, groaning at the taste of her, the feel of her, the sounds she makes. "Leo."

It's a warning as she approaches the edge, her hips shifting faster. It's been weeks of teasing and foreplay, so I'm not surprised by the speed of her approaching orgasm, but it sounds like she is. "Leo!"

My lips wrap around her clit and suck hard as I fuck my fingers into her hard and fast, on a mission. It happens a few moments later, her pussy tightening around me as she screams out my name, her fingers gripping almost painfully in my hair and making me groan again into her. The vibrations move through her, and her hips buck, drawing her orgasm out longer before she slowly loosens. I continue to move my fingers inside of her slowly, my tongue licking and sucking gently. Her fingers tug on my hair, pulling my head back, and I look up at her.

I've never seen anything more beautiful than a naked Willa, fresh from an orgasm, cheeks rosy, chest panting, lips parted as she looks down her body at me on my knees. I wish I had a single artistic bone in my body that I could use to paint or draw and immortalize it.

"Fuck me," she groans, and all thoughts of capturing the moment are gone, burned away with my own need. I slide my fingers out of her, and the mewl that leaves her lips has my cock stiffening painfully. I run my tongue over her one last time. "Leo!" Her hand still in my hair tugs again, desperate now, and I laugh as I follow her unspoken command, moving between her legs. Her hand fumbles between us, undoing the button of my jeans as I strip my shirt off. I'm not worried about getting fully naked, knowing that this is going to be quick, what with it being so long since I had her last, but I want to feel her skin against me as I slide back home. My shirt is on the floor by the time she's pulling my cock out, and I groan at the feel of her soft fingers wrapped around me. Her grip is tighter than normal, and my hips buck. When I look down at her, her lips tip up.

"Noticed you're a bit rougher than I am," she murmurs, referencing the numerous video calls we've had. "What do you like, baby? Do you want me to stroke you harder? Or do you like it when I tease you?" She gives examples of both, and each is its own perfect torture.

"Don't care, so long as your hand is on me," I say, then bend a bit, dipping my head to press my lips to hers, my arm wrapping around her back to pull her tight, until her upper half is pressed against mine. She sighs into the kiss, feeling that same consuming sensation of rightness as it slows, becoming everything I feel for her and everything she feels for me. Her hand around me shifts, guiding the tip to her entrance, and when I slide into her, we both sigh.

"Fuck," she whimpers as I settle in deep, staying there for a moment to catch my breath, to soak in the rightness of it.

"I know," I groan.

Because I do.

I've never felt this whole in my life, having Willa here in my arms, in our home, in the office I built her, after being away from her for so long. And right then, I decide there is no universe where we're going back to the way things were, back to that emptiness I feel without having her near.

I am never going to keep away from her for that long. Fuck my job, fuck contracts, and fuck the press. Willa Stone is mine, and I'm tired of pretending she's anything but that.

But all thoughts of the future and plans fly out of my mind as my hips slide back and then back, leaving me firmly in the present. Her hands slide up my chest, nails digging into my shoulders. Mine move to her knees, holding her open for me before I look down to where I'm disappearing between her legs. A deep, guttural moan leaves my lips at the sight, the perfection of it. We move together like that, her pants and my groans filling up the room as pleasure builds in me, as she tightens around me. After a few minutes of that, I can feel that, just like me, she's holding off, trying to put off the inevitable for as long as she can, to bask in this moment of being together like this again for as long as possible.

That is, until her hands move to my cheeks, tipping my head up to look at her, and pulling my face to hers. She kisses me, nipping at my lip, and it feels fantastic. My thrusts quicken, and her legs move, wrapping around my hips as I fuck into her.

"Come for me, honey. I need to feel you," I murmur against her lips. We can no longer kiss, our breaths too labored, so we are just holding our faces close to one another.

"You too," she begs.

"I'll follow you always," I groan, meaning my orgasm, but I think she knows that I mean it in all ways, because I really will follow Will to the ends of the earth if that's what she wants. Her head snaps back, her body tightening and shaking as she comes hard. I do as I promised, slamming in deep and filling her as she moans my name.

And even though we have a lot to talk about, so much to figure out, I know to my soul that none of that matters.

Because I have Willa, which means I have it all.

THIRTY-SEVEN

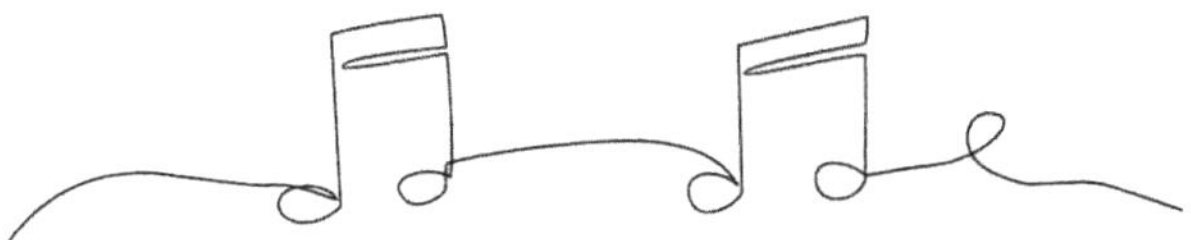

WILLA

On Monday, two days after I fled the city, Gabe drives me to the Perfect Image offices. The closer we get, the more anticipation brews in my chest, familiar to how I felt months ago—nerves, excitement, and a hint of resentment—though all now experienced through a much different lens.

When we pull up, and I spot photographers waiting outside, the scene feels both familiar and unexpected.

"Who gave them the heads up?" I ask, and Leo smiles from beside me, his hand tight in mine.

I woke up in his bed in Holly Ridge, and he made love to me before we took a shower together. Nat came over with coffee and bagels and helped me get ready in full Willa Stone glam. I have on a full, perfect face of makeup, my blue contacts, and the platinum wig, this time styled in soft waves down my back, but instead of black or white or beige, Nat directed me to wear a pretty burgundy dress with a pair of over-the-knee dark brown boots I'm borrowing from her.

It's exactly the shield and confidence boost I need for today's meeting.

"I did. No need to hide," Leo says.

I grin and shake my head. The car stops in front of the building. Butterflies erupt in my chest—not the happy, love-induced kind, but sharp, nervous ones. Their presence makes me momentarily doubt how the next two hours will unfold.

Leo squeezes my hand. "Ready?" He searches my face. I nod. "Do you need a minute? Did you do your routine?"

His eyes meet mine, and my chest fills with gratitude for his support—and for how well he understands me and my needs. He knows me better than I could ever express.

The truth is, I will never be able to thank Leo Sinclair for what he has given me over the past few months.

Not a dozen first-time experiences and the promise of a million more, if I want them.

Not elaborate dates or grand gestures or small moments of love.

But the grandest gift Leo has given me is the gift of *me*.

Leo, whether he realizes it or not, gave me myself back, and I will never be able to fully thank him for that.

So, for the first time in years, I don't need to prepare when I step out or put on a shield. I don't panic about being perfect because Willa Stone is just an extension of Just Willa, more extravagant, but still me. Both versions are deeply loved by Leo, my friends, and my chosen family, so I don't care if the cameras find my flaws.

Because I have people in my life who love me, not despite those imperfections, but *because* of them.

So I shake my head, feeling steady. When Gabe opens the door, we walk in past the cameras, smiling and waving without hesitation. The questions shouted from outside barely graze my attention, and I move quickly and efficiently into the building. Leo kisses me quickly in the elevator, fingers twining with mine. When we get to the offices, the receptionist gives us wide eyes, but says nothing as we walk to the meeting room. Jackie and Jefferson are already waiting, as requested. Leo closes the door behind us, and Jackie stands quickly, her face transformed by the worried mask of a mother.

There was a time I would have seen it as genuine, but now I

know nothing about Jackie; nothing can be trusted. I thought I created my masks and personas as protection, but I recently realized she taught me by example how to craft what people wanted most from me.

"Willa, my goodness, I was so worried," she says, moving towards me. "What happened?"

She pulls me in for a hug that I don't return, something she seems not to notice.

After Leo and I had time together Saturday night, we let Gabe call Jackie. He told her he found me, but said I was having a hard time and wanted to be alone. He assured her I was safe and that I'd meet her at Perfect Image on Monday to discuss a revised plan. Then, Leo spread the word that I'd gotten sick, which is why I didn't show up at the charity gala. We hunkered down together during all this.

She has no idea what has been going on over the past few days or the firestorm I've brought with me today.

She pulls back and scans me, her face twisting with irritation. "What are you wearing?"

I roll my eyes. I step toward the table, sidestepping her. I'm done with this act.

"Enough, Jackie. Sit down," I say.

Leo lets out a laugh that he hides behind a cough beside me. I look down my nose at the woman I trusted with everything, only to find out later that my trust was wholly misguided.

Leo pulls out a chair for me before sitting beside me. Jefferson and Jackie sit across from us. It's almost like a divorce mediation in some comedy. Honestly, it's probably the most accurate description of what is about to happen.

"Willa—" Jackie begins gently, concern etched in her voice, but I reach into my bag, pull out a folder, and place it on the table. I fold my hands over it, fixing her with a blank stare that halts her words.

"What was the plan?" I ask after a moment. "For the next press cycle. Because it's become very clear to me that you had a plan, and I was not aware of it."

"The...plan?" Jackie asks, and for a split second, I see it there—a flash of nervous energy. Panic.

Good.

She has a reason to be worried. Given what I've learned in the past two days, she has *every* reason to be anxious.

"The, um, plan? The plan is," she moves to the notebook before her, flipping pages and stuttering a bit. "To date Chris from August 20 through February, in preparation for your album release that we will be announcing in January." *We* would be doing no such thing. "I don't understand what is going on, I–"

"Chris seemed pretty sure I was going to marry him."

Jackie's eyes dart away, shifting to Jefferson. He nods, as if giving her permission to speak.

"I did become aware of that intention of his. I'm not sure where he got that idea," Jefferson says, voice fake and almost fatherly. "I am very apologetic over this miscommunication, and I want it to be clear that we had no idea that was something Chris was contemplating."

"Jackie did. She suggested it," I say bluntly, turning to my manager. "Multiple times. Each time, I argued it would not happen."

Leo's hand reaches under the table to rest on my knee. This weekend, I finally filled him in on everything I had been holding back since we separated. He understood why I kept quiet, but he made me promise never to do it again, a promise I quickly and willingly made. While I don't think things would have been any different if I had told him earlier, it would have been less stressful. I wouldn't have felt like I was gaslighting myself into believing things were normal when they clearly weren't.

"It was just a suggestion, of course," Jackie says, waving her hand.

I tip my head and narrow my eyes because we both know that's a lie. I let it go.

"Imagine my surprise when he entered my room Saturday," I say. "He told me that if I didn't accept his proposal that evening, he would release private and sensitive photographs to the press." The room goes quiet. "Where could he have possibly gotten those photos from?"

My eyes lock on Jackie.

"I don't—" she starts, and anger swirls in me at her immediate denial.

"Where did he get the photos from, Jackie?"

"If I can interrupt," Jefferson says, looking at me with pity. "I spoke with Chris, and he informed me that he was given those photographs directly from Leo." His eyes shift, and he gives Leo a smug smile, "I already have paperwork written up to fire him once this meeting is over, but I wish for you to know that Perfect Image takes blackmail extremely seriously, and we will ensure that the publicist who takes over your account when he is gone will be one you can trust. In fact, Jackie and I agreed that I am the most qualified to personally take over the Willa Stone brand."

I turn to Jefferson blankly.

"I'd rather choke, but thanks," I say with a tight smile. Leo does, in fact, choke out a laugh. This time, he doesn't bother to hide it. "But I do find that information interesting—and directly contradictory to what I learned. Since my privacy was so deeply violated, I had Jaime Wilde of Wilde Security recommend a team. They conducted a full inspection of all my tech and checked for weaknesses and breaches. That team included a digital specialist who audited my phone and my digital cloud's history. They found that an IP address accessed and downloaded files from my cloud on Wednesday. He used some questionable methods to trace the IP address to its source. To your credit, Jackie, you did try to hide it."

I open the folder, pull out a paper with the report findings, and slide it across the table, Jackie's address highlighted in bright yellow. Her face goes pale. My stomach churns, though I hide it behind sass and attitude. I shift towards Jefferson and give him a copy of the same paper with a sickly-sweet smile.

"Unfortunately, these findings aren't valid in court, due to their unconventional method of retrieval. Still, the team is confident that, with a warrant, they could do it by the book. Either way, it's clear Jackie downloaded the photos via my cloud using her access to my calendar and email, then handed them to Chris. That connection was easier to make because the unsaved number Chris sent messages from matched Jackie's assistant's area code and the first three digits of her cell number. I could only memorize the first six in those moments. While I can't say for certain without further investigation, I'm confident my assumption is correct."

At the look on Jackie's face, I don't think I need that full investigation. Her perfectly made-up face is losing all color, her lips parted, eyes wide with shock. It's clear that she underestimated me and never thought in a million years she would be here, caught red-handed.

I maintain my facade, using that long-established shield of mine, this one more vicious and cutthroat than my normal sweet Willa Stone one. "Now, I'm sure you know what decision these findings led me to." I pull out a thick packet of paper, filled with legal jargon, and slide it to Jackie. "This is for the full, amicable termination of our relationship, effective immediately." Jackie pulls them closer with a shaky hand, eyes flitting over the page before pushing it away. Her own mask comes back, a cocky look taking over as she crossed her arms on her chest.

"I'm not signing that."

"We are not leaving this room until you sign this, along with the iron-clad NDA requiring you to never speak about me, my brand, business, or any of the other items specified on page three." I push the papers back to her, and begrudgingly, she pulls them close. Jackie flips through the documents and shakes her head before fixing me with a look I've seen many times—her attempt to assert control over me.

It worked before, but I'm not the same person I was six months ago. If she hasn't noticed, she's paid less attention than I thought.

"This is ridiculous—" Jackie says. I slide another packet of papers forward, ignoring her and continuing on.

"This removes you from all previous materials and rights,

meaning you will rescind any right to ongoing royalties for past works and any future endeavors."

"You're out of—"

"You may retain all previous earnings, including those from brand collaborations you accepted for me and were paid directly to your personal bank accounts—not mine. If you do not sign this, along with the termination document and NDA, I will be pressing charges to recoup the entirety of what I am owed."

"I'm sorry?" she says, but her voice is frail. The last shred of hope I had fades away with the knowledge that she won't fight—because she can't.

"You should be, because for years, you insisted I wear certain outfits, going so far as to get angry if I went off script. I thought it was a bit strange, but you know, it's all about the brand, so I went with it. What I didn't know at the time was that many of those were high-value deals, often in the mid-to-high six figures, which you accepted on my behalf and never informed me of. If you refuse to sign these papers, I'll have no option but to pursue legal action for compensation. My private investigator estimates those missing payments total millions of dollars. You'd be entitled to your ten percent, of course, but once we factor in court costs and damages, I'm not sure how much you'd have left."

On Saturday night, after we called everybody up and made sure our friends knew I was safe, we called Jaime at Wilde Security. Between him and a few of his own PI and investigative contacts, we were able to quickly find everything we needed and more to paint the picture of the past ten to fifteen years.

Over the years, Jackie had accepted brand deals with dozens, potentially hundreds of brands, from clothing to workout gear to restaurants, promising them that I would get photographed by the paparazzi using their product if they paid me. It's why Jackie was so determined to always have my clothing set out. It wasn't that she needed to protect the brand, as she always told me; it was that she needed to hold up her end of the contract.

Silence rings in the room as Jackie slides the papers closer, hands shaking as she scans them over, then shakes her head before pushing them away with disgust.

"I'm not signing these. I'll come out with my side of the story. I'll tell the world the truth. If I go down, you go down with me."

I smile then.

A big one.

A *genuine* one.

One that probably edges on evil.

"And who would believe you?"

I ask, tipping my head to the side and looking down my nose at her.

"Excuse me? Everyone would. I would make a killing telling people this story, I bet I could—"

"You built the brand, Jackie, and I'll admit, you did it well. You're the cutthroat agent to Willa, my closest advisor, my right-hand woman, but I am *Willa Stone*. America's sweetheart. I am the one people love. Recently, I've come to dread the box you forced me into, but right now, it would work in my favor. To the media, to the world, I am sweet and innocent and untouchable. You could absolutely book fifteen interviews, try to tell the world 'your side,' but I would just have to go on *one*, tell my story, cry, bring the decades of receipts I've accumulated, tell everyone how you manipulated and used me, and I would win. And with that, I would destroy you. Your clients would all leave. You would be left with nothing. In fact, I think I am being incredibly generous by ending our relationship as amicably as I am."

When the full picture became clear, Leo wanted me to do much worse than just end things with Jackie, but I just wanted it all behind me. "But if you want to try and beat me at this game you trained me for, have at it. We can battle both in the media and the courts," I say.

With my words, I watch something change in her face, in an instant morphing from her being the one in charge, the one who controlled me, to seeing me as the one now in control of her. I put a hand on the stack of papers and make to slide them away. Panic flashes, and her hands slap over the papers, pulling them back to her.

"I can't believe you'd do this to me, after all of these years. After everything I've done for you."

I sigh, genuine sadness in the sound. I've gone through the stages of grief, what feels like a dozen times in the past two days, and I'm sure I'll feel it over and over for what might be years, each time I remember a small moment in time that twists the knife in my chest again. Something that was said or done or hidden that I ignored, a dozen of them that added up until I couldn't ignore it anymore.

There's no betrayal like one of someone you trusted, someone you loved, someone you thought of as family. There is no worse feeling than a person who never actually cared for you, who used you for their own benefit, and now that you're not complicit in it, you're being shifted into being the villain.

But that's fine: I can be the villain in her story, because I know she'll be living in a revisionist history no matter what, putting a spin on the truth to create something she can live with.

"You know, it's funny, because I thought the same exact thing."

Silence settles before I slide a pen her way. "Now sign the fucking contracts so I never have to see you again."

Then she grabs the pen and starts to read the papers, signing and initialing where I was kind enough to put little pink tabbies I borrowed from Wren.

"Now, Jefferson," I say as she does, turning to Leo's boss. "You are going to release Leo from his contract. And–"

"The fuck I will. You might have her tied up, but I don't—"

"I have a written and sworn testimony from Chris that you supplied him with the incredibly personal photographs, told him to blackmail me with them, and to inform me that Leo Sinclair was to blame. When he balked at first, because it seems even an asshole like Chris has a line, you had your *own* photos of Chris that you threatened him with."

His face blanches, and I smile.

This one hurt less.

Taking Jefferson down is far less personal and thus far more satisfying.

"Now, you are going to sign *this* contract that my lawyer so kindly also wrote up, releasing Leo Sinclaire from his contract." I take out another stack of papers from my folder and slide it his way. "It will allow him to start up his own firm, as well as take whatever clients of his who wish to go with him without contest. If you do not, I will approve Leo to submit this article I wrote about my experience with Perfect Image and the way they manipulate and control both their clients and their employees in order to create fear and ensure loyal." He looks from me to the contract before him. "I wouldn't suggest arguing with me on this, Jefferson, because I could easily be charging you with revenge porn."

"Is this not blackmail?" he asks, his voice smug, still trying to retain higher ground. "I could come out and say you are blackmailing me."

"You can't be this stupid, can you?" I turn to Leo, who is grinning now, wide and thoroughly entertained. "He can't be this stupid, can he?"

Leo just shrugs.

"I never said he was smart, honey."

Jefferson turns to Leo, anger and hatred on his face.

Yesterday, when I asked if he wanted to be the one to do all of the talking, to take down Jackie and Jefferson with his normal skill and sharp attitude, he declined, saying he wanted me to realize just how powerful I am. I was shocked, and it seems that Jefferson is too, though he's being stupid about it.

"Oh, so that's it, is it? The big, tough Leo Sinclaire is just going to let some bitch do his dirty work for him?" Jefferson asks, venom snapping at Leo. I tighten my hand in Leo's, nervous that he'll snap, that he'll bite the bait that Jefferson is clearly dangling, but if anything, he relaxes more, leaning back in his chair and grabbing a pen from the table, clicking the end carelessly.

"I guess so. I've gotta say, it's pretty entertaining to watch you be felled by a pop star you underestimated."

"Seems people have done that a lot to me," I murmur, and Leo looks to me, giving me a wide grin.

"Not anymore."

"Never again," I say, and despite the urge in my veins, I fight the desire to kiss him.

But barely.

"Now I have things and places and people to do, so if you two could get to signing, that would be just great."

Jackie and Jefferson glare at me, but when Leo offers the pen in his hand to Jefferson, he takes it before he starts signing.

"You'll be nothing without me," Jackie says as I walk out fifteen minutes later. "In two years, you'll have nothing, Willa." I look over my shoulder at her, then shrug a shoulder, Leo's hand in mine, the contracts secured in my bag.

"I'll be happy, and I'll be free, and with that, Jackie, I'll have it all." Then I turn back ahead and walk away with my head held high.

I hold it together in the elevator.

I hold it together as my heels click down the hall.

I hold it together as we step out into where a dozen cameras scream my name, my fingers twined with Leo's as we step out into the blinding sun, smiling.

But once we're in the car, it cracks.

The brave facade I've been keeping held high cracks, crumbling at my feet. Leo reaches over and unbuckles me, ignoring road safety and pulling me into him as Gabe drives away.

"I know," he murmurs before I say anything at all, which is good as I begin to cry into his shoulder.

I sob there, snuffling and hiccupping as I let it all out, as the emotions move through me, relief uncomfortably twining with disappointment and hurt. Because the truth is, I'd held the smallest kernel of hope. Hoped that it was all a huge misunderstanding, and that Jackie would somehow prove she really did care for me, that it wasn't all just a play for power and control and money all along. And when she didn't, I wasn't surprised, but I was disappointed.

Thankfully, I've had this cry a few times over the past few days, so it's only a few minutes in Leo's arms before I start to calm down, start to even out my breathing.

"This is probably the wrong time to tell you that was the hottest thing I ever saw, right?" Leo asks as my sniffle starts to fade out. I have so much to work on, to figure out. Lawyers to contact, things to put in place to ensure Jackie has absolutely no access to anything in my life anymore, but despite all of that, I laugh.

I laugh, and I do it hard, my sad tears turning to humorous ones, and as I do, Leo grins down at me, a thumb brushing over my cheek, wiping at the wetness there as I know he always will.

And there, in my relief and my sorrow, in my love and my acceptance and humor and joy, I know that I finally, *finally,* have it all.

THIRTY-EIGHT

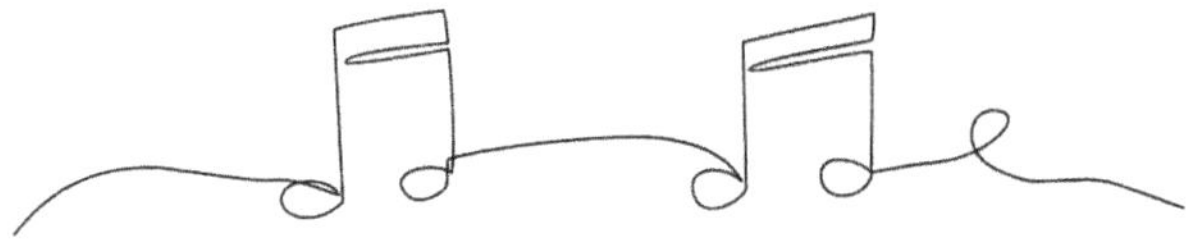

WILLA

I'm almost done getting ready when my phone rings. Normally, I would ignore it as I've been doing all this week, but considering what an important day it is, I check the screen. Instantly, I regret it when I see my mom's name written across it.

It's not the first time she's called, and it surely won't be the last time. Since my showdown with Jackie, she's been calling regularly, a few times a day. I genuinely missed her very first call, and when she left a voicemail demanding that I call her so she could *talk me out of this silly temper tantrum,* I decided I wouldn't answer for a while.

The truth is, I'm not ready for another disappointment from someone who, with distance and a shift in my mindset, I realize also used me most of my life.

It would be one thing if Jackie had simply gotten in my mother's ear and was spinning tales, if my mother had no idea of what Jackie has really been up to over the years, but as of Tuesday this week, the story of blackmail, fraud, and money mishandling by both Jackie and Jefferson has been splashed across newspapers, websites, and tabloids worldwide. Knowing how much she loves staying on top of all media, she has absolutely seen everything and is still trying to convince me to talk it out with my former manager.

Unfortunately for Jackie and Jefferson, neither of them ensured that the papers they signed included any disclosure that Leo or I couldn't speak about the heinous things they've done. While I won't be taking either of them to civil court, a few hours after we left the offices, the FBI contacted both parties regarding their crimes. It wasn't something I wanted to do, since I genuinely just wanted to put it behind me. But both Leo and Jaime reminded me that just because I was free from their bullshit, it doesn't mean that they wouldn't do the same thing to others, or that they weren't *currently* doing the same thing to other clients.

While I didn't have Jaime or his team look into my mother, her insistence that Jackie is innocent and that I call her to iron this "mess" out tells me that, until I'm ready for another painful conversation, I should ignore her, as well.

Despite my brave demeanor, the day after we came back to Holly Ridge, the emotions hit hard. Waves of pain, thoughts, and memories crashed over me, and small moments I'd brushed off began to make sense, revealing just how much control Jackie had and how deeply she had manipulated me.

That first day, I cried.

A lot.

I barely left my bed, barely ate, barely did anything, really. Through it, Leo held me the entire time. He made sure I drank water, told me I was strong, and kept me from wallowing. He reminded me that I had been working with her since I was a literal child, and that there was no feasible way for me to know what "normal" relationships would or could look like. He told me over and over that he was so proud of me for taking this step.

Leo is how I survived that first day.

The second day, I woke up with a killer headache and a heavy heart, but at least my appetite was back. Always seeming to know exactly what I need, even when I don't, Leo invited the girls over.

Although I spent that day crying a bit, I also laughed. A lot. We gabbed, and we bitched, and we moaned, and Nat threatened to track Jackie down and "beat her ass," a ledge Wren and I worked hard to talk her off of. We ate more junk food than anyone should in a single day, and by the end of it, I felt a lightness I didn't expect. Hallie pulled me aside before she left to tell me she was proud of me, and if I ever wanted to talk about moms and mother figures not living up to what I hoped, she was there.

That, too, made me cry, but in a good way.

Because that day reminded me that while I lost some people, I gained even more, and the friends I now have are there purely because they care for me.

On the third day, I decided I was done wallowing. Jackie had taken enough from me, and I had a beautiful, thriving career behind and ahead of me. I asked Leo if he could contact his therapist for some recommendations, and I began reaching out to any industry contacts I had to find an agent I might click with. I tried to convince Leo to become my manager and agent, but he insisted that was a line he didn't want to blur. He told me that, given my history, he didn't want me to ever question any choices he made, or for the professional and personal lines to overlap any more than they already do, since there was no way he would ever trust handing my PR to anyone but himself.

Days four and five were filled with calls, inquiries, and scheduling two weeks' worth of meetings.

But today, a week from the charity event, I'm getting ready for Hallie's wedding, and while I've been to some of the most sought-after parties, events, and awards shows, I've never been more excited for a night than I am right now.

Since Nat and Wren are both in the wedding as Hallie's bridesmaids, I'm getting ready by myself. It's a status I've experienced a million times throughout my life, but strangely enough, now it feels quiet and lonely. Putting on my blush and curling my hair without the constant chattering and laughter feels foreign in a way. Hallie told me I was more than welcome to get ready with them, which I appreciated, but I didn't want to be in the way during Hallie's big day, so I politely declined.

But unfortunately, it means I have no one to help me with my clasps.

Biting my lip in the mirror, I grab the bracelet I plan to wear with the outfit Nat helped me pick out over the summer, and make my way to the kitchen, where Leo is waiting. When I enter, his back is to me, broad shoulders beneath one of his signature, perfectly fitted suits, as he stares out the sliding glass doors. The trees are starting to change, creating pockets of orange, red, and yellow amongst the green, and I find Leo taking it in more often than not, telling me this is the view that made him buy this place, and envisioning what it would look like during each season. It's why he picked this place, part of why he settled here in Holly Ridge when he did.

In a way, it's part of what led him to me.

Because of that, I fucking *love* those damn trees.

But when he hears my heels on the hardwood floors, he turns to look at me. I smile as his face softens, and I take in his high cheekbones and his sharp jaw, clear since he shaved this morning. His hair is combed back, and he looks like the badass publicist I've known for eight years, the one I used to secretly pant over even if I knew I couldn't have him.

Illegally hot.

"Can you help?" I ask, biting my lip and lifting my wrist to him. His eyes go molten as they roam over me, taking slow, measured steps towards me before grabbing my outstretched hand. His hand is rough and warm on my skin.

"Jesus, fuck, honey," he murmurs, doing the tiny clasp before lifting up that arm and having me twirl beneath him as they do in the movies. My heart falters with the simple move, and when I face him again, a nervous smile is on my lips.

"You like?"

"I like a little too much," he says, looking me over again, his voice low and gravelly. The front of the dress has draping fabric that frames my cleavage, and the same draping and gathering runs across the dress, accentuating my hips and making my waist look tiny, the silky burnt orange fabric clinging in all the right places and ending mid shin. Even though I know I look hot in this dress, I suddenly wonder if it's *too* hot based on his look.

"Is it...too much?" I ask, eyes wide. "I don't know what you wear to a wedding in the woods." I look down my body at my outfit. "Nat picked it out, but—"

"No, no, Willa, it's perfect. God, you look...you look amazing."

"Really?"

He pulls me into him, body pressing against mine, and grins at me. "You look like completely fuckable but in a sweet, untouchable way."

"Well, I'm glad. That's what I was going for," I murmur, and he groans, sliding a hand to my ass and pulling my hips into his. For a moment, I melt into him, pleasure moving through me at the mere *idea* of what he could do to me when he's looking at me like that, but then common sense kicks in, and I push on his chest.

"No, no, you don't," I say, stepping away. "I sent Nat pictures of my hair and makeup already, and if it's fucked up, I'm going to get in trouble."

"We're still home, you can fix it." His voice is low and hot.

I have to admit, I hesitate, if only for a moment.

"*No.* Come on. We have a wedding to get to," I say with a shake of my head. He sighs, then puts a hand to my lower back, grabbing both of our jackets before leading us out the door.

The ceremony is simple, in the woods, and, in true Hallie fashion, beautiful. There's an aisle and a small archway that she and Jesse stand before, with Wren, Nat, and Emma beside her. Madden and Colt are standing with Jesse on the other side. The girls are in gorgeous light-blue dresses, the men in dark suits with light-blue accents, and the flowers are simple and colorful. Hallie told me the other day that they would all be cut from Mrs. King's flower field that the King brothers helped cultivate this summer, another extremely personal touch that is so Hallie.

Apparently. Madden begged to be the officiant, something both Jesse and Hallie instantly shot down, but it gave Hallie an idea. That's how Mr. King came to be standing behind Jesse and Hallie, watery eyes and shaking words as he married his son and the woman his family claimed as their own long before Jesse and Hallie realized they were meant to be together.

It's perfect. They didn't go with personal vows, something that Hallie told me she pretended to fight Jesse on, giving him a hard time even though she didn't actually want to, but Jesse's voice still holds strained emotion as he repeats his father's words to Hallie. My throat aches as I watch them vow to love and cherish each other for the rest of their lives.

"Are you crying?" Leo whispers, and I slap him.

"It's beautiful."

He looks at me with a soft smile on his lips.

"It is," he whispers, then presses his lips to my hair as I rest my head on his shoulder.

It doesn't take long for Mr. King to announce Jesse and Hallie as husband and wife, for Emma to cheer louder than anyone before the wedding party makes their way back down the aisle. I wave and smile at everyone as they pass us, sticking my tongue out at Emma when she walks past on Madden's arm, Nat on the other side, and making her giggle.

"Tits look *good* in that dress!' Nat squeals as she walks by, and I laugh, shaking my head.

"Hey, Will!" Wren says with a small wave, her eyes still watery from watching her oldest brother and best friend marry as she walks by on Colton's arm. "Hallie wants you for pictures!" My brow furrows, but she tips her head towards where everyone is moving. "You two follow."

"I don't—" But Adam is coming up the aisle behind her, ushering Leo and me to step ahead.

"It's best not to argue with Hallie, especially not on her wedding day," Adam says, and I can't argue with him.

And even though I refuse to be in *all* of the bridal party photos, Hallie eventually convinces Leo and me to stand with them for a few, and once again, I'm reminded that Holly Ridge is, and will from now on, always be my home, and these people are the family I've chosen for myself.

The reception is utter chaos.

It's in one of the storage barns that, according to Leo, the guys spent most of the last two weeks moving tons of holiday decorations out, cleaning, and then decorating as per Hallie, Wren, and Mrs. King's vision. It truly is gorgeous. There are two long tables for everyone to sit at instead of small assigned seats, and a huge buffet of more food than this number of people could ever eat. The entire place is decorated in flowers, greenery, and more fairy lights than I've seen in one place, but from what I understand, Wren has an arsenal, and this is only a small fraction of what she normally puts on *her* house for the holidays.

At the back end of the barn is a small stage with a band, and there's a sweetheart table at the front, though Hallie decided she hated being away from the excitement and ended up forcing Jesse to eat sandwiched between everyone. In one corner is a huge bar, apparently a wedding gift from Colton to his sister, with Colt's tenant-slash-alleged dream woman, Sloane, making drinks. According to Hallie, she doesn't actually know how to make many drinks, but Colt doesn't seem to mind leaving the excitement of the party to help her out as needed.

When Hallie throws the bouquet, Emma catches it, making everyone laugh as she races around, fist pumping the flowers in the air.

"Well, that's that, a freaking twelve-year-old is going to find her true love before me," Nat grumbles, and I laugh, putting an arm around her shoulders and pulling her in close.

"We'll find you a man. You'll meet a million of them on tour with me, of course."

Her body goes still before she turns to look at me. Her dark curls are a bit more tamed today, the top half pinned back, and her green eyes are huge when she takes me in.

"What?"

I lift a shoulder.

"I mean, if you want, of course, I know you have a job here, but... I'm gonna need someone I can trust to do my hair and makeup." I bite my lip, feeling like I should hide the smile spreading over my face. "And someone to dress me."

"No way," she whispers.

"Did you break her?" Leo asks low, and I elbow him.

"Oh. My. God," she whispers. "Oh my god."

"Though, if it's too big of an ask, I totally understand, I—" I start, but I'm stopped.

"Shut up," Nat nearly yells. "No take-backs, Wilhelmina."

"My name is not Wilhelmina," I inform her with a laugh.

"I know, but you need a big girl name when I need to be stern with you, and if you're going to be all nice girl and feel bad about asking me to be your stylist, and go on a world tour with you, you need to be big girl-voiced back into reality." I roll my lips in and nod, trying to hide my humor and failing.

"Can I take that you mean you'll think about it?"

"You can take that to mean that tomorrow, once I'm not hungover, you and I are getting on a call with Harper, because I have *ideas*. Big ones." She puts her hand in front of her, looking off in the distance. "Glitter. Sparkles. Rip away dresses. So much color, you're going to be a walking rainbow. And then I'm going to start shopping because if I'm attaching my name to your brand, your streetwear needs a total revamp. We can keep the cutesy stuff for Holly Ridge, but you're about to be a colorful hottie when you're Willa Stone." I laugh then, joy uncontrollable. She grabs my hands tightly and starts jumping. "This is so exciting! I promise you won't regret it!"

"Everything okay over here?" Madden asks with a smile and an eyebrow raised, appearing out of seemingly nowhere. I have noticed that whenever there is a ruckus featuring Nat, I've found you can always find Maden coming around to see what's going on.

"Get out of here, King," she says, pushing on his chest. "I'm about to go on tour with Willa-fucking-Stone as her stylist. I was out of your league before, but now I'm not even in your *stratosphere.*" She hugs me tight again, whispering a *thank you, thank you, thank you* in my ear as I laugh before running off to tell Hallie.

"What?" Madden asks, confused, but Nat is already gone.

"Will asked Nat to be her stylist and do her hair and makeup on tour," Leo explains.

"On tour?" His brows furrow, and a look I can't quite understand crosses his face, and I nod.

"I need people I can trust. She's good with fashion, hair, and makeup. Kind of the perfect all-in-one choice for me."

"No one more trustworthy than Nat," he murmurs softly, watching her jump excitedly with Hallie. "When's that going to be?"

I shrug.

"We're still working on exact dates, but this summer. April or May should be the first dates." He looks away again, wheels turning, but after a moment, something comes over his face, something I recognize intimately.

A shield.

And with it, he goes back to flirty, funny Madden.

"Well, make sure you save me some backstage passes. Definitely can get some hotties if I have the connections."

I roll my eyes and shake my head, but agree.

"You tell me how many you need and they're yours."

He nods, then looks into the distance.

"I gotta go, I see someone I know," he murmurs, then walks off without another word. I turn to Leo.

"Was that—"

"Weird? Very. What's going on there?" he asks, and I shrug, genuinely. unsure.

"I don't know, I thought they hated each other."

"You also thought I hated you, so you're not the best judge of character there," he says, looking as if he knows something I don't. I grin.

"Very true."

"If everyone doesn't mind, it's time for speeches," Mrs. King says a bit later. There aren't a huge number of people here, just forty or fifty of Jesse and Hallie's close friends, but the microphone is necessary with how loud this crew is. We all move, sitting at the tables and turning towards the center of the room where Emma is now standing on the little stage. She looks to me and gives me a small thumbs up, and I wink at her. When Leo turns to me, giving me a skeptical look, I ignore him, keeping my eyes on Mrs. King, who is now handing the microphone to Emma, before shifting my gaze across the room. I spot Adam standing in the back corner, removing his guitar from a case, and butterflies loop around in my chest.

"Hey, everyone. Uh, thanks for coming tonight. I'm just as shocked as I'm sure you all are that he conned Hallie into doing this," Emma says, and everyone laughs. I know she's not actually Hallie's biological daughter, but my god, is she so much like her now-step-mom. When I look over at the bride and groom, Jesse, is rolling his eyes and shaking his head, while Hallie looks pleased.

"I've known Hallie my whole life, since she's always been an honorary King. She thinks it's because she and Aunt Wren were always best friends, but if you know Hallie, you know that she's just... she's a King. She was always meant to be a king. She's funny, and she's loyal, and she's honestly too cool for my dad, but she slummed it a bit so that I could have someone cool in my life."

Another laugh, and Jesse covers his face, Hallie tipping her head back and laughing as she leans into her husband's side.

"But as I said, she was always supposed to be a King, and really, Dad was the only choice since she and Uncle Madden can't be in the same room without fighting."

"Because I'm always right and she hates that!" Madden jeers from the back of the room, and Hallie turns around to give him the middle finger.

"There's so much I could say about my dad, about how he's selfless and gave everything up when he knew I was coming into the world and how he's the best dad I could ever ask for, and how I'm so honored and glad he's my dad, but it's not Father's Day, it's his wedding day, and everyone knows that means the only person who matters today is Hallie." The women in the room cheer, and I melt when I watch Jesse press his lips to Hallie's hair. Emma turns her attention to the redhead, and her face goes soft before she bites her lip nervously.

"Hallie, I know you know how cool you are, like, *way* too cool for my loser of a dad, but I'm really, really happy that you agreed to give him a shot. I know he's really grumpy and annoying and has a lot of boring rules, but you two just work together. You make our house happier, and I'm happy you're in it with us." Hallie gives Emma a shaky smile, and I hear a sniff from behind me. When I turn, I see Nat is dabbing at her eyes, and Wren is full-out crying. "You're also kind, and you're patient, and you're the best person I know. Every single time I've needed you, you've been there. You've never treated me as anything other than a friend, and you've been the closest thing to a mother figure I've ever had." My own throat aches as I try not to let my own tears fall.

"I've been trying to think of something I could do to show you both how happy I am that you got married. I know the cliche is that daughters hate their stepmoms, but Hallie's kind of the best, and we all know my dad is the best. He made me after all." The room laughs, and she preens with the attention, but with the distraction, I start to stand. Leo grabs my hand, but I wiggle free, giving him a conspiratorial smile before quietly moving toward Emma.

"And honestly, I think I deserve a raise on my allowance for pulling this off," she says with a laugh and a flip of her hair. "But last night, I came up to my close, personal friend to ask for a favor, and she came through." I let out a laugh, though a couple of faces around us look utterly confused.

"Obviously, since I'm twelve and essentially poor, I couldn't afford anything for your registry, but Hallie's always shown me that memories are more important than anything, so I thought what better thing than making your first dance the most epic thing ever." That's when Adam and I move onto the stage, Adam shifting one of the microphones to the center of the mini stage.

When I look out of the room, it's the smallest venue I've played... possibly ever...But I already know it will forever go down as my favorite. I almost said no, not wanting to take the spotlight during Hallie's wedding in the least, but as Hallie has warned me time and time again, Emma is very convincing when she wants to be.

"Hey, Willa," Emma said last night at the rehearsal dinner. Just like with the photos, even though I was not in the wedding party, Halle insisted that Leo and I attend the rehearsal dinner.

"Hey, Em. How's it going? Are you excited for tomorrow?" She nodded, but when she bit her lip nervously, looking to the side, my gut dropped. Maybe that was the wrong thing to ask? I knew she and Hallie were close, but maybe there was some drama I didn't understand.

"Yeah, totally. But I only have a minute, and I have a favor to ask of you," she says, voice soft.

"Oh," I said, relief moving through me swiftly. A favor I can do. "Of course! What do you need?" She looked around nervously again before taking in a deep, nervous breath and spitting out her request.

"I want you to sing for Hallie and my dad tomorrow."

Unease settled in my chest.

"Oh, honey, I don't—"

Nerves moved through me, trying to figure out how to explain that just because she was a fan didn't mean that taking the spotlight away from Hallie would be a good idea, but she interrupted, explaining before I could decline.

"Just for their first dance, not the whole night. Just...just the first dance. I want to help make it special."

I open my mouth, but she kept on going.

"She told me you're like us. That your mom isn't the best, and that you get it. Hallie is...Hallie is everything to me. Everything my mom isn't, and I want everything to be perfect for her." Something warm moved through me at the sincerity in her words, at the clear evidence of just how close Hallie and Emma are. I know a good bit about Emma's mom, both because Leo stepped in earlier this year and because of stories I'd heard from Hallei. I know that a large part of the reason Hallie and Emma bonded so quickly is their shared trauma of being raised by mothers who left them early in childhood.

"They're dancing to 'Landslide,'" she continues, probably seeing my argument faltering, and warmth moves through me. Based on the story of their relationship, Hallie has shared, it's the perfect song for the two of them, a couple always meant to be, a couple where both of them were terrified of commitment for their own reasons. "And I know the recording would be fine, but I want it to be special. And I'm a pretty resourceful twelve-year-old, but unfortunately, I'm broke, so I have to get creative. I don't think asking my dad to pay for a gift for his own wedding would really send the same message."

I smiled then, my decision mostly made up now.

"That's probably true."

"I want to surprise them with you singing their song. You're basically family now, anyway. It would be special for them."

Her eyes are soft, sweet, and genuine, and I didn't have a choice.

I nodded.

After that, I went to find Adam, both to see if it would be a bad idea and to see if he could play with me, and he agreed not only that it would be something Hallie and Jesse would like, but also that it would be incredibly special for them.

And now, as I watch Jesse lead Hallie to the center of the room with tears in her eyes, I know that to be true. When Adam starts playing the opening chords, her tears fall. Jesse pulls her in closer, brushing the tears away before dipping his head to her ear to whisper something that makes her smile. They sway, turning as I sing, and when she faces me, her eyes lock on mine, and she mouths a heartfelt *thank you.*

And with Adam at my side, I sing a song about change and growth and finding love and conquering fears, a song so perfect for my friend and her new husband that I couldn't think of anything better.

But when I sing, I look at Leo the whole time.

✿✿✿✿✿✿

Later that night, another slow song, and Leo pulls me into his arms, swaying me as I soak in everything about the night. Despite the chaotic, stressful, and sometimes saddening past week, this right here makes every moment of heartache worth it: being here, in Holly Ridge, surrounded by my friends, held by Leo. I'd do it over and over and over again if it meant I would end up here at the end of it all.

"Do you want this one day?" he asks low, catching me off guard as I'm lost in my own thoughts. I pull back to look at him, a bit confused.

"What?"

"A wedding. Do you want that?" I sit on his question as we sway to the song, thinking about his question and trying to decide how to answer.

"Honestly?" I ask.

"Always," he responds. I smile and lift a shoulder before answering.

"I don't know. I never really thought too much about it."

He pulls back, giving me a confused look. "You don't know? Isn't this the kind of thing little girls dream about?" I let out a small laugh as we sway.

"Yeah, well, the other dream little girls have is being a popstar, and I got that one instead. It wasn't until recently that I thought I might be able to have both." He hums a low acknowledgment, holding me a bit tighter, and although I think he isn't going to push anymore, I continue explaining. "It was always the one thing I refused to fake," I murmur. "A wedding. It felt wrong, or like bad karma, to bring something so fake into something that would be incredibly real. I think a part of me always held out hope that one day, maybe, I'd find something genuine."

I look up at him and find he's already looking down at me and presses his lips to mine.

"Will you freak out if I tell you that we'll be here again one day?" he asks low. I stare at him, heart racing, before he continues. "You and me, dancing at a wedding. You in some white dress Harper made, your hair done by Nat, your girls at your side." My breathing hitches, but he keeps swaying us gently. "I don't think we'll be able to get away with something this small, but if you want it, I'll make it happen."

"Is this you asking me to marry you?" I ask with a tip of my lips, shockingly not thrown off by this development.

"Not at all. It's me telling you that's where this is headed. That one day, this is going to be made real in a permanent kind of way. I'll need that, tying you to me forever."

I grin then.

Wide and full of joy, because *telling* me he's going to marry me is so very Leo.

And in this new era, it's Leo and me: stating plainly what we want, what we need from life, and doing everything we can to make sure we get it.

Thankfully, it won't be a sacrifice to give him this.

"Good, because, when the time comes, you gotta ask me better than that," I whisper, pressing my lips to his. "I *am* a world-famous pop star after all."

There's a moment before his head tips back, a deep, full-bodied laugh falling from his lips.

"Noted," he murmurs. "The whole nine. Fairytale stuff."

"You've got time to plan it."

"I've got forever," he murmurs, and I crunch up my nose.

"I hope it doesn't take *that* long," I whisper, though when he dips his head and kisses me with a smile on his lips, I know he heard me. And I know I won't have to wait that long. The song ends as we kiss, slowly fading into another recognizable song, and I break the kiss instantly, looking around.

"OH, MY GOD!" I hear shouted.

"WHERE'S WILLA?" another voice calls. I turn back to Leo to tell him I need to go, that I'm being summoned, but he's already stepping back.

"Go. Have fun, honey."

And then I go sing *Wannabe* with my girls, screaming it at the top of our lungs. The wedding photographer takes shots of us, and the flashes are so familiar, but they don't even faze me. And later, when Hallie sends us all the photos from the night, the one of the four of us holding hands and jumping, singing this song at the top of our lungs while the guys watch from the sidelines with lovestruck looks on their faces is my favorite, the one I get printed and framed for my office.

I thought for the longest time that having it all was a lie, some sweet fairytale.

I once believed the lie we are told—that having it all is simply not possible. That you have to choose at some point what you really, truly want most in the world, and let the rest fall to the wayside.

You can't have the dream career and the movie-worthy love and the friendships that make you finally feel like you belong somewhere.

But the truth is, you can have it all. You just have to fight for it.

Having it all means fighting for it all, and so long as I have Holly Ridge and Leo by my side, I know I will fight tooth and nail to get—and keep—all of it.

ABOUT THE AUTHOR

Morgan is a born and raised Jersey girl, living there with her two sons and daughter, and mechanic husband. She's addicted to iced espresso, barbeque chips, and Starburst jellybeans. She usually has headphones on, listening to some spicy audiobook or Taylor Swift. There is rarely an in between.

Writing has been her calling for as long as she can remember. There's a framed 'page one' of a book she wrote at seven hanging in her childhood home to prove the point. Her entire life she's crafted stories in her mind, begging to be released but it wasn't until recently she finally gave them the reigns.

I'm so grateful you've agreed to take this journey with me.

Stay up to date via TikTok and Instagram

Stay up to date with future stories, get sneak peeks and bonus chapters by joining the Reader Group on Facebook!

Enter the Morganverse by catching up on your favorite Morgan Elizabeth books!

All books are interconnected standalones, which means you can jump in wherever you'd like, regardless of series or number in that series!

The Springbrook Hills Series

The Distraction

The Protector

The Substitution

The Connection

The Playlist

Season of Revenge Series:

Tis the Season for Revenge

Cruel Summer

The Fall of Bradley Reed

Ick Factor

Big Nick Energy

The Ocean View Series

The Ex Files

Walking Red Flag

Bittersweet

Evergreen Park Series

Passenger Princess

If This Was a Movie

Never Been Worse

Down the Shore Series

Tourist Trap

Mavens Series

Maneater

Holly Ridge Series

The Bright Side of Christmas

The Promise of Forever

The Mastermind Duet

Ivory Tower

Diamon TikTokress

All My Love

www.ingramcontent.com/pod-product-compliance
Lightning Source LLC
Chambersburg PA
CBHW071446140726
47997CB00005B/1609